Pretty Maids

Pretty Maids

Barbara Vaka

Copyright © 2011 by BARBARA VAKA.

ISBN: Softcover   978-1-4628-5452-3
            Ebook   978-1-4628-5453-0

All rights reserved. No part of this book may be reproduced or transmitted in any form or by any means, electronic or mechanical, including photocopying, recording, or by any information storage and retrieval system, without permission in writing from the copyright owner.

This book was printed in the United States of America.

To order additional copies of this book, contact:
Xlibris Corporation
1-888-795-4274
www.Xlibris.com
Orders@Xlibris.com
87343

Forward By The Author

My newest novel PRETTY MAIDS is a fictional story based on the truth about the growing exploitation of unsuspecting women by human traffickers. Much of the information I discovered through my own research while visiting Egypt on three separate occasions and from reviewing thousands of websites about human trafficking in Egypt and Israel.

Although my story takes place in the Middle East, the problem of human trafficking is worldwide and includes Europe, Asia, and North and South America. After the fall of the Soviet Union, many young women were forced to look outside the country for work. Those who stayed and were unable to find a job, frequently became prostitutes. Today in the countries that make up post Soviet Russia these women are enticed to apply for advertised jobs that promise an opportunity to earn money for themselves and their families. The jobs appear to be genuine in nature such as a nanny for a wealthy man's children, waitress in a restaurant, companion for the elderly, extras for movies, stage shows, and various other occupations far removed from the sex trade.

Following a brief interview, they are given an airline ticket and told they will be met by a company representative at the airport who will take them to an orientation before delivering them to their new job. At the orientation they discover the truth; the jobs they applied for do not exist. Their identity papers are confiscated and burned, their cell phones smashed before being whipped and beaten into submission and sold as sex slaves to work in the brothels or for wealthy individuals.

Human trafficking is for the most part an unreported crime. Victims are threatened with physical abuse and told any attempt to escape will bring harm to their families back home. Human trafficking of women exists in every country in the world. Some countries turn a blind eye and the practice continues with government officials and the police being some of their best customers. The women that manage to escape have no money, no identity papers, and are frequently jailed when caught and sentenced to prison for prostitution and entering the country illegally.

In Israel, the government does not criminally prosecute or convict any employer or recruiting agent for labor trafficking. Trafficking for forced commercial sexual exploitation is prevalent and the many brothels in Tel Aviv are allowed to operate without any interference from the police or the government. The women are smuggled through tunnels under the border between Israel and Egypt that are large enough to drive a truck through.

Wealthy Arab men from the Gulf travel to Egypt each summer to purchase "temporary" or "summer marriages" with Egyptian or trafficked women from the East European countries. Many are girls under the age of eighteen, some of whom have not reached puberty (seven and nine year old little girls). These 'marriages' are sometimes facilitated by the girl's parents and marriage brokers. It is a form of commercial sexual exploitation of children. It is estimated by UN Gift (Global Initiative to Fight Human Trafficking) that 1.2 million children are trafficked each year. Jobs are offered as maids for the summer, but the job goes beyond cleaning and in some cases consists of unusual sexual practices including bondage, whipping, and sexual humiliation in front of an audience consisting of men of wealth and power.

My husband and I learned of this through a travel agent we met, and a concierge at a hotel we stayed at in Cairo, Egypt. The concierge told us not to try and find a room in the summer as the wealthy Gulf Arabs came to town and rented almost every available apartment and hotel room. The merchants looked forward to summer because their businesses do well in an otherwise slow tourist season. These hotels, rated four and five stars, are located along the Cornish in Cairo and the Mediterranean in Alexandria. In other fashionable tourist cities in Egypt feature hotels known to provide 'live-in' maid service with no questions asked.

For the most part, Egypt is known as a transit country for women coming in from Eastern European countries to Israel for the commercial sex trade organized by international crime cartels, primarily Russian mobs and the Russian Mafia. Unsuspecting women tourists traveling alone are also fair game for these traffickers.

One of the leading cities in the world known for its trafficking of children is St. Petersburg, Russia. Men from Western Europe and the United States are among their best customers.

When I attended University in the 1960s, a friend had the opportunity to spend her junior year in France. The American women were warned by their supervisors on arrival not to visit certain parts of Paris during the school year. Many students ignoring this warning disappeared and were never heard from again.

The United States Department of State lists several countries as not fully complying with the standards for the prevention of human trafficking. These countries are referred to as "Tier 3" countries. What follows is a list of several countries referred to as Tier 3: Bolivia, Burma, Cambodia, Cuba, Ecuador, Jamaica, Kuwait, North Korea, Qatar, Saudi Arabia, Sudan, United Arab Emirates, Venezuela, and Togo. I listed them alphabetically so no prejudice is obvious. http://www.state.gov/g/tip/rls/tiprpt/2009/123132.htm (This is a website that lists all tiers and countries belonging to each Tier.

This next list is the countries that receive the most trafficked individuals: I listed them alphabetically so no prejudice is obvious. Australia, Brazil, Cambodia, France, Germany, India, Israel, Italy, Japan, Netherlands, Nigeria, Saudi Arabia, United Kingdom, United Arab Emirates, and the United States. Many other countries serve as destinations, but those listed are the most notorious for receiving these victims of trafficking. Some wealthy men on holiday will see an interesting woman that they desire and pay for her kidnapping and delivery to their yacht while at sea. These cartels charge huge sums of money for accommodating these wealthy men; twenty-five to thirty-five thousand dollars or more is not unusual. The men willingly pay for their perversions.

Over 95 percent of victims experience physical or sexual violence during trafficking and are often raped, tortured, forced into having abortions, and into performing manual labor.

According to statistics, 2.5 million people are in forced labor including sexual exploitation at any given time as the result of trafficking Of these, 1.2 million are children that are trafficked every year.

This horrific twisted business affects more than 161 countries and nets $32 billion dollars a year. (US dollars). Forty three percent of victims are used for forced commercial sexual exploitation and ninety-eight percent of those are women and girls.

Join me and help put a stop to this hideous violation of human rights. If you suspect someone is being sexually exploited or being used for slave labor you are urged to contact:

The National Human Trafficking Resource Center (NHTRC) Call the Hotline from anywhere in the United States 24 hours a day 7 days a week: **1-888-373-7888.**

The hotline is operated by the Polaris Project, a non-governmental organization working to combat human trafficking. Callers can report tips and receive information on human trafficking.

Go to their website at: http://www.polarisprojectnetwork.org

Barbara Vaka

16 July 2011

Acknowledgments

A book is a team effort. Without the tireless work of my husband, best friend, and terrific editor this book would never have happened.

This book is dedicated to my husband, Peter, Nicholas and Stacy Vaka, Nicole Vaka, Christian and Krystal Vaka, my grandson Nathan Poplar, and my granddaughter, Lucy Vaka. They have always given me their love and support.

I would like to extend our thanks and special recognition for our good friend Mohamed Sidky, Cairo Egypt. You have shown us the Egypt that few get to see and experience. Your kindness and generosity will always be remembered.

Love Is

A woman's body is meant to be clothed in the arms of the man that loves her.

Her eyes are to drink in the passion of his embrace.

Their lips meet and it is an explosion of emotions as they inhale each other's essence

His hands caress her body like a soft breeze on a hot summer's day.

Her fragrance is intoxicating and he is lost to his surroundings when he holds her close.

Love is a passion beyond words, beyond emotion, beyond the senses of our psyche.

Love is telling a woman you love her, not with words, but with your embrace.

Chapter 1

It was a muggy, oppressive steamy evening in January 2004, on a narrow back alley in the Geylang section of Singapore. The neighborhood reeked of raw sewage, exhaust fumes, and garbage in the streets. Three young Russian men were walking through the steady downpour. They were wearing blue jeans, pullover shirts, rain soaked dark blue jackets, and black, Greek fishermen's hats.

"The only good thing about Singapore, Yuri, is it is a warm rain, but I feel chilled to the bone. I hate the constant downpour. What we need is to do is kick back a few."

Yuri was a handsome young man in his late teens, 196 centimeters tall, muscular, strapping, that robust athletic look that women found seductive, wide through his shoulders, and narrower through the hips, with a deep husky voice that women found sexy and walked with a swagger. His jet-black hair and light blue eyes were in stunning contrast and in another era would have been regarded as a rake, even a debauchee. In Moscow, he had a different woman clinging to him every night of the week.

Anton, was average build, brown eyes, brown hair cut short and at least fifteen centimeters shorter, and his other friend, Feliks, the shortest of the three, had blonde hair to his shoulders and blue eyes. They were not the womanizers that Yuri tried to be nor were they into erotic diversions and thought an agreeable and appropriate thing to do on a wet dreary night was to get inebriated. The threesome entered a shabby run-down bar not far from their hotel and sat at a table off to the side in the dimly lit establishment. On the raised platform in the front of the room, a couple of men were singing very bad karaoke. The place smelled of cigarette smoke, used condoms, and stale liquor. A haze of smoke filled the air causing some patrons to cough. There were a number of entertainment girls standing around the bar eyeing up possible clientele for the night.

The sleazy establishment was located in one of the few red light zones tolerated in Singapore. Yuri had read that women in these seedy bars were registered prostitutes with clean bills of health. Like the Red Light District of Amsterdam in this part of the city, prostitutes were common.

Yuri turned to Feliks with a grin on his face, "See that unsophisticated young woman over there; she is giving me the sign of approval."

Feliks replied, "Yuri, she is too young. She looks about thirteen or fourteen."

"No, they would not let her in here if she was not at least eighteen, the legal age in Singapore. You two have fun drinking or whatever; I am going to have company tonight." Yuri took another gulp of beer. "Nothing warms me like a naked woman's body next to mine. I have been practicing 'I love you' in Mandarin, *wo ai ni*."

"How many languages do you know how to say I love you?" Anton asked.

"I know all the European languages plus Mandarin, Japanese, English, Arabic, Spanish and Portuguese. I never actually counted them, but I have used most of them at one time or another. I love women."

"Yuri, Feliks and I are not interested in some whore from Singapore. It is raining; we are soaked to the skin; we are returning to the hotel and getting out of these wet clothes,"

Yuri smirked. "You two have fun; I need a woman."

Feliks and Anton tired of drinking, not interested in whoring the night away, paid their bar tab, walked outside into the steady rain and began to walk back to their hotel.

"Look at that Feliks." Anton shouted over the sound of a jet flying overhead.

"Look at what? I had five bottles of that Tiger Beer and have trouble seeing anything." Anton replied slurring his words.

"It is a can of red spray paint by the curb; we'll paint Yuri is a lecherous bastard on the wall over there in Cyrillic letters. No one around here is literate in Russian, but Yuri will see it on his back to the hotel."

Anton painted while Feliks watched; he had only painted Yuri on the wall when two Singapore police officers apprehended both of them.

"Drop that paint can, it is illegal to vandalize our beautiful city," demanded one of the police officers in perfect English.

"There is nothing beautiful around here; it is filthy." Feliks replied in his broken English.

"Shut up. You two are under arrest."

The two police officers, shorter than Anton and Feliks were lean and muscular and easily put them in wrist restraints despite their efforts to resist. They ushered the two drunken Russians into the back of their cruiser and drove off to the station house.

"There are strict laws in Singapore against many things, including painting graffiti. It is a punishable offense," one of the police officers told them in an angry tone of voice.

Back at the bar, Yuri approached a young woman named Chen Mei Ling, only 150 centimeters in height; she had long black silky hair, heavy make-up and bright red lipstick, wearing a short black skirt and red blouse. She was hanging around with another woman who looked older.

"*You wan beer?*" Yuri asked in his interpretation of Singlish, the corrupted English that the local's spoke.

"*No lah, drink five botol oreddi.*" She answered him.

"Come pretty lady, we no drink, have fun, make luv. *Wo ai ni.*"

Yuri paid his tab and took Chen Mei's hand and he led her down the squalid alley toward his hotel. They had not walked far when he noticed 'Yuri' painted on the wall with red streaks of paint running down. He thought to himself, "Those two bastards. It has to be Anton and Feliks that did that."

Yuri and Chen Mei, both soaking wet from the rain, arrived at the hotel; the lobby reeked of stale cigarette smoke. The man behind the reception desk was smoking and a gray cloud of smoke circled over his head. The ashtray on the counter overflowed onto the floor.

Yuri guided Chen Mei toward the dark stairway to the second floor. She pulled back a little, but Yuri urged her on and they began to ascend the stairs. Just as they got to the second floor, Chen Mei began to scream at the top of her lungs "*Banzhu*! *Banzhu*! Help me! Help me!"

Yuri spoke no Chinese but he spoke English and was dumbfounded that she was screaming for help when he had not done anything. Prostitution was legal in parts of Singapore and Geylang was a red-light zone according to the Internet.

Suddenly, a muscular man about twelve centimeters shorter than Yuri wearing a jacket emblazoned with the name of the hotel grabbed his arm and threw him against the wall. The porter dragged him down the stairs and shoved him against the desk as the reception clerk called the police. The porter punched him in the stomach so hard Yuri grimaced and bent over from the impact of the man's fist into his mid section, and vomited on the floor. Yuri was too drunk to fight back. The police arrived and strong-armed him into the backseat of a police car and drove him to the closet detention center.

On entering the jail, he saw his friends Feliks and Anton in a large holding cell off to one side. The officer shoved Yuri into the same cell as his friends. He staggered and fell onto the floor.

"What the hell happened? Why are you both here?" They spoke in Russian so the guards could not understand them.

"It seems painting graffiti is illegal in this damn city. Why are you here? Prostitution is legal. What did you do, get rough with her?"

"Hell, I did not even get her to my room when this *blyad'* (bitch) starts to scream. Then some bastard in a porter's jacket slams me into a wall, drags me down the stairs, shoves me into a desk, and punches me so hard I threw up. He pinned me there until the police arrived. I don't know what the hell I am doing here. I do not speak Mandarin Chinese, and they do not seem to be inclined to speak English even though it is one of their four official languages. I know they speak no Russian and I do not speak Mandarin Chinese, Malay, or Tamil."

Feliks managed to get the attention of someone who understood English and persuaded the police to let him call his father; he told him what had happened.

"Well, what did your dad say?" Anton asked.

"He said he would fly to Singapore in the morning and would contact both your fathers before he left. He said he would call and find out how much of a fine would keep us out of jail."

"I think my father will help," Anton interrupted, "but Yuri's father is of the old school; you get into trouble after a certain age and you get yourself out."

"My father is an old bastard." Yuri snarled in response to the conversation. "I am always on his bad side. He'll probably be happy if I go to jail."

The next day, Yuri and his friends found themselves in a courtroom before a judge.

Feliks and Anton stood before the judge. Feliks' father, slender with blonde hair and blue eyes, slightly taller than his son, stood in the back of the courtroom clutching a black briefcase.

In perfect English, with no emotion, the judge in an angry tone of voice, glared at them as he spoke, "You have defaced our beautiful city for which you will suffer three strokes of a caning rod, and pay a $2500 fine each. Your fathers have agreed to the fine rather than have you go to jail for six months."

"I cannot believe you are serious. It was paint; it will wash away," Feliks protested.

"If you do not keep quiet, I might recommend twice that number of strokes and six months in jail along with the fine." The judge's voice was loud and angry." Take these young ruffians to the punishment area. There is still time this morning to have them checked by the doctor and punished today."

Feliks' father approached the judge.

"I have brought 160184 Rubles or 7000 SGD to pay Anton and my son Feliks' fines. When can they fly to Moscow?"

"They may return with you tomorrow. The crime the other young man committed is more severe. Did you bring money for his fine?"

"No, Yuri's father refused to pay anything."

"Wait for the jail to call you at your hotel. They will tell you when they are ready tomorrow."

Yuri watched his two friends dragged off to the prison for their punishment. Unlike him, they would be back in Moscow the next day.

"Yuri Berezovsky," the judge intoned in an angrier voice, "is found guilty of attempted rape of fifteen-year old Chen Mei Ling. The hotel porter stopped you from taking her to your hotel room. Eighteen is the age of consent in Singapore, not fifteen."

Yuri tried to explain, "She was in this bar, and in the company of several women; I know they were prostitutes. If she was only fifteen, she should not have been in the bar. She dressed like a prostitute. How could I know she was so young?"

The judge glared at him and said nothing that would indicate he had heard anything Yuri said. "The sentence is ten strokes of the rod and three years in prison. You will be notified of the caning the morning the punishment is to take place."

Yuri stood there glaring at the judge. "I demand to speak with the Russian Embassy. I did nothing wrong. I never touched that girl."

"If you do not shut up," the judge roared, "you will get the maximum of twenty-four strokes of the cane and six years in jail. I am being lenient." He nodded at the guards who dragged Yuri still protesting from the courtroom.

Yuri talked a guard into allowing him to call the embassy and his father. The Russian Embassy refused to get involved with a sex crime.

"You should have known better. Singapore has no tolerance for any crime. You should have asked for her identity papers. If she had none, then you would have known she was underage," came the unsympathetic reply from the Embassy.

His father had advised the boys not to go to Singapore in the first place. When Yuri reached his father on the telephone, all he heard was parental indifference.

"Perhaps Yuri you will learn from this," Shouted his father in an angry voice. "I am tired of your whoring and not doing anything with your life. I cannot and will not get involved. You got into this mess; you have to be man enough to handle it. Feliks and Anton just got back. They told me what happened. Grow up Yuri. A good whipping may knock some sense into you."

Yuri's father hung up on him and the guards took him back to his cell at Changi prison to await his punishment.

Yuri had been in prison for three months when he got word that his punishment was that morning.

Two well-muscled guards arrived at his cell at six.

"Strip you bastard. The judge should have sentenced you to twenty-four strokes. You will not be so pretty after my friend lashes you. I told him to strike you harder because of your light sentence. How dare you try to rape a fifteen year old girl?"

The guards laughed as they watched Yuri take off all his clothes.

"Put your hands in front of you."

Yuri put his hands in front of him and one of the guards cuffed his wrists together.

The guards led him to the punishment area of the prison. There were ten men stripped naked with their wrists cuffed together squatting down on their haunches.

"Squat like those other bastards and listen for them to call your name. No talking to anyone," he barked in English.

Yuri squatted until he heard an announcement.

"Yuri Berezovsky, you are next."

Yuri walked to a desk where there was a doctor.

"I am going to check your blood pressure. You seem healthy enough."

The doctor checked his blood pressure, wrote something on a chart, "This one is ready to go. He should be able to take ten strokes with no problem. I will check him again at the prison when his punishment is over."

The guards led Yuri into the punishment area. He faced an ugly structure called a trestle.

"See that trestle, bend over that wooden beam and grab the bar in front of you with both hands."

Yuri bent almost ninety degrees from the waist and had to reach forward to grab the bar. The guards strapped his wrists with heavy leather straps to the bar, his legs to the bottom of the trestle sides, and placed a pad across his back to protect his kidneys from a misaimed strike of the rod. Bound the way he was, his bottom made a perfect target and he could not move in any direction.

The flogger was a powerfully built, well-muscled, broad-shouldered giant of a man about twenty-eight years old. He was much taller than the average Singapore citizen was. His body was wet with sweat from previous canings he had administered that morning. He was making practice strikes against a dummy off to the side of Yuri. Yuri could hear the rod whack against the dummy and the whoosh of the rod. Yuri braced himself for excruciating pain. These men, trained to strike with maximum force, to inflict the greatest amount of pain, but with minimal permanent damage to the accused. A man had recently sued the prison for disfiguring his son and maiming him for life. The judge was not sympathetic, but gave the father the equivalent of one hundred dollars American money. A good flogger could strike ten times without an overlap of strokes.

The rod used in Singapore is made of rattan and is soaked in water overnight to make it flexible. It is 1.2 meters in length and 1.3 cm in diameter. Some reports state the rods are soaked in brine so they stung more when they stroke the prisoner.

The call came, 'one,' and the flogger swung the rod and scourged Yuri's bare buttocks with maximum force. A thin raised white line crossed his backside from one cheek to the other side of the other cheek. Thirty seconds later, the call came again, 'two'. The second strike struck with a thwacking sound, as it smacked above where the first rod had landed, causing the white line to split open and bleed. A second line appeared. Yuri was screaming in agony and when the call 'three' echoed in the room, the rod landed a third time with agonizing force across his posterior. It was five minutes later when the call, 'ten' was made and the rod pummeled his bloody buttocks and was as vigorously delivered and forceful as the first.

By this time, Yuri was almost numb from the pain. He was unbound hurried into a van, laid on a blanket on the floor face down, and transported nude to the new Bedok Reformative Training Centre for offenders between the ages of sixteen and twenty-one. The doctor checked his physical condition, wiped his damaged skin with antiseptic, and declared he needed several stitches. Yuri lay face down in his cell moaning in agonizing wretchedness from the torture he had endured while the doctor stitched his bloody bottom. He could not eat, sleep, or stand up on his own for three days. The pain was unremitting. The guards gave him water to drink until he was able to walk steadily on his own. During this time, he began to contemplate why he had gone through this.

He was developing a loathing for women, all women. He remembered his one time girlfriend in Moscow, Katerina, telling her father he had raped her. Yuri was sixteen at the time and had sex with her, but she consented. She was afraid she would get into trouble and lied to her father who did not believe in the justice system and took matters into his own hands by hiring a couple of muscle bound thugs to beat him unconscious. That was when he had begun to visit brothels. Sex with no commitment was better than sex with unintended consequences. Relationships would have to wait until he was much older. Women had always caused him great difficulty. The plan was revenge, to torture women and however and whenever possible inflict great pain, so they would suffer in agony as he had agonized and suffered at the hands of his tormentor in Singapore. Yuri had never hit a woman, but was contemplating the first time and the great relief it would give him to punish a woman. As the days passed, his physical wounds began to heal but the emotional scars from his father's betrayal and memories of the women responsible for his unjustified suffering fed his rage.

In the solitude of his cell, Yuri began to formulate a plan. When he returned to Russia, he would get involved with the human trafficking trade. He had heard rumors that Russian Jews made millions of dollars in the trafficking of women, transporting them through Egypt into Israel. The women, locked in cells, were beaten, raped, and sodomized into submission. Once their spirit was broken, they were sold to pimps who would beat and ravish them again. Each women saw twenty to fifty patrons a week, sometimes more. Those who attempted escape were made examples, whipped so severely they often died; their bodies dumped along the highway to become another 'Jane Doe' found murdered. Labeled prostitutes, no one cared.

It was reported, that Israeli-Jewish money launderers handled the money and that the Jewish-Russian Mobs made millions. It is a billion dollar a year industry. After all, for over two hundred years, Jewish traders have been importing female sex slaves from Eastern Europe. White women under twenty-four bring the most money. With the breakup of the old Soviet Union, young women from poor Eastern European countries seeking work were deceived into believing that they would get good jobs outside of Eastern Europe and return home, rich and able to support their families. Once they got off the plane in Cairo, they are cast into a living hell, taken to a warehouse, their identity papers destroyed, stripped naked, beaten and raped. Following more indoctrination in the art of lovemaking, the women are driven across the Egyptian desert and smuggled into Israel through a network of underground tunnels where most spend the rest of their lives as sex slaves. Others are auctioned off to buyers in different parts of the world. It is no wonder this abominable and damnable trade continues.

Yuri became obsessed with the idea of inflicting pain while imposing his will to satisfy his carnal desires. Using twisted logic, he rationalized that what he contemplated was justified, payback for the pain and indignity he had suffered. Women had become objects to do with what he wanted. Easy money made it even more appealing. It was mainly an International Jewish Mafia business and in places like Germany, they controlled organized crime. Because saying anything against these groups in some European countries was dangerous, they were rarely prosecuted. The victims feared reprisals against their families if they said anything.

Upon completion of his sentence of three years, Yuri arrived home in Russia. Prison had changed him, physically and mentally. The once jovial and fun loving young man who loved women was now bitter and disillusioned. His body bore disfiguring scars that would last the rest of his life. His eyes were sunken, his skin a pasty white, his once robust features drawn.

Felixs and Anton met him at the airport.

"Yuri, if it was not for those baby blues of yours, I would not have recognized you." Anton said half in shock at the sight of his old friend.

"How many kilos did you lose?"

"I must be down by thirteen or fourteen. My muscles are weak. Where is my father? I thought the old goat would delight in seeing me broken this way."

"I'm sorry to tell you but your father died six months ago. Some say he was poisoned. Your uncle tried to get the Singapore authorities to let you go early so that you could be at his bedside. They refused. They said you would never be anything but trouble."

"I'd like to say I am sorry and that I will miss him, but now I need to get back in shape. I plan to work out every day for the next six months. By then I should be my muscular handsome self," he boasted. "My uncle told me to move in with him."

"What do you plan to do then?"

"I want to get even with Chen Mei. If I could go to Singapore and find her, I would delight in giving her ten strokes of a caning rod."

"If you ever go back there they will lock you up. They told us never to return. We were, as they put it, 'unwelcome visitors'."

"They made a stronger threat to me. They threatened to give me another ten strokes of the rod and six years in prison. I hate those people."

Yuri was becoming agitated at just the thought of the girl responsible for his ordeal.

"There are a lot of opportunities for someone like me. My uncle knows some very influential people in the sex trade. There is a lot of money to make, not to mention the side benefits."

"Those rings are run by dangerous men, Yuri. I have heard how ruthless they are. Once you join, it is for life. They will not let you quit. The only way to out is when you are dead of natural causes, or they kill you and make it look like natural causes. You have always been wild, but do not do this. Get over the punishment you received, find a good job, a nice woman, enjoy life. Anton and I have good jobs. We can get you a job working with us. We make good money, have a nice apartment and lots of women visit us."

"No, my mind is made up. I want revenge. If my father was not dead, I think I would cane him with a rod for letting me suffer and for doing nothing to help me. Three years in a Singapore prison seemed like ten and all that time my cellmate spoke nothing but Arabic. Now I speak fluent Arabic. It is good that I catch on to languages quickly."

Yuri thanked his old friends for meeting him and for offering to help. It was clear he had made up his mind and nothing his friends could say would change that.

Yuri had dinner with them and walked out of their lives.

Soon after moving in with his uncle, Yuri had no trouble finding a group that specialized in trafficking women through his uncle's connections. It took him six months to rebuild his body to its former muscular build. Every day, all day he spent punishing himself in the gym getting stronger. By eating a diet that was high in protein and taking supplements that contained branched-chain amino acids (BCAA), glutamine, essential fatty acids, meal replacement products, pro-hormones, creatine, thermogenic products and testosterone boosters, he was soon as buff as before.

The next step was to pay a visit to one of Moscow's brothels. The Russian mafia now controls much of the Israeli underworld including prostitution. In Russia, Jewish gangs control the trade along with their Russian counterparts. Yuri's hatred of women made him a prime candidate for them to hire. Soon he was a recruiter using his handsome good looks to attract women. They loved his thick hair, pale blue eyes, tall muscular build, and deep sexy voice.

It was not long before a prosperous Yuri developed his own side business unbeknown to the mob. He planned to eventually break away and become independent using his newfound alliances for protection. Yuri would seduce an enchanting woman as his companion, become involved with her, and then kidnap her. Wealthy men were willing to pay almost any price to have a woman that could fulfill their needs. Yuri had handpicked and trained women to yield to every command, no matter how perverse. It was an endless market with a clientele that demanded the best and never questioned the price. When they became bored, they would send them back to Yuri who then sold them to other traffickers. On rare occasions, the woman was married to her abuser. For wealthy executives they were toys to provide diversity in their otherwise dull lives. They wanted control, a woman who would serve them, and be at their beckon call. A price of $35,000 in American money was not uncommon.

The mob suspected what Yuri was doing, but he had become one of their best recruiters using his good looks and charm with women. Desperate, these women were willing to do anything to escape the poverty of their home country with the promise of a good job and enough money to support their family. The dream soon became a nightmare once they arrived. Yuri arranged their trips to Egypt or Greece, and then with connections the mob had developed, they would eventually end up in Israel. After all, raping a non-Jewish woman was not against the law in Israel.

In just four years, he had accumulated the equivalent of one million dollars American and hid it safely in a bank account in Switzerland. In another six months or less, he planned to disappear assuming a new identity that he bought four years ago in Greece, move to a tropical paradise, buy a yacht, find a beautiful woman that would love him, and retire a wealthy man at the age of twenty-five.

In his quest to find one last special woman Yuri traveled to London and began romancing the beautiful, pampered, naïve, and spoiled daughter of a British Member of Parliament, Cassandra Cavendish.

Seducing such a naive and gullible woman for Yuri was almost too easy. Personally, Yuri liked a more sophisticated woman, a woman capable of handling life on her own. It was not long before he was enjoying the beautiful Cassandra every day in his hotel suite, teaching her ways to pleasure him. "This is an exceptional woman who will require an exceptional client, someone who will appreciate her talents and upbringing," Yuri reasoned. Recently, when he needed an emergency operation while staying in Cairo he had met an Egyptian doctor and decided that he would be the perfect customer for Cassandra. The two men had discussed the fact he was looking for a companion very much like Cassandra. Yuri would offer her vacation to an out of the way port city east of Suez and while there sell her to the doctor who owned a large yacht. There was only one condition; the doctor insisted she not be touched. Yuri wanted the pleasure of breaking her spirit for himself. Every time he whipped or spanked a woman, he felt he was getting even for what happened to him in Singapore. There is an art to applying the whip to a woman's bottom with maximum sting without breaking the skin and Yuri had become a master. His instrument of choice was a flogger with nine strips of thin rubber cording, fifty centimeters long with diagonally cut tips that gave an extreme sting. For his less cooperative subjects, he had another flogger that had eighteen strips of hard-core rubber twisted together with hard rubber barbs that stung with double the intensity and if not handled properly broke the skin. For pure pleasure and stimulation, nothing equaled spanking them with his bare hands and watching their bare bottoms blossom into a fiery red. It was personal and he enjoyed doing it. Yuri had never injured a woman severely, but he always got aroused when spanking or whipping their bottoms.

Chapter 2

Yuri first met Cassandra Cavendish, the daughter of Lord Robert Cavendish, an influential, forceful member of the House of Lords at a restaurant near Trafalgar Square where she was having lunch alone. Her long honey-blonde hair caressed her shoulders as she moved her head. Milk white and unblemished, her complexion was flawless. Sensing his approach, she turned and flashed a smile that reflected in her brilliant blue eyes. Yuri approached the table where she sat with her bare legs casually crossed. On her feet, she wore what appeared to be very expensive Italian shoes. Just above the knee sat the beginning of light tan wool skirt that led to a form fitting coral sweater set. A long camel hair coat sat draped over the back of her chair. Sophisticated and cute, Yuri thought to himself.

Even seated he could tell she was shorter than he was. Women taller than him were intimidating. Casually he approached and began a conversation. Most women perceived him as a handsome, suave man of the world, obviously wealthy, brawny and robust, a real prince charming. Cassandra was obviously no exception. Precisely tailored, his wardrobe was impeccable with dark blue slacks, a light blue oxford button down collar shirt adorned with a beautiful floral silk necktie tied in a full Windsor. His coordinated blazer festooned with brass buttons completed the look. On his wrist, he wore a gold and diamond encrusted watch. Cassandra recognized it because her father owned one similar to it. He had paid less than 5000 pounds.

"Hello, my name is Yuri Berezovsky. I am in London on business for few weeks. May I ask why is beautiful woman eating alone?" Yuri greeted her in his heavily accented English.

"I was shopping and stopped for something to eat."

"May I join you and treat you to lunch. I hate to eat alone. I am from Russia, but I love to practice speaking English, especially with alluring woman."

"You speak English very well. Please join me. Honestly, I hate to eat alone also." She answered in a high-pitched flirty voice that had a soft caressing tone to it.

Cassandra and Yuri spent over two hours having lunch and she was glad he had joined her.

Yuri asked her, "May I see you again for dinner this evening at my hotel, the Dorchester on Park Lane. We will dine and attend play. I am in London for three weeks and then I must fly to Moscow, Tel Aviv, and Cairo on business. I return to London frequently. I have three weeks before I leave London, and we could have fun during that time getting to know each other."

"I find you charming. Dinner and theatre sound wonderful. Do you suppose you could get tickets to *Flash Dance, the Musical?*" she asked.

"I am sure I can purchase tickets for show this evening."

"I will let my father know not to expect me for dinner."

Yuri showed surprise at her comment.

"I cannot believe that you are that close to your father at your age?"

"I am his only child, he is overly protective, and he is trying my tolerance by interfering with my social life. I will not introduce you to him. He never approves of my men friends. Where should I meet you?"

"Meet me at the Dorchester. We will get to know each other over dinner, and I will drive you home after the show."

They left the restaurant together promising to meet that evening as planned.

Yuri managed to secure two orchestra seats for the musical Flash Dance directed by Nikolai Foster.

Cassandra told her father she was meeting friends and would be home after midnight. She took a taxi and met Yuri inside the lobby of the Dorchester. They had a wonderful meal. Yuri was charming especially when Cassandra laughed and giggled at his jokes hanging on every word as he told her of his plans for the next three weeks while he was in London.

In the theater, Yuri reached across and placed his arm across her shoulders, kissed her neck, and held her hand as she watched the stage production. Cassandra seemed to enjoy the attention even more than the show. When the actors had taken their last bow and the curtain came down, he turned and whispered into her ear.

"Please join me at my hotel for drink before I drive you home."

Cassandra whispered back, "That would be lovely. Did you enjoy the musical?"

"I delighted in your company; I paid more attention to you than show. Come, I want to show you my suite at the hotel and treat you to a special Russian drink. They do not have it in the restaurants here. I bring it with me from Moscow. Please, join me."

"All right, Yuri, but I should really return home; it is late."

When they arrived at his suite, he opened a bottle of his favorite Russian Vodka, *Pyatizvyodnaya*. "This vodka is special. It has touch of honey."

"*pust'sbudutsyavse tvoivashi mechty*, it is Russian saying, 'May all your dreams come true.' You are very pretty woman. I think we could become close friends."

Cassandra took a tiny sip, "No, you must drink like a Russian. Watch me."

Yuri tipped the shot glass and drank it down in one swallow. Cassandra tried to do the same.

"Vodka is not for sipping. Here is another glass, *Zdorovya*, 'good health'"

"Oh Yuri," she coughed, "I feel light headed and dizzy. It burns my mouth and throat. Please no more."

Yuri pulled her to him, held her close, and passionately kissed her on the mouth. His hands slipped under her silk blouse and he gently caressed and fondled her ample breasts.

Cassandra pushed back from him. "Yuri, I think this has gone far enough tonight. We just met. I am not going to have sex with you. Take me home, please."

"Of course, please forgive me. You are so enchanting; I could not control my feelings. May I see you again; tomorrow? We will go on a drive to countryside. I love English countryside. I will ask hotel to prepare picnic lunch for us."

"Yes, that sounds like a wonderful idea; I too like the countryside."

Yuri drove her home and kissed her again in the car. "Cassandra, I have only met you, but you are woman I have only dreamed of meeting. I am very smitten. Until tomorrow."

Cassandra kissed him in return and hurried into the house. She ran to her room and thought of the handsome man she had met. "My father is not going to meet Yuri and spoil everything. Yuri is so handsome and must be wealthy to afford staying in London's finest hotel. His kisses excite me. Maybe he is the prince charming I have always dreamed of meeting."

Yuri had sprung his trap. A naïve Cassandra failed to ward off his overtures and was hopelessly under his spell. She was falling in love with the man that would eventually betray her.

Over the next three weeks, Cassandra visited his hotel room on many occasions to spend a lecherous afternoon in Yuri's arms completely smitten by his charm. Her training had begun and he taught her many ways to make love to him.

The day before he left on his business trip, Cassandra came to his hotel. "Oh Yuri, Must you go? I will miss you so."

"It can't be helped. I have business responsibilities. Perhaps we could say good-bye for few hours in my bed."

"Oh Yuri, you are a wicked man, but I love you."

Yuri pulled her to him and before she could say anything, had her dress off and his arms around her. Pressing her closely he kissed her deeply. Cassandra lay insensible in his arms. Yuri covered her body with burning kisses and love bites working his way down to kiss her vaginal lips and proceeded to flick her gate of pleasure with his tongue. He turned her on her stomach and had her get on her knees providing him complete access. Lubricating her bottom, he entered her from behind, moving fiercely in and out, she let out a moan and her body moved with his. The voluptuous agitation of her entire body brought them together as they climaxed in unison.

Physically exhausted, they fell to the bed facing the ceiling unable to speak. Yuri broke the silence.

"I have great feelings for you. My ecstasy is consummate. Knowing you are waiting for me, the next week or two will pass quickly."

"Must you go, I need you."

Cassandra pleasured him with her mouth and he instructed her to swallow his ejaculate telling her it had spiritual properties and would enhance her body chemistry. Again, he took her in his arms and they kissed passionately. From the bed, she watched as he packed his suitcase. Cassandra gathered her clothes and dressed without saying a word. Sitting in continued silence, they drove back to her home. Yuri pulled the car to the curb and shut off the engine, turned to her with a look on his face she had not seen before.

"Cassandra, do not date anyone else while I am away." His words carried the import of a threat, not a request. "I am jealous lover when it comes to sharing my woman."

Cassandra pushed toward him and starred into his blue eyes.

"Oh Yuri, I promise. I will await your return. Call me often; you have my cell phone number."

"You will always be on my mind. I promise you. I will call whenever possible."

Ten days later when Yuri returned to London, he was still recovering from an emergency operation in Cairo, but now he had a buyer for Cassandra. Yuri could not wait to see her again to seal the deal.

"Poor innocent Cassandra, she will bring a pretty price," Yuri thought to himself as he dialed her number on his cell phone from the terminal.

"Hello Cassandra?"

"Yes."

"It's Yuri, Cassandra I have missed you so much. Meet me at Dorchester in one hour, room 513."

"I want you to meet my father, Yuri. It is time you met him."

Cassandra had promised herself that she would introduce Yuri to her father, whatever the consequences. Yuri was now an important part of her life, her future.

"I do not think that is acceptable recommendation. Your father sounds like man who does not like any of your friends; perhaps in another week or two. I want you to myself this week."

"No, I insist. Just come by the house and say hello, please Yuri. It would mean so much to me. Father wants to meet the tall, dark, handsome man I have been seeing. Please Yuri, just come in and meet him. I have been chattering about you for over a month."

Yuri knew it was useless to argue and this was not the time to raise suspicions or seem to be anything but the ideal love interest.

"I will be there in an hour."

Yuri arrived at Cassandra's home and for the first time walked up to the house, a three-story townhouse near Hyde Park on the West side of London, and rang the bell."

The door opened to reveal a beaming Cassandra standing next to her father.

"Father, this is Yuri Berezovsky. He has been out of town for over a week. He is the man I have been dating."

"Pleasure to meet you sir. Won't you come in?"

Yuri stood shaking hands and looked around the well-appointed sitting room. Dark burgundy upholstered furniture contrasted against the parquet wood floor. Heavy brocade draperies, the same dark burgundy as the furniture hung on the windows and framed sheer curtains made of fine lace. On a mahogany table sat a lead crystal decanter of whiskey or bourbon and a matching crystal ashtray. Yuri detected the aroma of a recently smoked premium cigar hanging in the air.

"What business are you in?"

Cassandra's father was direct and to the point.

"I deal in expensive commodities, sir. I am sorry to meet you and run, but we have reservations. I enjoyed making your acquaintance."

"I understand. Perhaps we can continue our conversation at another time over a glass of good whisky and enjoy a fine cigar."

"Thank you, I would like that very much but we really must go." Yuri headed Cassandra to the door and they left.

He immediately took her to his hotel room where he handed her an elegantly wrapped box. "I saw these in Cairo, and I had to buy them for you; they were irresistible."

Cassandra opened the box to behold a stunning diamond bracelet with matching earrings.

"Oh Yuri, "she gasped, "They are so exquisite. Help me put them on."

Yuri fastened the clasp and she removed the earrings she had been wearing and put on the new two carat diamond studs.

"You look like princess. Make love to me."

Yuri unfastened her dress and took his time sliding the zipper down kissing her bare back as he undressed her. As she stood to face him, the dress fell to the floor at her ankles. Yuri took her hand and motioned her to lie on the bed. Naked and vulnerable she shook with anticipation at his touch.

"Excuse me, I am not strong enough. I had surgery while I was gone. We will make gentle love until I heal." Their bodies entwined and they kissed each other passionately.

"Oh Yuri are you all right, I missed you so much. London was not the same after you left. What kind of surgery did you have?"

"I had an emergency appendectomy while away. I need you to help me recover. I have two tickets to Egypt where we can spend time together in a small port city on the north coast where we could relax on beach for week. We leave in four days, yes?"

"I don't know Yuri. My father might not let me go."

"Cassandra, you are grown woman. Your father seems stern, strict, authoritarian, and unbending. Why not just come with me? Do not tell him you are going anywhere and call him once we arrive."

Cassandra looked away and shook her head. "I could not do that. Please, I'm sure he will not object once I tell him how much you mean to me."

Yuri drove her home after they had dinner and parked in front of the house. "I will pick you up tomorrow evening at seven and dream of you until then. I have business to transact during afternoon."

"Tomorrow cannot come soon enough; I think I am falling in love with you."

Cassandra put her arms around him and they held each other tightly and kissed good night.

Cassandra's father was waiting for her when she came through the door seated in his favorite chair with a cigar burning in the ashtray.

She barely had time to take off her coat when he spoke.

"Cassandra, on first impression, I do not like this man. He seems distant. He was so evasive when I asked what he did for a living."

This was not the first time Cassandra had fallen for what her father considered a less than reputable man of questionable means.

"I am going to see him tomorrow Father. We have a dinner date. Look at the diamond bracelet and earrings he gave me. I really care for him."

Cassandra placed her hands around his neck and gazed with a puppy dog stare into his eyes. Gently he removed her hands and spoke sternly to his daughter.

"Cassandra, this is too expensive a gift. Return them."

"Are you having sex with this man? You are a genteel woman; act like one. With a gift such as this he expects more than a kiss on the lips."

"Oh Father, that is none of your affair." She said in an annoyed tone of voice.

"It is my business as long as you are my daughter and live under my roof. Cassandra, you do not know what this man does for a living. Has he ever told you exactly what he does?"

"Yes, he said he was in the business of importing valuable commodities; he told you that. He said his main business was with Israel, he is Russian and Jewish."

"I have nothing against his being a Russian Jew, my dear. I do not like the way he treats you. He is rude, ill mannered and apparently did not want to talk with me tonight. He seems aloof, and I do not like the look in his eyes. This is not a man to be trusted."

"Oh Father, he has bewitching blue eyes. He does not have the manners of a Lord, but he is such fun. Did I tell you he is recovering from an operation? He wants to take me to Egypt to a beach resort to recover from having his appendix removed. We will have separate rooms. The bracelet was to make up for the time he was away."

"I want you to say no. Unless you are formally engaged to this man, the trip is off. You have only known this man for a few weeks. Before you go on holiday, you should know him a lot better and be engaged to marry him. You have a reputation to uphold."

"He said he wants to meet you and socialize, once we decide to marry. I think he is going to give me a ring tomorrow night."

"I want you to put him off when he asks you. The sure way to find out how he feels is to be hesitant. You should wait until you know him better. If after six months you feel the same, we will talk again."

With hands on her hips, Cassandra turned and fired back.

"I guess a month is not a long time to know someone. We have dinner and the theatre planned for tomorrow night. Yuri is so warm hearted; it is impossible not to love him. You will never accept or respect the men I date and always find something immoral, unethical, or improper with them. I am afraid that I am the one who has really discouraged his meeting you. You never approve of my friends. Sorry I introduced you."

"Be careful my dear, I have a feeling about this man that he cannot be trusted. I have tried to research his background through a friend at the Russian Embassy. They found nothing about him except a birth certificate, address, and a visa. I would like to know what he really does for a living. His vague answer told me nothing. Most men are eager to talk in some detail about their business. Cassandra, you are a very wealthy young woman; you must be careful. If he offers you a ring, say no."

"Father, that is the last straw; I know what I am doing. I cannot believe you have the nerve to have spies trying to find out about him," she shouted angrily.

Yuri arrived by cab at Cassandra's home the next night unaware of the argument between Cassandra and her father. He sat nervously in the front room waiting for her, saying as little as possible to her father. When she finally came into the room, Yuri stood up and said, "You are late. I have been here for twenty minutes. We will miss the opening curtain, hurry."

Robert Cavendish glared at Yuri as he took Cassandra by the arm, and rushed her outside to a waiting taxi.

"You made me wait, why?" Yuri asked in an agitated voice.

"My father and I had an argument last night when I arrived home. It continued tonight just before you arrived."

"I have impression that your father does not approve of me."

"Oh Yuri, you know how fathers can be. I am his only daughter and he wants what is right for me. He is old fashioned and feels we do not know each other well enough to travel together to Egypt."

"I have tickets; plans are made. Do you want to go or not?"

"I think we should back up a little until we get to know each other better. We have only known each other a month. Perhaps we should plan the trip for the end of the year. It is September, and Egypt may still be too hot. I think I would rather go in late November or early December."

"Your father cannot control your life. You are mature woman; you will go with me, now." Yuri was almost shouting at her.

Cassandra was taken aback by the change in Yuri's demeanor since his return. In the short time they had been together, he had been tolerant, patient and eager to indulge her every whim. It was what she loved most about him. "It must be the result of his operation," she thought to herself.

"I do not believe you are so angry with me. You told me you go to Egypt and Israel every few weeks. You are getting over an operation; perhaps we should go when you are stronger. I think Father is right, we should wait."

Yuri was enraged and threw the ticket at her.

"Here is your ticket to Egypt. The hotel reservation is in El-Arish. Consider it parting gift. I cannot believe at twenty-four you would rather listen to your father than me. I have business to handle. You need to grow up Cassandra. You are silly little girl. Russian women are much more sophisticated. I am going to change my reservation and go to Moscow to spend time with my uncle, and recover. Go by yourself if you wish. I had special gift for you, but I am not giving it to you now. Keep the bracelet and earrings."

Yuri paid the driver to take her home and then sped off in another taxi.

Cassandra rushed into the house with tears streaming down her cheeks.

"Father," she sniffled. "He left me. He gave me the ticket and said it was a parting gift. He said he preferred Russian women. I never should have listened to you. He was going to ask me to marry him. He had a ring for me. You have ruined my life. I will never forgive you, never."

"I do not suggest you use that ticket." Her father shouted after her.

"I am going to use the ticket. I think El-Arish sounds like a wonderful place to recover from losing Yuri. I love him. Besides, he said he was going to change his reservation and go to Moscow to visit his uncle." Cassandra shouted back and slammed her door.

"If you insist, Cassandra, call me when you arrive. I worry about you." There was genuine concern in his voice as he spoke to her from the other side of her bedroom door.

"Father, I am a grown woman. I will call you when I arrive, but then do not expect to hear from me again until I return home. I need to be alone for a while. I really love Yuri. You have broken up too many of my relationships. No man will ever be good enough for your little girl. I have a feeling he really needed me and time to relax on a beach to recover. How could I have been so cruel to him?"

Crying, Cassandra flung herself across the bed and lay sobbing.

"If he really loves you, he will return. I guess if I had been in hospital having surgery, I would be a little distant."

Robert Cavendish went down stairs, settled his tall, slender frame into a chair, and poured himself a glass of whiskey from the crystal decanter on the table and drank the fiery liquor with tears in his eyes. He poured a second drink and swallowed it quickly.

Pushing his fingers through his graying hair, he thought to himself, "What would her mother say in a situation like this? She always understood our daughter. I am so afraid of losing her."

Robert poured himself another shot of whiskey, turned out the lights, and went upstairs holding the handrail to steady himself. "I have lost my daughter," he thought as he closed the door quietly behind him, wiped the tears from his eyes, and retired for the night.

Chapter 3

Three days later, over 3500 kilometers away, Dr. Jameel al Basara was standing at the helm of his thirty-five meter yacht carefully maneuvering it away from the dock in Alexandria, Egypt as his five-man crew tended to lines and pulled fenders on the deck. He was just shy of two meters in height, muscular, the result of regularly working out at the hospital gym. A long, white robe, *thobe,* loosely clung to his sculpted body. On his head, he wore a *thagiya,* a traditional Arab cap with holes in it to hold his thick black curly hair in place. On top of the thagiya was a *gutra,* a white scarf worn to keep the hot summer sun off his head. Holding it in place was an *ogal,* a black band with gold threads. Black framed holographic sunglasses costing more than 195 Euros shielded his eyes from the glare. An expensive chronograph on his tanned wrist sparkled in the sun. Jameel wanted for almost nothing, living in luxury he looked more like an Arabian prince from the tales of Scharazade than a medical doctor. When he spoke, his voice was rich, deep, and comforting. Women hearing him speak thought of him as virile, sexy, and reassuring.

As soon as the yacht cleared the harbor, one of his crew took the helm and Jameel walked to the fly bridge, laid back on one of the comfortable loungers, and closed his eyes enjoying the soft sea breeze and the warmth of the late summer Egyptian sun.

Thoughts of his upcoming adventure raced through his mind. At last, he would have the one thing still missing in his life, a woman at his disposal subject to his every wish and desire.

"Am I really going to buy a woman and make her my slave? It would ruin my family's reputation if anyone found out."

Jameel found the thought of a woman at his beckon call twenty-four hours a day without the right to say no appealing.

"If she is as desirable as Yuri says she is, I will enjoy her body and she will obey me; unlike my wife who never agreed with me or did anything, I asked. I am going to enjoy this adventure. If it does not work out, I only need to contact Yuri on his satellite phone and he will arrange to take her off my hands. Yes, yes, I will go through with this. It will be an amusing break from the stress of being a surgeon at Cairo's busiest hospital."

A crewmember arrived topside with a tray of sliced cheese, cold cuts, fresh fruit and an iced pitcher of fruit punch.

"When will we reach the coordinates I gave you?" Jameel asked as he sat up in the chair.

"We should be there shortly, maybe an hour and forty-five minutes."

"Good, the boat we are looking for is a twenty-one-meter sport fisherman. Her hull is white and the name on the transom is in Cyrillic letters. It should be easy to find if the coordinates are correct."

"We will notify you as soon as it is in sight. Why are we meeting this other boat if I may ask?"

"I am meeting a foreign woman and she is a very private person. When she comes on board, she will speak to no one. This will be a very private affair. Mention this meeting to no one; do you understand?"

"Yes sir, I will inform the rest of the crew."

"Thank you. I trust you and know this rendezvous will be our little secret."

The crewmember got a smirk on his face as he turned away and returned to the lower deck with the other crewmembers.

"Jameel is meeting a woman. I do not know who she is, but we are not to mention this trip to anyone. Personally, I am glad to see he is meeting someone. I am tired of his complaints about his wife and the divorce. Jameel used to be fun before he got married to that bitch Zahrah. Hopefully this woman improves his temperament."

Jameel thought of how his parents just two months ago following his divorce had given him this new yacht out of concern for his happiness and well-being. They knew he loved the sea and hoped a new, larger yacht would help him to forget his bad marriage. Since the divorce, occasional trysts with several prostitutes left him unsatisfied and unhappy. The divorce had left him bitter about women, all women. This would be different, a great adventure.

His marriage to Zahrah was arranged and took place following his graduation from college with honors at just twenty-six. By Islamic culture, he was very young to take a wife and was disappointed that he had never had a chance to experience life as a single man. Repeatedly he had replayed the events that had led to his failed marriage. Zahrah was twenty and madly in love with her childhood sweetheart, Abdullah. Once, during their brief courtship, he overheard them speaking to each other.

"Abdullah, I would rather leave home than go through with this marriage. I love you."

"You cannot run away. Your family and Jameel's have planned this marriage since you were little. You must go through with it. If the marriage fails, I know Jameel; he will divorce you. He will not keep a woman that does not love him. He told me he would have rather picked his own wife."

"I love you; I cannot marry him."

"You will for the honor of your family and his. I want you so much; but Jameel will let you go. I know he will. Please, for the honor of all our families, marry him."

Zahrah was in tears, but took his advice. The marriage was stormy at best and she continually found fault with everything Jameel did including his attempts to appease her. They could not talk to each other without arguing.

During one of their arguments she told him, "Abdullah said you would divorce me. I do not love you. I have never loved you. Let me go."

"It is not up to me, our families planned this; give it a chance. We have only been married five months."

"It seems like twenty years to me. Let me go! Let me go!" She shouted at him and hit him in the face with her open hand. "You gave me everything but a divorce. I told you I was not in love with you before we were married, but our families insisted."

"Zahrah you have gone too far. Enough!" he shouted. "How dare you scream at me, give me orders and hit me. I have never struck you, but you hit me and deserve to be punished. Perhaps a good spanking of your bottom will make you think before you do something like this again. I have given you everything you asked for and tried to make this marriage work."

"Go ahead, beat me. Give me a reason to hate you more. You are a bastard and a coward if you hit me. I will get a divorce."

Again, she smacked him in the face, this time leaving her hand print. As his cheek reddened, she stomped off.

Jameel followed grabbing her roughly by the arm and dragged her down the stairs into the basement, closed the door behind him and locked it. He did not want the servants to hear what was going on. There was a wooden bench against the wall and he sat down, pulled her across his lap, pulled her dress over her head, and despite her screaming and wiggling, ripped her panties off exposing her bare bottom.

"Let me go you bastard."

"You deserve this," he shouted at her as he began to spank her bottom with his hand. "You have not even tried to get to know me. I will spank you until you settle down."

Jameel spanked her until she finally stopped screaming and her bottom was a fiery red.

As soon as he released her, she got up, her dark brown hair in disarray and pulled her dress down. Despite the fact, she was thirty-three centimeters shorter than Jameel she started pounding her fists into his chest.

"I hate you, I hate you. Let me go."

She kicked him in the shin.

Zahrah screamed at him. "*Inta Khaywan, Inta humar*. How dare you spank me as if I was a child? Abdullah would never hurt me."

"You call me an animal, a donkey, I have had it. When a woman hits and curses her husband, severe punishment follows. How dare you kick me? I have a gag someone gave me before we married as a joke; it may shut you up for a while."

Jameel grabbed her arm and she continued to hit him. He pinned her arms behind her back and held them with one hand as he removed his belt. He took her to a pole that ran from the basement floor to the ceiling, bound her wrists behind her with his belt, and fastened them to the pole.

Zahrah was in tears, but still swearing at him. "*Wad al haram,* I will report you."

"I am not a bastard. I have a right to discipline my wife. This gag will shut you up. After an hour, if you continue to swear at me, I will put it on for three hours and spank you again."

"Please no, Jameel, I will be quiet." She pleaded.

He grabbed a five-centimeter diameter ball gag off a shelf. It had leather straps on each side. He put a leather strap around her forehead and fastened it tightly to the pole so she could not move her head.

"Stay still while I put it on you."

"Open your mouth." He ordered her.

Zahrah obeyed.

"Wider. Wider." He shouted.

Zahrah complied and he took the ball gag, placed it into her mouth, and buckled the straps tightly. Her mouth was wide open but she could not utter a sound. She began to drool and streams of saliva ran from her mouth.

"Stay that way for an hour. I do not want to listen to you say another abusive word to me. You deserve this."

Jameel left her bound and sobbing and ran upstairs, opened the door, slammed it behind him, relocked it and went to the master suite on the second floor. He entered the room and pounded his fist into the wall, breaking through the wallboard and leaving a ragged hole. His knuckles were bloody.

"I must let her go. I cannot do this. She deserved her punishment, but I cannot hurt her."

He picked up the telephone and called his father,

"Father, I cannot do this anymore. She drove me to the breaking point. She hit, kicked, and cursed me. I spanked her, bound her to a pole in the basement, and put a ball gag in her mouth."

"Jameel, I had no idea you and Zahrah were that unfit for each other. I will call her parents and the cleric. We will make the arrangements. The divorce will be discreet. Now get down there and release her."

Jameel hung up the phone, washed the blood off his hands, changed his blood spattered shirt, and walked slowly back to where Zahrah was gagged and bound. A half hour passed by the time he walked back to the basement. Zahrah was sobbing and her entire body was shaking.

"I am so sorry. Forgive me. My father is arranging our divorce."

Jameel carefully removed the gag, wiped saliva from her face, and he unbound her. He took her in his arms and held her as she sobbed.

"Forgive me Zahrah. I did not realize you were that unhappy until today. Forgive me. Hit me again if it will make you feel better."

Zahrah was sobbing as she told him, "You are a decent man Jameel. I should not have hit or cursed you; I deserved to be punished. I know you have tried to make me happy. It is just that I have always loved Abdullah. I am so sorry it got to this point. I do not hate you; I just love another."

Jameel held her and kissed her cheeks. "We never should have gotten married putting our families ahead of our own feelings. I am sorry I punished you. Forgive me if I hurt you."

Zahrah looked up at him, her eyes filled with tears.

"It was my fault also. I wish today had never happened but I am also glad that it did. Thank you for trying. That is more than I ever did. I did not give our marriage a chance. Forgive me for hitting you and cursing. You did not deserve that abuse. My hope is that we will part friends."

Overcome by a rush of regret, Jameel suddenly realized that his marriage to Zahrah would soon be over.

"I will never forget you Zahrah. I wish it had ended better or perhaps not at all. Only our families will know and they will understand."

"Thank you Jameel. I am truly sorry."

She hugged him and kissed him affectionately. Tears streamed down her face and she hurried upstairs.

Jameel was alone in his huge house when his parents called two weeks after the divorce.

"Jameel, drive to Alexandria with us. We have a surprise for you."

His parents arrived in their luxury sedan. His father wore an Arabian Thobe and his mother wore an embroidered black abaya and a hijab. When they arrived at the port, Jameel saw the huge yacht at the dock.

"I cannot believe you did this. You know how I love boats and the sea. Thank you, thank you. I am sorry my marriage did not work."

"It was not your fault. We must change from traditional ways of arranging children's lives. You have a right to choose. Enjoy the yacht and find a good woman. Mother and I hate to see you so unhappy."

Jameel had tears in his eyes and hugged both of his parents. "I will name the yacht *El Jumanah*, The Silver Pearl."

"I will contact my crew from the old boat and we will go sailing next week."

"Your mother and I look forward to it."

When Jameel returned to the hospital the next day, a young Russian executive was in emergency with an acute appendix attack. Jameel was the doctor on call that day and remembered the conversation he had with his patient after the operation.

"How are you today, Yuri. It was lucky for you that your appendix had not burst."

Yuri spoke in Arabic, "I am feeling well, but you look down. Women problems?"

"Is it that obvious? I divorced my wife a couple of months ago. I am afraid to start a new relationship. It was a terrible ordeal, but I miss making love to a woman. Women for hire are not human; their movements are mechanical. They have no emotions. They are robots, cold and unemotional."

"Have you ever thought of having a concubine?"

"No, not really. Right now I am open to suggestions."

Sensing he had an excellent opportunity Yuri decided to take advantage of this young and vulnerable doctor. He could tell Jameel had the means and Yuri would give him the desire.

"You would be in control. Your concubine would obey your every command; she would have sex with you anytime, anywhere, any way. If she dared to talk back, punish her and spank her bottom; it will remind her you are in charge. This kind of woman makes a man forget a bad marriage. I will personally find this woman for you."

Jameel was already fantasizing about what it would be like to have his own personal sex slave complying with his every wish.

"It sounds tempting."

What Jameel could not know was that Yuri had already found his perfect woman. Cassandra was just what the doctor ordered.

"I work for a large organization that finds women for discriminating businessmen. I have a side business of my own and many satisfied customers. This conversation is between you and me and must never leave this room. I can trust you, yes?"

"Of course, I am intrigued by your proposal. Explain what you can do for me. I do not want to have a prostitute or call girl."

"What I do is bring you a young, alluring woman trained in the art of love. It is expensive, but she would be yours to do with as you wish. She will have no identity papers, no money, and no passport. Escaping from you is impossible. This woman is yours for as long as you want her. If you tire of her, I will take her back. I am part of a very large organization that specializes in finding women for lonely men. The woman I find for you will be special. What type woman would you like?"

"A beauteous blue-eyed blonde would be nice." Jameel took a deep breath.

No sooner than the words left his lips, desire began to overcome his common sense.

"Will not this woman try to escape? I am a doctor and my family has status. I cannot risk a scandal should this, this indiscretion get out. I already perform illegal circumcisions of women on the side."

Yuri was already starting to like his perspective client even more knowing he was willing to risk his reputation and license to practice medicine by performing illegal circumcisions.

"I have heard many doctors do that."

"It saves them from mutilation by the people who still practice this. I charge nothing and the little girls are not mutilated."

"Little girls?"

"Yes, most of the girls are under ten when they are circumcised. I even circumcised an adult woman, once. She was from Germany and married to an Egyptian; he insisted on circumcision. He made me do it without anesthesia while he watched and directed how much he wanted cut. I was paid a lot of money."

"I cannot imagine doing that to a little girl or an adult woman."

A look of disgust flashed across Yuri's face as he experienced an emotion he thought he was no longer capable of feeling. Mutilating children was too much, even for Yuri.

"It is a culture that has existed for hundreds of years among the Coptic Christians, Nubians, Muslims, Africans, and some Bedouins. Some of the Israeli Jews still practice circumcision of their girls."

"In Russia, we like our women au natural in that area. I do like the way Muslim women shave their bodies; they feel soft and silky like newborn babies." Jameel acknowledged Yuri's comment with a smile.

"If the woman creates a problem, call me, I take her back, no risk. I will even train her to be submissive. When she arrives, she will do anything you ask."

"I think I am capable of training a woman myself,"

"Of course, I understand." Sensing the hook was set, Yuri gave Jameel a price of 100,000 Egyptian pounds. The doctor did not question the price nor attempt to barter him down.

"My life needs some excitement. Give me a call when you find someone. Do not abuse her. I do not want her beaten or whipped into submission. If there is a mark on her body, I will not pay you anything. You will give me her identity papers."

"Agreed, the price is 100,000 Egyptian pounds."

"Where would I meet this woman?"

"You told me you had a yacht. I also have a yacht. We will exchange money and the woman at sea off El-Arish."

"How long will it take to find my woman?"

"Give me at least two weeks to make sure I have the right one. Your woman will be special, handpicked, and trained in the art of love by me."

"I have a satellite phone, call me, and let me know what size clothing she wears."

"The woman I have in mind is English, the daughter of an English lord. She is very charming, has long honey blonde hair that falls almost to her waist, dark blue, almost violet eyes, long lashes and a flawless complexion. In dresses, she is a perfect thirty in England or a size thirty-six on the continent. In shoes a five and a half British and size thirty-eight continental. Blouses she would be a forty British or forty-six continental. Her only flaw is she is naïve, and allows her father to make her decisions for her. We met several weeks ago. I will continue to see her and teach her all ways to make love so she will be experienced."

The thought of a woman of noble birth was more than Jameel had hoped. With a title came means, not only money, but also influence. The thought of an angry English lord marshaling his considerable resources to find and reclaim his missing daughter was a daunting possibility he would deal with later once he had a chance to think it through.

"I will expect your call."

Jameel checked Yuri's incision. "You may leave the hospital this afternoon. You are recovering nicely and there is no sign of infection. Do not do any heavy lifting for at least two weeks."

Jameel finished eating, laid back, closed his eyes again, and waited for the sighting of Yuri's boat.

Chapter 4

One year ago in Cairo, Egypt, Shamsa, a graceful petite woman in her early twenties with shoulder length dark brown, almost black hair wearing a long sleeved tunic, and long skirt with Arabian embroidery, was hurrying around her large and well-furnished penthouse apartment getting Suhail, her son ready for a luncheon with her husband Hassan. Dressed in a cute outfit his grandmother had bought for him, Suhail looked so grown-up in his white shirt decorated with the little ducks and dark blue overhauls. On his feet were brand-new white shoes. Placing him into his stroller, she picked up the bag she always carried containing a change of clothes, two bottles of breast milk she had expressed that morning, diapers and wipes. Suhail was nine months old today and advanced for his age. He could walk holding on to the furniture with one hand while holding his favorite toy, a set of multi-colored plastic keys his father had given him. The small boy clutched the keys in his hand as they rode the elevator to the garage. His mother buckled him into the child restraint seat, put the stroller in the back, and got behind the wheel of their dark green SUV.

It was an exceptionally clear day in Cairo; the sky was a dark blue with little puffy white clouds drifting over the monochrome colored city. Brightly colored laundry, draped over the balconies of the tall apartment buildings to dry in the warm sun provided the only color in the drab landscape of the city. It was normal traffic for Cairo when they entered the main thoroughfare. The cacophony of horns and squealing brakes filled the crowded streets of the bustling city with a constant din.

Shamsa turned and cooed to Suhail, "We are having lunch with Papa. You are such a big boy. I love you so much."

Suhail was a handsome baby boy with a full head of hair and gorgeous brown eyes framed in thick lashes like his father. He looked up at his mother, and smiled. Shamsa carefully maneuvered the large vehicle through the narrow, crowded streets. Traffic was heavy as usual and some cars had so many multiple dents and patches on their bodies it was difficult to tell what model or year they were. A bus passed her with passengers clinging to its sides like barnacles on an old boat. There were traffic signals, but they were rarely functional and when they did operate, drivers ignored them. Crowded together drivers pushed their way ahead ignoring the painted lanes creating four confused lanes of traffic squeezed into three lanes. Pedestrians took their life in their hands racing between cars to cross the street. There were crosswalks, but most people preferred finding their own way darting across wherever there was a slight break in the constant flow of traffic. Suddenly, the car in front of her stopped to avoid a pedestrian and Shamsa slammed on the breaks just missing the back bumper of the car in front of her. Everyone was upset and sounding their horns creating a frantic chorus. A motorbike carrying a family of four wove between the cars.

Shamsa's husband Hassan and his brother Rafiq owned several hotels in Egypt. Hassan had his office in their largest hotel, Pharaoh's Pyramid Hotel in Cairo along the Nile with a view of the Cairo Tower. Rafiq was usually in the smaller hotel in the city, Horus Towers in Giza near the pyramids. The brothers owned three other hotels: a five star hotel in El-Arish east of Suez, two four-star hotels-one in Aswan, and the other in Luxor and were very successful.

Hassan had been in the military and was considering it as a career when he met Shamsa. She was college educated and her family had left her their hotel business when they died. Rafiq and his brother ran the business and later added hotels in Aswan and Luxor. The two brothers were very influential businessmen in Cairo and their hotels catered to diplomats and wealthy tourists.

Shamsa called him on her cell phone, "Hassan, I am wearing the exquisite embroidered skirt and scarf you bought me. Suhail and I will be at the hotel in five minutes. The new outfit your mother gave him makes him look so grown up and the keys you gave him have become his favorite toy. Love you so much."

"Love you back. See you soon."

Shamsa turned onto the one-way street near the hotel and was almost finished singing a song to Suhail, "*Fiha wezza wa bata Bi ta'mel quack quack, quack*" (there's a duck that goes quack, quack, quack . . .)"

In disbelief, she saw a car heading straight for her going the wrong way at an unusually high speed. Shamsa screamed just before the cars collided head-on. The driver in the other car was not wearing a seat belt, and his head now protruded part way through the windshield despite the fact the airbag had deployed. The air bag popped up in front of Shamsa and held her captive between the wheel and seat until it deflated. Frantically she tried to open the door. It was jammed. She climbed over the seat to get into the back of the car with Suhail who was screaming. The force of the collision had jammed the back doors as well. Shamsa tried in vain to open the windows in a futile attempt to escape. The impact had stalled the engine and cut off power to the windows.

Holding Suhail in her arms, she pounded on the windows screaming for help, "*il-Ha'ni! il-Ha'ni!* Help! Help!"

The smell of gasoline from a ruptured gas line permeated the car's interior and Shamsa panicked. In seconds, flames engulfed the car trapping Shamsa and Suhail. The intense heat from the inferno prevented those trying to help from doing anything but watch in horror. Police and firefighters arrived at the scene moments later and extinguished the fire, but it was too late. Shamsa and Suhail were dead, burned beyond recognition. The police identified the owner of the car as Hassan al Gaafar.

Back at the police station one of the officers recognized Hassan's name on the accident report. "I know this man; I met Hassan and his wife at the hospital the day their son was born. He owns that large five-star Pharaoh's Pyramid Hotel along the Cornish."

Hassan's office phone rang.

"Hula," Hassan's secretary Adiva answered the phone.

"*Assalaamu' alaykum.* (peace be upon you) Who is calling?"

"*Wa Aleikum Assalam.* (and peace upon you also) It is Sergeant Akar Sawalha. "Is Mr. Gaafar in his office? There is an emergency situation, I must speak with him."

"I will ring you through immediately."

"*Assalaamu' alaykum.* Hassan Gaafar speaking."

"*Wa Aleikum Assalam.* Mr. Gaafar, this is Sgt. Akar Sawalha; we met nine months ago. Our wives had babies the same day. It was a wonderful day for our families."

"Yes, I remember you. What is wrong? I sense there is a problem."

"Something terrible has happened."

Hassan knew it was personal and had nothing to do with the hotel business. He sat down at his desk.

"Your wife and son were involved in a horrible accident. I am so sorry."

Hassan interrupted him, "No, no, you cannot be telling me they did not survive."

"I am so sorry. The vehicle caught fire and your wife and son were not able to escape. The accident was not your wife's fault. I know this must be the worst day of your life. Please accept my sincere condolences for your loss."

Shock, disbelief, Hassan could not comprehend what he was hearing.

"Where are they now?"

"They were taken to hospital. The police identified the driver of the other car as Vasilli Sviatoslavich. Identification came through the Cairo International airport car rental. It was determined that he was drinking. A half-empty bottle of vodka was on the floor in the front of the car. Is someone there with you?"

"Yes, yes, my secretary."

Hassan let out an anguished scream. Hula rushed into his office.

"What is wrong, sir?"

"They are gone, gone, dead, burned alive in the car." Hassan fell to his knees pounding his head into the carpet weeping.

"Who?"

"Shamsa and Suhail."

Hassan got up, slumped back into the chair and slammed his fist onto the desk sending papers flying across his office. "I must go to them. I just spoke to her on the phone."

"Please, please, I will call Rafiq. Do not drive in your condition," Adiva implored him as she burst into tears.

Mohamed, the hotel's manager, heard the commotion and rushed into Hassan's office.

"I heard what happened. Adiva, make the phone calls. I will stay with him."

Mohamed put his arms around Hassan and held his trembling body. Tears streamed down Hassan's face and he had trouble breathing.

"Sit down, sit down, please, Hassan. We notified your father and brother. Can I get you anything, a glass of water or tea?"

"No, I do not want anything. They cannot be gone. They were my reason for living. How can I go on?"

The secretary called Rafiq who was in the city that day at the Giza hotel and told him what had happened.

"Do not let him leave Adiva. I will get there as soon as possible. Stay with him."

Rafiq called their father, Sabir, who was a surgeon at one of Cairo's largest hospitals. Sabir, wearing surgical scrubs, and Rafiq, wearing a dark blue designer business suit arrived about the same time. Both men were dark complected, about 195 centimeters each with black hair and mustaches. They left their cars running at the entrance to the hotel, and rushed through the lobby and into Hassan's office. Mohamed had his arm across Hassan's shoulder trying to console him.

Hassan was distraught. "Why, why, I should have gone home for lunch as usual? Suhail was nine-months old today. It is my fault. I am to blame. I suggested we go out to lunch because it was a special day. Shamsa said she would drive to the hotel."

"It is not your fault." Sabir tried to comfort his son. "Their leaves fell from the tree of life. You must not blame yourself."

Rafiq hugged his brother as tears streamed down his own face.

"We will get you through this. Your life must go on. Mother, Rafiq and I are here for you."

Hassan's body trembled, as he fought to gain control of his emotions.

"I must go to them. They are at the hospital."

"We called the hospital. They are being prepared for burial as we speak."

"No, I must see them again. I must hold my wife and son once more."

"No, Hassan, remember them as they were. Do not do this. I will see you through this. We called Shamsa's mother and sister. The burial is tomorrow. Come, we must go."

Eight Months Later

"Hassan, you must get involved with something," Sabir pleaded with his oldest son. "You cannot mourn the dead forever. Look at you. You have lost ten kilos, your eyes are blood shot, and you are not sleeping. Rafiq says you are always angry and unreachable. Your mother is in tears from worry. Your life must go on."

Hassan sat opposite his father fingering the melted remains of the plastic keys that he had given Suhail. They were misshapen and grey from the fire, but he never went anywhere without them.

"Why, I cannot get her out of my mind. Her last words on the cell phone, I love you so much. Then she was gone. I am having trouble living without her and Suhail. My son never lived to see his first birthday. They were a part of me."

"Rafiq and I need you. Your mother needs you. Listen to me please."

Hassan settled back on the sofa spread his arms across the back and looked away, lost in self-pity.

"Listen, I am involved with some former military friends of mine. We are working to put an end to the sex trade that passes through Egypt. These women are driven in the back of a truck, and sometimes marched across the desert, smuggled into Israel, and sold to the brothels to service the wealthy Jews and other businessmen. I have treated two women who managed to escape while they were still here in Cairo. They tell tales of horrible degradation and beatings at the hands of these ruthless people. It has got to stop."

Sabir continued, "It's the Russian Jews and the Mafia doing this and the Israeli government permits it. We have to stop this barbaric slavery. It will keep your mind involved. Perhaps the man who killed your Shamsa and Suhail was part of this filthy business. No one ever claimed his body and Moscow denied he ever existed. They said no one by that name at that address ever held a Russian passport. Cairo denied he had a visa. All of his documents were forgeries—good forgeries."

Hassan took a deep breath, "What can I do?"

"You can help by watching for single women traveling alone. You and Rafiq own five hotels in the busiest tourist attractions in Egypt. That small hotel in El-Arish is not far from the border with Israel. Did you know that several single women each year arrive in Egypt with all the proper paperwork and visas but there is no record of their ever leaving? They just disappear."

"I must do something. Sleep only comes when exhaustion takes over; I might as well have died that day."

Sabir left and for the next three months, there were only scattered rumors of missing women, but none where Rafiq and Hassan's hotels were located. It had been almost a year since Shamsa and Suhail died.

One day in September, a report came across Sabir's desk that a British woman, the daughter of a prominent member of the House of Lords had disappeared from Cairo. She was last seen boarding a bus to El-Arish. Sabir worked with Henry Ewing at MI6 in London on cases that involved missing women trafficked for sex. They had met years ago when Sabir had been a doctor during the war with Israel over the Sinai and remained close friends.

Sabir called Hassan, "There may be a major shipment of women in the next month; we have learned this from our intelligence. We do not have a date. Perhaps this woman was to be a part of this shipment."

"If that man was part of this, I will have my revenge. My life needs to be normal; I do not even feel like a man," Hassan told his father.

"Talk with Rafiq. Plan to move your office temporarily to El-Arish. We have been expecting this break. It will not be a permanent, a month, six weeks at the most. Rafiq will manage. For the past year he has managed to run the hotels with very little help from you."

"Too many memories are here. I hate going home at night. Shamsa is everywhere. I wake up thinking I hear Suhail crying."

"Talk to me. Talk to my friend who is a psychologist. You must go on with your life. It was not your fault. Stop blaming yourself."

"I will talk with Rafiq. He will be angry that I have not been in Cairo for so long, but I must do something. I am more dead than alive."

Chapter 5

One year earlier, Alex MacKay entered a bookstore on his way home from Heathrow Airport. "May I help you Mr. MacKay?" The old lady never forgot a customer, even those who visited the shop less frequently.

Alex looked up at the woman standing before him. She looked like a character from a Dickens's novel come to life from one of the books on the shelf. Her grey hair was done up in a bun and she wore an old Victorian style dress with lace. She peered at him over her reading glasses perched almost to the tip of her nose flashing a warm smile of recognition. The twinkle in her blue eyes said welcome back. Alex responded with a smile. It had been some time since he last visited St. Sithyn's Book Store on Portobello Road.

"Yes, Mrs. MacDougal, I'm here to pick up the children's book you kept for me." Without a word, she disappeared behind the counter reappearing an instant later, book in hand.

"Thank you, that's the one."

"Shall I wrap it?"

Alex nodded, "Please."

The old woman carefully wrapped the old book in brown wrapping paper and placed it inside a plastic bag.

"Here you are Mr. MacKay. I'm sure your Lassie will love this book and when your little one arrives, the stories will be his favorites."

"Thank you, Mrs. MacDougal. I have been out of town for three weeks and I can 'ardly wait to get 'ome." Alex spoke in a deep husky voice letting his Scottish brogue come into full play. It would not be long before he walked through the door to greet his wife Catherine who neither appreciated nor tolerated his Scottish brogue. He knew he had to slip back to London English when he got home.

Alex Branford MacKay buttoned his raincoat and looked out the window for any sign of the cab he had called. It had started to rain. He was a very tall handsome man, 194 centimeters in height, with dark brown hair and gray eyes. Alex had a medium, well-proportioned muscular build, wide through the shoulders and slim through the hips.

Moments later a taxi pulled up and beeped its horn; Alex grasped his package tightly, opened the door, and turned toward Mrs. MacDougal.

"Guid day, back soon. I luv your bookstore."

As Alex stepped out, the wind driven rain assaulted him immediately. Sloshing through ankle deep water he made his way to the cab. Just as he grasped the door handle, a flash of lightning streaked across the sky illuminating a jagged scar that passed over his left eye and continued to his chin. He got in, gave the driver his address, and carefully placed the plastic bag containing the book on the seat next to him. Starring out the window deep in thought, Alex sat quietly as the driver maneuvered his way through moderate traffic to the west side of London near Hyde Park and the address Alex had given him. The rain beat a steady tattoo on the roof of the cab as it planed like a boat through the wet streets.

The driver pulled to the curb and stopped. Alex paid him and without putting up his umbrella, clutched the book, hurried up the stairs to the house that had been in his wife's family for over a hundred years and stepped inside. Alex preferred his ancestral country home in Kincardineshire, Scotland near Fettercairn. An ancient castle stood on the property that he had reconstructed at his father's insistence. It was only because of Catherine's obstinacy that they lived in the city at all.

As he entered, rock music, which he disliked intensely, played so loud it seemed to make the whole house vibrate. An exotic aroma drifted through the air from an incense burner on a table in the hall. Opera, light jazz, classic rock, or musicals were more to Alex's taste in music. He put down the package, removed his dripping raincoat, and placed his umbrella near the front door. The noise emanating from the front room was Metallica, his least favorite rock music. Taking the book from the bag, he walked toward the music. Decorated in expensive designer modern furniture and abstract art that covered the walls, the room was totally out of character with one exception, a wing back chair upholstered in the MacKay tartan and above the fireplace a framed coat of arms of the MacKay family. On the bar sat a bottle of his favorite MacKay whiskey and a crystal decanter filled with the same, along with a humidor of his favorite Cuban cigars. A dark blue oriental carpet covered the wood parquet floor.

Catherine sat in the corner with her legs crossed in a black leather and chrome chair. She looked up as he entered the room. Her piercing blue eyes connected with his, her honey blonde hair draped softly across her shoulders, poised in a designer dress, she held a glass of red wine in one hand and a lighted cigarette in the other. A wry smile graced her lips.

"I missed you the last three weeks, Catherine. Come my love, give a hug; I bought a book on my way home at the old antiquarian bookstore on Portobello Road. It is an ancient book, leather bound with gold edged pages. It contains stories from my childhood. Mrs. MacDougal sends her best."

Alex stood there with his arms outstretched, Catherine remained seated as though she was part of the chair, said nothing, and a sullen expression replaced her smile.

"Could you turn down the music, I can hardly hear myself think. Does that incense contain one of those synthetic cannabin oils?" Irritation crept into his voice.

"Just because you hate my music, does not mean I cannot listen to it when I want. I like it, I like it loud, but we do have to talk, I will turn it down. I like the incense, it makes me feel good all over," she answered angrily.

Catherine reached over and turned down the volume.

"You do not sound glad to see me. What is the matter?" His voice became stern and angry. "You are drinking wine, and smoking my love? You know what the doctor said about alcohol and tobacco while you were pregnant. What is wrong with you?"

"Alex, look at me. I have been here alone while you have been out of town playing spy, or whatever you do, working for the government. I am not ready to be a mother. I hate to tell you this dear, but while you have been serving your country, I have been serving a gentleman who appreciates me. He takes me to hard rock concerts and sporting events. We dine in the finest restaurants and go for rides in the country to his estate. He smokes fine Nicaraguan cigars and drinks the best brandy. He knows what a woman wants. Unlike you, he does not mind a woman that smokes. He gave me the incense. Look at yourself Alex, that scar on your face makes you look like a thug recovering from a knife fight. You may have the deep husky voice of Sean Connery complete with his brogue, but you are nothing to me. You are more concerned with those women you rescue. Besides, I no longer carry your child. I suppose you thought the little mother would be waiting for you."

Alex dropped the book on the floor and slammed his fist onto the table causing a crystal ashtray to tumble to the floor and shatter. He clenched his fists and the vein on his forehead started to pulse as his rage built.

Catherine's voice changed into a snarling tone, her demeanor changed, and she spewed forth the venomous words, "I had an abortion the day after you left. Now, it is time for me to leave, my bags are packed. Bernard asked me to move in with him; I always hated this old house of my parents, keep it. Alex, you are a loser. Do you really think you have the allure of a James Bond? You do not. You are nothing. I never did like children or children's stories."

She reached down, pulled her wedding and engagement rings off her finger, and flung them in his face as she went to stand up. "You are a . . ."

Alex swung his arm sending the table lamp flying across the room. He rushed toward Catherine with tears streaming down his cheeks.

"You murdering bitch. How could you? You knew it was a boy, our first son, our flesh and blood. How could you? Five months pregnant. You fucking bitch."

Alex shouted and his voice had deteriorated into his Scottish brogue. He grabbed her by the arm and pulled her out of her chair sending her wine glass crashing to the floor. His hand slipped from her wrist wet with wine, and the momentum with which he grabbed her catapulted her into the fireplace. Her head caromed against the corner of the stone mantle making a cracking sound. Catherine slumped to the floor without saying another word. The blood from her head wound pooled onto the floor. Alex rushed to her side and tried to feel a pulse, but he knew she was dead before he made the effort. He sank to his knees sobbing.

"What have I done? What have I done? I did not mean to kill you. How could you have killed our son? Oh God, what will I do?"

Alex got up and sank into the wing back chair opposite where Catherine had been sitting. He picked up the decanter of whiskey, took a long drink straight from it. His eyes stared at the fireplace and his mind raced.

"What am I going to do?"

He got up from the chair, walked to the window, and stared at the torrential rain. The wind was still raging and the lighting lit up the street. The lights blinked out, he stumbled in the dark into the other room, and sat at his desk. He took an encrypted cell phone from his pocket and made a call while looking back at the body of his dead wife, "You will not destroy me. I am not a murderer. I will survive this." He dialed a number and a man's voice answered.

"Henry, I have a problem. We need to meet. I must have time off. I am in major trouble and need help. We must meet immediately."

"I am in the area, be there in less than five minutes."

Chapter 6

In a suburb outside of Denver, Colorado, Emunishere woke up in a sweat screaming from a nightmare concerning events that unfolded a year ago, "No, no, they're all dead."

The nightmare had woken her from a sound sleep several times over the last year, but this was the worst. Everything replayed in her mind remembering every detail of the events of the past dreadful year.

It was the day before her and her husband Greg were to leave on their first vacation since being married six years ago when they had gone on a quick four-day honeymoon in Las Vegas.

Emunishere thought back to when she was eighteen and dropped out of art school to marry Greg, the love of her life; a brilliant businessman on the road to success who was ten years her senior. Love won out over her dream of being an artist. Every endeavor Greg entered into resulted in success. They had just moved to a suburb outside of Denver, Colorado into a large, five-bedroom mansion, and were still unpacking. On the day before they were to leave on their dream vacation, Greg called at four in the afternoon.

"Hello Kitten." Greg and her parents often called her Kitten, an affectionate nickname, because that was the meaning of Emunishere in Arabic. Everyone else called her Sher, which she did not like, but had gotten used to in school because her name was so unusual and Americans had trouble pronouncing it.

"I'm going to stop and buy a bottle of wine for dinner on the way home. I will be home by six. This vacation is so over due and I can hardly wait to relax in the sun for a week, just you and me, maybe we'll think about starting a family."

"We have a large house, plenty of room for children. I planned steak on the grill for dinner; buy that Australian Shiraz we like so well. Love you."

Greg finished his work, left full instructions for his assistant, and said good-bye to his staff.

"I'll think of you when I am lying on the beach or riding a camel around the pyramids."

His secretary laughed. "Mr. Bishop, I can't picture you on a camel, careful you don't fall off."

"Looks easy. Remember the movie *The Mummy*. If those actors can ride a camel, so can I. They don't even need a bit like a horse."

"Send us a postcard and a picture of you and Sher on camels."

"That I will."

Greg left his office, went into the garage, and pulled his new sports car that could go 0-60 in 3.9 seconds, onto the highway. Rush hour traffic was heavy and after fifteen minutes of stop and go, Greg pulled into the parking lot of a small shopping center with a large wine import shop. As he was getting out of his car, a man wearing a mask ran over, grabbed him by the arm, and jerked him out of his car.

Greg staggered and tried to pull his arm free and shouted, "You bastard."

"Get outta the car man," shouted the man who was wearing a balaclava.

Greg was struggling and before he could say another word or pull away, the masked man pulled a twenty-two caliber gun out of his waistband and shot Greg at point blank range in the head, "Ousta la vista senior, thanks for the car man." He grabbed Greg's wallet, got into the car, and drove off the tires squealing. The sound of the gunshot attracted people in the center and they ran to where Greg lay dying in the parking lot.

"Call 911," someone shouted.

At least six people using cell phones dialed 911.

"Did you see that car leave, the tires were smoking?"

"It was one of those new models. Wow, what a car."

The police arrived within minutes and began asking questions.

"Did anyone see what happened?"

Answers came quickly.

"It was a silver car. One of those new sleek sport jobs, I've seen the ads, 0-60 in less than 4 seconds."

"What kind of car was it?" the police officer asked.

"I don't know man; one of those new sporty models advertised on television all the time."

"What color?"

"Silver."

"No it was grey." A man in his late seventies called out.

"No, I think it was white."

Sergeant Bill Russell of the Denver City Police asked. "Did anyone see the carjacker?"

"Perp was short and stocky, wore a mask." A young blonde replied.

"No, he was at least six foot, black." A tall obviously Latin man answered.

"Hispanic for sure, maybe Mexican," a tall African-American with a shaved head answered.

"I know what he looked like, and he was black, just like you, only shorter," shouted the tall Latin man that had answered previously.

The police could not find two witnesses to agree on anything. The dead man had no identification on his person, and his car was missing. The wine shop owner saw the blinking lights from three patrol cars that now were in the parking lot and came out to see what was happening.

"Officer, that man is a new customer of mine. He and his wife moved here about two weeks ago. They are from Chicago. She's a lot younger than him and very tall, at least an inch taller than her husband, a drop-dead gorgeous red head with a perfect figure."

"Do you know his name?"

"His first name is Greg, his wife has a really weird name, and I have no idea what he told me when he introduced her, but I may have some old charge slips. He always charged his purchases. I will look in my records. What a shame. He was a nice guy. The wife is stunning, never understood what he called her, foreign sounding name, but she looked American. Shame she's a widow at such a young age."

Bill Russell, who was first to arrive on the scene along with two officers followed the shop owner into the store and waited while he searched his old sales slips.

"Here it is, Greg Bishop. I don't have his address and the receipt doesn't have his entire credit card number."

"We can research that. Several people saw the car drive away quickly. Do you know what kind of car or the color of the car Mr. Bishop drove?"

"It was a newer car, maybe 2010, silver, sleek design. I am sure it was silver; I own a silver car. Don't know the make or model, real sporty and I am sure very expensive."

The police took the information, went back to the car, and called in their report.

"I hate carjacking cases. It happens all too often and it is so quick, witnesses are unreliable. It's over in less than thirty seconds."

"I got a hit sergeant." The answer came in less than five minutes." He is Gregory Harrison Bishop, age thirty-four, lives in that new sub-division across from the Gateway Mall, 3467 Granite Place."

Bill Russell answered, "I'll drive out there and notify the widow. This is a part of my job I can't stand, and I get to do it more often than I care to remember."

Emunishere finished packing her suitcase and went into the kitchen to prepare the steaks for the grill. Greg liked to do all the grillwork. She had prepared an appetizing Caesar salad with fresh croutons that she had made herself. The baked potatoes were almost finished. It was six o'clock. Greg should be walking through the door any minute. She knew the traffic this time of day in Denver could be impossible and turned on the six o'clock news just as they were covering the scene of a carjacking when the doorbell rang. Emunishere looked out the window and there was a police car in the driveway. She hurried to open the door.

Bill Russell, thirty-five years old, tall with blonde hair and blue eyes stood at the door wearing his neatly pressed uniform. In a soft voice filled with concern he said, "Mrs. Bishop, I have some very sad news. Your husband was the victim of a carjacking gone terribly wrong."

"Oh no, you can't be telling me this. They, they," Emunishere stuttered. "They were talking about it on the news when you rang the doorbell. Where is he? Was he hurt badly?"

"He was taken to Mercy Hospital, but they could do nothing. If you call the station in the morning, we can give you the full report. Here is the phone number of the hospital."

Tears were streaming down her face, her body trembling, "Did you catch the person who did this? Greg was so proud of his car; he must have put up a fight. No car is worth your life."

"No, we have not found the car yet, but we have an all points bulletin out. There are not many cars like that on the road. I'm very sorry for your loss. Let me help you into the house and get you a glass of water, can I call someone for you?"

"No, there is no one to call. We've only lived here for two weeks. I don't know any of the neighbors. Thank you."

Bill Russell asked again before he left, "Are you going to be all right. I can have someone from our department come by and talk with you."

"No, no, thank you. I'll call my parents and they can come. Thank you. You are most kind."

Bill Russell closed the door quietly behind him when he left and got into his squad car and called his wife. "Betty, I love you. Rough day and I'll be home soon."

"I can hear it in your voice. See you soon." Betty hung up the phone and thought to herself, "I know he loves his job, but I worry every time that phone rings."

He wiped tears from his own eyes and headed back to the police station.

It took Emunishere a few minutes to pull herself together. She called her parents on their cell phone and told them the news.

"I am so sorry Kitten. Dad and I are en route to Mesa Verde. We will have the pilot land, refuel, and head to Denver. See you later tonight."

"I need you. We were leaving for Egypt tomorrow night at six."

A few hours later, Emunishere phoned the airline and canceled the flight to Cairo. The airline requested a copy of the death certificate before they would issue a credit.

"Those unfeeling bastards, do they think I would lie about my husband's death? What is wrong with people?" She shouted into the empty house.

It was ten o'clock and her parents and had not arrived. Emunishere took some aspirin and laid down on the sofa. She had drifted off to sleep when the telephone rang. "Mrs. Bishop."

"Yes."

"I am with a small airport in Mesa Verde, Colorado. A charter plane with four passengers bound for Denver crashed on take-off in the rain. Two of the people on board the plane were identified as your parents. It has taken us quite awhile to find you. Fortunately, one of your neighbors in Chicago was home and told us your new address and phone number. Your mother had your address and phone number in her wallet to call in case of an emergency."

"No, this cannot be happening. My husband was shot and killed when a man stole his car earlier today. What time is it?"

"It is two in the morning Mrs. Bishop. My condolences for your losses. Where can we send this information, and when will you be arriving in Mesa Verde to take care of your parents?"

"I don't know, I don't know. Email me the information. I can't think straight now."

Emunishere gave them her email address, hung up the phone, and sat on the sofa staring into space.

That horrible day left her in grief for the next six months. Greg had an insurance policy, because of the manner of his death, the premium doubled and the insurance paid two million dollars. The pilot of the small charter plane did not pay attention to the warning not to take off because of the weather, and the airport that hired him as a pilot on call, paid her another million dollars. She did not have to worry about finances, but her life was in shambles. She ventured out and went to one of the large shopping centers in Denver; it was two weeks before the holidays. Emunishere had spent the entire day at the mall shopping for presents for her friends, aunts, and uncles. It was closing time and she was walking to her car carrying three large bags from her shopping spree. A man jumped out from between the parked cars and attacked her. He grabbed her arm sending her packages flying, and then tried to steal her handbag.

"Help me; help me," she screamed.

The man looked around and saw another man rushing toward them. He was a Japanese businessman screaming at him, "Let that woman go, get away from her. Leave, I am on my cell phone to the police."

When the attacker understood that he had no option and Emunishere's screams were drawing a crowd, the assailant ran down the stairs and was soon lost in the crowd of holiday shoppers.

"So sorry," the polite gentleman bowed his head. "My name is Toshira Takama; You are okay?"

"I'm fine; he didn't hurt me." She answered in an excited tone of voice.

"I am a student at a martial arts school. You should take self-defense lessons. My class meets twice a week on Wednesday evenings and Saturday mornings. I would be glad to introduce you to my instructor. He offers special classes for self-defense. My wife and I take lessons from him; we feel safer knowing that my wife can defend herself if she is alone."

"Thank you so much. You have been most kind. I don't know what I would have done if you had not come along. I will see you Wednesday evening. What is the address?"

The middle-aged man carefully wrote the information on the back of his business card and helped her pick up her packages waiting until she securely locked the door to her car.

Emunishere drove home, put her presents down, and collapsed onto the sofa. She pulled out the card and studied the address.

The next Wednesday, she went to the martial arts class and spoke with the instructor. The classes met in a store located in a strip mall. The To

Shin Do Martial Arts School called the Tiger's Den was located between an ice cream shop on one side, and a large sport emporium on the other. Class was ending and youngsters between the ages of six and twelve were putting on their jackets, and proud parents were escorting the children to the mini vans and SUVs that filled the parking spaces. They looked so cute in their white and black uniforms and belts with brightly colored stripes. Some older women and men were entering the building and carefully laying their coats on the benches that lined each side of the room. They were wearing uniforms in a different color from the younger children.

"Good evening," Mr. Tokama entered the school.

"Good evening. I took your suggestion," Emunishere turned to him. "Thank you again."

The instructor walked over to Mr. Tokama when he entered.

"Is this the woman you told me about?"

"Yes," Mr. Tokama answered him.

"Mr. Tokama told me to expect you. The school will prepare you to defend yourself if you are ever attacked again. My name is Koichiro Nokozama; this is my school."

"I am Emunishere Bishop, my husband was killed by a carjacker, and someone attacked me a few nights ago in the parking garage. I have a gun in the house, but I need to defend myself when I am not at home. What kind of private lessons do you offer? I don't want to be part of a group. I don't want a blue or black belt. I only want to know how to defend myself."

"I offer private lessons in the morning before the schools let out in the afternoon, but never on weekends. They are expensive. What I teach is a form of Taijutsu that emphasizes timing, balance, angles, and the use of leverage. It does not rely on sheer strength as some other martial arts."

"It sounds like what I need. When can I start? I'm available five days a week."

"We can begin tomorrow. I am free from eight until nine every day."

"Great, I will see you in the morning."

Emunishere took the lessons two days a week for the next four months. She was becoming an expert in self-defense. She would never need help again if faced with a similar situation as what happened in the mall-parking garage. She thought, "If Greg had taken lessons, he might not have been killed."

Emunishere thought back on the vacation that she and Greg had planned. They were to fly to El-Arish, a port city east of Suez in Egypt where her parents had gone there on their last vacation. The city deteriorated when the Israelis captured Sinai and returned it to Egypt in 1982. El Arish was a delightful port city with endless groves of bowed palms lining the beach. Several four and five star hotels were there. The main event in the city was the Thursday market where the Bedouins came to sell their fruits and vegetables, clothes, camels and livestock, along with the traditional Bedouin handicrafts. Her mother had loved the elegant beadwork and silver jewelry and had a huge collection from trips over the years. She had given Emunishere a fetching bracelet, earrings and necklace from their last visit. After a week on the beach and shopping at the market, she and Greg were to fly to Cairo, take in the ancient sites, then continue by air to Luxor. There they would board a boat and cruise down the Nile to Aswan, fly back to Cairo and home.

"I am going to take that trip," she thought to herself.

As soon as she arrived home, Emunishere called the travel agency and made plans to leave in September for Egypt.

The next day, she enrolled in private classes at a language school to learn to read and write Arabic. She had spoken Arabic since childhood, but never learned to read or write the language. The school arranged private classes for her and guaranteed in four months, she would be able to read and write the language.

Emunishere decided to list the large house that she and Greg had bought and hoped the house would sell before she left. Upon her return, she planned to buy a small ranch in the mountains, preferably with a room that had large windows facing north that could be used as an art studio along with the horse she had always wanted. The realtor assured Emunishere that her home in Denver would sell in a short period of time for the listing price and that she could begin looking for a ranch property that suited her requirements.

One evening after her Arabic class, a man in the same language school asked her to join him for a drink after class.

"Hi, my name is Brian Edwards, I see you every week leaving about the same time I leave. What is your name? What class are you taking?"

"Emunishere Bishop, but some people call me Sher. I am taking private lessons in reading and writing Arabic."

"That is an unusual name, no wonder you go by Sher."

Emunishere glared at him, "I prefer you call me Emunishere; it means kitten in Arabic."

They walked to a restaurant near the language school and he ordered a bottle of white wine.

Brian tried to pronounce her name, but kept getting it wrong. Emunishere finally relented and told him, "Call me Sher."

"This is my favorite wine. I hope you enjoy it as much as I do."

"It is delicious. What do you do for a living?" she asked.

His answer was somewhat evasive, "I have my own business. I am a consultant for small businesses and teach computer skills to business owners."

"I'm not very good with computers. Perhaps you could teach me. My husband never had the time."

"I would be glad to teach you everything I know."

"Are you married?"

"No, my husband died some time ago in a carjacking."

"Why Arabic, why not take Spanish? I find I cannot go to a fast food restaurant without speaking Spanish."

"My mother was Egyptian. I lived in Egypt from the age of one until I turned six. I spoke Arabic before I spoke English. My parents were archeologists."

"Is it safe for a woman to travel alone to Egypt?"

"I will be fine. When I arrive at the hotel, they will have a private car, driver, and guide available. A guide will always be with me."

"If my finances were better, I would like to join you."

"I would love to have your company, but perhaps another time."

After accepting several dates with Brian, one evening he asked her, "I have a great business opportunity that just presented itself to me. I would not ask anyone else, but I am fond of you. There is room for one more investor. For $120,000 you could invest in my company and be sure to at the least triple your investment in no more than five years."

"I don't really have any interest in investing in a business. My husband was involved in his own business and did contracting with a large corporation on the side. He never had time for anything, but business. What makes you think I would have that much money to invest in your company?"

"You live in a large house and it is for sale. I checked you have no mortgage. When it sells, you would be able to invest in my company. I thought you might want to help me get my business on a firm footing. We seem to have fun when we go out. I thought you enjoyed my company."

"You know what I think; I think you have been stalking me. I think you figured I would be so interested in you that I would fork over that amount of money because I was a young widow. Listen to me Brian; I am not interested. Don't call me again. I know a swindle when I see it. Do you think I am stupid? Good-bye."

"Emunishere," Brian called to her, "What about all the dinners we have had? I have an investment in you," Brian whined.

Emunishere stopped and turned to face him. Now she was really angry raising a clenched fist.

"I could not imagine why you were so interested in me when we have nothing in common. I like the desert, the mountains, and the sea; you like the big city. Why did it take me so long to discover what a creep you are? I can hardly wait to leave on my vacation."

Emunishere turned and walked away from him and never looked back.

Brian called after her, "Bitch. I wasted three weeks of my life on you."

Brian got into his ten-year-old compact car squealing the tires as he pulled away from the curb.

Emunishere watched him leave, "There is something about a wealthy young widow with several million dollars in the bank that attracts the worst men. I am doomed to a life of solitude," she started to cry.

Emunishere was packed and ready for her vacation with an entire month to relax and try to forget the past, but the nightmares continued bringing back memories of that horrible day. Would they ever pass? In the past year, she had mourned the loss of her husband, and her parents. Now she was returning to the land of Egypt where her parents had met. The last time she was in Egypt, Emunishere was a six-year-old child.

"I will return to Colorado, buy a ranch, and live the life of a reclusive artist. I don't think I will ever meet another man I can trust. Will I ever love again or am I destined to live alone?"

Chapter 7

It was late in the afternoon on a hot summer day. The sky, as usual, over Cairo was clear blue except for the slight haze that always hung over the city. Rafiq and his brother Hassan were sitting at a table by themselves at an open-air restaurant next to the Nile River having an argument. They both had expensive taste in clothes and wore custom tailored business suits and white dress shirts open at the collar.

The air smelled of fresh baked bread from brick ovens at the front of the open-air restaurant next to grilling chickens turning on a chain driven barbecue rack. Two women wearing galabeyas, sat on the ground in front of the ovens attending to the baking bread, absorbed in a conversation between them. They did not look up at customers entering the restaurant. More than fifty chickens slowly turned on the spits, the smoke drifting over the patio restaurant toward the nearby Nile. Brightly painted tables sat under a canopy of large flowering trees and colorful umbrellas. A wall of flowering vines climbed trellises along one side of the restaurant blocking the clientele from the traffic noise.

Hassan, the older of the two, slammed his fist onto the table making the dishes jump. Startled, the other patrons in the restaurant turned to see what was happening and then went back to eating their lunch.

"I will do what I feel I must do to help our father stop the sex slave trade from Egypt into Israel. Do you know how many women are smuggled from the ports East of Suez into Israel? El-Arish is less than fifty kilometers from the border and is one of the worst areas."

Rafiq sat patiently until his brother had finished.

"What about the hotel business we have built? You have not focused on business for almost a year. The hotels have suffered; I need you full time. You cannot leave Cairo for a month or six weeks. These are our busiest hotels and it takes the two of us. This human trafficking business has existed since time began; it is not your fight. You need to get your life back together. I know how difficult it has been, but there are better ways to get your mind off what happened. Are you seeing anyone? It has been almost a year since the accident."

Hassan leaned forward and spoke in a hushed voice.

"It is none of your business. Do I ask you about your personal life?"

Rafiq threw up his hands.

"What personal life? I work sixteen hours a day trying to keep the business going. How long will you be gone, for a month? You will have to fly back to Cairo every time I need you. I do not like this at all."

Hassan suddenly had a vacant stare as if caught in his own thoughts. After several moments he spoke.

"It was a Russian Jew that killed my family. He had had too much vodka to drink. My wife and son are dead. The car exploded and there was not enough left to recognize. I hate the Russian Jews; he was probably involved with trafficking women. They have to be stopped."

Hassan continued, "I have nightmares about that phone call telling me my family was dead. I will never forget them. Shamsha's and Suhail's clothes were given away; Mohamed took them to the City of the Dead along with all of Suhail's toys, except these keys." Hassan held the keys in his hand as though they were his most precious possession. Rafiq reached across the table to calm Hassan who was on the verge of tears.

"I know how difficult that must have been."

Hassan clutched the keys in his hands along with his *komboloi* (worry beads) as tears streamed down his face. His body visibly trembled as he sat opposite his brother.

"No, no, you could never know the pain I suffer."

Hassan took a deep breath and sighed.

"Father is right, helping a good cause may help me, but I am not leaving the business."

"Something has got to help Hassan. We need you. Mother needs you. She cries every day seeing you like this."

"I feel I am getting it together. This may be my one chance to get back to a normal life."

"It better be," Rafiq responded.

"I cannot mourn my family forever. I will still be managing one of the hotels, and if you get in trouble, you can call me. The hotel in Aswan and the other in Luxor have good managers. If you run into difficulties in Cairo, El-Arish is a short flight away."

"Did father talk you into joining his crusade against the trafficking of women? You really need to be more involved with our business, not this sex slave trade." Rafiq continued. "How dangerous is this going to be?"

"Whenever there is a lot of money, there is a lot of danger, especially if you are going to stop the source of the money."

Rafiq was getting agitated and shaking his finger into his brother's face, "Most of these women are from Eastern Europe. Let the Europeans handle it."

"Their hands are tied. They do not report the Russian Jews because they fear reprisals. These mobs are dangerous, ruthless people. They have taken advantage of their untouchable status and used it to promote many immoral businesses. People are afraid."

Rafiq shook his head and pushed his fingers back through his dark brown almost black hair as he listened to his brother.

"We have suspicions that more than a few tourists have disappeared. They are usually single women traveling alone between the ages of eighteen and thirty. Look at it this way; I am protecting our hotel clients. A British woman, daughter of a member of the House of Lords, disappeared when she did not check into a hotel in El-Arish only last week. I will not be gone long my brother. I am moving my office to El-Arish for a month at most. My main thought is to focus my efforts on stopping the traffickers in that area. It is close to the Egyptian border with Israel. Father heard a rumor that a shipment of women from Eastern Europe is due to arrive in a few weeks, smuggled across the desert, through the mountains, and on to Israel. If all goes as planned, I will be back in Cairo in less than a month. This is not a permanent move."

Rafiq sat back in his chair, resigned that Hassan could not be dissuaded.

"You are my older brother. I hope you know what you are doing. It has been a difficult year, as I have had to do more than my share. It is time that you were working on our business full time. I love you and could not think straight if something happened to you. Father has always thought of you first. You are his favorite."

"Now that isn't true. Father treats us equally. I will be careful. Do not worry. If nothing happens within three weeks, I promise to return to Cairo and get myself back into the business. You deserve three weeks' vacation."

"I will hold you to that."

The brothers embraced and walked to their cars parked in front of the restaurant along the narrow street.

Chapter 8

Hassan moved his office to El-Arish into a suite of rooms on the top floor of the Sinai El-Arish Hotel. His job was to watch the port and then go on night patrols outside of the city with others involved in the movement to stop smugglers crossing the border into Israel.

He was at the reservation desk when an American woman traveling alone arrived at the hotel. Security stopped Emunishere's taxi at the entrance to the drive leading to the hotel. Bomb sniffing dogs walked around the car and armed security guards asked for her identification and that of the driver. Following a careful inspection, he waved them through. Once inside the lobby, Emunishere approached the security checkpoint. Her bags passed through a scanner similar to what was used at the airport. She placed her handbag and camera case on the conveyer belt and walked through the scanner. A beep sounded. Emunishere checked and removed her watch and walked through again. No beep the second time. She apologized in Arabic that she had forgotten to remove her watch. The security guard smiled.

As she walked to the reception desk across the spacious lobby, everyone turned their heads to follow her. The glass doors at one end offered an unobstructed view of the beach, but no one in the room seemed to notice. Emunishere Bishop was just shy of 180 centimeters in height, with long auburn hair that fell to her waist. Her complexion was flawless and she wore no make-up except to accentuate her green eyes that had flecks of gold in them. She looked like a fashion model wearing a long green skirt and black long sleeved top with a green scarf around her neck. In perfect Egyptian Arabic, she gave her name, "Emunishere Bishop, I have a reservation, and the room was paid in advance for nine days." She spoke with breathiness to her voice that made her sound sultry.

"Yes, all is in order. You are traveling alone?" Hassan asked.

"Sadly, the answer is yes, my husband was killed over a year ago. We had planned this trip for two years and it is long overdue." Tears seemed to well up in her eyes, but did not flow down her cheeks.

"Is there a problem in the area? I had to pass through two security check points to get into the hotel."

"No, there is not a problem. All hotels in Egypt are protective of their guests. We are near the Israeli border and you will notice many security checkpoints throughout the area. Do not be afraid, Egypt welcomes and protects her tourists."

"Thank you for the explanation. It is somewhat reassuring to know."

"It is not wise for a woman to travel alone in Egypt." He cautioned her.

"I plan to spend several days relaxing on the beach in the sun. Could the hotel arrange a private car, driver, and guide to see the sights of El-Arish, the mosque, bird sanctuary, and the Bedouin market to shop for crafts and jewelry by Sunday or Monday at the latest?"

"The Bedouin market is famous and meets every Thursday. Today is Thursday; plan to spend time at the Bedouin Market this afternoon. By Monday, we can arrange a car, driver, and guide to take you to the historical sites in the area. El-Arish has few tourist sites; but it is best known for its beaches."

"That sounds like an acceptable idea. I plan to eat a light lunch and shop. Is the market far from the hotel?"

"Your Arabic is flawless, not many American women speak Arabic."

"Thank you."

"The market is very close." Hassan continued with a smile, "I will have one of my hotel staff accompany you to the market after you have lunch. It is not wise for a woman to go to the market alone. The Bedouin men are there on market day, some go there in search of available women to marry, and it is also an opportunity for the Bedouin men to meet and resolve their differences. It is not uncommon for fights to break out on market days."

"Thank you. Should I come to the desk when lunch is over?"

"Yes, a driver and guide will meet you."

"How late do you serve dinner?"

"We serve dinner until eleven. You can get lunch in the restaurant across the lobby."

"Thank you."

The porter handed her the key and she followed him into the elevator. She opened the door and waited for the porter to step in. "Set the bags anywhere, I'll get to unpacking later"

As instructed, he set the bags on the floor and turned to leave. "Excuse me." The bellman turned back and took the tip from her outstretched hand. "Thank you." She watched as the door closed behind him.

Emunishere walked to the window and looked out at the pristine beach lapped by the glistening waters of the Mediterranean Sea. A light breeze blew through the open window stirring the curtains. Inhaling the sea air, she thought, "If only Greg were here to share this with me."

It was not to be. Never before had she felt so alive and yet so alone. Was this a new beginning or another attempt to forget what she had lost? Forgetting was less painful if only for a little while.

Using the bathroom, she freshened up, and immediately left for lunch.

She chose a seat next to a window where she could look out at the sea. The restaurant had a large gourmet menu featuring local dishes for which the hotel was famous. Speaking in Arabic, she ordered lentil soup, a seafood salad, bread, and a cup of mint tea. A smile of satisfaction crossed her lips as the waiter acknowledged her with a nod. At the airport, with the taxi, the reception desk, and now the restaurant she had spoken only Arabic; reading and writing Arabic was still a problem. The class had helped, but it was still difficult for her to read.

After lunch, she went to the desk where a young man, no more than twenty years old, wearing black slacks, white shirt, and a blue blazer with the hotel emblem was standing. The young man recognized her immediately as she approached.

"Mrs. Bishop, I am Mohamed, your driver, and guide for the market. The hotel car is ready."

"What is the price?"

"It is very reasonable, fifty dollars American for half the day. It will be added to your bill."

Hassan watched her intently as she gracefully moved across the lobby.

He turned to Kateb, a young man in his late twenties, one of his desk clerks, as Emunishere left with Mohamed for the market, "I have never seen such green eyes. They had flecks of gold in them. I do not usually like American women, but this one is extraordinary. She speaks Arabic fluently and dresses conservatively unlike most Americans. I may invite her to dinner so she does not have to eat alone."

Kateb shook his head in agreement. "She is not like any other American that has stayed here." He smiled as Hassan left the desk and went to his office.

Once outside, Mohamed opened the door of a tan sedan with the hotel name painted on the sides and drove to the market less than twenty minutes from the hotel. The market was a riot of color and bustling with locals and tourists. As they approached the entrance, a cacophony of sound filled the air and the aroma of saffron, garlic, onions, and baking bread filled the air. Each week Bedouins from numerous tribes came into the town to buy supplies and sell their wares. Stands covered with fresh fruits and vegetables lined the narrow street. Hung above on wires were colorful dresses blowing in the wind. Cages of chickens squawked, protesting vehemently their incarceration in the small cages as if they knew they would be someone's dinner that evening. A very dark complexioned man with a colorful purple band around his head had brought two camels to sell. The camels towered over his short stature. Emunishere, her senses assaulted by the sounds, smells and sites did not know where to look next. A sense of adventure overcame her. To her right two Bedouin men wearing typical attire of white shirts, handkerchiefs on their heads tied in place with twine were engaged in a loud argument. Mohamed took her arm and guided her away toward a booth filled with exquisite ornate Bedouin silver jewelry, dresses with elaborate beadwork, and woven rugs from goat hair. Emunishere was unaware of the danger. The shop owner was a woman who peered at her through a slit-eyed veil. Her calloused hands, stained with henna, held an elaborate garment adorned with beaded embroidery. Her eyes were black coals behind the veil she wore. Mohamed helped her bargain for the best price. Emunishere bought two pieces of silver jewelry and a dress with beadwork.

"Never pay what they ask. They expect you to bargain with them. They look forward to it. Let me bargain for you and arrange best price."

"Thank you so much Mohamed. I would have paid much more without your help."

"That is why Hassan had me accompany you. Never go out alone to that market; it could be dangerous for a woman by herself."

They left the market and returned to the hotel around six in the evening. After passing through security, Mohamed drove to the entrance of the hotel. Emunishere handed him a U.S. twenty-dollar bill and asked him to give her a wakeup call at eight-thirty. Inside, she put all of her bags containing her purchases through the scanner. This time, she carefully removed her watch before walking through so as not to set off the alarm. Back in her room, she carefully placed her purchases into her suitcase and undressed, before collapsing on the bed, exhausted from her day at the market. She had been asleep for several hours when suddenly she awoke in an upright position, tears streaming down her face crying, "Why Greg, why did you have to fight to save a car?"

Frightened by her own screams, she opened her eyes to find she was in a dark room. Reaching for the light by the bed, she got up and headed for the shower. Changing into a different outfit, she left the room and took the elevator to the lobby. It was nine in the evening, when Emunishere came into the dining room. Hassan had been watching for her.

"Good evening, Mrs. Bishop."

"Please, don't be so formal. Call me Emunishere."

"I am Hassan Gaafar, the owner of the hotel. You speak Arabic like a native. Was your family from this part of the world?"

"Yes, my mother was Egyptian and I spoke Arabic before I spoke English. It has been almost a year since my parents died in a plane crash. That was the last time I spoke Arabic. Reading and writing the language is proving to be a challenge."

"May I buy you dinner this evening so you do not have to eat alone?"

"That would be lovely. Thank you."

Hassan gestured for her to follow the Maitre'd to his personal table. He held her chair and waited until she was seated before taking a seat opposite her.

"Thank you so much for arranging my trip to the market with Mohamed, Mr. Gaafar."

"Please, call me Hassan."

"Mohamed is a very nice young man and quite helpful. His bargaining skills saved me a lot of money. The market was very crowded and the Bedouin men did not appear to be that friendly toward American or European women that were shopping. I hope that it was not a mistake traveling in this part of the world alone. My husband and I planned to leave on this trip the day after he was shot."

"Traveling alone is not a problem provided you stay in the tourist areas and go with an escort elsewhere as you did today. We do not worry about someone stealing our car, but it is not safe for an attractive young woman like you to be on the streets alone at night. Those foolish enough to try have been known to disappear."

"Disappear?" Emunishere face showed concern.

"Yes, there are criminal elements at work in this part of Egypt that prey on unsuspecting women." Sensing she was afraid, Hassan decided to change the subject.

"My schedule is busy tomorrow, but if you would permit me, I could drive you to the sites near here and out to the fortress and bird sanctuary. Tomorrow is Friday and I attend the Mosque. A Bedouin store is on the way, the owner is a friend of mine, and he will treat you well. His jewelry is of a better quality than what you found at the market today."

"That would be so nice. Thank you so much. Would it be possible, after your services at the Mosque, for me to look inside? My mother was Muslim. She used to read to me from the *Qur'an*, and we prayed together five times a day when I was a little girl. She had me memorize all the prayers in Arabic. I still know them, but haven't prayed in several years. My father was not religious and never went to church. I know, according to Islam, they should have divorced when he did not become a Muslim, but she loved him and they ignored the rule."

"I would be glad to show you the Mosque. You must wear a head scarf, long sleeves, and a long skirt."

"That is no problem. Except for one pair of pants, all my clothes are long sleeved blouses, long skirts, ankle length dresses, and headscarves to match. My mother missed Egypt and often told me interesting things about her growing up in Cairo and Egyptian culture."

Emunishere continued speaking of her past while they finished dinner. "When we moved to Colorado, I was six years old. There was no Mosque in the small town where we lived. My mother practiced her religion at home, and when my parents were away on frequent trips to archeological sites in different parts of the world, they did not want to take me out of school. They sent me to live with my aunt and uncle who never approved of my mother or the Islamic religion. They left me at home when they attended church. Uncle always complained to his brother that I was just like my mother, a pagan, according to him. Mom and Dad never discussed religion and my husband Greg was not a religious man. My parents did not live near us, and we only saw them a few times a year. It's late and I really should get some sleep. Thank you for a lovely evening."

"The pleasure was mine. May I walk you to your room? Is ten o'clock tomorrow morning a good time to meet you in the lobby? We will drive into the city, give you a little tour, and take you to the craft shop."

"Ten is fine. I am looking forward to tomorrow already."

"Perhaps you will become a practicing Muslim while you are here."

"I have often given consideration to becoming a Muslim, especially since the death of my parents and my husband. Perhaps you can help me decide."

Hassan walked her to her room and opened the door for her. "Until tomorrow."

"Good night."

Emunishere watched him walk to the elevators and then closed her door. She got undressed and took out her diary.

> *"Dear Diary,*
>
> *You are my constant companion. I wish Greg or my parents were here. Why am I here alone? I should never have tried to go on this vacation. One nice thing happened today; the owner of the hotel arranged for me to go to the Bedouin market with an escort and later treated me to dinner. Tall, muscular, with black hair and a thick mustache, Hassan is oh so handsome. His voice is deep and husky. He is a Muslim. I understand from what mother told me, Muslim men do not date, especially non-Muslim women. Families arrange everything or they go out in the company of others to meet new friends. When he offered to take me sightseeing and shopping I said yes without thinking. Strangely, his mind seemed to be on something else when he spoke. There was a distant look in his deep brown eyes. I know that look. He is suffering from the loss of someone close."*

The next morning, Emunishere ate breakfast in her room. She dressed in a long black skirt, long sleeved orange blouse, and orange scarf around her neck. At five minutes before ten, she walked into the lobby of the hotel. Hassan was getting off the elevator as she sat down in the lobby.

"Have you been waiting long?"

"No, I just arrived. It is a lovely day. Perhaps I will go to the beach this afternoon when we return to the hotel."

"El-Arish is far off the beaten track for American tourists. How did you choose it for a vacation?"

"My mother and father spent their last vacation here. She would tell me stories about a little paradise kissed by the sun that no one knew about. Greg and I needed a secluded place away from the hustle and bustle to relax for a week. Next week, I will travel by bus to Cairo to see the magnificent sites Egypt has to offer. I barely remember seeing the pyramids and the museum when I was a little girl."

"I think you will find El-Arish to be a real paradise. Your mother was so right. Few tourists outside of Egypt or the Middle East ever visit here. We have a few Europeans but rarely see Americans."

They drove into the city and Hassan walked her into a huge Bedouin shop. It had jewelry, pottery, clothing, embroidered scarves, and lots of rugs and crafts hand made by the local Bedouins. Hassan spent some time speaking with the owner of the shop and told Emunishere he would return in a little over an hour. She felt safe knowing the owner was a friend of Hassan.

Emunishere bid him goodbye and proceeded to look at everything in the the shop. As was the custom, the owner offered her a cup of karkade tea, made from the flower of the Habiscus plant.

"Thank you. It is delicious. My mother always had hibiscus or green mint tea."

While she sipped hot tea, the owner showed her some ornate and antique silver jewelry.

"I do not know which I like the best," she smiled. "This is my first visit to El-Arish. I went to the market yesterday, but your jewelry is so extraordinary, I cannot resist."

She chose two antique heavy silver and amber necklaces, five heavy silver bangles, and two pair of silver and amber earrings.

The shopkeeper wrapped them carefully and she continued to browse while waiting for Hassan. When he finally arrived, she was buying some paintings on papyrus that the shopkeeper had shown her.

"You have bought a lot of things. Do you want to tour the city while we are here?"

"Yes, that would be wonderful. This is an amazing store. I have bought too much; there will be no room in my suitcase."

Emunishere was beginning to like Hassan more and more. Being with him made her feel safe and comfortable and wishing she had more time to get to know him.

"Not a problem. I'm sure you will collect other treasurers while you are here."

Starring into his eyes she smiled, "I'm sure I will."

"Come, I will show you the mosque."

Driving along the narrow street the minarets of the mosque came into view. Hassan parked across from the entrance. Upon entering, she covered her head and proceeded to remove her shoes. Strings of lights suspended beneath the dome illuminated a small band of worshipers and a circle of small windows provided natural light. Oriental rugs covered the marble floor. Along one wall was the mihrab, or niche, inscribed with elaborate Arabic calligraphy indicating the direction of Mecca. To the right was a set of stairs leading to a platform upon which a decorative gold chair sat. From here the imam, or leader, would deliver his sermon during Friday prayers. No pews or seats were in evidence as followers sit on the floor.

"Let me show you the women's section." Hassan took her hand.

Emunishere stood in the Mosque, her bare feet upon the thick carpet, awakened new feelings in her; memories of the past and her mother. Perhaps, she thought, "This is what I have been looking for, this is where I belong."

After leaving the mosque, Hassan took her around the small port city. As they drove along the waterfront, she noticed a great many fishing boats at anchor or tied to moorings.

"Is fishing an industry here?"

"Yes, it is. Many people own boats. Do you like boating?"

"My husband did not like the water even though we lived in Chicago on Lake Michigan. We moved to Colorado which does not have very much boating except on reservoirs or rafting down river rapids."

They finished their tour and he brought her back to the hotel. His car was checked the same as the taxi and Mohamed's car from the day before.

"Why did they check your car, surely they know you own the hotel?"

"All vehicles are checked. Someone could have tampered with it when I parked at the mosque and again at the shop. Our security checks everyone. You are safe here."

"I never see this kind of security in the states except at airports."

"Egypt is not like America. We are always vigilant."

"One terrorist bomb and American hotels and shopping centers will have similar security systems; some politicians say we need better security now."

"Egypt has already had too many terrorist attacks on tourists. We have learned to be watchful."

Hassan parked the car and escorted her to the lobby.

"Please forgive me but I have business to attend to this evening, but I will take you to the Zaranik Protectorate Bird Observatory tomorrow. It is Egypt's first bird observatory with over seventy-five different species of birds. If you enjoy taking pictures, bring your camera."

"Yes, I look forward to seeing it. Thank you so much for today and for accompanying me. I had a wonderful time."

"Until tomorrow."

Emunishere went to her room and ordered her dinner from room service.

> *"Dear Diary, I had a wonderful time today. Hassan took me shopping and showed me the city. I went inside the mosque and memories of my mother filled my mind and brought tears to my eyes. Hassan shook my hand and said good night. He is not like any man I have ever dated. By now, most American men would have at least kissed me once or put their arm around me, or tried to get me to have sex with them. It is refreshing for a change. He looks into my eyes for the longest time. I wonder if he likes me or just doesn't approve of a woman traveling alone. He seems so distant. Something from his past troubles him."*

The next day, Hassan took her to the large bird observatory where she took dozens of pictures of sea birds. They decided to have lunch there at an outside café and watched birds migrating from Europe to their winter haunts in Africa.

"I have never seen so many different birds at one time. They are beautiful. I have taken over a hundred pictures. Why are there so many tourist police and checkpoints? We were stopped several times coming here."

"El-Arish is only forty kilometers from the Israeli border. Tensions are high because of the Gaza war and border control is strict. People come here to relax on the beach and attend the Bedouin market on Thursdays. There is not much else to do."

"Not to change the subject, you are from the American west, yes?"

"Yes I am, why?"

"Do you like horses, Emunishere?"

"Yes, I want to own a horse, Greg promised he would buy me my own horse when we returned from Egypt. It is so nice to hear someone call me by my full name. Most Americans have difficulty-pronouncing Emunishere and call me Sher; I don't care for the nickname. My parents and husband called me Kitten on occasion, but always used my given name."

"Emunishere is a charming name for a lovely woman. My father's stud farm is near here. Our horses are famous all over Egypt and Saudi Arabia. Would you like to visit his horse farm tomorrow?"

"I can't think of anything else I'd rather do."

Upon returning, Hassan excused himself, left for a meeting, and attended to business at the hotel.

Emunishere changed and went to the beach in the afternoon and took a long nap before ordering dinner in her room. As the day replayed in her mind, she pictured Hassan in her mind and finished a sketch of him that she planned to give him the next morning. Satisfied, she began to sketch one of the hundreds of sea birds that she had photographed earlier at the Observatory.

Emunishere awoke early, anxious to get started and to see Hassan. She dressed in a long black skirt, long sleeved blue blouse, and matching scarf. Under her arm, she carried the sketchpad with her drawing of Hassan. She took a small bag with a change of clothes.

Hassan spotted her from the front desk as she stepped off the elevator.

"Good morning. Why are you carrying a sketch pad?"

"I love to draw and paint. My favorite subjects are people and animals. Come, I have something to show you."

Emunishere set the pad on the counter and removed the sketch of Hassan in artist pastels from the pad, rolled it, and handed it to him.

"This is for you. It is what occupies my time in the evenings in my room."

Hassan carefully unrolled the paper. "You are a very talented artist. I do not remember posing for you."

"Remember, I took your picture the other day and used it as a reference. I also started a sketch of one of the birds we saw at the observatory."

"Please, when you finish, show it to me."

Hassan continued to stare at the likeness as though it were a mirror. "I have never had a portrait of myself. This is exceptionable. I want to show it to my father while we are at the stud farm today."

"I am glad you like it."

When they arrived at the farm, there were about thirty horses in different fenced paddocks. A tall chestnut stallion caught her eye immediately.

"I love that tall chestnut stallion. He is magnificent."

"You have a good eye for horses, his name is Nabil, and he is my favorite."

"Come into the house first, I would like to introduce you to my father. He is a surgeon at the largest hospital in Cairo and this is his day off."

Emunishere took Hassan's out reached hand. They walked up to the front door and before he could turn the knob, it opened. Standing in the doorway was Sabir, tall, like his son with black hair that was just beginning to turn gray around the temples. Dressed in black slacks, riding boots, and a white long sleeved shirt, he looked the part of a rancher. Sabir embraced his son and kissed him on each cheek.

He then turned to Emunishere. "You must be Emunishere. Hassan has told me about you. Your mother was Egyptian. Where was she from?"

"My mother was from Cairo, born and raised on the island of Rawdah." She replied in perfect Arabic.

Clearly impressed, Sabir responded in Arabic.

"Hassan said you spoke Arabic like a native. I know Rawdah well. Welcome to my home."

Servants had prepared a beautiful lunch and served it on a covered veranda overlooking the horse paddocks with the desert as a background.

After they had lunch, Emunishere excused herself and left to change into her riding pants. Alone, Sabir took the opportunity to talk with his son.

"I am glad to see you in the company of a woman again, she is striking."

"Her husband died during a carjacking. I am just her escort while she is in Egypt. I did not think it safe for a woman traveling alone. Do not try to make it seem more than it is or that we are on a date."

"You must move on and get back to a normal life. You need to get married and begin a new family. You need the love of a compassionate woman."

"She is not only compassionate but very talented."

Hassan handed the sketch to his father.

A smile graced Sabir's lips as he glanced from the drawing to his son's face. "She is."

Hassan took back the drawing and carefully rerolled it.

"I promised to take her riding."

He left to change into his riding boots.

When Hassan had left, Emunishere returned to the great room where Sabir was sitting. Sabir stood to greet her and took her hands in his.

"My son is fortunate to have made friends with such an artistic and compassionate woman. Hassan has had more tragedy in his life than anyone should have to bear. He showed me the portrait you drew of him. The artist is a woman who truly cares for him."

"What happened?"

Sabir smiled. "Give him time. He will tell you what happened. Be patient."

Emunishere got tears in her eyes. "I knew something troubling had happened in his past. It is in his eyes."

"He is very alone."

Sabir stopped at the sound of Hassan's footsteps on the stairs.

"Here he comes. Enjoy your ride," he said quietly.

"Are you ready, let's go?"

Hassan escorted her to the corral. The groom waited for them with two saddled horses. As she was looking at the horses, and not where she was going, she tripped. Hassan caught her before she hit the ground. It was the first time he had touched her except to shake hands. He held her for a moment and looked into her eyes. Her skin tingled at his touch.

"You could have hurt yourself."

"Thank you for catching me. I wasn't looking where I was walking."

They mounted the horses. Hassan got up on his stallion Nabil and Emunishere rode a white mare.

"Nabil, what an interesting name," Emunishere remarked.

"Nabil means noble in Arabic and he is my prize stallion. The mare you are riding is Baraka, her name means fair. She is one of our brood mares and was my wife's favorite horse. We will ride to a small oasis and rest the horses before returning."

They rode for an hour before arriving at the oasis, a large lake in the middle of the desert. Trees and grass lined the bank. Hassan spread a blanket on the ground, and they sat under a lone palm tree and talked. The breeze off the water was cool after the hot ride over the sand. They enjoyed two bottles of mineral water Hassan had brought that were still cool.

"My wife used to ride with me." His voice cracked.

"You are no longer married?"

Hassan looked away before he answered, "My wife and son were killed in an automobile accident a year ago. I miss them terribly."

He told her the entire story and his eyes were wet with tears when he finished. Emunishere gently put her hand on his.

"I knew you had suffered a loss. It is in your eyes. Forgive me, I didn't mean to pry into your personal life."

"No, no apology is needed. It is getting late. Let me help you mount." They rode back to the farm, and said good-bye to Sabir.

Hassan went to change into his shoes and Sabir walked over to Emunishere.

"He told you; I can tell."

"It must have been horrible. The baby was only nine months old. I lost my husband and my parents the same day, but to lose a child, the pain must have been unbearable." Her eyes filled with tears that streamed down her cheeks.

"He is doing better and is more like himself every day. Today is the first time in almost a year that he smiled. You made that possible. Take care. I am sure I will see you again." Sabir handed her a neatly folded handkerchief.

Emunishere wiped her eyes and handed it back to Sabir, "Thank you. Hopefully we will meet again soon."

Hassan came down stairs and kissed his father good-bye.

"She is a lovely woman, Hassan. She has made you smile."

"She is a delightful woman and a talented artist."

"That portrait was drawn from love."

"Let me go at my own pace."

"I will; she is good for you." Sabir smiled knowingly.

"Thank you. I do like her." Hassan cleared his throat.

They drove back to the hotel and Hassan was deep in thought as he drove. It was after six in the evening when they returned.

"I would like to take you to dinner tonight. There is a charming restaurant near the waterfront that overlooks the harbor. Could you be ready by eight?"

"That would be nice, thank you."

He walked her to her room and opened the door, took her in his arms, and kissed her on the cheek. "I had a wonderful time today. Meet me in the lobby at eight."

Emunishere started to cry as soon as she closed the door. Memories of Greg flashed across her mind. She brought out her diary and began to write. *"I don't want to live as a reclusive artist with a horse any more. I am falling in love with Hassan. He has suffered so much; he lost his wife and only son. When he talked about it, there was so much pain in his eyes. I wanted to reach out to him. He is so alone and blames himself. We are going to dinner by the waterfront tonight."*

Chapter 9

Yuri Berezovsky had just arrived in El-Arish when his satellite phone rang.

"Berezovsky," a deep voice speaking Arabic greeted him. "Do you have the special package you promised me in your possession? My yacht is at sea and I am paying a lot of money for this package and do not want to wait too long."

"The package will arrive in El-Arish on the bus from Cairo. I will take possession in less than an hour and be on my boat."

"I want the package delivered today. Remember, not a mark on it. Do you understand me, Yuri? It is a very expensive item. Do not damage it."

"Not to worry. It will be as promised and ready for delivery. I have the coordinates and will meet you in four hours to transfer the package. Make sure you have my money. I must be in Cairo for a big shipment next Friday."

"Excellent, I like the idea this once belonged to a British Lord. I never much cared for the British. See you at the agreed location."

Yuri closed the connection. To the untrained ear, it sounded like nothing more than the sale of an expensive commodity. No one overhearing would suspect the handsome man in the business suit was capable of such a despicable act.

Yuri arrived at the bus station to welcome Cassandra. The bus was a little late and he watched as she exited the bus and walked toward a taxi stand. She was wearing a long skirt trimmed in lace with a long sleeved blouse that matched the blue in the skirt. She had a silk scarf around her neck that blew behind her as she got off the bus.

"Cassandra, I am glad to see you took advantage of tickets I gave you."

"Yuri, what are you doing here?"

"When I heard you left for the airport to fly to Cairo, I knew I had to meet you in El-Arish. Please, Cassandra, I like you so much. Please let me drive you to your hotel."

"All right, Yuri. It is good to see you. We had such fun in London."

"A matter of fact, why not spend tonight on my boat with me. If you decide you would rather go to hotel and never see me again; I will do as you ask." He winked at her before putting on his sunglasses.

"Oh Yuri, I couldn't. What would my father say?"

"How would he know unless you told him? Please give me one more chance. You will have very exciting time with me. It will be an adventure. I have expensive yacht and besides, it is early and we have all afternoon to enjoy each other. It will be fun. Look, you are wearing bracelet and earrings that I gave you."

"I could not stop thinking of you after you left that night. I was so angry with my father I did not speak to him for an entire day. I am glad you met me when I got off the bus. We will see how tonight proceeds. I do like you. Father made me angry, he never approves of my friends."

Cassandra got into Yuri's car and he put her suitcases in the back. They arrived at the dock where Yuri's boat was moored. It was a twenty-one-meter yacht with long sport fishing poles on each side of the boat that looked like huge antennas. Two large fishing chairs sat bolted to the deck in the stern.

"Here we are."

"I didn't know you were into fishing?"

"It relaxes me; I love to fish."

"It is an impressive yacht; I want to see the interior. What is the name of your boat? I cannot read Cyrillic letters."

"*Radost 'MoyA*, which translates in English to *My Joy*. I am very proud of my yacht. It is three years old, like brand-new. A customer of mine was so happy with merchandise; he gave me this boat as payment. When I am not dealing in expensive commodities, I cruise, sometimes for month at a time. It is my only home. I hope to retire on this yacht and cruise the Mediterranean."

"I never thought of you as a yachtsman or a man that enjoyed fishing."

"There are lots of things about me my dear that you do not know."

Yuri showed her into the cabin. All the woodwork was in a high gloss finish, and the sole was matching wood and holly planks. They walked through the galley that had a four-burner stove, two refrigerators, and a microwave oven. In the main salon was a fifty-inch LCD television. Yuri turned it on and inserted a DVD of an old James Bond movie starring Sean Connery.

"This is one of my favorite bond movies, *Goldfinger*."

"Never pictured you as a Bond fan."

"I love James Bond. Sean Connery is still my favorite actor for the character of Bond. I own every Bond movie ever made. We will watch later tonight." He turned the television off.

Yuri guided her into the owner's stateroom. The bed was queen sized on a raised platform that had the same high gloss cherry wood as the main salon. The master head was large and had a glass-enclosed shower and garden tub.

"This seems more like a luxury hotel room than the interior of a yacht. It is breathtaking. I love it."

"It can cruise at twenty-four knots. While I get us underway, change into a bathing suit and join me on the deck."

Yuri changed into a very brief black Lycra men's swimsuit, and a shirt that he did not button, and went topside to put into the navigation system the coordinates Jameel gave him.

Cassandra changed into a very skimpy pink string bikini with a thong bottom.

Yuri watched her move, studying her body as she came on deck.

"It is good I met you here. That bikini is not acceptable on beaches at El-Arish or anywhere in Egypt. Remember this is a Muslim country. You will have to buy more modest suit tomorrow. The local women bath while fully dressed. I on other hand love to see woman's body. All of woman's body."

"I never thought of that."

"I tell you what, when we are out of sight of land and there are no boats near us, why not sunbath nude, no strap lines. The boat has high sides and no one will ever know, except me." Yuri gave a sexy laugh.

"Oh, Yuri, you are so wicked."

Cassandra placed a towel on the deck and took off her bikini. She rolled over face down on the deck.

"Yuri, could you put sun lotion on my back, please," she asked.

Yuri put the boat on autopilot, came to her side, and knelt next to her. His strong hands rubbed the lotion onto her body. Cassandra purred as he massaged her and touched every inch of her. He ran his fingers the length of her long supple legs.

"I will let you bake for hour and then I will put lotion on front of you."

Cassandra giggled, "Oh Yuri, Father was so right, you are so conniving. I never should have trusted you, but we have such fun together."

She lay there baking in the sun and Yuri took off his shirt and let the sun bath his body. He steered the boat further and further away from shore. The coordinates were in an area that was out of the shipping lanes where there were no fishing boats. He checked the GPS that he was on the right heading.

An hour later, Yuri had her turn over, he kissed her, his hands cupped her breasts, kissed her nipples, and he could feel them begin to swell with pleasure. He stripped off his swimsuit and made love to her. His body slipped along her freshly lotioned skin. "Put your legs over my back so I can push further into your luscious body."

His thrusts became fierce and his rapid movement soon brought them both to an orgasm. He kissed her passionately and stared into her eyes.

"You are lovely woman and I like you, but someone has to steer the boat."

Yuri left her baking in the sun, put on his swim briefs, and went back to his navigation station to make sure he was in the location he wanted, checked his watch, and knew he would link up with Jameel in an hour.

"Come on, sleepy head. We will go below and have some erotic fun together. Have you ever had someone bind you and then make love to you? We'll pretend you are captured slave girl."

"Oh Yuri, no, but it does sound exciting. You seem so much more relaxed than when you were last in London with me."

"I am more relaxed. I love Mediterranean area. It is such change from Russia. I love warm sun of Egypt. It makes me forget cold dreary weather of Moscow."

They walked into the large main cabin. He tossed his sunglasses on the bed.

Cassandra noticed there was a ring in the ceiling with a pulley at the top and a rope tied off on the side of the cabin.

"You have done this before."

"Yes, but never with anyone as seductive as you. Give me your wrists and let me put these cuffs on you. I will wrap your wrists with gauze so it does not hurt your delicate skin."

Cassandra allowed him to put cuffs on her wrists and ankles. She giggled as he prepared her.

"Now, I am going to attach your wrists to that ring from the ceiling and pull your arms over your head. Then I am going to attach your ankles to the two rings on floor."

"Oh Yuri, I am getting wet just from your binding me. I never thought this could be so erotic."

Yuri finished binding her and smiled at her naked body, still glistening from the sun lotion, with her legs spread wide. He placed a chain around her neck. Yuri kissed her on the mouth and his fingers stroked her body and entered her gate of pleasure. He kissed her breasts and sucked each nipple until it was erect.

"You are aroused much quicker when you are bound. We should have done this before." He laughed. "No rings in hotel room ceilings."

"Oh, Yuri, this is so erotic." Yuri removed his brief not much larger than a jock strap, and his naked body rubbed against her. He brushed her hair back away from her face, pulled her body toward him, and having reached a princely state of erection, he began thrusting into her moving her body back and forth. He engulfed himself completely and drove himself into her by pulling her body toward him. Their bodies collided with every thrust. At every insertion he slapped against her body; she sighed and let out a howl as he pushed more deeply into her; he distilled his very soul into Cassandra. Yuri kissed her passionately and held her close. Perspiration was streaming down his body and his masculine scent was intoxicating. Cassandra was panting and sighing because of his amorous attack. He left her and went into the head, took a quick shower, and dressed.

"Can you untie me, you bound me very tight." Cassandra pleaded when he returned. "I imagine you are a ruthless pirate and I am your helpless captive."

"You have no idea how close your imagination is to reality. My lovely captive, today, you will meet another Yuri. Remember my mentioning that I traded in high priced commodities from the Middle East and Eastern Europe. On occasion I sell very special commodities from other parts of the world, such as London."

"Yuri, what are you talking about? What commodities?"

"My business pays very well Cassandra. I make many thousands of dollars. You will make me much money in few minutes."

"Yuri, what are you talking about? Release me," she struggled and twisted from side to side, but she could not move much the way he had tightly bound her.

"We have just begun to play, my dear. I have very special customer who wants you."

"You are talking about selling me. Let me go. My father was right, you are no gentleman. You are a wicked, not to be trusted, just like my father said." Realizing she was about to be sold into slavery to a perfect stranger she began to scream. "Release me this minute you bastard."

"Scream all you want. We are not near anything. No one will hear you. I have used this boat before to train many lovely women. In the end, they all become quite submissive. Unfortunately, I have orders not to touch you. It would have been enjoyable whipping or preferably spanking your lovely bottom, but it would cost me too much money."

Yuri took some ice cubes and held them against her body.

"These ice cubes will cool your temper." He smirked.

He held the ice against her nipples, slid them down her body, her thighs, and pushed them into her gate of pleasure and held them there.

She screamed and tears rolled down her face, "Yuri, please stop, it is too cold."

"No one ever was hurt by an ice cube, my dear. If only you had been more, mature. My father told me on my eighteenth birthday to make it on my own. Be consoled, this is when I usually spank a woman bound this way or lash them to quiet them with a flogger for about a half an hour until their bottoms are fiery red and their bodies striped. When I finish, they do anything asked of them for fear of another whipping."

Cassandra tried to struggle, but was so upset she could only sob.

"My father is very wealthy. If I give you money, will you release me? My father will give you 50, 000 pounds Sterling."

"Cassandra, I do not want your money. Understand this; I love to have sex with women, but no long relationships. Trusting women is poison for me; I have been hurt too many times. You have seen my scars. They are the result of an underage girl who lied to the authorities in Singapore when I was a young man. I suffered three years in prison and ten strokes of caning rod because of her. I enjoy making love to women, but when I finish with them, I like to spank them, sell them to men who want special kind of companion, or walk away and never see them again. Your money is not important to me. Your father ran your life and now you will make the right man good sex slave. I have taught you many ways to make love. Grown women should think for themselves, and never listen to their fathers."

"I am tied too tight and my feet barely touch the floor. I liked you Yuri, but my father was right. If I ever get free, you will end up in prison for rest of your life."

"Not going to happen. Your father will think you disappeared in Cairo, and if he does manage to check the hotel in El-Arish, you never registered. There is no trail and no escape."

"I hate you. Maybe your customer will ransom me to my father."

"My customer hates British and what they did during war on Iraq. He can hardly wait to own the daughter of British Lord. Perhaps," Yuri paused, "he may circumcise you. Can you imagine how painful that is? He is wealthy divorced surgeon from Cairo that wanted a blue-eyed blonde. When he desires to have sex, submit to his desires and he will not hurt you. All he wants is willing woman to love."

"Please let me go."

"No, I cannot do that. A Czech woman I sold two years ago emailed me six months ago that she was so grateful for making it possible to meet the man of her dreams, as she put it, the most marvelous man in world. She actually thanked me for selling her. At first, she also hated me. Perhaps you will like him. Remember though, he has paid much money. He will expect something in return."

"I hear a boat. I think the good doctor has arrived. May you have exciting life Cassandra? You are the last special woman I plan to sell. I am planning to retire to tropical island in month or two with the money I earned from finding and selling alluring women to wealthy men. Forgive me, but this conversation is over. Wear this gag until he removes it."

Yuri kissed or on the mouth, then put a five centimeter round ball gag with breathable holes in her mouth, fastened it securely with a leather strap so it fit tightly so she could not make a sound.

He whispered to her, "This man will not hurt you. I picked him special. Trust me. Do everything he asks and he will be very temperate and not want to spank your bottom." Yuri tied a blindfold across her eyes. "It is a shame you were so unsophisticated."

Cassandra moved her head side to side and the only sound she made was a kind of muted mewing. Tears streamed down her face.

Jameel's boat gently tapped the side of Yuri's boat and a crewman tied the two boats together with large fenders in between. Yuri was in awe of the size of Jameel's yacht.

"Could I look on board your magnificent yacht?" Yuri asked in Arabic.

"I am here for one purpose. I plan to leave immediately."

"The woman is ready. Do you have the money?"

"I want to see her first."

Yuri took Jameel, to where Cassandra was tied in the cabin. "I told her you would circumcise her if she didn't do everything you told her to do."

"I should never have mentioned I circumcised women." Jameel stopped and looked at Cassandra as her body was squirming against the rope that bound her. "She is lovely, exquisite; her skin is flawless. You did not exaggerate her beauty."

Jameel walked to her, fondled and kissed her breasts, slid his hands along her lotioned body that seemed to gleam from the sun piercing through the cabin window, and probed her gate of pleasure with his fingers while Cassandra pulled and squirmed. He walked behind her and slapped her playfully on each cheek. "I want to see her eyes."

Yuri removed her blindfold to reveal her eyes, bloodshot from crying.

"She looks terrified. Did you hurt her in any way?"

"I have done nothing per your instructions. She did not like the idea of being a sex slave when I told her. Her anger will pass. Make believe you are a sultan and she is part of your harem. Everyone needs to live a fantasy. She is a woman to enjoy. If she is not agreeable, call me. I would love to condition her. Do you wish for me to make her submissive? She will be at your beckon call."

"I will take charge of making her submissive, and enjoy having sex with her before I return to work in ten days."

Jameel looked into her eyes and whispered in her ear in English?" Has this man brutalized you in any way?"

Cassandra was frightened, but managed to nod her head, no.

"Did he do anything to hurt you?"

Cassandra nodded yes.

"What did you do to this woman? I said not to touch her."

"I chilled her down with some ice cubes I slid along her body. Her temper flared when I bound her; the ice cooled her off. She shivered a little, but that is all."

Jameel looked at Cassandra again. "Did you make love to this woman?"

"I made love to her and she made love to me, willingly. I told you we dated for several weeks. Of course, I made love to her that is how I train women in the art of love. She is a delight in bed; sexy lady, and good kisser. I will miss her. She knows all ways to make love and bring a man pleasure, which is the training I provide at no charge." Yuri smirked.

"Where is the burka including *hijab* (head covering) and *niqab* (veil) I told you to have ready?"

Yuri handed him the black burka. Jameel untied her legs and released her arms from the hook in the ceiling, but left the handcuffs on her wrists and the gag in place.

"I am going to cover you with this. It has a veil to cover your eyes; you can see out, but no one can see into your eyes. I am leaving your wrists cuffed and the gag in place; you must be quiet and not pull away from me. You will cooperate with me, or I may reconsider having Yuri condition you."

Cassandra cooperated and was soon standing fully covered.

Jameel took a case that he had placed on the floor, opened it, and handed Yuri the money.

"I hope she is worth the money I am paying. I have never done anything like this before in my life. I am a very conservative, private man. Give me her identity papers."

Yuri handed him her passport, driver's license, and credit cards from her purse including her cell phone. He kept the cash.

"Wait, I have something for you." Yuri handed him a flogger with many rubber strands with pointed tips. "Here, it is my favorite flogger. Use it if she refuses to cooperate, as it will sting her bottom without breaking the skin. A few lashes with this and she will become very submissive. Her name is Cassandra Cavendish."

"Thank you, but I prefer using my hand for spanking, but this may come in handy if she fights me." He smiled admiring the phallus shaped handle.

One of the deck hands from Jameel's boat helped Jameel pass her from boat to boat. Then, he boarded the yacht, picked her up in his arms, and told his man to make way. "Get underway, I want to dock at Alexandria by six this evening. Once we are moored, wash down the decks before my guests arrive; they are due at nine o'clock. I will be in the lower cabin. Do not disturb me."

The first mate nodded his understanding and turned barking orders to the crew to pull in the fenders in preparation to get underway. The yacht had a fly bridge, an upper deck, a main deck, and a lower deck. Because of the nature of this trip, he carried his special package below to the lower deck and placed her on a bed in a large guest cabin. The owner's cabin was on the upper deck.

The two boats went their separate ways.

Chapter 10

The day after selling Cassandra to Jameel, Yuri left his boat in El Arish tied to a mooring, and flew to Cairo. He was a man on a mission to get ready for Friday's shipment including arranging for a doctor to be at the cave in the mountains to help with the women. One of the Bedouins wanted the doctor to circumcise his young daughter and two nieces. It was illegal to do this surgery, but Yuri offered to have the doctor do it in return for a large sum of money. The doctor had agreed but did not know that twenty enslaved women would also be under his care for a few days.

Yuri arrived at Dr. Ahmed Ishmail's office wearing jeans and a long sleeved sport shirt. The doctor, a man in his fifties with graying hair, almost twenty centimeters shorter than Yuri, had assembled a full surgical kit, sterile sheets, and blankets. Yuri carried the equipment and supplies to the car, and they commenced to drive Yuri's four-wheel drive vehicle toward El-Arish and into the mountains. They had been on the road for two and a half hours when Yuri pulled the car to the side of the road.

"Before we continue, doctor, it is important that you wear this hood. This is a secret place of the Bedouins, and they dislike visitors. I am sure you will not mind, it is for your own protection. Besides, you are well paid."

The doctor complied and put on the hood and they continued to the foot of the mountains. Yuri drove through the desert avoiding security checkpoints. At the end of the road, a Bedouin with four camels was waiting for them.

Yuri stepped out of the car and addressed the man.

"Load the supplies on the one camel and we will ride up the trail on the other. Come doctor, we are almost there." Reluctantly, Dr. Ishmail followed orders keeping the blindfold on while they helped him to board the camel. The trek by camel took forty-five minutes to arrive at a large cave that the Bedouins had carefully camouflaged.

'Adey greeted them as they entered the cave. He was not a tall man, dressed in typical Bedouin style with a white thobe with a striped *kibr* over the front and a sleeveless coat in shades of blue. He wore a *kufeya* held in place by an *ogal* of camel wool. He had a black leather belt around his waist and a long curved knife or *khanja* in a scabbard under the belt. "Doctor, my wife and sister will have the girls here tomorrow morning at 6 a.m."

Dr. Ishmail replied, "I am prepared for the surgery, Type II circumcision. One word of this and I could be jailed and loose my license. The government does not want this barbaric practice to continue."

"You will do as you are told. My wife will tell you how much to cut. This is part of my culture and you will cooperate. I don't think you want to continue life as a eunuch doctor," 'Adey laughed.

The next morning five women arrived with three young girls. Two of the girls were six years old and 'Adey's daughter was seven. 'Adey's wife was there along with her sister and mother.

"You will do the surgery without anesthetic. If not, we will operate on you," 'Adey smirked.

"I will do it. Strap the first girl to the table and make sure she cannot move."

'Adey's daughter removed her shift and willingly climbed onto the table, and allowed them to bind her tightly. The doctor directed them to spread her legs wide exposing her entire vaginal area. The doctor cleaned her with antiseptic and prepared to make the first cut. He was to perform Type II circumcision or an excision. The girl let out a piercing scream as the scalpel made the first cut. The doctor would remove the entire clitoris along with the inner vaginal lips. The mother told her to be brave as this was necessary to becoming a woman. The doctor continued to cut as the young girl screamed from the intense pain.

"Cut more," the mother directed. "I know how I was cut. You must cut more. If you do not, I will do it."

Blood ran onto the table as the doctor continued to cut and by the time the mother was satisfied, the girl had fainted from the pain. He stitched her, wrapped her in a blanket, and laid her gently on one of the beds in a cell along the side of the cave. The women would take the girls immediately to their home in the desert when the operations were complete. The other girls were also snipped under the direction of their grandmother and mother. The girls screamed and screamed, but the doctor continued.

"Well done doctor. The girls look good. My wife and the other women will take them to our home in the desert."

"Give them these pills to prevent infection."

"We are of the 21st century doctor. Your directions will be followed."

The women were happy, 'Adey was delighted as the girls lay unconscious. 'Adey and the other man carefully carried the girls to the foot of the mountain pass where a jeep was waiting. Yuri helped them put the girls carefully into the back of the car and watched as they drove back to the Bedouin camp.

Yuri had been in another part of the cave when the doctor had started but ran to see what was going on when he heard the little girl's scream, The sight of the women telling the doctor to cut more as the blood ran, caused him to turn away. He became so nauseous; he vomited.

When the screaming stopped and he composed himself, Yuri walked over to the doctor. "Doctor you will be staying on at the cave for awhile. There are twenty women arriving here on Saturday morning about five o'clock. You will check them and give each a complete physical."

"I want to return immediately. You said nothing of more women. Take me back to Cairo now."

"You will do as I say doctor." Yuri grabbed the doctor and shoved him into the wall of the cave. The man was terrified and in fear of his life. "My two friends will make you comfortable. You are paid well for your services. I will see you Saturday."

Yuri got on one of the camels, headed back to his car, and parked it at the marina near his yacht. He decided to have dinner at his favorite hotel, the Sinai El-Arish before flying to Cairo.

When Yuri arrived at the hotel, he felt strangely refreshed, despite the incident in the cave. The rest had done him good; he had almost recovered from his surgery. He walked into the lobby, cleared security, and noticed a tall American woman getting off the elevator. She caught his eye, no ring, and Yuri thought to himself, "That redhead would sell for a great deal of money. Cassandra was to be my last private sale, but this woman is exceptional." Then he noticed that she was not alone, but was met by a very tall, well-dressed Egyptian executive.

Yuri looked in their direction and then walked over to the registration desk so he could see her better.

"I am expecting friends; what is the rate per night?"

The reception clerk answered all his questions. Yuri paid little attention, as he could not take his eyes off Emunishere. He took a seat in the lobby to watch the American red head. Yuri got up and slightly bumped into Hassan, said excuse me, stared at Emunishere and left the hotel. A short time later Hassan and Emunishere left together. Elegantly dressed in a long black skirt gaily decorated with rows of colorful rickrack and a long sleeved pink top that picked up one of the colors in the skirt along with a pink scarf, Emunishere looked exceptional. Yuri watched them leave while sitting in his car in the parking lot. Seeing no opportunity at the present to snatch the woman, he returned to his boat.

Hassan and Emunishere went to dinner at one of the restaurants in El-Arish. After dinner, they returned to the hotel where he escorted her to her room.

Emunishere unlocked the door and asked him if he wanted to come in.

"I leave on Friday afternoon for Cairo. Tomorrow is my last day in El-Arish. I have had a wonderful time and I will miss you." She handed him three sketches of sea birds.

Hassan looked at the sketches and smiled, "It is like being there again. Have you ever thought of being a professional artist?"

"It was my dream once, but everything changed when I got married. My husband didn't want me to work."

Hassan took her in his arms, kissed her lightly on the mouth, and said, "I will miss you. Tuesday morning I will be in Cairo to attend a meeting. I understand that you are staying at another of my hotels managed by my brother. I will call him and arrange for the best room."

"Emunishere, I have become quite fond of you. You are not like most American women. You have made me feel like a man again."

He kissed her passionately, looked deeply into her bewitching green eyes, and held her close.

"Good night. We will do something special tomorrow. I cannot meet you until one in the afternoon. We will meet in the lobby."

She kissed him good night and he left for his own room. Emunishere wrote in her diary again,

"Dear Diary. I wish I did not have arrangements to go to Cairo. Tuesday is not far away. I have one more day with Hassan; we will spend the afternoon together. He kissed me passionately on the lips, but I want more. I want him to make love to me, hold me, and tell me he doesn't want me to leave. Perhaps it is too soon after the death of his wife and son; he is not ready for a relationship with a woman. I never felt this way when Greg kissed me."

Thursday morning Yuri was just off shore in his fishing boat looking through his binoculars when he noticed Emunishere sitting on the beach by herself. She was wearing a conservative one-piece black bathing suit, leaning with her back against a palm tree, with her eyes closed enjoying the sun. The beach was empty. There would never be a better opportunity. Yuri took the dinghy, headed toward the beach and walked quietly toward Emunishere. Before leaving the boat, he had filled a syringe with an intramuscular anesthetic that would render her helpless. Kneeling next to her, she suddenly became aware of his presence. Just as he was getting ready with the syringe he spoke in a low whispering tone next to her ear, "You will be my pretty maid for the next few days like Cassandra, and join my other pretty maids all in a row."

Emunishere, sensing danger, kicked his leg, Yuri lost his balance, dropped the syringe in the sand, and as he went to stand, she took her hand, palm out, and slammed it across the bridge of his nose using a wedge movement she had learned from the martial arts school. She heard the cartilage break and blood ran down his face. Yuri let out a groan. Quickly she rolled to her side and sprang to her feet. Yuri, taken by surprise, could do nothing; Emunishere struck him with a powerful kick to the jaw and followed with another kick to his thigh. By this time, Yuri was back on his feet. He tried to strike her, but was having trouble seeing because of his broken nose and she was too fast, a blur. Spinning around she landed another powerful kick to his groin. He grunted and started to fall forward when she followed with a slam to the side of his head with another wedge movement. Yuri collapsed in the sand. Emunishere started screaming help in Arabic as loud as she could as she ran toward the hotel. *"ilHa'ni!-ilHa'ni!."*

When she was far enough away, she looked back over her shoulder and saw Yuri stumbling the other way toward the dinghy. Emunishere stopped and watched him push the dinghy away from the beach, jump on board and power toward a fishing boat anchored off shore. She turned and ran quickly the rest of the way to the hotel. Breaking through the door, she ran across the lobby to the concierge's desk. Her bathing suit and arm spattered with blood from where she had kicked Yuri.

"Help me, help me, a man tried to kidnap me off the beach. Is Hassan here?" she shouted while gasping for breath.

"Mrs. Bishop, what has happened you are covered in blood?"

"It is not my blood. It is from the man who attacked me. I think I broke his nose."

"Hassan is not here. I will call him immediately, and summon the police, and a doctor."

Emunishere suddenly became aware she was standing in the hotel lobby wearing only a bathing suit.

"I need to get to my room."

The man behind the desk sensing her embarrassment walked around and offered her his jacket.

"Thank you so much. Call me when the police or Hassan arrives. I do not need a doctor. I am just out of breath."

"A porter will escort you to your room and stay outside until Hassan or the police arrive. Someone will get your things from the beach."

Yuri quickly got on board his boat, his hands strangling the wheel as he brought the *My Joy* up to its full twenty-four knots and steered away from the other boats coming to a stop when he was about twenty nautical miles out to sea. There were no other boats in the area and he put the boat on autopilot. Fearful that someone might have heard her screams for help and followed him he scanned the shore to make sure that there were no boats in pursuit. To his relief, he saw nothing but empty ocean behind him. For now, he was safe. Pain from his injuries reminded him that he had other problems. Blood started to flow again from his broken nose. He went below to get some ice and a towel.

This meant that he would have to put in at another port and take a bus back to El-Arish under the cover of darkness. Regardless of what happened, he would have to get to Cairo airport to greet the women coming in from Eastern Europe. His job was to indoctrinate them before bringing them across the desert to the mountains, check his arms shipment, and smuggle the women into Israel.

"That bitch on the beach will pay for what she did to me. I will find her. She will wish she never met me before I am finished with her." The only thing hurt more than his pride was his nose; he screamed as he tried to bandage it.

The desk clerk reached Hassan on his cell phone and told him what had happened.

"I am on my way to the hotel. Tell Mrs. Bishop to stay in her room until I get there. When the police arrive, have them wait in my office. Start asking around and see if anyone saw what happened."

Hassan hung up the phone, got into his car and headed back to the hotel.

Chapter 11

Alex MacKay had not been active in MI6 for almost a year and had just arrived in London from his restored castle home in Fettercairn, Scotland when his encrypted cell phone rang.

"Alex, Henry Ewing."

Henry Ewing, head of the MI6 division special agent in charge of crimes involving the trafficking of women for the sex trade was calling him.

"Yes, what is it?"

"Alex, we need your services in conjunction with a very sensitive matter. The daughter of Lord Robert Cavendish has disappeared in Egypt while on vacation. He suspects she has been kidnapped, but he has received no request for a ransom."

"How old is this young woman?"

"Cassandra is twenty-four years old."

"Possible she ran away with a boyfriend?"

"Her father said she was dating a Russian Jew and he did not trust the young man and that he told her to stop seeing him. This young man, Yuri Berezovsky, gave her tickets for a trip to El-Arish for a week and a pre-paid hotel reservation. They were to travel together, but when she told him no, he threw the tickets at her and said it was a parting gift, that he had other plans to return to Moscow."

"Sounds like nothing more than a young woman angry with her father."

"The other possibility is that she was kidnapped by human traffickers and will be indoctrinated and smuggled into Tele Aviv or Saudi Arabia as a sex slave. She might still be in Egypt imprisoned by a wealthy man who is keeping her in his home for his enjoyment. Women traveling alone frequently disappear in Egypt."

Alex interrupted, "The Russian Jewish mobs are the most active groups in the Middle East with the sex trade. It is a billion dollar a year business. What is his full name? It is possible our paths have crossed in the past."

"His full name is Yuri Berezovsky, a very tall, olive complexioned man in his mid twenties with piercing blue eyes. Our contact in Cairo reports that the Egyptian authorities have no record of him entering the country. That's not to say he slipped across the border without them knowing."

"Berezovsky is not a name I have come across before."

"Last year over one hundred women from various parts of the world traveling alone entered Egypt on visas, and never officially left the country. Even though you have been on rescue missions in the past, be careful. Every time I see that scar on your face, it reminds me of the woman that tried to kill you when you attempted to rescue her against her will. Turned out she was perfectly happy with the man that enslaved her."

"Our intelligence indicates that Egypt is still the main transfer point for the Russian mobs to smuggle women into Israel. I want you to fly to the port city of El-Arish, near the Israeli border. Check with our local branch to see if they have heard anything. Alex, this is a priority assignment. If she has been abducted, every hour we delay makes it less likely we will find her."

"I understand. Thanks for the call. I need to get back to work, besides, I owe you."

"What happened was regrettable but it is in the past. I need you to focus on finding Cassandra Cavendish." Covering up Alex's involvement in the accidental death of his wife was an unpleasant necessity to save an experienced operative.

"No one else could have gotten me out of the mess I got myself into with Catherine. My career would have ended and I would have served time in prison even though it was an accident."

"I remember, Alex, that when you introduced me to Catherine, she struck me as the wrong woman for you. You had nothing in common. Glad I could help; she was an evil bitch. You will never forget what happened because you are a descent man, but no one ever questioned the story I told the police."

Henry continued.

"If the sex slavers are involved, I welcome the opportunity to shut them down. This syndicate is like a multi-headed snake, cut off one head and two more grow back. Since the breakup of the old Soviet Union, the sex slave trade has blossomed and reached epidemic proportions. Russian capitalism, what an oxymoron."

"I still cannot believe that woman cut me. I heard that after being repatriated, she went back to that bastard and they were married. I have great difficulty in understanding women." Ewing chuckled. Alex had not changed.

"I am working on getting you a clearance through the Egyptian government that will allow you to freely move about even though this is not a sanctioned mission. You have a reservation for the afternoon flight leaving from Heathrow to Cairo. From there you will take a charter to El-Arish. When you arrive, go to the Sinai El-Arish Hotel. The room is registered in your name."

"Is this hotel where the missing woman was staying?"

"No, she had a reservation at another hotel but never arrived. The owner of the hotel where you are staying is a man named Ibn Sabir Hassan al-Admad Gaafar. Hassan and his father, Sabir, are involved with a group of ex-military volunteers in Egypt with the approval of the government that are fighting for the same cause we are."

"Am I to work with him?"

"This is off the books, Alex. The man that heads up the group in Egypt is Hassan's father, Sabir Gaafar. Sabir is a skilled surgeon and works with many of the women who have escaped. Our sources tell us that they are planning to smuggle a group of women across the desert into Israel in the next few days."

"I will pack and be on my way."

"Alex, this is not an official operation; be careful. Sabir Gaafar is the head of the operation along with his son, Hassan. If you do discover a group, I will see that your operation is sanctioned with the full approval and support of her Majesty's government. Think of this as a reconnaissance mission."

"I understand."

"You are one of my best Alex. I am depending on you. Find this British woman. Lord Cavendish is a very influential man and I cannot imagine she will object to your rescuing her. He has already left London on an earlier flight and will be at the hotel when you arrive. Make sure he stays at the hotel and does not try to investigate on his own."

"I will make that clear to him."

Alex drove directly to his town house in Notting Hill, situated in West London, and picked up his "to go" bag. Boxes were everywhere as Alex was in the process of moving his things to his castle in Scotland when Henry Ewing had called.

The flight to Cairo was uneventful. Twenty minutes after boarding the charter to El Arish he landed. Alex took a cab to the hotel.

Arriving two days earlier, Robert Cavendish was waiting in the lobby when arrived at the hotel. Stressed, his eyes almost sunken because of lack of sleep, Cavendish was a man in need of answers, answers he hoped, Alex MacKay would provide. Since the disappearance of his daughter, Cavendish had thought of nothing else. Horrible thoughts of what she might be subjected to raced through his mind.

Chapter 12

Jameel laid Cassandra gently on a bed in a cabin on the lower deck, fastened her ankle cuffs together, and left her gagged with her wrists cuffed wearing the full burka. Looking at his captive lying on the bed, afraid to move, he could see the terror in her eyes. Would she ever accept him as her benefactor and friend, or only obey out of fear. The thought of having a woman that would obey and respect him was appealing. Beyond physical pleasure, he wanted a companion, someone with whom he could share his life. That would come later, for now he would enjoy finding out how much she had learned from Yuri.

Cassandra lay staring up at him as he watched her, "I cannot believe Yuri has done this to me." Her wrists were beginning to hurt from the tightly wound gauze and her feet were tingly from the straps cutting off her circulation.

"This gag is causing me to drool. Who is the man who bought me? Yuri said he is a doctor and might circumcise me. I don't even know his name."

Cassandra was in fear of what might happen next. In the last two hours, she had gone from a love struck girl to the slave of a man she had never met. She lay there sobbing in the middle of the bed.

Without saying a word, Jameel removed the ghutra and thobe he was wearing revealing a carpet of thick, black hair on his chest. His tan face was adorned with a bushy black moustache. The hair on his head was as thick and black as his chest. Jameel cut an imposing figure, standing tall with a muscular build. Bending over Cassandra, he removed her burka, gently running his hands across her body, and fondling her breasts.

Passion ignited by his caresses, started to overcome her fear that this man was about to rape her or worse, sodomize her and beat her into submission.

His hands were everywhere, touching every part of her body while his lips gently kissed her whispering in Arabic as he looked into her eyes.

"Oh my God, I am drooling like a pig with an apple in its mouth from this gag. What must he think of me? Jameel seemed not to notice, entranced by her naked vulnerability. As he touched her moving his hands ever faster she thought, "His hands touch parts of my body so gently it is like a soft breeze flowing over me."

Jameel continued using only his hands and kisses. Aroused, her body responded. "What is wrong with me? This man is going to punish and discipline me until I do whatever he asks." Physical attraction suddenly gave way to the realization that she was in real danger. "If he unbinds me, I will make a break for it and dive overboard. I'd rather drown than become any man's sex slave." Cassandra began to sob.

In a gentle reassuring voice, Jameel spoke to her as he sat on the bed next to her. "Cassandra, my name is Jameel al Basara, you may call me Jameel. I am going to unbind your ankles. I will take you and clean your body inside and out. Do not struggle or resist me. If you try to kick me, I will punish you. The gag will remain in place for now; I know it is uncomfortable, but I will remove it shortly."

Jameel unbound her ankles, but left the leather cuffs attached. "Yuri tied you very tight. Your ankles will tingle as the blood begins to circulate."

Jameel gently removed the strips of gauze, massaged her ankles, and kissed the tops of her feet. He smiled at her, pushed her hair away from her face, and in an assertive tone of voice said, "Come with me." He helped her up from the bed.

When they entered the bathroom, he lifted Cassandra onto a table, his naked body rubbed against her. "I am going to shave your body and use a special wax to remove all your body hair from your private parts. You will look like a newborn baby when I am finished. Do not move; I might cut you."

Jameel flashed a straight edge razor in front of her eyes. Cassandra lay still with tears flowing down her cheeks as he carefully applied shaving cream and shaved her body with the straight edge; finishing with a safety razor, and lastly, applied warm wax to remove any body hair he missed. With a warm cloth, he wiped the area he had denuded of hair leaving her body smooth and silky. Cassandra shuttered, but lay still afraid to move. He kissed her body where he had shaved her, flicked at her private parts with his tongue, and kissed the entire area he had shaved. His sucking gently at her delicate portal of pleasure caused Cassandra to let out a sigh.

Jameel stood up beside her.

"Turn on your stomach; I am going to give you an enema. Your body must be cleansed inside and as well as out. Do not resist me. I have two deck hands that would be most eager to help me do this."

She would have screamed, but she was gagged and unable to make a sound. Lying on her stomach, she continued to wiggle her body. "Keep still," Jameel shouted, smacking her several times with his open hand on her bottom to make his point. Cassandra stopped moving.

Gently he inserted a tube into her bottom releasing the enema consisting of one pint of a warm solution of much diluted coffee. He proceeded to massage her shoulders as she lay still and kissed the small of her back. After a few minutes, he removed the tube, lifted her off the table, and put her on the toilet.

"It is time for a shower. I am going to go into the shower with you and scrub your body. If you attempt to move away from me, I will bind your wrists to a hook in the ceiling."

Jameel took her into the shower. She stood there with the warm water cascading over her body. He lathered a sponge and gently scrubbed her body with a fragrant soap. Their bodies brushed against each other and it was obvious that he was in a state of arousal. With a white cotton towel, he carefully dried every part of her before applying a lotion to her skin. His hands were strong yet soft. Picking her up in his strong arms, he held her body close to his as he carried her into the stateroom and laid her gently on the bed face down.

"I am going to make love to you. Because you are my slave, I will never have vaginal sex with you. You will learn there are many ways to pleasure a man. I am going to insert some lubricant into your bottom and promise to be gentle. My intention is not to injure you, but enjoy you. Please, try to relax. You may find this arousing. Yuri said he trained you in all ways to make love to a man; this should be nothing new. I am going to secure you this first time; I don't want you to fight me."

Jameel fastened her wrists to the headboard, spread her legs apart, and fastened each ankle to straps he had installed at the foot of the bed. He shoved a pillow under her to elevate her bottom and inserted a tube of lubricant into her anus. He pushed his fingers into her, first one finger, then two then three.

Cassandra tried to squeeze herself together to prevent his entering her; attempting to wiggle free of him, but he spanked her bottom with his hand several times causing it to bloom into a rosy blush. Her futile attempts to escape only increased his determination.

"Relax, stop trying to fight me; you cannot escape. I have made love to a woman in this manner many times with no complaints. It is very pleasing for me."

From the bedside table, he picked up a phallus, liberally applied lubricant gradually inserting it into her tight ass before slowly pulling it out, while Cassandra moaned and wiggled her body. After several minutes of using the phallus, he had come to a full erection, removed the phallus, placed his erect manhood against her, and pressed hard. Gradually she opened and he was fully inside of her. He knew she must have been feeling his presence to her naval and continued to push in and out slowly at first, then with increased fierceness until Cassandra stirred beyond bearing by the furious agitation it caused, tried to cry out, as he fingered her other gate of pleasure now wet and pushing against his fingers. After close to an hour, he was now master of the situation and finally gave all his energy with an explosive release of the voluptuous joy of his senses. Reticent and still, his chest heaving with every breath, Jameel felt the tension drain from his body. He stayed inside of her until he was completely relaxed collapsing on the bed beside her.

"You have a very tight ass, my dear. We will spend many pleasurable hours doing this. I will teach you many positions for anal sex. Now, I am going to release your ankles and uncuff your wrists. Do not try to strike me or I will punish you. Lastly I am going to do is remove the gag. When I do, say nothing or I will put it back in."

Sitting on the bed next to her, Jameel released her wrists, unwound the wet gauze, and massaged her wrists to get the circulation going. He brushed the back of her hands with his lips.

"Yuri bound your wrists more tightly than your ankles. You will be fine; it will burn as the blood starts to circulate again. I am going to remove your gag, say not one word; listen to me."

The second he removed her gag and she was completely free; Cassandra sprang off the bed and screamed at him, "You fucking bastard. Let me go. How dare you rape and sodomize the daughter of an English Lord? My father will pay any ransom you ask. Release me. I hate you; I hate Yuri. I demand you set me free. She pounded his chest with her clenched fists, turned, and tried to run away from him."

Jameel grabbed her roughly by the arm and shouted at her, "You dare strike me, scream, and curse at me. The first punishment you will receive is for disobeying me. The second punishment is for cursing and screaming when told to be quiet and listen. You will become submissive and hold your tongue." Jameel's voice was forceful and angry when he spoke to her.

Cassandra continued to try to escape from his strong grip, but to no avail.

"I think what you need is a good spanking."

"You would not dare," she screamed. "You have already spanked me several times; my bottom smarts."

Jameel cuffed her wrists despite her struggling and pulled her across his knees. As he spanked her bottom, she cursed each time he struck her. "You bastard, you and Yuri will pay for this. Fuck you both."

"Stop cursing and screaming and I will stop spanking you."

Her bare bottom blossomed into a fiery red as he continued to spank her until she finally stopped, and lay across his lap sobbing uncontrollably.

"I am now going to place an old fashioned gag in your mouth that you will find most unpleasant. I will bind you to that pole that runs from the cabin sole to the ceiling. Where did a genteel woman like you obtain such a vocabulary? It is most unladylike." Jameel spoke in a softer tone this time.

He bound her hands over her head and tied them securely to the pole. Likewise, he took a leather strap and bound her body to the pole. A third strap secured her ankles and stopped her from kicking. The last strap he put around her forehead so she could not move her head from side to side. From the galley, he picked up a clean kitchen towel, brought it to the bathroom, soaked it in warm soapy water, and wrung it out tying one end into a tight knot. Cassandra was frightened he might really hurt her and did not fight him.

"The ball gag will not inflict pain or discomfort; this will cure you of cursing and speaking when told to be quiet. Open as wide as you can. I am going to place this knotted towel into your mouth. It is soaked in warm soapy water to remind you not to curse. I will tie it tightly and let you stand there for an hour. The next time you curse, it will be soaked in hot sauce, and your mouth will burn."

Jameel tied the gag securely, slipped into a thobe, left her in the bedroom, closed the door, and went topside for an hour to relax with a glass of fruit juice and scanned the horizon for any sign they were getting close to Alexandria. Thoughts of how to tame her went through his mind.

When he returned to the cabin, Cassandra was sobbing, tears rolled down her cheeks and her body was trembling. Releasing the strap holding her head, he removed the towel, placed his hands on both sides of her face, and looked directly into her tear-filled eyes.

"Will you stop screaming and cursing? No more hitting."

Cassandra looked at him and in a quivering voice answered, "I will stop. Please, please let me wash my mouth with water; that soap tastes terrible. I won't hit you again."

He unbound her, led her into the bathroom, and handed her a glass of cold mineral water.

She rinsed her mouth. Jameel picked her up in his arms, kissed her gently on each cheek, and placed her in the middle of the bed.

"Lay here quietly. If you leave this cabin, I will call your friend Yuri and send you back to him. Hurting you is not enjoyable for me; you must do as I ask. Please try, I know you are upset and unhappy with your current situation."

Cassandra looked up at him with tear-filled eyes, "I will be quiet, please do not hurt me. You frighten me. Please, I will do anything you ask."

Jameel smiled at her, smoothed her hair with his hand, and kissed her on the cheek.

"I need time alone and will return shortly. There are things I must discuss with my crew before we arrive in Alexandria."

Jameel went onto the bridge with his men.

"How much further do we have before we make port?"

"We will be at the dock at six," responded the first officer.

Jameel sat outside on a deck chair enjoying the sea breeze off the water thinking about his captive. "She is a very alluring woman. After my ten-day vacation, I will send her home to her father. It was arousing spanking her lovely bottom. I want her to be a lover, not a terrified slave."

Jameel entered the cabin, Cassandra had not moved.

Cassandra sniffled, "Please let me go. I am not a slave to anyone. My father is very wealthy and will pay you anything you ask."

"Money is not important to me; I want a loving companion for the next ten days."

"If I agree, does that mean you will let me go?"

"We will see when that time comes."

Sitting on the bed in a gentle voice, he told her, "Roll onto your stomach."

Jameel took a soothing lotion and gently applied it to her abused bottom. He kissed the small of her back, brushed her hair to one side, and kissed the back of her neck.

"This should ease any pain you are feeling from when I spanked you. I am going to lie next to you and rest before we arrive at the dock. If I fall asleep, do not attempt to leave the cabin or I will spank you again, twice as long and twice as hard. Yuri gave me a flogger; I might try it out on your lovely behind."

Jameel removed his thobe and before he lay down noticed tears welling up in Cassandra's eyes. Catching a tear on his finger, he kissed it.

"Your tears are salty, but I have only begun to taste your sweetness. I enjoyed making love to you. You will learn that hurting a woman is not in my nature. Now, use the bathroom; take a warm shower while I rest. There is a dress in the closet that should fit. Yuri gave me all your sizes before you came aboard. No one will bother you for the next two hours."

"Thank you for not hurting me." She sniffled. "Would you mind if I stayed here with you? I'm exhausted."

Jameel kissed her cheek and smiled at her before he lay next to her. Cassandra slept most of the two hours with him at her side under an unbelievably soft cotton sheet. When she awoke she lay there watching him take long deep breaths, relaxed and at ease. Cassandra's mind was racing to make sense of what was happening to her. "He sleeps soundly. What is to become of me? He kisses me and I return his kisses. When he embraces me, I want to hug him in return. How is it possible to hate him for what he has done and still find him physically attractive? When I gaze into his deep brown eyes there is an inner fire to them." Cassandra closed her eyes and fell asleep snuggled next to his naked body.

The alarm on Jameel's watch went off and woke him to find her sleeping next to him.

In a soft voice he whispered, "We will dock in a few minutes at the port of Alexandria where I keep my boat. Guests are coming for dinner. Wake up lovely lady," he gently kissed her ear and she rolled toward him. "I want you to get dressed and we will go to the dining room. Your seat will be under the table, where I am sitting; you will pleasure me."

Cassandra awoke sitting straight up.

"I will not be seated under a table like a dog." She shouted at him.

"Must I spank you, again? You will do exactly what I tell you. Remember, at the present, you are my slave and will do what I demand. The next spanking will be harder and longer; you will be gagged, left bound in the engine room where it is very hot, and beg me to release you."

Cassandra glared at him. "I will do it, but when I get away from you, you will pay for this humiliation."

Jameel handed her an exquisite emerald green ankle length dress of pure silk, with a high neckline and long sleeves from the closet. It slid over her body and she looked in a mirror as he zipped the back of the dress. It was elegant and fit her to perfection. Jameel put his arms around her and held her close.

"Trust me. Loving you is what I desire, punishing you, believe it or not, makes me feel bad."

He handed her a comb and brushes to do her hair.

"There is make-up on the table by the mirror. A woman should look alluring, especially around the eyes."

"Not that anyone will see me under the table."

When she finished, she stood up and he walked to her, kissed her on each cheek, and held her face between his hands.

"You are a very lovely woman, do not be frightened.; I understand this is not your choice."

Jameel paused and placed a gold chain around her neck.

"When you are outside of my cabin wear this," he handed her a burka. "I share your beauty with no one. You really are striking." Jameel paused to look at her.

"Come, I am taking you to the dining room before my guests arrive and while my crew is busy elsewhere. There are several cushions on the floor in front of where I am sitting. The table has a white cloth that falls to the floor. I am the only one will know that an enchanting woman sits at my feet at my beckon call. They will have no idea why there is a smile on my face while eating dinner. No one, but me, will know you are there." He kissed her on the lips.

When they arrived in the dining area of the yacht, he pulled the cloth aside, removed the burka, and helped her arrange the cushions so she could sit comfortably, placed a cuff on her ankle, and chained it to the table leg. "The chain is not strong enough to hold you captive, but is a symbol of your captivity." He handed her a cold bottle of spring water.

"Do not even think of announcing your presence while I am here with my guests. A severe whipping by me will follow. Yuri said the flogger he gave me would not break the skin, but had a terrible sting. My hand hurts from spanking you earlier."

"I will be quiet," she said to him with tears in her eyes.

"I know you will. Don't cry." He smiled.

Jameel left with the burka, tossed it in his cabin, and greeted his guests topside. They spent some time on deck before coming into the dining room about an hour later sitting three on each side of the table. Some of the guests were wearing thobes and others were wearing slacks. Cassandra watched each pair of legs imagining what the man attached to them looked like. All she could see were their legs and feet clad in leather sandals. Jameel wore a thobe, and sat alone at the head of the long table with her sitting at his feet. He bent down as if picking something from the floor and whispered. "You will pleasure me. If I am not satisfied, I will spank you again after my guests leave." He added, "I enjoyed spanking you. You have a luscious bottom."

Cassandra lifted Jameel's thobe to discover there was nothing to hinder her access. She proceeded to pleasure him, as she was familiar with the art of fellatio. Yuri had taught her well in London. He told her oral sex was not really sex, but brought great pleasure to a man. He instructed her on how to pleasure him in many ways. Cassandra stroked Jameel with her fingers and ran her tongue along the bottom of his penis and it began to swell. She flicked the tip with her tongue, put her mouth around him, and moved back and forth each time taking him deeper into her mouth. When he came, Cassandra swallowed as Yuri had taught her and she pulled back and released him slowly from her lips, kissing him. She kissed his lower stomach, the inside of his thighs, his legs, and the tops of his feet. Cassandra settled back at his feet and gently kissed his bare legs. Jameel attempted to keep his composure as one of the guests suspecting something gave him a strange look.

He leaned down pretending to have dropped his napkin and whispered. "That was most enjoyable. You have many talents. Sit quietly and be patient with me. Food is coming soon and I do not want you angry with me for not feeding you dinner." He laughed just loud enough for her to hear him.

When the food arrived, Jameel prepared a small plate of nuts and fruit, reached under the table holding the pate in his hand. Cassandra took the food and ate quietly. A short time later when his guests were engrossed in a debate about horses, he handed her a plate with meat and vegetables. Famished from her earlier ordeal, she ate everything he gave her. The last plate he handed her contained a delicious honey-drenched pastry along with another bottle of water.

They remained seated at the table for another two hours discussing buying sperm from his father's prize stallion. Jameel represented his father in all business regarding horses. Not understanding what the men were talking about, Cassandra fell asleep from exhaustion under the table, curled at Jameel's feet.

Jameel and his guests went on deck where they enjoyed smoking sheesha and drinking licorice mint tea. They left around two o'clock in the morning; he walked into the dark dining room, and gently woke her.

"Come with me. I will take you to bed."

Jameel removed the cuff and led her to his personal quarters, the main salon on the boat.

"You will sleep next to me, but I will not touch you again tonight. Thank you for your silence during dinner. Yuri taught you the art of fellatio well" He smiled at her and unzipped the back of her dress, kissing the back of her neck.

"Get undressed and feel free to use the bathroom before joining me. We will not have sex again tonight; I promise." Jameel held up his hand with a boyish smirk on his face.

When she returned, he was already in bed. She slid under the covers next to him facing the wall, but could smell his strong masculine scent. Reaching over her, he pulled her body next to him and whispered softly several phrases in Arabic as his lips brushed her ear sending goose bumps down her arm. *"Ahlam Sa'ida, Ashourou bel farahi maak, Yahabibi."*

He whispered in English, "This is what I said; sweet dreams, being with you has made me happy. I like you." He kissed her on the back of her neck as he gently brushed her hair to one side and. put his arms around her holding her close to his body.

She turned to face him and spoke in a quiet voice, "Sweet dreams, and good night." Tears ran down her face as he kissed her again.

She fell asleep in his embrace.

The next morning, Cassandra found she was alone in the stateroom, as he did not wake her when he left. There was a note written in very poor English script.

Use bathroom,
Dress clothes bed.
Leave at eleven

I have trouble writing English. My Arabic script is much better.
Jameel

Cassandra got up, rinsed her face with cool water, put on make-up, and dressed. He had laid out a meticulously embroidered galabeya, hijab, and nijab. She admired the long gold chain he had given her. One of Jameel's men knocked on the door.

"I bring breakfast." He announced in very heavily accented English. "Tray is outside door."

Cassandra opened the door and found a tray filled with delicious pastries, sliced meats, and fresh fruits, glasses of fruit juice, coffee, and tea. She ate her fill, and as she was finishing, Jameel entered. He was wearing western clothes, black slacks, a long sleeved white shirt open at the neck and no head covering. He had a thick gold chain around his neck, dark sunglasses, and gold and diamond encrusted chronograph on his wrist. This was a side of Jameel she had not met, all business, and no small talk, not even good morning.

"We are some distance from my country home and will ride in two cars. You will ride in the second car, but do not attempt to speak to the driver. He will tell me if you say anything. Do you understand?"

"Yes, I understand. You are no longer wearing Arab attire."

"I dress as the gulf Arabs when I meet with them on business, and always on my boat. It is cooler and the tagiyah and gutra keeps the sun off my head." He laughed. "The rest of the time, I wear Western clothes."

"I will be quiet; I promise."

"We have a two-hour drive to my home." He kissed her on the cheek, hugged her close to him, and escorted her to the car.

The driver pulled the large, luxurious, white four-door sedan away from the dock and followed the car in front of him. Cassandra rode in silence as instructed staring out the window as the port of Alexandria, faded and the landscape changed. Her odyssey was not what the tour book described. The tour of Alexandria where Cleopatra's palace lay under the Mediterranean Sea, the lighthouse known as the Pharos, one of the seven wonders of the ancient world, had toppled from a severe earthquake, the city where the greatest library of the ancient world was located, had not gone as planned. Kidnapping, sodomy and rape were definitely not mentioned in the itinerary. Alexandria, where the Romans destroyed the ancient library with fire; home of the great woman philosopher mathematician, Hypanthia, killed by a Christian mob, and now the site where her innocence was taken along with her freedom.

"Will I ever be free to travel to this ancient city and visit its Catacombs and Pompey's Pillar?

Is there a time in my future when I will be free to walk through the Fortress of Qaitbey, and visit the new library, the most advanced library in the Arab world? Or am I to be a slave in the service of a wealthy man until he tires of me and returns me to Yuri or worse sells me to another?" Cassandra sat there staring out the window as tears welled up in her eyes.

The driver was playing a CD of Egyptian music called *sha'bi*. She recognized the singer as Hakim. His music was often heard in news shops and coffee houses owned by Middle Eastern businessmen in some areas of London. Looking out the window, the barren landscape dotted with walled compounds, donkey drawn carts, and occasional banana groves. It was so different from anywhere she had ever traveled before. In its own way, the desert was captivating, a vast inland sea of endless sand and scrub under a cloudless blue sky. Soon she noticed there were trees coming into view in the distance. As they got closer, the trees parted to reveal a gated entrance leading to a huge house situated on an oasis. The gates opened and the two cars proceeded to the front entrance under a portico and stopped. As Jameel opened her door, the loud music poured out of the car.

"I hope the music of Hakim did not bother you. My driver loves his music; I forgot to tell him not to play it."

"It is okay. I have heard his music before. Middle Eastern shops in London often have his music playing. I like his music," she laughed.

"I did not realize Hakim was popular in London. I have several of his albums on CD."

Jameel directed the staff in Arabic to take the bags into the house.

"My servant, Abbas, will show you to my bedroom. You must want to freshen up after your long ride. Please use the bathroom; there are lotions, fresh make-up, a new comb, and brush. Help yourself to one of the outfits hanging in the closet. You will find an entire wardrobe purchased just for you. Under garments are in the second drawer of the chest. Touch nothing else in the room. You may walk onto the balcony if you like. It is a beautiful view."

Cassandra walked into the master suite. A servant locked the door behind her. It was a palatial room with floor to ceiling windows hung with sheer white curtains. French doors opened onto a spacious balcony. Against the wall facing the windows was a king sized bed with deep blue silk sheets and a canopy of blue silk. Bouquets of flowers were everywhere filling the room with their fragrance, a feminine touch in an otherwise male dominated decor. Reminders of male influence were everywhere. Several large framed photographs of horses hung on the white walls. The bathroom was enormous with dark azure blue sinks set in stunning white marble counters and walls. The fixtures were gold plated or perhaps even gold. The floor tiled in the same white marble was covered by a blue, silk oriental rug in front of the sinks. The shower had marble tile and pulsating showerheads on both sides. Along with a toilet, there was a bidet. Cassandra looked in the closet and found at least twenty outfits. She removed the clothes she was wearing and took a long shower with fragrant soap and enjoyed the cascading water as it gently stroked her body. Shampoo and conditioner were on a shelf in the shower. She found some lotion with a label in Arabic that she could not read; it smelled of roses. There was a hairdryer and she blow-dried her hair. A selection of exotic and expensive fragrances sat in beautiful bottles. She selected one named Khaliji. The fragrance was spicy and intoxicating. Looking in the mirror, her bare bottom showed no signs of her spanking. She selected a pale pink silk nightgown that clung to her body revealing her features, went into the bedroom, and climbed in between the silk sheets. With everything that had happened to her, she could feel her heart racing from the stress of not knowing her fate. The warm shower had relaxed her and she was beginning to feel drowsy. It was late morning; she fell into a deep sleep for the remainder of the day. The sun was setting when Jameel entered the bedroom and woke her with a kiss on the lips.

"Time to wake up sleepy head. I did not wake you for lunch; you were sound asleep."

Jameel handed her an Egyptian galabeya that was hand embroidered with intricate Arabic geometrics as a design to wear along with a hijab, but no veil. They walked downstairs and out into the desert along a gravel path. Jameel carried a basket of food and fresh chilled fruit juice and a blanket with him. The sun dropped below the horizon and darkness enveloped them. They continued to walk in the dark far away from the house to the other side of a sand dune. Jameel spread the blanket on the sand, removed her hijab, and ran his long fingers through her hair.

"I thought a picnic dinner under the stars would be nice. Please sit. The stars at night are enchanting. On occasion I fall asleep out here and get up with the sun."

Cassandra sat spellbound gazing up at the night sky.

"They are brilliant against the pitch black sky. In London, the sky is never this clear."

Jameel proceeded to spread the contents of the basket on the blanket.

"Tomorrow you will begin to learn to speak Arabic; I will teach you. I hate speaking English. It is a terrible language."

"Where did you learn to speak English? You speak English very well."

"My father sent me to a boarding school in England. I went to Oxford and on to Cambridge for my doctorate."

"Yuri said you are a surgeon."

"Yes, I practice at the largest hospital in Cairo."

"Why are you involved with sex slaves? You are a handsome man; there is no need to kidnap a woman to make love to you."

He proceeded to tell her his story.

"Your friend Yuri came to the hospital one day for an emergency appendectomy and we got to talking. I had recently divorced my wife and swore I would never be involved with another woman for a long time. He offered to find me an enchanting woman and told me about you and offered to pay him the absurd sum of money he was asking."

"Did he show you a photograph or offer any details?"

"Yuri is a consummate promoter and claimed he did not have a photograph but gave me a description of a woman that most men only dream of leaving me alone with my own fantasies. He said a captive woman would submit to me and do whatever I wished until I tired of her. She would come with a return guarantee, no questions asked. It sounded so exciting the way he described having a concubine, a way to forget a bad marriage. Before I would agree I made him promise, he would not terrorize or whip you. That is why I examined you on the boat; you seemed to have been untouched."

"Yuri never whipped or spanked me, but tortured me by sliding ice cubes over my body and inserting them into my vagina before you arrived because I swore at him. Until he sold me to you, Yuri was an impassioned and affectionate lover teaching me many ways to pleasure him. In return, he bought me exquisite jewelry and took me to fine restaurants. I thought he loved me as much as I thought I loved him. Why did you get divorced?"

Jameel seemed surprised by her question and after a long pause decided to answer. He explained his circumstances in a gentle reassuring tone of voice.

"The marriage was arranged by the two families. We did not know each other and she loved another man. We tried. We obeyed our parents, but it was a failed marriage from the beginning. When I marry again, my parents will be the last to know. I will be married to a woman I love and respect before I tell them. She will be a woman that I chose."

"Will you ever let me go?"

"I have not decided."

In a more concerned voice, she asked him, "What do you plan to do to me? Yuri said you might circumcise me."

"Unlike some Middle-Eastern men, I do not believe in circumcising a woman. I plan to enjoy your company and make love to an enchanting woman during my ten-day holiday. Submit to my amours and make love to me. You are no virgin; you have made love to other men and have the skills to pleasure me. Saturday of next week, I must return to Cairo." Jameel continued, "If you become my concubine, this country home will be your residence. Until then I expect you to pleasure me, make love to me, be my companion, and do what I ask. In time we will have to see if we are compatible."

Jameel's response was not what Cassandra wanted to hear, her fate at the whim of a man she hardly knew. A woman of title and privilege, she was not ready to become a kept concubine at the disposal of a wealthy doctor. Resistance was futile. Jameel kept her locked away with no opportunity to alert her father as to where she was and what had happened. She was sure he was looking for her and would spare no expense to find his daughter. It was just a matter of time. Until then she would submit to her captor.

"You have a gorgeous yacht. What does the name mean?"

"The name in Arabic is *El Jumanah* which means The Silver Pearl in English."

"What a magnificent name for a yacht."

"It was a gift from my parents. They felt badly about my failed marriage."

"I hate being thought of as a concubine or slave. What is the difference between slave and concubine?"

"A slave is an unwilling captive often whipped into obedience; a concubine is a willing lover well compensated and provided for. My preference is a concubine, not a slave."

"My preference, like you, is to be free to choose whom I love and marry."

Cassandra's voice changed and in a cool tone replied, "It is getting cold, I would like to return to the house."

"First, pleasure me as you did under the table. Then we will return to the house."

Cassandra repeated what she had done the other night. Jameel put his hand on the back of her head forcing her down on him until he was half way down her throat. She gagged and tried to pull back but not before he came in a rush.

Gasping for air Cassandra could not speak.

"Yuri taught you well. You are right, it is getting cool; we will return to the house."

Jameel put his arm around her and held her close. Cassandra did not pull away from him or reject his kisses. His tongue darted around her mouth as he held her close to him. He relaxed his hold and she kissed him in return and put her arms around him.

"Thank you for returning my kiss. It was nice. Did you have enough to eat?"

Cassandra was afraid to tell him what she really thought and smiled politely.

"Yes, the food was delicious. I loved eating under the stars. It was very romantic. You seem very attractive, seductive, and charming; I do not understand why your wife did not love you."

"She was in love with another man who convinced her that if she complied with our family's wishes I would soon divorce her to be with him. When I refused, she became violent and abusive. We both said and did things we later regretted."

Jameel packed up the basket and started toward the house. The temperature had dropped fifteen degrees in a short time causing Cassandra to shiver.

"Here, put the blanket around your shoulders. You will sleep in my room again tonight. When my work demands I will return to Cairo and you will have separate quarters in another part of the house. Do you know how to ride a horse?"

"Of course, I am an expert rider. At our country home in England, I have an Arabian named *Humam*."

"That means clever in Arabic."

"I named him myself. Father owns an estate where I used to go foxhunting, before they made it illegal."

"I like the name. Tomorrow you will accompany me on my morning ride. Riding for two or three hours relaxes me. Being a surgeon is stressful. I find taking time to relax weekends when I am not at the hospital is essential. Riding in the country and sailing the Mediterranean aboard my boat are my greatest passions, until I found you. Now I have something else to look forward to in my leisure time."

Placing third after a horse and a boat was not Cassandra's idea of a compliment. She had become nothing more than a rich man's plaything, a diversion to relieve his stress.

Once in the bedroom, Jameel disrobed and climbed into the bed.

She took off her clothes in the dressing room, turned off the light and climbed in next to him.

"I like the feel of your naked body next to mine."

Cassandra pulled the covers over her and tried to sleep with his arm around her holding her close. He kissed her on each cheek and then on the mouth. Again, she returned his kisses.

"You are a very desirable woman. Trust me when I say that I will never hurt you. Go to sleep; let me enjoy the warmth of your body."

The next morning she awoke to discover Jameel had already left. At the foot of the bed was a riding outfit, including riding boots and the ever-present hijab. She took a shower, dressed, and sat down to wait because he had told her never leave the room.

About half an hour later, Jameel entered and smiled at her. "Thank you. I appreciate your waiting and not leaving the room. My servants have prepared a large breakfast for us downstairs in the dining room. Do you ride English or would you like to try an Arabian saddle?"

"I will ride whatever saddle you choose," Cassandra replied obediently.

After breakfast, they walked to the barn where two horses stood saddled with Arabian saddles and glimmering silver tack. The mare, a light grey, stood about fifteen hands. The stallion was white and stood about sixteen hands.

"Your horses are stunning. Their coats look like silk."

"They are groomed every day."

"I will boost you up on *Badra* my favorite brood mare. Her name means Full Moon as the moon was full the night she was born. My stallion is my prize stud. His name is *Altair*, The Flying Eagle. Both horses have custom-made Arabian saddles made from buffalo leather. The saddle on your horse is smaller and should fit you well; I had it made for my first wife."

They mounted and a groom adjusted her stirrups. Without a word, Jameel turned his horse out of the corral and galloped full speed into the desert. "Follow me," he shouted.

Cassandra was a champion equestrian and had won many contests; turned the mare, dug in her heels giving the horse his full head and galloped at full speed right behind him. Looking back, he had a broad smile on his face and slowed his horse to a canter allowing her to catch up.

Cassandra came along side without saying a word.

"You are an impressive rider. I find the desert beguiling; the feel of the wind against my face and the sun beating down is a part of my life I embrace whenever possible. We will ride for about two hours and then rest. I have arranged a picnic lunch at a small oasis."

Cassandra felt at ease as they rode across the desert following Jameel. The two things she loved most in the world were riding horses and singing. In another life, she studied opera with the hope of a career in music. She dreamed one day of having a part in a major musical production.

Jameel reined in his horse, dismounted and walked to a small oasis where there were five or six trees and a small pond. Cassandra followed. Removing the saddle, he then hobbled him leaving him free to drink. He did the same with Badra and gave each horse a handful of oats sweetened with molasses. A large picnic lunch basket sat under a tree on a blanket spread on the ground. There was ice-cold mineral water and fresh chilled fruit juice to drink. His servants had prepared a delightful lunch of eggs, meat, cheese, and fresh fruits.

"Your horses are handsome. Do you sell them outside of Egypt?"

"I sell sperm outside of Egypt but some of my horses sell in Egypt or the Gulf States including Saudi Arabia, but my prized horses I would never sell, they are part of my family. I charge a stud fee for Altair. In English pounds, it would be 2,000 pounds sterling to have him service a mare. We should have something to eat then relax a bit before going back."

The sand shimmered in the heat of the noonday sun but in the shade of the trees, the breeze was cool. After lunch, Jameel removed his boots and shirt.

"Lay back on the blanket. We will relax before we ride to the house. I will help you with your boots." He removed her boots and massaged her feet then lay next to her on the blanket. Jameel pulled her closer to him.

"You are an alluring woman. I do not usually like European women, but you are exceptional. I am looking forward to spending the rest of the week with you before I have to go back to work. A little love making in the desert in the open air is always pleasurable." His hands started to unbutton her blouse. "Allow me to undress you."

"Must we have anal sex? I prefer other ways."

"Yes, I will try to pleasure you at the same time. I desire you, but unless a woman is my wife, this is how I make love. You have no choice. Am I that bad a lover?"

"No, it is not that. You are a wonderful and passionate lover," she began to cry.

Jameel undressed her slowly, kissed her breasts, and moved his hands along her body. She moved her hands across his naked chest and kissed him in return. He undressed completely and held Cassandra in his arms for the longest time as though he was lost in thought. He gently laid her on her back on the blanket.

"Spread your legs a little, I want you to derive pleasure from my love making as well."

He kissed her breasts, sucked each nipple until it was erect, and ran his tongue along the middle of her body. He gently held her vaginal lips apart and kissed her and his tongue intruded her private gate of pleasure. The more he kissed and sucked the more aroused she became. She began to sigh softly.

"Turn over and get up on your knees."

Cassandra turned and he came from behind her and ran his tongue between her vagina and anus several times. His tongue circled her opening and as she relaxed, he pushed it inside. Holding her bottom, he spread her cheeks with his thumbs as he continued to kiss and lick causing her to sigh even more. Applying lubricant, he pressed his now fully erect manhood against her, and slipped into her with ease. With his fingers, he rubbed her other gate of pleasure and they moved together as his in out motions became fiercer until they climaxed together. Both lay breathing heavily on the blanket. He kissed her neck and whispered in her ear words of endearment in Arabic. The sun was hot and their bodies were wet with perspiration.

"Did you derive pleasure from my amours? You seem to respond to my loving you."

"I have never experienced such feelings while making love, my passions run wild at your touch and you leave me breathless. I am still a little frightened of you."

"You have nothing to fear. I promise. Whipping a woman is not my nature. Having a woman willingly make love to me is all I want."

Cassandra was confused. She was starting to have feelings toward her captor. Was this just a physical attraction or the beginning of love?

"I wish we had met differently."

"A woman should respect the man she is with and pleasure him." He paused, "It is very hot today; it is not a huge body of water," he said pointing to the small pond, "but very refreshing. Jump in, it has a sandy bottom and is about three meters deep."

Cassandra jumped in and was surprised at how cold the water was. He dove in next to her and drew her body next to his.

"It is cold," she shrieked. "I thought it would be warmer."

"Most people do," he laughed. "It is artesian well water." Holding each other, they kissed for the longest time, but the cold water soon convinced them to swim to shore.

"I have business to attend to this evening. When we return, I will give instructions to have dinner sent to your room."

Using a towel he had brought with him, he dried her body, and held her. His wet body glistened in the sun, and she sensed his strong masculine aroma as he kissed her on each cheek and looked into her bewitching blue eyes.

"We should get started. It is a two hour ride back to the house."

"You are a compassionate lover."

She reached up, put her arms around him, and kissed him on the lips. He kissed her passionately in return, their tongues began to duel as he held her in his arms for several minutes; they said nothing.

Jameel dressed, saddled the horses, and they took their time riding back to his home. When they got to the house, the same groom took the horses, they went upstairs, and took a shower together. As the water streamed over their bodies, he took her again from behind and thrust into her repeatedly with the water cascading over them until he exploded in a total release. Cassandra's body shook as it awakened new sensations in her. Motionless, he remained inside her and whispered in her ear.

"I like you very much, *Anti rashiiqata l qzwaam*, in English, you have a gorgeous body." Withdrawing he faced her pressing her against the wall with his body.

Tears filled her eyes and she hugged him. "Oh Jameel, you have made me feel more of a woman than I could ever imagine. I want to be your concubine, not a slave. I will make love to you anyway you desire."

"I am glad you have decided to willingly make love to me."

Jameel got dressed in western slacks and a blue dress shirt that he wore unbuttoned half way. Cassandra dressed in a pull over caftan that was in a winsome shade of azure blue that brought out the color of her eyes. He took the heavy gold chain from his neck and put it on hers along with the first chain he had given her. "*Ya Amar*. It means like the moon or translates to quite beautiful." He kissed her passionately and held her in his embrace.

"Now I must go. Do not touch any of the electronic devices in the room including my computer, the television, or the CD player while I am gone. They are very complicated to use if you do not understand the system. Upon my return, I will teach you and then you may use them.

Help yourself to the books on the shelf; several are written in English. At university, I practiced by reading English translations of books I had read in Arabic. I will see that you get a delicious dinner. I do not want to do something silly again and put you under the table. That was wrong for me to do that. Forgive me for being so stupid."

"It felt strange sitting by your feet, but it was erotic at the same time. I forgive you," she smiled.

"I expect to get back quite late, so go to bed when you are tired. Put your head on the pillow and have pleasant dreams. My meeting is with several Saudi men here to here to talk horses and to arrange to buy sperm."

Jameel kissed her cheek and cupped her face in his hand, "We had an enjoyable day. This is the most relaxed I have been for a long time. I enjoy making love to you, *habibi*."

"I had a pleasant time also. Thank you for a lovely day. I will wait for you to come to bed. Good night." She reached up on her tiptoes and kissed him affectionately on the mouth.

He left her and closed the door. He did not lock it.

Cassandra looked around and picked up a book of poetry, *The Prophet* by Kahlil Gibran. The lines of a poem from that book flashed across her mind, '*When love beckons to you, follow him, though his ways are hard and steep. And when his wings enfold you, yield to him.*'" It was one of her favorite books of poetry. He also had Love Poems of Rumi, from the thirteenth century who wrote poems of mysticism and desire. She read *The Alchemy of Love* and *Desire*, two of her favorites. "*I desire you, more than food or drink, my body, my senses, my mind hunger for your taste.*"

An English translation of a book by Naguib Mahfouz, *Palace of Desire* was on one of the shelves; Mahfouz had won a Nobel Prize for literature. After reading the book for a while, she walked out on the balcony. The view was of endless desert. It was alluring and the sun was low in the sky as two large luxury white sedans approached the house. Cassandra went back to reading.

A short time later, there was a knock at the door. "Who is it?" A woman's voice answered in Arabic. It was a woman servant wearing a hijab carrying a sumptuous meal. In broken English, the women told her to leave the tray outside the door when she was finished. Cassandra thanked her in Arabic and sat down to eat. She had not eaten much lunch and suddenly realized how hungry she was. When she was finished, she set the tray outside the door as the women had instructed. Glancing down the hall there was no one in sight. She could hear Jameel's voice speaking in Arabic and understood enough to know what they were saying. Closing the door she went into the closet and changed into an elegant nightgown. All the clothes fit her as though they were custom made for her. Jameel certainly has good taste in women's clothes. The price tags were missing, but reading the labels Cassandra noticed they were all by French and Italian designers. With nothing to do, no television to watch, she decided to practice her singing. She loved to sing and had a trained operatic voice. She began to sing some of her favorite songs from the *Phantom of the Opera* and other Andrew Lloyd Weber songs. She often pictured herself starring in the role of Christine.

The seven men who had joined Jameel for dinner were just finishing when they heard her singing from upstairs. Cassandra had no idea that the room she was in was directly over the dining room and that the heating and ventilation ducts in the floor would carry her voice to anyone in the room below.

One of the men asked, "Jameel, who belongs to that magnificent voice? I know it is not a recording. Is she a famous opera singer that you are holding captive?"

"No, it is a friend of mine from England. I will tell her to be quiet."

"Please, let her sing. I feel like I am at the theatre in London. If she is not professional, she should be."

The men listened to Cassandra sing for an hour while smoking their expensive Cuban cigars, and then it was quiet.

"I guess your little song bird went to bed," one of the men laughed.

They left the dining room, walked outside, and talked for another two hours while sitting on the veranda smoking sheesha and drinking licorice mint tea before they left. The aroma of oranges drifted in the air and into the bedroom.

It was little past two in the morning when Jameel walked upstairs and found Cassandra sound asleep in bed, the book *The Prophet* next to her.

Cassandra heard him come into the room, but lay still, watched him go into the bathroom, and heard the water running. Unaware she was watching him he emerged a short time later and walked over to the French doors and out onto the east-facing balcony, to pray the *'Isha* or evening prayer. Finishing he stood looking out at the dark desert under the star-studded sky. Reflecting upon the events of the past week, Jameel realized he was developing a real affection for Cassandra. It was becoming more than a lustful escape.

"I have become comfortable with Cassandra and really do not want her to leave her. Making love to her, kissing her passionately, and holding her in my arms is most agreeable." Starring at the stars, he remained on the balcony for some time before he undressed and went to bed. Slipping in behind Cassandra, he put his arm around her and drew her close kissing her and whispering in Arabic. "*Ana bahibik*, I love you."

Cassandra felt his naked body pressed against her and snuggled next to him.

"I am falling in love with Jameel," she thought to herself. "What will I do if he sells me to another or leaves me here, a personal play thing to be enjoyed on weekends and special occasions? Does he feel the same way as I do? I hope he makes up his mind before he leaves for Cairo on Saturday morning. By now, my father must be frantic with worry but going back to London is not an option. If only I could contact him and tell him that I am all right."

In the morning, before the sunrise, Cassandra watched as Jameel repeated his actions of the night before walked onto the balcony and prayed the *Fajr* or pre-dawn prayer. He looked so serene and peaceful, she thought to herself, as he finished, gazing across the desert at the rising sun. Quietly she got out of bed and joined him on the balcony. He put his arms around her and kissed her tenderly.

"I will teach you how I pray five times a day. Each prayer has a name, *Fajr*, pre-dawn, *Dhuhr*, noon, *'Asr*, afternoon, *Maghrib*, sunset, and last night you watched me pray *'Isha*, evening before going to bed."

Cassandra answered him with a smile. She envied the solace that Jameel derived from his faith. Finding inner peace and her true identity were goals that had alluded her all her life. Cassandra had never truly been independent. Her life had been series of relationships with men starting with her father; each with their own needs and desires without any concern for what she wanted. Yuri was just another disappointment, although he was the first to sell her. This relationship of slave and master was not so different, except Jameel had explained the rules going in. No illusions, no deception just raw emotions, and lust, perhaps that attracted her to this man of mystery from another culture who seemed strangely connected to her past.

"I did not wish to disturb you." Cassandra was embarrassed that he knew she was watching.

"Join me as I pray at noon. I will teach you the prayers."

Tears filled her eyes and she kissed him, "I want to learn from you."

Several days passed before he taught her how to pray and she joined him. They made love every day exploring different ways to arouse each other. She pleasured him with her mouth and they French kissed passionately.

Jameel hated having to speak English and patiently proceeded to teach Cassandra many phrases in Arabic. Only two days remained of his holiday and he had many things on his mind when they retired for the night. Unable to get to sleep, he thought about going back to work and the difficult choices he had to make. Was he ready for a serious relationship so soon after his divorce, or should he let Cassandra go? If he chose to keep her and it did not work out, he would have no one to blame but himself. This time he would make the decision, not his family.

Cassandra went immediately to sleep dreaming of Jameel holding her, marrying her, loving her, then her dreams turned to a nightmare and he was whipping her and putting that awful towel in her mouth. She screamed before she woke up. Her body was sweating and she was out of breath. Jameel reached for her and held her close to him. "What is wrong? You screamed."

"I had a nightmare."

"Tell me about it." He asked in a soft concerned tone of voice.

"You were whipping me and putting that horrible towel in my mouth only this time it was soaked in hot sauce and my mouth was on fire. I was strapped to a table and you were standing over me with a scalpel in your hand ready to circumcise me. I was so frightened."

"I have not touched you in a brutal way since that first day, but I did enjoy spanking you." He smiled and winked at her.

Cassandra was still afraid and clutched the sheet in front of her. She failed to see the humor in Jameel's response. Eventually she relaxed reassured by his gentle touch.

"I should not have cursed and struck you, but I was angry and frightened. When I was a little girl, my mother made me bite into a bar of soap for swearing. It tastes awful."

"A genteel lady should never curse." He smiled at her and laughed. "You deserved to be spanked."

"You did not hurt me. When you spanked me, I was more embarrassed and humiliated than injured."

"I would never whip a woman, but I might spank you again if you make me angry," he smiled. "As for circumcision, I perform such operations on women and small girls to save them from being mutilated by their mothers and grandmothers, but personally, I would never cut you. I love that you get pleasure from our love making."

In a soft quiet voice while looking into his beguiling eyes, she whispered, "I am in love with you. I would rather stay your concubine than go back to England." Tears filled her eyes streaming down her cheeks.

Jameel had tried to summon the courage to tell her what he really felt and had failed; partially because of fear, his attraction was more out of lust than love. Leaving her, even for a week, was not an option. His passion transcended the physical; he had come to love her.

"*Ente Habibi*, you are my love."

Cassandra exuberantly flung her arms around him.

"How would I say I love you in Arabic?"

"Ana uhibbuk."

"Ana uhibbuk, Jameel." She kissed him affectionately.

"I have heard your singing on several occasions; you have a wonderful voice. My friends and I sat and listened for an hour after dinner. *Phantom of the Opera* is one of my favorite musicals that I attended in London a few years ago. Sing for me tomorrow. Sing just for me?"

"There is nothing I would rather do. *Phantom of the Opera* is one of my favorites. I did not know you could hear me."

"I will look forward to it. Now, go to sleep Cassandra. I should not have gotten involved with Yuri in the first place; what was I thinking buying you as a sex slave. Upon my return to Cairo, I will contact a doctor friend of mine, Sabir Gaafar at the hospital. He breeds horses at a stable near El-Arish and is working with a group of men attempting to stop the slave trade in Egypt. I will give him Yuri's name."

"What if Yuri comes back while you are gone once he finds out you are looking for him?"

"As far as Yuri knows I am nothing more than a satisfied customer. He has no reason to think otherwise. You are safe here."

"Jameel, I am glad you did want a slave, this once. We never would have met otherwise. What do you plan to do with me?" She laughed.

"You said you are in love with me," he took a deep breath, "*hal atatazawwajiinii,*

Jameel placed his hands on her shoulders and peered into her blue eyes intently with a look she had not seen before. The words in Arabic meant nothing to her.

"Will you marry me? You are an extraordinary woman. Riding horses, singing, making love to me, I feel as though I have found the counterpoint to my soul. I never thought falling in love the way I have with you possible. Say yes and I will arrange for a cleric to be at the house in the morning. Become my wife, and return with me to Cairo."

Cassandra turned her head in a vain attempt to conceal her delight. This was more than she had hoped.

"*Aiwy (yes)*, Ana uhibbuk. Being your wife would be wonderful. I was so afraid you would not want me. When you made love to me, I had feelings I have never had before. The touch of your hands and lips on my body made me want to kiss you and hold you. I want to make love to you and bring you pleasure. My life is in your hands." Tears welled up in her eyes.

"Dear Cassandra. Do not say yes immediately. Listen to what I have to say. My culture is different from yours. On many occasions, you will find yourself eating alone or with other women apart from me. You will wear a burka when we travel, and sometimes, just a hijab and long sleeved dress to your ankles. I will share you with no one. At home, you will have dresses of your choice. We will have many children." Jameel smiled at her and kissed her before he continued; "I will demand respect and will punish you if you do not obey me." He paused and smiled, "I must admit you have a cute bottom and spanking you was very arousing. I might spank you before we make love, just for the fun of it."

"If you did not spank too hard," she giggled, "I would not mind; it was arousing."

Jameel continued. "You must learn to speak, read, and write Arabic. You have already joined me in prayers but you must become a Muslim, and accept an Arabic name."

Cassandra was a reflection of every man she had ever been with except her father with whom she frequently disagreed. This was her chance to break away and live her life in a manor to which she had become accustomed. She thought she had it with Yuri until he sold her to a stranger. If becoming a Muslim was what it took, she was ready.

"I was never much on going to church. My father lost faith when my mother died and we did not attend any church. Praying with you has been insightful into your religion. I want to become a Muslim; you have already taught me many prayers. My goal has always been to learn Arabic and with your help, I have learned many phrases already. Loving you and being loved by you are all I desire."

He took her in his arms and kissed her long and sensuously on the mouth. "Once we are married, I will make love to you in many other ways, and kiss you all the time. I enjoy making love in many ways, but with slaves and concubines, vaginal love is never possible. Good night Cassandra, have no more nightmares."

"I will only have enchanting dreams and look forward to making love to you. When you touched me with your fingers, I wanted you so badly. Your lips touched every part of my body; no man has ever made love to me that way. It was erotic; I became a woman in your embrace. I will be an obedient and loving wife. I want to give you pleasure. I will make love to you any way you want me to, even though I do not like anal sex; it does give me feelings that are exciting and lascivious. I feel so much a woman when you hold me, touch me with your fingers, your lips brush against my body and it makes me almost climax without you inside me. I have never met a man like you. What name will you give me?" She asked.

"I will call you, *Fatinah*. It means fascinating, captivating, alluring, enchanting. You are all of those to me."

"I love the name. I love children and want a great many; all sons, all handsome like their father."

"We will see what we can do," he smiled. Now get some sleep.

Next morning, Cassandra rolled over to find she was alone in her bed. The sun was streaming through the open window backlighting Jameel who stood at the foot of the bed. Throughout the night, they had sat up talking.

"Come, we cannot keep the cleric waiting."

The cleric had already arrived at the house after being summoned earlier by Jameel who had insisted he be there early in the morning.

"I must take a shower first."

"There is no time. Put this on." Pulling on a fetching outfit he chose for her to wear, he guided her into a great room of the house where the cleric sat along with a magistrate.

The cleric had her repeat some phrases in Arabic, and Jameel whispered to her that she was now a Muslim. She followed the cleric into a separate room and he presented her with a *nikaah, a* contract stating what Jameel would give her to provide for her in the event they divorced or he died. The Imam translated for her. Jameel was also signing a contract. The marriage was official. Two members of his household served as witnesses. They repeated some more Arabic phrases and the cleric left. Cassandra, now Fatinah noticed that Jameel handed the magistrate a large sum of money. She seemed confused. In less than thirty minutes, she had become a Muslim and Jameel's wife with barely enough time to brush her hair before she was in front of the Imam.

She looked at Jameel expecting him to say something or at least offer a traditional kiss. It was all business like buying a car or a house. Actually, she remembered that both of those had taken longer. There was no walk down the aisle in the Mosque, no "Do you take this woman?" Just a few Arabic phrases and she was a married women with a written contract she could not read.

"I am entertaining some friends this afternoon and again this evening. I will introduce you as my wife. A Muslim wife speaks very little to her husband's guests, unless she knows them well. I will request you leave after the introductions. Your lunch will be brought to our room."

"I will take you shopping for a wedding ring later this afternoon." Jameel sounded more like the wedding planner than her husband. She had wondered if they exchanged rings.

After the guests left, they drove to Cairo, about an hour's drive. Cassandra sang songs of love to him as he drove.

"You must sing for me every day; you have a marvelous voice." Arriving at an area of Cairo with small shops, they went inside a store that sold clothing. Jameel bought her a very expensive abaya with brilliant sequined embroidery in gold, white, and blue for the evening and several other abayas, galabeyas, and dresses with designer labels from Paris to wear under them. He then took her to a fine jewelry store, and sat her in front of a showcase with rings.

"Which ring do you like best?"

"Please choose for me."

Jameel picked a platinum ring with a pink diamond surrounded with several blue white diamonds. He also chose a matching necklace, earrings and bracelet. He never asked the price and paid the shopkeeper in cash.

Jameel placed the ring on her finger. "It is time we return to the house. Our guests will arrive shortly. I love you Fatinah."

Upon their return Fatinah went to her room, showered and dressed in an exquisite black abaya with a teal blue inner lining and delicate silver and gold geometric embroidery on the neckline and sleeves and an intricate Arabic design in fine embroidery decorated the front. Hidden underneath, she wore a lovely teal blue dress by a French designer. She combed and styled her hair, applied her make-up perfectly, and was a vision. Jameel insisted she wear a hijab to cover her head. The new couple entered the dining room, Cassandra on his arm. Everyone was anxious to meet the blond, blue-eyed European woman who had captured Jameel's heart. For the first time Cassandra felt out of place. All eyes were upon her. Suddenly there was silence as Jameel introduced her as his new wife. "The servants will bring your dinner the same as lunch," Jameel whispered.

Without hesitation, Fatinah excused herself using what little Arabic she had learned and went to the master suite. It felt odd not to be included after so much preparation. Better to be the center of attention for only a moment than to be ignored back home, she reasoned.

Changing into something comfortable see decided to listen to music. Jameel had taught her the intricate control system for his electronics and the sound of Egyptian music filled the room.

It was after midnight when Jameel joined her. She had fought to stay awake and was waiting for him. They prayed together and undressed. Jameel pulled her to him. He kissed her passionately on the mouth and held her close. His strong hands caressed her breasts; gently spreading her legs he exposed that which he had proclaimed untouchable before marriage. Cassandra quivered in anticipation of his touch as his lips lightly caressed her naked Venus mound denuded of hair the day he took her. While kissing her on the mouth, he suddenly sheathed himself inside her; his in and out movements became faster, and he went deeper with each thrust of his body against her, Cassandra groaned with pleasure, her arms clutching his body to her. Their bodies moved as one. As her muscles grabbed hold of him, he could hold back no longer and it was as though he poured his entire being into her. Breathless, they both lay exhausted on the bed, their bodies wet with sweat from the heat they generated.

Satisfied, Jameel took her in his arms and held her close. "Good night my love, no man should be as happy. *Uriidu an abqaa ma'ak lil'abad* (I want to stay with you forever.) Tomorrow we will drive into Cairo where I have an imposing home in the heart of the city. I will introduce you to my parents. I called them, told them about this extraordinary woman, and that I was in love. They are looking forward to meeting you." Jameel kissed her filling her mouth with his tongue re igniting his passion much to Cassandra's surprise. Stopping he continued to talk, "On Saturday, we will stop at the hospital and I will let them know of my honeymoon for the next two weeks. I want to introduce you to my staff. We will leave for Alexandria Saturday night, and sail early Sunday morning for the exotic Greek islands."

"Jameel," she said seriously, "I should call my father. By now, he has launched a full-scale search for me. I do not want him to worry any more than he already has. He needs to know I am safe."

"Of course, I understand, you should call him. Before I return to work, we will fly to London. I would like to meet your father. I hope he approves of me."

"Do not expect too much, he is a difficult man."

"Kidnapping his only daughter is not the best way to win his approval, but I will try to convince him that I love you and will make you happy. Eventually he may come to accept me."

Jameel handed her the satellite phone and told her how to place the call.

Chapter 13

When Hassan returned to the hotel, the police were already waiting for him in his office.

"Gentlemen, please wait here. I will go and escort Mrs. Bishop to my office."

Hassan went to Emunishere's room and dismissed the porter by the door. Cautiously, she looked through the peephole before opening the door.

"Oh Hassan, I was so frightened." Her body was trembling.

Hassan put his arms around her and held her close. She started to cry as he held her.

"Are you all right? Where did you learn to fight? Mohamed told me you fought free from this man and broke his nose."

"I studied self-defense for four months after my husband was killed. It is a long story. It was frightening not knowing if escape was possible; he was a very tall muscular man. It will haunt me forever."

"We must go to my office. The police have arrived. I will stay with you."

"Hold me a little longer before we go. I need you."

"I am not leaving you. Whenever you are ready let me know."

Hassan stood in the doorway, his arms folded around her.

Emunishere lifted her head from his chest and kissed him.

"I couldn't handle this without you by my side. I'm ready now."

Hassan took her to his office where she told her story to the police.

"The man was over six feet tall, maybe six foot three inches, or six foot four inches. I don't know what that is in centimeters. He had thick black hair, brilliant blue eyes, olive complexion, a muscular build, and spoke English with a Russian accent."

"Did he say anything to you?"

"He told me I would be his pretty maid, like his friend Cassandra. He also said he would be taking me into the mountains before a trip across the desert."

"Did he mention any other women?"

"He referred to a group of pretty maids all in a row. I don't know what that meant.

"When he went to grab me, I kicked him in the thigh and groin and broke his nose with a martial arts strike. Once free, I ran in the direction of the hotel. He started to chase me, then stopped, turned around, and stumbled along the beach in the opposite direction of the hotel. I watched as he got into a little boat, and headed to a fishing boat anchored off shore. The boat then headed out to sea."

"What color was the fishing boat? How big was it?"

"It was white in color with large fishing poles that resembled antennas. It was forty or fifty feet long, again, I don't know metric measurements. It was quite a distance off shore. I did notice a name on the transom, but it was in Cyrillic letters and I couldn't read it."

"Thank you Mrs. Bishop.

We have a sketch artist. Would you mind working with him?"

"I'm an artist myself. I think I can draw a sketch of this man."

"When will you finish the sketch?"

Emunishere responded to him, "It will be ready later this evening."

"We'll send someone for it. Leave it at the desk."

"Wait a minute." Emunishere interrupted. "I recall seeing this man before. Hassan, remember that night we had dinner at the restaurant in town. The man that attacked me this morning was sitting in the lobby of the hotel that night. He kept staring at me, and then got up and walked to the reservation desk."

"I remember a man bumped into me but I did not really take much notice. My mind was on someone else," he smiled at her.

"Will there be any more questions for Mrs. Bishop?"

"Hassan," the police officer addressed him by his first name. "Have you seen this man in your hotel before that night in the lobby?"

"I remember now. He was here two or three times in the last month but we have never had an incident like this."

"If he comes back, please call us. We are checking with the marina when we leave here. How many boats with the name in Cyrillic letters could there be in this area? Call us when the sketch is ready."

The police left and Hassan took her to his suite of rooms on the top floor of the hotel.

"You will stay here with me until we resolve this problem. I do not want you to leave El-Arish until I can travel with you. I have made the necessary arrangements to cancel your reservations with the bus company and the hotel in Cairo. Everything in your room will be packed and moved to my suite. This man is likely angry that you escaped from him and broke his nose. He may come back."

Emunishere started to sketch a likeness of Yuri.

"Do you mind if I watch you sketch?"

"No, please don't leave me alone. I'd like you to watch."

"When you finish that sketch, I want to talk to you about something. In addition, this evening an agent from MI6 is meeting with me. He is working on the disappearance of an English woman, Cassandra Cavendish, from this area a few days ago. Her father Lord Robert Cavendish will be here shortly."

"That awful man mentioned I would be like Cassandra."

"This is obviously the same man that kidnapped her. Agent Alex MacKay will be here along with Cassandra's father. He is due to arrive soon."

Emunishere finished the sketch and handed it to Hassan.

"This is the man; I will never forget his face."

"I have seen this man at the hotel in the past. Yes, he was the man who bumped into me that evening. You were of more concern to me at the time," he smiled at her and held her hand.

Hassan pulled her into his strong arms, held her close, and kissed her on the cheek. "If you had been kidnapped this morning, I would never have forgiven myself."

They held each other for a long time; the phone rang.

"Hassan, I am sorry to disturb you, but Alexander MacKay and Robert Cavendish are here to see you."

"Send them to my suite." Moments later Alex knocked on the door and Hassan welcomed the two men in. "*Ahlan wa-sahlan*, (welcome)."

Agent Mackay was wearing black slacks, a blue shirt, imported Italian leather shoes, and wore an expensive Swiss watch. Robert Cavendish wearing a grey pin stripe suit and white shirt looked pale and harried.

"I would like to introduce you to my friend, Emunishere who was almost kidnapped this morning off the beach in front of this hotel."

"You are a fortunate woman to have gotten away."

"Please, Mr. MacKay, have a seat."

"Call me Alex. This gentleman is Lord Robert Cavendish, Cassandra's father; I am not here officially as part of the government. My mission is off the books but I will do everything possible to aide you and the other men in capturing this group. In the past, my assignment involved investigating the trafficking of women. Do you have a description of the man?"

Hassan handed him the sketch Emunishere drew of Yuri. "Here is a drawing Emunishere drew of the man who tried to kidnap her. He mentioned Cassandra, Lord Cavendish's daughter and pretty maids all in a row."

Suddenly Lord Cavendish became agitated and red in the face.

"That is the man my daughter was seeing in London," he said shaking his finger at the drawing. "He told her he was an executive trading in expensive commodities. His name is Yuri Berezovsky. I never liked him and warned Cassandra not to trust him. It was nothing he did, but the look in his eyes. He had the bluest eyes I have ever seen."

Alex studied the likeness in the picture while trying to remember if he had ever come across him.

"I have been on leave for a year," Alex said. "Most of the cases I investigated were connected to Russian mobs, but this man was never involved in any of those cases. His is a new face, Lord Cavendish."

"Please call me Robert, I dislike using that title outside of Parliament."

Hassan was satisfied that Emunishere's attacker had been identified. That information along with her description of the boat would give the authorities something to go on.

"Join us for dinner. I will order room service. I think it best if we are not seen together publically."

Chapter 14

At the Sinai El-Arish Hotel, Hassan, Alex MacKay, and Robert Cavendish were talking after dinner in Hassan's suite.

"I never liked Berezovsky when my daughter was dating him." Robert interrupted, "Can we try to find something about him? I know he is the man my daughter was seeing in London. The sketch Emunishere drew is an exact likeness of him?"

"Robert," Alex responded. "I have contacted Henry Ewing, my division commander at MI6and he is trying to find out as much as possible about this man. Obviously, this is a new player in this business. In the past, we have captured some of these Russians, but despite the evidence, Moscow categorically denies the existence of these mobs."

Hassan spoke to Alex and Robert, "We will meet here in my suite at ten tomorrow morning. I have arranged for you and Robert to have adjoining rooms. They are one floor down. Here are the keys. Your luggage will be in your room when you get there. Until tomorrow morning."

Alex turned to Robert, "I will join you shortly, Hassan and I need to discuss something that happened on one of my past missions."

Robert took the magnetic key and went to his room.

Hassan and Alex walked out onto the balcony.

"I see you have done close-in combat, Alex. That scar is a bad one. You could have lost an eye or even your life."

"That is why I wanted to speak with you. That cut is from a woman I rescued a few years ago from a man who had bought her as a sex slave. Seems she was content in her new life. I have learned that you must be careful. Women are difficult to understand and unpredictable."

Hassan smiled at him, "Yes they are. I will keep that in mind. People do not always want to be rescued. I have never been cut, but I have had to deal with difficult women in the past when I was in the military and at the hotels I manage."

Alex just smiled and shook his hand.

"See you at ten."

Alex left for his room.

Hassan closed and locked the door securely before turning to Emunishere who had listening from the other room.

"Emunishere, take a nice warm shower; I will massage your muscles. After the fight you had this morning, they will cramp if you do not take care of yourself. It has been a stressful day. Your suitcases have not yet arrived; use my robe, it is hanging in the bathroom. I am a great masseur."

Emunishere showered and put on Hassan's blue silk robe that was several centimeters too long. When she entered the bedroom, she noticed that Hassan had removed his sports coat, unbuttoned his shirt, and rolled up his shirtsleeves.

"Lay face down on the bed." Hassan had a lascivious grin on his face.

"I don't think you can give me a proper massage while wearing your robe," she giggled.

Emunishere unbelted the robe and let it slide slowly down her body; forming a dark blue puddle of silk at her feet and stood naked in front of him; he took her into his arms and kissed her passionately. She lay face down on the bed while he opened a jar of amber scented massaging oil and started to massage the exotic oil onto her body. A unique blend of vanilla, rose, bergamot, and sandalwood produces the mysterious fragrance known as amber and the oil known for its healing properties.

"You are a very beautiful woman. Let me know if I press too firmly. I can feel the knots in your muscles."

Emunishere lay there as his strong hands pressed deeply into her sore muscles. He massaged her back, her arms, and the length of her long limber legs. She was very relaxed as he continued to massage her body while he kissed the back of her neck and small of her back. She rolled onto her back and they embraced for the longest time before he continued to rub the oil onto her body; he massaged her thighs, and fondled her breasts, kissing them until her nipples were erect. His kisses continued down her body; gently holding her lips apart, he kissed her gate of pleasure. His tongue moved deeply into her with a mind of its own, flicking from side to side causing her to sigh deeply and her body moved against him. He took in her sweetness and embraced her body as it trembled in his embrace.

Emunishere looked at him with tears in her eyes. "I am falling in love with you even though I have only known you for a week; *Anahibbuk (I love you)*. I was dreading having to having to take this trip to Cairo by myself. Promise me you will be careful; Berezovsky is a dangerous man. I got lucky only because he was not expecting a woman to fight back. He is a solid, powerful man; my leg hurt when I kicked him."

"I am glad you surprised him. You have surprised me many times since we met. I hope to get to know you much better. We will have a future together; I promise."

Hassan placed the robe about her shoulders, showed her into his second bedroom, and closed the door to his. "I will see you in the morning before I leave."

Emunishere pulled Hassan's robe around her, brushed her teeth, got into bed, and slipped naked under the soft Egyptian cotton sheets. She could not sleep and wept thinking to herself, "If anything happens to him, what am I to do? I love him so much even though we have not made love, but the touch of his hands on my body and the caress of his lips, I am enraptured."

Exhaustion from the day's events caught up with her and a restless sleep finally arrived. It was only an hour later, she woke up screaming as the attack filled her mind; only this time, she lost the fight, Yuri kidnapped, and dragged her across the desert soon to be a sex slave bound for Tel Aviv.

Hassan rushed into the room.

"You screamed. What is wrong?"

He sat on the bed next to her.

"It was a nightmare; the fight today went the other way."

He held her in his arms and then slipped under the covers next to her.

"Don't be afraid. We will see this through together."

Emunishere felt his body next to her and realized he had not gotten dressed. She kissed his chest, her tongue caressed his nipples, and they hardened at her touch. She kissed his body until she reached his penis and held it in her hand and stroked it until it began to swell. She took his manhood in her mouth and caressed him with her tongue. Hassan sighed as she made love to him and when he climaxed, she took his emanation and savored it, as it was a part of him.

"I know you will not make love to me unless we are married. *Oriido an akoona ma'aki ila al-abad* (I want to be with you forever) *ana ataajok* (I need you)."

Tears filled his eyes as he took her in his arms and kissed her passionately and his tongue explored her mouth.

"*Hayet albi enta* (you are the life of my heart) *tatazawwajni* (will you marry me)? Emunishere, I never thought I could ever love again."

She kissed him in return and whispered in his ear, "I love you so much. Being your wife is all I want."

They prayed the *'Isha* and fell asleep in each other's embrace.

Chapter 15

Yuri arrived at the airport to pick up the first six women that were arriving on a flight from Romania. Yuri escorted them to a warehouse in the Heliopolis district of Cairo about fifteen minutes from the airport. He had two of his friends from the Russian mob, Aleksandr and Dobrashin, waiting for the women. They drove to the warehouse with five women in the back of the van and a petite young girl no more than twelve or thirteen sat in front next to Yuri.

Yuri entered the warehouse while holding the young girl's hand and directed the other women along a dimly lit narrow hallway, down a flight of stairs, into a musty smelling dark basement. They walked across the first room and he opened a door into another section of the basement. Along each side of the large room were four closed doors. Yuri opened the first door and told five of the six women to get comfortable. Aleksandr and Dobrashin, two Russians working with him, stayed with the women while Yuri took the petite young girl aside. Yuri towered over the young girl. Her skin was pale in contrast to her black hair and her eyes were teary.

Yuri knelt next to her and whispered in Romanian, "Adriana, remember me? I spoke with your parents. They wanted this for you."

"Yes, I am frightened."

"You will be with a new family soon and they will care for you."

He gave her a piece of paper. "This is my email address. If you can, send me a message; I will let your parents know you are well."

He escorted her through a large room with overstuffed sofas upholstered in a rich gold colored brocade fabric, an exquisite oriental rug in shades of blue covered part of the floor, and draperies covered the walls. A small room was located at one the end of the room.

"Wait in this room until I come for you. No one will bother you. It has a bathroom and there is a bottle of spring water and a candy bar and fresh fruit on the counter."

Yuri kissed her on the cheek, and she kissed him in return. He closed the door, locked it from the outside, and returned to where the five women waited for him in another room. Three single beds were arranged along two walls. The Russian guard, Aleksandr, almost two meters tall, well muscled with an acne pocked face opened the first door and motioned for one of the women to come with him. He led her into a large room to meet with Yuri who was sitting behind a large desk. An incense burner sat on one end of the desk filling the room with kyphi, a scent that went back to the Old Kingdom of Egypt. A half smoked cigar sat in an ashtray with a thin wisp of smoke drifting upward.

"Give me your identity papers, your wallet, and your clothes." Yuri told her in a lascivious tone of voice.

The frightened woman screamed at him, "What are you saying? Hand you my clothes. I am here for a job interview."

Yuri shouted at one of his men, "Aleksandr help her undress and toss me her purse."

Aleksandr snatched her purse and tossed it onto the desk. Another guard, Dobrashin, shorter with black hair and a stocky build, fierce dark eyes, almost black in color, held her arms behind her back as the first guard stripped her naked by cutting her clothes with a knife. Aleksandr picked up a flogger with thin strips of leather with pointed tips and whacked her across her bottom several times until it was red while Dobrashin held her.

Yuri shouted at her in Romanian, "You will be beaten into submission and do as you are told. Stop fighting us and you will not be punished."

The woman shrieked in response in Romania, "You filthy pig. *Futu-te* (Fuck you). Let me go. Let me go."

"Take her into that first room and punish her for fifteen minutes. Then bind her to the bed face down with her hands cuffed behind her back and each ankle secured to the bed frame. Gag her; she is a noisy bitch."

They dragged the screaming woman into a room and fastened her wrists to a large metal ring suspended from the ceiling. They took turns whipping her back, thighs, and bottom until she stopped shrieking. Dobrashin unfastened her wrists, carried her to the next room, tied her wrists behind her back, and fastened her ankles to a bed. He placed a ball gag in her mouth.

"When we initiate the other women, I might be back to have you pleasure me, you bitch." He laughed and smacked her bottom five more times with his open palm before he left and rejoined Aleksandr. This continued until the men indoctrinated the four additional women by whipping, gagging, and binding them. They burned their identity papers. Yuri and the two guards divided the money from their purses between them, smashed, and discarded their cell phones.

"It is almost time to pick up the next group. There are twelve this time. Aleksandr, stay here with the women, their bottoms are yours to enjoy. Dobrashin and I will meet two more of my Israeli friends at the airport and escort them here."

The second group arrived and the same procedure took place.

The first woman screamed and cursed. Dobrashin grabbed her and Aleksandr began to whip her bottom. He whipped her until her bottom was a bright red blush. The thin hard rubber long tailed floggers they used delivered a painful sting. The first lash stung, but continually lashing in the same place multiplied the pain to extreme levels. When she had stopped screaming from exhaustion, Dobrashin slathered her bottom with a lubricant and worked the phallus shaped handle of the flogger into her back door of pleasure and vaginal cavities. He continued to sodomize her with rapid in and out movements as she wriggled her body to free herself from his torture, when Dobrashin tired, he held her down and Aleksandr raped her. After her initial whipping and rape, they dragged her to another cell, tied face down on a bed, and a gag placed into her mouth. They left her in her cell and called the next woman.

Yuri picked one of the women for his own indoctrination. She was a stunning red head, 170 centimeters tall, fair complexion, rounded figure, but not overweight and captivating gray eyes.

"This woman will make up for the red head that broke my nose this morning in El-Arish. Aleksandr you and Dobrashin initiate the others. I will be very busy enjoying myself."

Yuri took the red head into a room set apart down the hall.

"I would hate to be her. Yuri is still furious that a woman got the better of him when he went to kidnap her off the beach. She turned out to be some kind of woman martial arts expert. She broke his nose and kicked him in the groin."

"Must have been a helluva of a woman, Yuri's a tough opponent."

"That or he had too much vodka for breakfast," Aleksandr laughed.

There were poles floor to ceiling, a wooden platform in the room along with a desk, one chair in the middle of the room, and a double bed along one wall.

"Sit down."

"Let's see, you are applying for a job as a nanny for a diplomat in Tel Aviv. You speak Russian, Czech, and English. Your name is Magdalena." Yuri spoke to her using a surly tone of voice.

"Yes, I was educated in England." She answered in a frightened voice.

Yuri walked around the high back chair she was sitting in and before the unsuspecting Magdalena could do anything, he wrapped a wide leather strap around her neck and bound her to the chair. He then pulled her arms behind the chair back and tied them together.

Magdalena began to cry, "Please, please do not hurt me. What are you doing to me? I am pregnant. I do not want to lose my baby because of a severe beating. You are traffickers."

Yuri towered over her as she sat in the chair sobbing. With a gentler sound to his usual harsh voice he used when speaking to these women, he knelt by her side; he asked her in Russian, "You are pregnant. Why are you applying for his job? You should be home having your baby. There are warnings about applying for jobs like this. It is a trip to hell in the brothels of Tel Aviv or Cairo or wherever. You must look at the Internet. It is filled with warnings about traffickers like me."

"I did not believe the warnings. My family will have nothing to do with me even though I was raped. By getting a job in another country, no one would know my shame."

Yuri started to pace.

"What am I to do with you? These men are animals; they will not care if you are pregnant. If I take you to Tel Aviv, they will take you to a butcher in a back alley and perform an abortion."

He unbound her and escorted her to the bed on the side of the room.

"I apologize, but you must undress."

Magdalena began to undress and cried so hard her body was shaking. Yuri walked over to her when she had all her clothes off, put his arms around her, and held her close to him.

"I will protect you, but you must do everything I ask." He whispered to her. "I will pay for you, and you will be mine. After the women are at the border, I will bring you back to Cairo, see you are safe, and send you to Russia where a single mother will not be in danger. I have two friends in Moscow who will help you."

"I want you to scream loud each time I strike the wall, they will think I am beating you."

She screamed each time he struck the wall with his hand. She was crying.

Magdalena looked at him with tears rushing down her cheeks and asked, "What is to become of me? I want to have this baby; it is part of me."

"I will see you through this. Now I must bind you to the bed and hope you look abused enough. Those men may enter the room at any time."

"Will they rape me?"

"No. not after I buy you. Once you are mine, no one will touch you."

"Are you sure you can get me out of this without being beaten or raped?"

"I will do my best Magdalena. Do not let on I was temperate. They think of me as a pitiless ruthless man; I do not want them to think otherwise."

Magdalena acted terrified as he bound her to the bed face down with pillows under her stomach to lift her butt high.

"I will spank you a little so they believe you are in great pain." He struck her bottom with his hand several times until it turned pink, and she screamed each time, he struck her.

"You are okay, I did not injure you?" Yuri asked in a concerned tone.

"I am fine." She sniffled.

Yuri kissed her on the cheek. He heard one of the other men coming into his room and he screamed at her in an angry tone of voice, "By tomorrow, you will be willing to do anything we ask of you. You will drink piss and eat shit; whatever we want. If you do not, you will be whipped the same as today."

He smacked her with his open palm once more.

"You *pizda*, (cunt)," Yuri shouted.

"Yuri, this woman has not been spanked enough, you barely touched her."

"I have decided to buy her for my pleasure. I want to take my time and enjoy torturing her. I will pay $5,000 for her."

"Why pay for her when you can do all those things for free?"

"Revenge for the red head on the beach this morning. My nose hurts like hell and my balls are still on fire. No one is to touch this woman. She is mine," he snarled.

"Yuri, you are not yourself. What is happening to you? We are not allowed to just buy a woman."

"I will buy her if I want to and there is nothing you can do about it. Ee dee nahooy (Fuck you)."

"*Otebis*'(Fuck off), Yuri."

Aleksandr left and Yuri whispered to Magdalena, "You are safe. No one will touch you. Trust me. I will get you through this."

"Thank you. Can you cover me, I am cold."

Yuri put a blanket over her and kissed her.

"Are you comfortable; I did not tie you too tightly?"

"I am comfortable."

Yuri left her and locked the door to the room.

"I am off to the airport for the last group of women. I will return soon. Do not go near that woman; she is mine," he barked.

"Yuri, you think you run this operation. We are tired of you having your way. Be careful or we will ship you back to Singapore and arrange for twenty-four strokes of a cane. Maybe that will beat some sense into you. You do not run this operation. Boris will be told how you are behaving."

"I will buy any woman I want. Back off. Do you want to buy a woman? I will sell you one."

"Hell no, I get everything I want free. You are deranged. Why pay for something you can get for free. She will not be touched, but you are out of control."

Yuri left for the airport and cursed as he drove the van to Cairo International.

He screamed inside the car, "I will get that red head from the beach if it is the last thing I do. My nose hurts and my groin is killing me."

Yuri returned about one a.m. with the remaining women. They indoctrinated them, and by three in the morning, they were finished for the night. In the morning the owner of the warehouse, Kahlil would arrive. From every shipment he picked at least five women, auctioned them off to wealthy Saudis or Egyptians he knew had the desire, and the means to own a women.

Yuri retired to his room, unbound Magdalena, and sat at the desk organizing all the paperwork and destroying the women's identity cards.

Yuri turned to Magdalena, "No one will know you are untied. This is the only bed. You will not be harmed."

Magdalena smiled at him, "I trust you. You have saved my baby and me. If you wish, make love to me; I will submit to you."

"Thank you for the offer. You are a ravishing woman and I respect you. A woman like you needs a man that will love you, marry you, and make a life for you and your baby. My life is in danger for buying you, but I cannot stand to see you abused. We still have a way to go but I cannot do anything until these women are at the cave. Then we will return to Cairo."

Yuri undressed and slid into the bed next to her. He put his arms around her, pulled her body next to his, and they slept until six the next morning. The room was dark as Yuri quickly got dressed before binding her to the bed and gagging her. She offered no resistance.

"I am sorry to do this, but this man will insist on seeing all twenty-five women."

It was around 0630 when Kahlil and five men arrived at the warehouse. Two of them were Saudi and the other three were businessmen from Cairo.

Kahlil showed them into a showroom and had them make themselves comfortable. Dobrashin offered them tea and placed a basket of fresh fruit on the table. The men were all smoking cigars and clouds of fragrant smoke drifted through the room. Judging from the aroma of the cigars, they were most likely Cuban. Egyptian belly dance music filled the room.

"I will be back in a few minutes. The women will be brought in one at a time."

Yuri, smoking a Cuban cigar, escorted Kahlil to the individual rooms.

"Where do you get those cigars, the fragrance is intoxicating, smells like wood, nuts, cocoa beans, and spice.?"

"My uncle has a friend in Cuba who sends them to him; I will get a few extras next time."

When Kahlil saw Magdalena, he turned to Yuri," I love women with red hair. I want her for myself."

"She has already been purchased by me."

"Berezovsky, that is not allowed and you know it. I have first pick.

"Not this time. Move on; there are lots of pretty women and the special one I told you about, arrived yesterday."

Yuri winked at Magdalena as they left the room.

Kahlil picked four women but was still angry with Yuri, "Do not ever choose before me again. I want a red head the next time, you hear me."

"I will make sure we have several red heads; you will have your pick."

He took Kahlil through the salon and unlocked the door where the young girl waited.

"This is Adriana, the young virgin you requested. Her parents agreed to this. Is it possible to place her with a descent man?"

"All five of these men are very wealthy and do not have a reputation of abusing the women they buy. She will be safe with anyone of them."

Yuri directed his men to take the four women and Adriana to a large bathroom. "Let these women wash, comb their hair, and put on make-up. I want them to look stunning." Turning to a stunning blonde, Yuri asked her in a quiet voice," I know you are terrified and angry, but please take care of this young girl. Her parents requested this."

Tears rolled down her cheeks, "For you I will do this. Magdalena is pregnant and I know you protected her."

Yuri wiped her tears away, "Thank you. The men in the next room will not brutalize you."

The first woman walked into the room where the five men were sitting.

Yuri told her to walk up to each man and let him feel her and do anything the men asked.

Yuri shouted at her in Romanian, "Bend over, touch your toes, he wants to check your ass. Walk to the next man. Wiggle, dance to the music. I want you to move. That man wants you to open your mouth; do it."

When all five men had fondled, pinched, and fingered her, the bidding began. She was about twenty-two years old, had long brown hair, a buxom woman about 165 centimeters in height. The bidding stopped at 50,000 Egyptian pounds. In American money, that was a little over $8500 American dollars. The woman returned to her cell, bound hand and foot.

The second woman arrived. She was twenty-two, a little heavier and only sold for 40,000 pounds. The next woman was the blonde women that Yuri had asked to help with Adriana. She sold to a Saudi who paid 55,000. Adriana, wearing a thin cotton shift walked to the center of the floor; she was in tears. The bidding was fierce and when it was over, she sold for 150,000 Egyptian pounds. The wealthy Egyptian that had won the bid on the blonde woman, smiled as he outbid the others for Adriana. The last woman sold for 40,000 pounds. One man who was out bid on all the women was angry and demanded another woman be available.

Kahlil told him, "Return in five days, you will have first choice."

The man left with the other buyers. Yuri and the two other Russians placed the women in the trunks of their cars and they left the warehouse. Yuri carried Adriana and she sat in the back seat of a large white luxury sedan. Yuri asked the Saudi to let the blonde woman sit in the back with the little girl. The Saudi agreed as Yuri slipped him 10,000 Egyptian pounds. Yuri kissed her on the cheek, winked at the blonde, and closed the door. He wiped a tear from his eye as he watched the car drive away. The sale was over by 0730.

Kahlil and Yuri went into an office near the front of the building on an upper floor.

"Here is your twenty-five percent Berezovsky. Excellent women this time, especially that young girl, and the blonde. Do not choose any women the next time until I have chosen. Do not forget my redhead."

Yuri was furious, he shouted, "Twenty-five percent. We agreed on forty percent. It has always been forty percent."

"The cost to keep the police away has gone up. There are several groups trying to put an end to this slavery. I have expenses to cover. You do not like my arrangement, go somewhere else. Several groups use my facility. Do you think you are the only ones?"

"You are doing this because of the red head."

"May be, but my costs are higher. Get over it."

"Next month is Ramadan. I always take that month off; no Muslim customers. The Jews are cheap bastards. I will see you in November when the Gulf Arabs and Saudis return. I insist on a fifty fifty split. Don't worry, they will all be gorgeous."

Kahlil was not buying Yuri's attempt to increase his cut. Now he had something to hold over his head. News that he had held one of the women back for himself would mean stern punishment and a warning if he were lucky.

"Thirty-five percent. We will talk again. Get your women out of here as soon as the sun sets tonight. Our agreement is for forty-eight hours only. I have another group in five days."

When Kahlil had left, Yuri gave orders to his men.

"I want the remaining nineteen women, fed and dressed in caftans. We leave at six this evening. The Bedouin guides will be here at four. They want to enjoy themselves with the women before we leave. You have all day, train them well. I am going to pick up food for the redhead and myself. I am planning to make love and sleep all day in my office. Do not disturb me."

Yuri left the warehouse, bought food and drinks for himself and Magdalena, and returned to his office and locked the door.

Magdalena lay bound on the bed. He untied her and gave her a colorful caftan to wear that he had purchased along with a delicate silk headscarf.

"We will stay here until this evening. You will be transported along with the other women, but will ride in my car to the end of the road where we will go by camel. I do not want you to have to walk up that treacherous dark narrow mountain trail."

Later in the evening four Bedouins wearing kefiyahs and thobes arrived at the warehouse. He gave them their choice of the remaining women for the next two hours. "We will leave at six."

The women were dressed, their arms tied behind their backs. Yuri took care of Magdalena personally and tied her wrists in front of her, but not too tightly. "You will ride in the lead car with me. No one will touch you."

Magdalena thanked him and kissed him on the mouth as he held her close.

Chapter 16

The next morning two Bedouins entered the hotel, went directly to the concierge, and asked him to call Hassan and tell him, Harb, and Mohned were there to see him.

It was usual to see Bedouins in the hotel. They owned a gift shop attached to the hotel that sold Bedouin crafts.

When Hassan got the call, he told the concierge to show them into his office and he would be down directly.

"Emunishere, I must meet with some men in my office. Do not leave the room. I will be back in less than an hour. Mohamed will be just outside your door."

Hassan kissed her on the cheek, dressed, and hurried to his office pausing briefly to talk with Mohamed.

"Please stay outside my suite until I return."

Mohamed left immediately and took the elevator to Hassan's suite.

Hassan entered his office and greeted the two Bedouins.

"Have you any news?"

"Yes, a doctor circumcised three Bedouin girls yesterday. My daughter is a friend of one of the girls. She told my daughter of a cave with jail cells in the mountains."

"This may be the cave we are trying to find. Keep surveillance, particularly at night. If you see trucks or vans, let me know."

"We will survey the area tonight. There is no road to the cave. They will have to park and walk the women to the cave using a narrow trail cut into the side of the mountain. It is almost an hour on foot to the cave because of the narrow path."

"Watch, when you see the women start across the desert, call me on the satellite phone I gave you. Your business will receive a large payment for this information. We need to protect our hotel clients. One of our guests was almost kidnapped yesterday."

"We are glad to help. We have known each other a long time Hassan."

Hassan returned to his suite. "Emunishere, we have received word on the location of the cave."

"Does that mean you will rescue Cassandra?"

"We must wait until the other women arrive, then we will make our move. It may be as early as tomorrow."

"I will call Alex and Robert with the news."

Early that afternoon, Hassan and Emunishere visited the jewelry store off the hotel lobby.

"I want to buy you something. Which ring do you like best?"

Emunishere did not know what to say.

"Choose for me. They are all dazzling."

Hassan chose a yellow gold ring with a large center emerald surrounded by diamonds. He slipped it onto her finger and it fit perfectly.

"Hassan, it is magnificent."

They left the store and returned to his suite. Emunishere put her arms around him and kissed him passionately. "I do love you."

Hassan kissed her in return and held her close to him. "You must stay in the suite the remainder of the day. Tonight may be the night we make our move on the traffickers in the mountains. When I return, we will get married and not leave this suite of rooms for a week. I want to savor your sweetness and make love to you night and day."

"Is that a proposal? I will be waiting. Be very careful. I could not live without you. Promise me you will return safely," she started to cry.

Hassan held her, brushed her hair from her face, and kissed her. "I will be back safely. Robert Cavendish is spending the night in the suite with you. He already volunteered to sleep on the sofa."

Hassan, Alex, Sabir along with thirty men that had been working with Sabir, met in a warehouse near the waterfront within the hour. The men, all ex-military had sleeping bags and provisions for three days. They would sleep on the floor of the warehouse until Hassan received a phone call announcing the news that the women were driving toward the mountain. It was almost an hour climb up the narrow mountain trail on foot to reach the cave, more than enough time to mount an attack. The plan was to intercept them on the trail before they reached the cave. If they were successful, these women would not face the degradation of becoming sex slaves in the brothels of Israel.

Hassan heard his satellite phone ring and answered. It was one of his Bedouin friends. "There is a caravan of four cars traveling together; we have followed them from Cairo to Port Said and they have turned onto El Kantra east-El Arish. We are seventy-five kilometers from El-Arish."

"How many women?"

"We count about twenty. They will arrive at the foot of the mountain around four in the morning. It is best to intercept them when they are on foot."

"Station some of your people in the mountains on both sides of the trail in case they make a break for it. We want to capture as many guards as possible."

"Were they armed?"

"We counted four Russians with Kalashnikovs. The Bedouins numbered six and all carried a variety of guns including Uzis. There may be two more Bedouins in the cave."

"Did you see Berezovsky?"

"He is in the lead car carrying a 9 mm handgun. We recognized him from the sketch; there is a bandage on his nose. A single woman is in the car with him."

"I want that son-of-a-bitch alive. Be careful. We will keep you informed of our location. We are beginning to move. Is the woman Cassandra Cavendish with them?"

"Could not tell, she may be the women in the backseat with a scarf over her head."

Hassan called Robert and told him to come to his suite immediately and stay with Emunishere. They were leaving for the mountains.

Robert arrived at Hassan's suite and she let him in. The phone rang and Emunishere answered. It was Hassan. "Let me talk with Robert."

Emunishere handed him the phone. "I want to come. They have my daughter."

"Robert listen to me, these men are armed and dangerous. They would rather fight than lose twenty women that would sell from $3500 American money to $10,000 or more. Slavery is over a billion American dollars a year business. I need you to stay there with Emunishere and will call you on the satellite phone the minute your daughter is safe. Please put Emunishere on the phone."

Hassan spoke with Emunishere in a reassuring tone of voice. "I promise, I will return to you. The men with me are all former military. Stay there with Cassandra's father and console him. He is so worried about his daughter."

Emunishere started to cry and tears ran down her face. "I love you. I hope you capture that Russian who tried to kidnap me. He must be punished for what he is doing to these women."

"Get some rest while I am gone. Order room service. I will return late tonight or early tomorrow morning. I love you."

Hassan, Sabir, and Alex had seven vehicles capable of desert travel. They would head toward the mountains on a different approach than the caravan with the twenty women. The Bedouins would meet them two kilometers from the trails end. From there they would travel by foot to the cave. They were two hours ahead of the caravan, and had time to set their trap.

Soon after the men left, the phone rang; the call came from a satellite phone.

Emunishere answered.

"Is Robert Cavendish there? This is his daughter."

Emunishere called to him. "It is a woman. She says she is your daughter."

Robert grasped the phone in his trembling hand.

"Father, I knew you would be anxious to hear from me."

"Where are you? I have been worried sick."

"For once in your life, Father, listen to me. This will be a very short phone call. Do not try to find me. You always interfere with my personal life; first with Joseph, then George, and last with Yuri. I have met an Egyptian doctor, fallen in love, and married him. You can do nothing about it. We are on our honeymoon."

"Cassandra, who is this man? Where are you?"

"My life is in the hands of my husband Jameel. I am twenty-four years old and happy for the first time in my life. I love you father, but I have my own life."

"Cassandra, you cannot do this."

"I have done it. Good-bye Father."

Cassandra pushed the disconnect button on the sat phone. Robert was in tears. He looked at Emunishere. "I have lost my daughter. She is married to an Egyptian doctor named Jameel that I do not know. Tell your friend Hassan and Alex, the search for my daughter is over. I am returning to London immediately."

"Where is she?"

"She wouldn't tell me."

"Are you sure she is all right?"

"I could tell from her voice, she is content. She never told me about this man and suddenly in two weeks, they are married. I have lost her."

Robert left Emunishere, returned to his room, called the desk, and arranged for transportation to Cairo by private car.

Emunishere called Hassan on his phone.

"You can tell Alex to stop looking for Cassandra. She called her father. Yuri has nothing to do with her disappearance. She married a doctor from Cairo."

"Did she give her father this doctor's name?"

"He thought she said his first name was Jameel."

"I will ask my father if he knows a doctor named Jameel. He has been in the hospital system in Cairo for thirty years."

"Please be careful. I love you."

"I will call Mohamed and tell him to keep watch outside your door until tomorrow. Love you."

Yuri got into the lead car and was in communication with the cave. "We are running a little late. We should be at the cave before 0500. The Bedouins were having too much fun."

Yuri spoke with Aleksandr before he and Dobrashin got into their cars, "When we get these women to the cave and settled in, I am leaving with the redhead to return to Cairo. I am not making the trip to Tel Aviv. Dobrashin, you will be in charge."

Aleksandr shouted in Russian at Yuri. "Boris will be told everything. You have broken all the rules. What is the matter with you? You did not whip or abuse any of these women, except that redhead. She did not even look like you spanked her."

"I cannot help it; I have a thing for redheads," Yuri smirked.

At four in the morning, the caravan arrived at the foot of the mountain trail. The women left the cars and proceeded on foot to the cave. The Bedouin guards herded them along. Some of the women were sobbing, some were screaming at the guards.

One of the women lunged at the Bedouin holding her, and bit him on the neck. She started screaming and running with her hands bound behind her back.

Yuri shouted, "Grab that woman and bring her to me. Bind her wrists in front of her."

Yuri stripped her naked. He had two Bedouins hold her, and he began to lash her with a flogger with thin twisted rubber cording with hard rubber barbs. He lashed her hard; the skin on her bottom split open after several violently delivered lashes one after the other in the same area, and blood trickled down her legs. Yuri was losing it. The woman managed to wiggle free and continued screaming and running when she tripped and fell off the trail landing on the rocks several meters below.

Yuri climbed down to where the woman was laying and determined she was dead. Her head had hit a pointed rock and she was lying in a pool of blood.

"This cannot be happening to me. Everything is going wrong. I was cheated by Kahlil, Aleksandr is threatening me," Yuri pulled his gun and fired a single shot into the dead woman's back.

"Anyone else has a complaint," he roared in Russian and Romanian. "You will cooperate. You will pay back the cash your trip cost. When you pay all debts, you will be free. You belong to us. You will be taught what you must do for the next two days and then you will be taken to the border and smuggled into Israel."

Aleksandr grabbed Yuri from behind, and slammed him with his fist making him bend double and groan with pain.

"Yuri, you owe us for that woman. We will tell Boris. This is your last mission. You bought a woman for yourself and cost us money and then a woman dies in our charge. You are out of control. What is wrong with you?"

Yuri straightened up, delivered a hard punch to Aleksandr's jaw knocking him off his feet, and pulled his gun.

"Hit me again and I'll shoot you the next time. I am in charge and I will do what I want. I will pay $3,500 for this woman and $5,000 for the redhead. Satisfied, I did not kill her. She tripped and fell, clumsy cow. I put a bullet into her to make a point. She killed herself. Look at them; they are quiet. They will not give you any more trouble."

Aleksandr got up rubbing his jaw and snarled, "Boris will take care of you; maybe he will ask me to kill you."

"You would not stand a chance against me Aleksandr; shut up and take charge of the women along with Dobrashin. Grab that body and bury it."

The women sobbed and gasped in disbelief that one of their group had been whipped and then shot. A hush fell over them and they meekly fell into line to trudge up the mountain.

"The walk ahead of you will take an hour. You should be more cooperative when we get to our camp. It is all uphill into the mountains." Yuri shouted at them.

"I want to check on the inventory of weapons and ammunition we are smuggling. There is a need to speak with the doctor, as he was upset about having to stay at the cave after circumcising those little girls.

The two Bedouins will come down to help with the women. I am taking the redhead with me. I need the doctor to fix my nose and check her; she seems to have a problem."

Yuri had them lift Magdalena onto the camel and rode to the cave with her seated behind him. "I will have the doctor check your condition. Trust me. No harm will come to you." He whispered in her ear.

Magdalena thanked him again. When they arrived at the cave, Yuri shouted in a loud voice, "Adey, I am back. Get your lazy butt out here. I want you and your friend to go down and help with the women. Where is the doctor?"

Unseen by the Bedouins and Russians, Hassan's men were closing in and they could hear the entire conversation.

Alex told Hassan to tell the men to circle around both flanks. "We will spring our ambush shortly. The men are in position up the trail. The strike will begin at exactly 0445."

"Alex and I are going back to the cave. We plan to take the Bedouins by surprise and capture Yuri."

Alex and Hassan mounted two camels that the Bedouins had brought with them. They approached the cave quietly so Yuri would not hear their approach.

The doctor shuddered with fear at the sound of Yuri's voice. He was cowering on the floor of one of the cells.

Yuri led Magdalena to a bed he had in the back of the cave and walked over to the doctor's cell.

"My good doctor, get dressed," Yuri unlocked the cell door and threw the doctors clothes in his face.

"Why are you doing this? I took care of the girls?"

"I have more women for you to check and my nose is broken. Some bitch broke it. In addition, I have a woman that you need to examine. She says she is pregnant and I need to know she and the baby are all right."

"I will look at your nose and the woman. Surely you do not want me to circumcise all of them."

"Your job is to check each woman, no cutting. See if they are in good physical condition, and are not infected. I hated to see you cutting those little girls. It made me vomit. Their screaming was horrible, how do you do perform such detestable operations on little girls?"

"I am paid well and it saves them from mutilation by old women who don't know what they are doing. I did not agree to help with the trafficking of women for sex."

"No, you did not. If you wish to leave this cave alive, you will do as I order you. Get dressed. I need to separate them as to their attributes and that includes their physical well-being. You will be compensated doctor."

"If I refuse?"

"You will become a eunuch. I will do the job myself and leave you in the desert to rot." Yuri shouted at him.

"You have made your point."

"Now, look at my nose."

The doctor looked at Yuri's nose. "The only way to fix your nose is to re-break it and set it. Otherwise it will always have that bend."

"How long will it take?"

"I should be finished in half an hour. I will anesthetize you, break your nose, set it, and you will be awake in a little over an hour."

"I do not have an hour. I will take care of my nose when I return to Cairo later today. Bandage it properly."

The doctor bandaged his nose and Yuri winced as he applied the bandages.

"This woman's name is Magdalena. She is pregnant. You are to tell no one of her actual condition. Tell anyone that asks; she is in shock. I have already paid for her; she will be unharmed and return to Cairo with me. I do not abuse pregnant women."

"You are not as tough as you pretend to be. Under all that gruff and growl, I think you are a descent man."

"That is our little secret, doctor." Yuri winked.

Yuri walked into the back of the cave and checked on the crates containing the guns and ammunition.

Hassan and Alex saw the two Bedouins headed toward them and hid their camels off the trail and dismounted. Hassan stood on a ledge near the edge of the trail and as one of the Bedouins came close, he leapt from the ledge and he and the Bedouin hit the dirt together. Alex grabbed the halter of the other camel and jerked so hard that camel and rider fell to the ground. Alex and Hassan disabled the two guards. They tied and gagged them and dragged them off the trail.

They were close enough they could hear the doctor and Yuri arguing. Carefully they climbed the rest of the way on foot. They radioed the group that the guards at the cave were out of commission. The plan was to capture Yuri in the cave. They gave the go ahead for the ambush.

Yuri was so involved with the crates of guns; he did not hear Alex and Hassan enter the cave. All of a sudden, he heard a footfall, but it was too late. Yuri pulled his sidearm, but Alex kicked it from his hand. He lunged at Alex. Yuri and Alex locked in hand-to-hand combat. Alex was a bear of a man and soon had the advantage since Yuri was still recovering from his injuries and could not fight effectively. Alex subdued him and Hassan handcuffed him.

"I hear gun fire, Alex. I will make my way down the trail. You stay here and check out those crates. Lock this bastard in one of those cells."

"If you need help, I have my radio."

Hassan left the cave and headed down the trail. He could hear gunfire and the women screaming. Someone was yelling to the women, "Get down, get down."

Just as Hassan came around a bend in the trail, a bullet ricocheted off the rock wall, and hit him in the shoulder. Holding his injured shoulder, he turned and managed to get back to the cave. Blood oozed between his fingers. He called out, "Alex, I am hit."

Alex hurried to his side and helped him into the cave. "You should have let me go. You have not been in the military for two years; you are out of practice. You should always keep your head down, Hassan."

"I know that. Get going."

Alex left to investigate who was shooting. Hearing the commotion Dr. Ismail emerged from the back of the cave catching Hassan by surprise.

"Stop, who are you?" Hassan shouted.

"I am a doctor tricked into coming here. Yuri paid me a lot of money to circumcise three young girls. I was greedy. They told me I had to stay because there were many women I might have to treat. Believe me. I do not want any part of this."

"Can you help me, I am wounded."

"Let me look at your shoulder."

Hassan got up on the table where the doctor operated on the girls; Ismail stripped off his blood-soaked shirt. It was an ugly wound and bleeding profusely. Hassan lay there as the doctor examined him.

"There is no exit wound; the bullet is lodged in your shoulder. I can try to remove it with the surgical instruments I brought with me."

"I will give you something for the pain."

"No," barked Hassan. "I need to be alert. I can handle the pain."

Magdalena came out of the back.

"Where is Yuri?"

The doctor looked up, "He is in a cell over there. Stay away from him."

Hassan asked the doctor, "Who is that woman?"

"Yuri rescued her. She is pregnant. He is trying to get her to safety in Cairo. Yuri is not as bad as you think he is. The man has a streak of decency."

"Yuri has a good side?" He asked questionably.

Magdalena walked over to the cell where Yuri was sequestered. She called to him quietly, "Yuri, what can I do to help you?"

"There are keys on the hook over the bed in the back. Get it for me; we will escape this cave together."

Magdalena ran into the back and grabbed the key off the wall. She returned and unlocked the door to the cell, released the handcuffs, and Yuri was free. He silently walked over to a table where Hassan had put his gun and picked it up.

At that moment, Alex returned to warn Hassan that Yuri might have a key and would try to escape. He quickly aimed his Sig Sauer 9mm and shot Yuri once in the arm and once in the thigh. The doctor was about to remove the bullet from Hassan's shoulder when two shots rang out. Unsure what had just happened he froze with the scalpel in his right hand.

Magdalena rushed to Yuri's side and was in tears, "Why did you shoot him? He rescued me."

Yuri screamed in pain as his leg gave out completely and he fell to the floor gripping it with his good arm and tried to stop the bleeding. Magdalena took off her scarf and tied it tightly above the wound to stop the bleeding in Yuri's leg.

"Get out of my way, now," Alex shouted at her.

"Don't hurt this woman, you bastard, she is pregnant," Yuri growled.

"Who the hell are you?"

"I'm Agent MacKay MI6."

Magdalena moved away from Yuri and Alex examined Yuri's wounds.

"Berezovsky, you will live. I will have the doctor patch you up once he is finished with my friend."

Hassan looked on and said in a faint voice, "I am glad you did not kill him; he may have information we can use. What brought you back?"

"I came back to warn you that he might have a key to the cell. Looks like I was just in time. He was picking up your gun when I walked in. Who is this woman that seems to care so much about him?"

The doctor answered, "Her name is Magdalena, and Yuri rescued her from the traffickers because she is pregnant. He was taking her to Cairo this afternoon."

Alex turned to Magdalena and in a gentler tone of voice told her, "He is going to be all right. I am an expert shot; I did not shoot to kill. Berezovsky, I am placing you under arrest for the trafficking of women." Alex motioned to Magdalena, "Please sit over there."

Magdalena sat down in a chair and began to cry.

The doctor continued to work on Hassan pulling out the bullet and closing the wound. He was in pain but more concerned with what Yuri knew.

"We must make Berezovsky tell us what he knows. I want to know who the head of this organization is. This slavery business has got to end."

"Be still," the doctor cautioned. "I am not finished yet."

Yuri groaned in pain from his wounds, "I will never tell you anything. Do not hurt Magdalena. She is not like other women. I need help before I bleed to death."

Sabir arrived at the cave and ran to Hassan's side. Hassan told his father, "This is the doctor they paid to circumcise the Bedouin girls. He is no part of this and was bribed into coming here; they made him a part of it." Grimacing in pain from the wound to his shoulder, Hassan explained to his father that they had not found Cassandra among the women.

"Emunishere called me and I told Alex, Cassandra ran away with a doctor from Cairo, and she is married. Do you know a doctor at any of the hospitals with the first name Jameel?"

"We have about four doctors with that first name. There is one doctor in his late twenties, recently divorced. He raises Arabians as do I." Sabir turned to Dr. Ismail, "I will tend to my son. See to Yuri."

The gunfire from the base of the trail had stopped.

"Doctor, make sure it hurts him a lot when you operate. Perhaps the pain will loosen his tongue."

"You bastard, I have suffered pain before at the hands of Singapore's best flogger. I tell you nothing," yelled a defiant Yuri.

Alex looked at Hassan and then at Yuri. "The doctor said you threatened to castrate him. We could have the good doctor castrate you along with tending your wounds. Maybe that will convince you we are serious."

Yuri screamed, "You fucking bastards. If I tell you, I am dead man."

"If you don't tell us, you are not even a man."

"If I tell you who is behind this, will you let me go?" Yuri asked in a more conciliatory tone of voice.

"Tell us what we want to know and we will not castrate you, but you will serve jail time for trafficking. The good news is you will live. That is as much as I can offer you now. The sooner we find the head of this organization the better your chances of coming out of this alive and a man."

Yuri was feeling faint from the loss of blood. He closed his eyes and went limp.

The doctor interrupted them, "If I do not help this man, he will die. He has lost a lot of blood."

"Okay doc; make sure you give him nothing for pain. I want this man conscious; he has things to tell us when you are finished. If he does not, I will castrate him myself. I will not need your help." Alex barked.

The doctor operated as best he could in the dim light of the cave. Yuri stirred and groaned as the doctor probed for the bullet in his leg and bandaged his arm where the bullet had grazed him.

"You are a lucky man," he told Yuri. If you had not helped that woman Magdalena, I would not have operated on you and just let you bleed to death. The bullet in your leg is lodged in the bone and I cannot remove it here. I have stopped the bleeding. You will need a transfusion when we get you to Cairo." Ismail stopped and whispered in Yuri's ear, "I am the prison doctor; perhaps I will pay you a visit."

When the doctor had finished, Alex locked Yuri in a cell where Magdalena sat next to him. Yuri was too weak to resist.

Alex helped Hassan to a chair.

"Are you all right?"

"I will be fine once we get this slave trader back to Cairo and in jail where he belongs."

One of Sabir's men appeared at the opening of the cave with a report.

"We have killed three Bedouins, wounded two, and captured a third. We found the two that you and Alex disabled. Three of the four Russians are dead, but the fourth is alive and I know we can make him talk."

Hassan was breathing heavily from the pain, "Alex, call in the army. We need help getting these women off the mountain. Keep them here until the military arrives. We will make it down on our own."

Alex walked over to Yuri. "We are going to have a long talk about what you have done to these women once we get to Cairo. We need to know everything you know. Until then your captivity will be kept secret. Sabir has made the arrangements. You will tell us what we want to know, or die a terrible slow death."

Magdalena broke in to defend Yuri, "Yuri is not a bad man. If it were not for him, I would have been raped and beaten like the others. He saved me." Magdalena pleaded with Alex, "Please, do not kill him. Do not hurt him anymore, please, I beg you. He saved my life and the life of my baby. Give him something for the pain. Please, I beg you." She threw herself across Yuri's body sobbing.

Alex looked into her tear-filled eyes, "I promise not to kill him." He called to the doctor.

"Give him something for pain before we transport him."

"I cannot give him anything for pain; he has lost too much blood."

"We will see he gets medical care." Alex reassured her. "Once we arrive in Cairo I will arrange with the authorities to get you to safety and back home with your family."

Yuri nodded in and out of consciousness leaning on Magdalena for support.

Alex approached and placed his hand under Yuri's chin lifting his face he stared into his eyes.

"Berezovsky, I was about to ask you about a woman named Cassandra Cavendish. We thought you had kidnapped her, but she called her father, told him that she had run away, and got married. Did you kidnap her?"

"I dated that woman in London for almost a month. We were quite involved. I do not understand women. I guess I never will," Yuri grumbled and closed his eyes.

Alex looked at Yuri, "I have trouble understanding women myself. Selling children into slavery is even below you. Some of the women you brought here were fourteen and fifteen. This has to come to an end."

"They lie about their ages. I am not to blame for that. They volunteered to come, no one forced them."

"Magdalena tells me you helped her. It is hard to believe you have a compassionate side Yuri."

"Do not tell anyone. I will lose my reputation." He grimaced in pain.

"Perhaps you are not the brutal beast you pretend to be. What is wrong with you? You killed one of these women, yet were kind to Magdalena. Why are you in this business?"

Yuri became defensive.

"I did not kill that woman. She broke away when I whipped her, fell, and hit her head on a sharp rock. I shot a dead woman. I make a lot of money. Go away. I am in pain. You shot me twice you bastard."

Yuri lay back and closed his eyes.

Alex called to the doctor, "Check him, he passed out."

Sabir answered, "Best he is unconscious, the pain is excruciating, and he has lost a lot of blood. If he isn't taken to a hospital soon; he won't make it."

The sound of approaching helicopters filled the cave. One of the guards went outside to get everything ready for the flight to Cairo.

The radio cracked to life. A soldier called to ascertain the number of weapons in the cave said they would stand guard until the army took charge. They unbound the women prisoners, gave them galabeyas and water.

"Keep the women here until the military arrives to drive them back to Cairo." One of Sabir's men shouted. "There they will be processed and sent back to their home countries."

Two soldiers helped Hassan and Yuri into the first helicopter. Sabir left one of his men in charge, and joined them along with an armed soldier to guard Yuri.

Alex got into the second helicopter with Magdalena, Dr. Ismail, and the wounded Russian. Two armed soldiers came along to guard the Russian. Both helicopters took off for Cairo.

Alex looked over to Magdalena, "I am here to help return you and the others to your homes. Yuri told me of your condition. I will have you examined at the hospital in Cairo."

Alex smoothed the hair out of her eyes and whispered to her in a soft voice. "I will personally return you to your family. I hate to see a lovely woman abused."

Magdalena smiled at him and answered in perfect English. "Thank you. Yuri never hurt me. He protected me from the other men. He saved me. He could have raped me and he did not. I even offered myself to him to show my gratitude; he only hugged me, held me close, and told me he respected me. He was sending me to Moscow with a friend of his who would care for me. I know he will help you; stop threatening him."

"I hope you are right. We need his help."

"You speak English quite well."

"I was a student in London and visiting a friend in Romania and we applied for these jobs. It sounded too good to be true, but we had just finished college and were about to go job hunting in a week. When my family learned I was pregnant, they wanted nothing to do with me. I told them a man raped me but it did not matter. They said I was a disgrace to them. I cannot go home."

Alex touched by the young woman's story remembered losing his unborn child when his wife decided to have an abortion.

"You can stay with me until the authorities sort things out. You are too lovely to have suffered so much."

Magdalena smiled for the first time since her capture.

"You are too kind. I could not impose myself on you after all you have done. What would your wife say?"

"I'm not married. My wife died last year."

"I am very sorry." A look of concern flashed across her face blocking her smile like a passing cloud hiding the sun. It was not long before it reemerged. "You are Scottish yes? I recognize the accent."

"Yes I am"

In the first helicopter Hassan sat in pain and muttered, "I need to go to El-Arish; Emunishere is alone." His father answered, "I have already called the hotel. Mohamed is helping Emunishere pack and she and Mohamed are flying to Cairo to meet us at hospital. She will be there when we arrive. Lay back and try to rest; you are in no condition to do anything but sit quietly. I will ask Emunishere to move in with your mother and me."

Chapter 17

Jameel and Fatinah arrived in Cairo and went straight to his villa in the Heliopolis section of the city, a short ride from the airport. A tall decorative iron fence surrounded the property with a gate that opened onto a long drive leading to the house. Two columns rising three stories supported a domed portico marking the front entrance. The colonial style villa harkened back to the reign of King Faruck surrounded by towering trees, flowering scrubs, and tall palms.

As the car approached, Fatinah remarked, "It is majestic."

"The house has been in my family for generations. My parents gave it to me when I married. My father is a retired bank president; he and my mother live in the penthouse of a twelve-story building located near here that they own."

Jameel pointed to a black Mercedes next to one of the four garages. "That is their car over there. I told them we were coming and they can hardly wait to meet you. Best we not tell them how we met. They would never understand." He smiled at her.

"That will always be our secret. It was an adventure. I am so glad Yuri sold me to you. My future could have been quite different. My father did not approve of my relationship with Yuri or any other man I ever dated; Yuri became angry when I told him I would not marry without Father's approval. At the time, I thought he was being overly protective; it turned out he was right."

"What would he think of me?" asked Jameel.

"It does not matter, that is all in the past. For the first time in my life, I feel totally free and happy." Fatinah paused, "I love you Jameel."

"You were dazzling the first time I saw you."

"I was naked with my arms tied above my head, blindfolded, and gagged."

"To me you were the most alluring woman I had ever met."

As the couple walked up the stairs to the front door, a man in his mid sixties along with a woman in her early fifties greeted them. His mother was wearing an intricately embroidered galabeya with a matching hijab. His father wore a dishadasha and an Arabian jubba. Fatinah could not help but notice he was almost as tall as Jameel.

"Jameel, your mother, and I are glad you are happy. Please introduce us to this lovely woman standing next to you."

"This charming woman is the love of my life. Her name was Cassandra Cavendish. Her father is an English Lord. I have given her an Arabic name, Fatinah."

"Fatinah, this is my father, Yusuf."

"Come, I will have your bags brought in. Jameel seems quite enchanted with you. We are anxious to learn more about how you the two of you met."

Jameel's parents acted as though they were still living there and that they had come as welcome guests.

Yusuf stepped forward and kissed her on both cheeks. "Welcome to the family. Where did you meet my son?"

"We were introduced by a mutual friend of ours." She turned to Jameel and winked. "It was love at first sight. I know how much you love your son and promise to make him happy."

"From what he has told us already, I am sure you will."

"This is Aliah, my wife of twenty-eight years. Jameel tells me that you sing. My wife plays the piano. Perhaps this evening you and Aliah will entertain us."

"I would love to sing."

Aliah had dark brown hair, a little taller than Fatinah, with dark brown eyes and a cheery smile. She hugged Fatinah and there were tears in her eyes. "I am glad to see my son so happy; he found a woman he loves. We have planned a delicious meal for you. It will be ready in an hour."

"Please excuse us, it has been a long day and we would like to freshen up. We will get settled and be down for dinner in an hour."

"Of course, we understand, his mother said. "Fatinah, there are fresh linens in the bathroom and I took the liberty of laying out something for you to wear."

"Thank you, you are very kind."

Not wanting to raise his parent's expectations, Jameel told them of their plans.

"Saturday evening we leave for Alexandria and sail on *El Jumanah* early Sunday morning for a two-week holiday. I will stop at the hospital Saturday afternoon and let them know that I am still on vacation."

Before going upstairs, Jameel gave Fatinah a brief tour of the house. "I want to show you my home. Today it feels different. The minute I walked in the door with you, the house came alive. I never was comfortable here with my first wife Zahrah. You have made all the difference in my life. If my parents were not here, we would not do anything but make love tonight."

The house was bright with full-length windows in the back overlooking a garden with a fountain.

The ornate décor and furnishings dazzled Fatinah. Original oils by well-known Arab artists and French tapestries adorned the walls.

"It is so beautiful. How did your parents come to give it up?"

"My mother has trouble with her legs and Dad is not getting any younger. Even with a full staff, there is a lot to do. They are very happy where they are now. Besides, they can come back whenever they wish. I spend most of my time at the hospital or on my boat. Come, you must be tired."

Jameel escorted her upstairs to his master suite. He removed her hijab and abaya to reveal a gorgeous light blue silk dress with long sleeves and a high neck. Like a butterfly emerging from its cocoon, she stood ready to try her new wings.

"In our home, unless we have business guests, you need not be covered."

The entry room was two stories tall with brass lanterns hanging from long chains filling the room with light. The floor was marble and on the sidewalls were mosaic tiles with graceful Arabic calligraphy as decoration in shades of blue. A large inlaid mother of pearl table held a huge arrangement of fresh flowers and their perfume filled the room. The living room was huge, ten by twelve meters. The outside wall of the room was floor to ceiling windows each draped in gold brocade drawn back to reveal sheer white curtains that covered the windowpanes. An oriental silk carpet covered the center of the marble floor. Black lacquer sofas, each large enough for four people, faced each other in the center of the room. The sofas were upholstered in cream color silk brocade. Behind each sofa stood a console table elegantly carved with thin curved gold legs, the tops decorated with intricate mother of pearl inlay. Matching end tables sat next to each sofa supporting elegant ceramic lamps with silk shades. Between the two sofas, was a large coffee table with a design of palm trees and feluccas going down the river Nile. Along the opposite wall were two large mosaic chairs with inlaid designs. Two large Syrian style chairs with inlaid shells and interlace wood Arabesque sat in one corner of the room. A small writing desk with a matching chair placed near the windows caught Fatinah's eye.

The dining room was large with a carved walnut table with a mother of pearl scroll design on in the top in the middle surrounded by ten matching chairs adorned with in laid mother of pearl backs and off white silk brocade seats. A massive glass front, walnut cabinet filled with antique silver pieces stood on one side of the room and on the other side a larger glass front cabinet held a china service for twelve of ornate Egyptian porcelain and sterling silver hollowware goblets with gold linings. Jameel showed her his study that was in stark contrast with the rest of the house. It had an intricate inlaid wood floor with a dark blue carpet in the center. His desk was black lacquer and chrome with a computer and two flat screen monitors. A fax machine and laser printer were on separate black lacquer tables. A humidor, lighter, and cigar cutter sat next to a large alabaster ashtray near the computer. It reminded Fatinah of her father's study in Britain. The chairs were ultra modern in black leather and chrome. The wall on one side of the room was floor to ceiling bookshelves. The other walls held paintings or prints of paintings by Baker Masad and Ahmad Azzrelbaidi. The wall his desk faced held six large paintings of horses by Saleh Almasri and Sadeq Ja'Far.

There was a music room next to his study. It had a large full size concert grand piano in black lacquer and several settees with rich brocade sat facing the piano. The walls held abstract art by many artists.

"Your home is magnificent. I feel like I am in a palace."

"Come, I will show you the master suite before we have dinner."

The master bedroom held a king-size bed in white lacquer with mother of pearl inlay and two large chests of drawers. It had a luxurious white silk duvet with gold embroidery and matching pillows. A large mirror with an ornate gilded frame leaned against one wall. Abstract modern paintings hung from the pale yellow walls in gilded frames. There was a balcony entered through French doors from the bedroom that overlooked the backyard and patio. A tall sheesha with a blue glass base sat next to a chair at one end of the patio and another matching chair next to it with a small round table in front of the chairs. The back yard was a maze of color with flowering trees and plants. A large fountain sat in the middle of a manicured lawn. On the patio below was a set of white wicker furniture with thick cushions in a colorful floral pattern.

The aroma of cumin, thyme, coriander, onions and other spices from dinner cooking drifted throughout the house.

"Your parents are very nice. Your mother had tears in her eyes. They are both glad to see you so untroubled."

"Yes, they are. We must not disappoint them."

Jameel had come to blame himself for the failure of his first marriage. Taking responsibility was the only way he could deal with it though in his heart he knew that she loved another from the first day.

"My mother is a fine cook. She probably spent all day preparing the meal with the servants. She is also a very fine pianist. I did not have time to show you, but there is an unpretentious wood paneled room the other side of my study with a deep blue Egyptian carpet and comfortable dark brown leather furniture. It is less formal than the rest of the house. It has a large LCD 1080 television; an exceptional sound system fills the room with music. I have a very large music collection and sometimes read in that room. There are three more bedrooms each with their own bathroom and in the morning, I will show you the kitchen. Now it is time for dinner. We do not want to be late."

They came downstairs to the dining room, the table held large platters of food and elegant blue silk and gold placemats. His mother had prepared a roast filet of beef, seasoned chicken with currants, almonds and vermicelli, along with numerous vegetable side dishes, Moloukhiya soup, lamb sausages rolled in pistachios, and a fresh garden salad.

The porcelain china was white with a black and gold border. Crystal goblets sat at each of the four place settings and the flatware was sterling silver in an intricate design. Porcelain tiles protected the wood from the heat of the many serving platters. An array of crystal pitchers with various juices sat in the middle of the table along with several bottles of mineral water. The kitchen staff appeared out of nowhere, served every one, and then vanished as though they had never been in the room. On one wall of the dining room high glaze porcelain tiles with an abstract calligraphy in a design in shades of blue, white, and gold were mounted. A large vase with artificial floral flowers sat at one end of the table. Directly above, suspended from the ceiling, hung a huge, multi-tiered crystal chandelier that gave off a brilliant glow filling every corner of the room with light.

They sat down to dinner and Yusuf asked Fatinah, "Are you related to Robert Cavendish, the English Lord who stood up against the Prime Minister over the war in Iraq?"

"My father is a very opinionated man. Hundreds of lives would have been saved if the PM had listened to him."

"I admire his courage. Britain would have done well to listen to your father. It would be nice to meet him someday."

"I was very proud of him. I am sure he would like to meet you also."

Jameel whispered to Fatinah, "If you do not like the Moloukhiya soup, it is okay. It is an acquired taste."

Fatinah responded, "I have heard of a green soup famous in Egypt. Is this that soup?"

"Yes it is."

"Will your mother mind if I don't eat it?"

"No, she will understand. Everything else is delicious. I eat it, but do not like it." Jameel smiled.

They finished eating and Fatinah turned to Aliah, "Jameel said you prepared this meal. I wish I could learn to cook a meal such as this. Would you teach me?"

Aliah was clearly delighted to have the opportunity to teach her son's new bride knowing he would get what he liked most.

"I will give you his favorite recipes. Teaching you to prepare them would be so much fun. Jameel has a wonderful kitchen staff but now I would like to hear you sing."

They walked into the music room and Aliah sat at the grand piano.

"Do you know any of Andrew Lloyd Weber's music?"

"I know them all."

"*Wishing you were somehow here again*, from Phantom of the Opera and *Memory* from *Cats*, are two of my favorite songs."

Aliah began to play and Fatinah sang both songs; they filled the house with music and Jameel and his father sat on one of the settees and listened.

"Please sing another one," Jameel pleaded.

"How about *Love Changes Everything*? It's another song by Andrew Lloyd Weber?"

"That is one of my favorites."

Fatinah sang and as usual, it brought tears to her eyes.

"I always get emotional when I sing that particular song."

Jameel put his arms around her and held her close. He looked into her face wiping away the tears with his finger. "I love you so much."

Yusuf walked over to them, "I am so glad you found each other. We never should have tried to plan your life. Fatinah, you are the daughter we always wanted."

Fatinah loved her father but she was always closer to her mother. Her death had left a void in her life. So much had happened since her passing. Moments lost and left unshared between a mother and daughter. How she wanted to tell her about Jameel and his family.

"Thank you. I lost my mother to cancer years ago, but now I have found another." Both women embraced.

"Yusuf, these young people do not need us staying any longer. They want to be alone."

Turning to her son she said, "Your father and I will drive to Alexandria and see you off on your honeymoon Sunday."

Yusuf pulled his son aside, "Someday you will have to tell me how you really met this woman. I sense there is more of a story than an introduction by a mutual friend." His father winked knowingly.

"Someday Father, I may tell you. We will see you Sunday morning."

No sooner had his parents had left, Jameel and Fatinah went upstairs, embraced, and made love until they were so exhausted; they fell asleep in each other's arms.

Chapter 18

Saturday morning Jameel drove to hospital with Fatinah to let them know he would be gone for two more weeks. When they arrived, he escorted her to his office.

"I want to introduce you to my staff and before we leave I want you to meet Dr. Sabir Gaafar and tell him about Yuri."

No sooner had they come through the office door, Jameel's secretary Nawar rushed to him.

"I am so glad you are here." Nawar said quickly, almost out of breath. "There is an emergency. Two helicopters are arriving with four patients in forty-five minutes. Two of them are in need of immediate medical attention as soon as they land. Both men have been shot with high caliber bullets and need blood transfusions."

"No other doctor is available?" He asked in an irritated tone of voice.

Newar continued, "Dr. Gaafar requested you personally. He is on the helicopter with his son who is one of the wounded men. He requested that you treat him."

Jameel answered her, "Give me the contact number for Dr. Gaafar. The reason I am here today is to introduce you to my wife, Fatinah and to let him know that we were going to leave on our honeymoon tomorrow and will be gone for the next two weeks."

"I did not know you were married." She turned to Fatinah and in English with a heavy accent said, "You are a lovely bride."

Jameel translated for Fatinah everything Newar had told him, "Fatinah, I have an emergency. Please wait for me in my office. Newar will get you something if you are hungry or want something to eat. Dr. Gaafar, the man I wanted you to meet, is flying in with his injured son for emergency surgery for gunshot wounds. He requested that I personally treat him."

"It sounds serious."

"Wounds from large caliber bullets are always serious. I should be finished in two or three hours after they arrive. I promise, as soon as I am done here we will go back to the house, pack the car and leave for Alexandria to board my yacht in the morning as planned."

"You are needed. I understand."

He kissed her on the cheek, whispered he loved her, and told his secretary, "Please bring Fatinah some tea."

Jameel contacted Dr. Gaafar on the radio. "Sabir, this is Jameel, what is the extent of the injuries to Hassan?"

"Jameel, praise Allah, I was afraid I would not be able to find you."

"You are lucky I had stopped by the hospital to notify you that I will be gone for the next two weeks when Newar told me what had happened."

"He has lost a lot of blood but fortunately neither bullet seems to have damaged his vital organs. There is a lot of damage, especially around the exit wounds, as you would expect from high caliber rounds. I have stopped the bleeding but he will need an immediate blood transfusion once we land. The hospital will have his blood type on record. Prepare at least two units and have a third ready if necessary."

"Sabir, I will be ready as soon as you arrive in operating room seven. I was told there were other patients."

"Another man was shot twice; he will be under my care. He is a Russian Jew that was caught trafficking women."

"What is his name?"

"His name is Yuri Berezovsky."

"I know that man. I operated on him a few weeks ago for an emergency appendectomy. I was going to call you today and inform that I recently learned that he is involved in human trafficking."

Jameel was beginning to understand the risk he was taking by exposing Yuri. His involvement would certainly raise suspicion and at the very least launch an internal investigation by the hospital.

"We should talk once we know my son is out of danger. You would think being a doctor would make this easier. I am always nervous when it comes to members of my own family. You have a reputation for being the best at treating gun-shot wounds."

"I will take the best care of your son. Blood for both men's transfusions will be ready. Yuri Berezovsky's blood type is still on file."

Jameel immediately went to the pre-op and scrubbed, called up files for blood types, and assembled his surgical staff including a surgical nurse named Helen recommended by Dr. Gaafar. He briefed the team on Hassan's condition and ordered two units of blood for each man and a third as a precautionary measure if needed. When they arrived, Jameel had them take Hassan to operating room seven, and Yuri to operating room eight next-door. Dr. Gaafar scrubbed and checked his patient.

"This man is very weak, begin with two units of blood, and call for a third unit immediately. The shoulder wound is minor, but the leg wound is problematic. That bullet caused some major damage."

Jameel cleaned Hassan's shoulder wound and ordered one unit of blood immediately. "The wound is dirty, a lot of particles of rock dust; it has the potential for getting infected. Shot must have ricocheted off something to cause the damage I am seeing."

Sabir and Jameel continued to operate on their patients and within two hours, both men were wheeled into a recovery room side by side. The military guard from the flight stood watch at the door to ensure that Yuri had no chance of escape.

The two surgeons scrubbed clean and went to Sabir's office to discuss Yuri before joining the women waiting in Jameel's office.

Fatinah was sitting in Jameel's office. She wore a black abaya with ornate turquoise and sequin embroidery and a hijab. The two women were busy talking when a knock came at the door.

Nawar opened the door. The desk nurse was with a well-dressed, young woman.

"I hate to disturb you, but this is Emunishere Bishop. She is the fiancée of Hassan; Dr. Jameel is operating on him. I told her she could wait in his office rather than in the waiting room."

"Certainly, thank you. Please come in, this is Fatinah, Dr. Jameel's wife. They were leaving on their honeymoon when the call came. Hassan is still in surgery and will go to the recovery area as soon as the doctor is finished."

"How is he?" Emunishere asked in a concerned voice with tears in her eyes.

"I do not know; he received some medical attention before flying here. Jameel is an excellent surgeon; he is in the best hands. Can I get you some tea or coffee? I was just bringing tea for Fatinah." Nawar answered in a reassuring voice.

"Yes, that would be nice, thank you."

Nawar left the two women alone.

"You look American, but speak Arabic and have an Arabic name?" Fatinah asked.

"Yes, I am American, my mother was Egyptian. You are English?" Emunishere asked.

"Jameel and I were married yesterday and were leaving on our honeymoon this afternoon when he learned about your fiancée."

"Fatinah isn't an English name. Is your family from the Middle East?"

"No, when I married Jameel, he gave me an Arabic name. My given name is Cassandra, Cassandra Cavendish."

Emunishere's expression changed, "I know your father."

"How could you know my father?"

"I was the one who answered the phone the day you called to tell him you were married. He thought you were kidnapped and was looking for you in El-Arish."

Emunishere could not conceal her anger. Hassan and Alex MacKay had risked their lives to rescue a woman who was obviously not in danger. Memories of what she felt at the loss her husband knowing she would never see him alive again gave her a unique perspective of what this woman's father had experienced when he knew his only daughter was missing. Imagining the worst, only to get a phone call, telling him that she had run off with a man he had never met halfway around the world.

Emunishere Wanted tell her what she thought of her and the consequences of what she perceived as a callous disregard for her father and others, but decided to hold her tongue.

Sensing Emunishere's hostility, Fatinah decided to make small talk rather than provide a detailed explanation of what had really happened.

"It is a small world," she remarked. "My father never thought any man would be good enough for me. I met Jameel, fell in love, and we were married in less than two weeks. I plan to introduce him to my father while we are in England on our honeymoon."

"Have you known Jameel long? Your father said he had never heard you mention an Egyptian doctor."

"We only met a short time ago under unusual circumstances and fell in love. He is an extraordinary man. I have never met anyone like him. I know my father will approve."

Emunishere was confused and decided to assuage her curiosity to learn what really happened.

"Your father said a man named Yuri; I cannot think of his last name, kidnapped you."

"It is a very long story about Yuri Berezovsky. He is a person from my past who enabled me to meet Jameel. How long have you known Hassan?"

"I have only known Hassan for nine days. Traveling alone, I booked a room at his hotel not knowing what would happen. When inquiring at the desk about seeing the sites he cautioned me about the dangers of going out unescorted. Sensing my dilemma, he gallantly offered to show me around. As my attraction grew, so did my desire and I found myself wishing he would be less of a gentleman.

When a man on the beach attacked me, Hassan was there to help and comfort me."

"Did they find the person that attacked you? How did you escape?"

"I took self-defense classes for four months after my late husband was killed at the hands of a carjacker. Using my training I instinctively went on the attack crippling his right knee and breaking his nose. The outcome might have been very different if he had known I was trained in self-defense. The element of surprise gave me the advantage.

With the help of Hassan and the authorities using my description of the attacker, he was identified as your friend Yuri Berezovsky."

Fatinah quickly distanced herself from Yuri without divulging the full truth.

"Yuri is not a friend."

"How was your fiancée shot? Is he in the military?"

"Not any more. He was in the military, but now owns and operates several hotels with his brother Rafiq. His father, Sabir is a surgeon at this hospital. Hassan's wife and son died in an automobile accident a year ago. Since then he has had great difficulty getting back to a normal life; he was helping his father who leads a group that is trying to stop the trafficking of women through Egypt into Israel. While trying to rescue several of these women, including you, Hassan was shot by one of Yuri's men."

Fatinah did not know what to say. She could no longer bear to look Emunishere in the eyes. With hands folded in her lap, she looked downward and spoke softly.

"I am so very sorry, for everything. Unlike you, I was not lucky enough to escape. Yuri pretended to be in love with me while he was planning to sell me to the highest bidder."

Emunishere looked on with compassion as Fatinah told her story.

"Once we were out to sea he told me of his plan. Yuri had taught me well in the ways of making love and pleasuring a man. In a moment, I went from lover to sex slave, bound to a bed and gagged. He later transferred me to another boat owned by the man I now love. I've come to forgive him for the humiliation and pain he caused me, but will never forgive Yuri for betraying me."

Emunishere reached out and held her hands.

"Self defense training would have helped. I might look into that myself, but I do not think Jameel would approve of my going to a class."

"Why not?"

"He is very protective of me. In addition, this is Egypt. Married women do not take martial arts classes."

"Tell me more about Hassan."

"He escorted me everywhere and I fell in love; he asked me to marry him and bought me an engagement ring just before this happened. We plan to marry once he recovers from his wounds."

Nawar returned to the office carrying a tray with sandwiches and two cups of Egyptian green mint tea. The two women talked together for the next couple of hours.

Anxious for word on Hassan's condition, Emunishere leapt to her feet at the site of Dr. Gaafar and Jameel entering the office.

"Is he going to be all right?" Emunishere asked.

"He lost a lot of blood but the operation was a success. I expect him to make a full recovery."

Emunishere felt a rush of relief at the news.

Jameel introduced Fatinah to Dr. Gaafar, "This is my wife, Fatinah."

"I am very pleased to meet you. Jameel has told me everything," winking at her with a wry smile. "I do not approve of what he did, but I am glad he accepted Yuri's offer. You are a very enchanting and fortunate woman."

Fatinah smiled, "What happened to Yuri?"

"Yuri's recovery will be long and painful. His leg muscles were badly damaged and he will need extensive rehabilitation before he has full use of his limb. Luckily, we did not have to remove it," Dr. Gaafar told her.

"It cannot be too painful or too long," Emunishere commented.

"Yuri is a strange man; he makes love to a woman and then kidnaps her and sells her into slavery because she displeases him. My father warned me about him, but I was having too much fun. Will the hospital fire Jameel because of what he did?" asked Fatinah.

"There will be an inquiry by the board but I have decided to recommend they keep him on and allow him to practice. He promised me never to be tempted again. I am confident that as head surgeon they will honor my recommendation. Before you and Jameel leave, I want you to meet my son, Hassan."

"Hassan's fiancée is a remarkable woman. We've been getting to know each other," Emunishere told Dr. Gaafar.

"Did she tell you she is a talented artist? When you and Jameel return from your honeymoon, we will all have dinner. You and Emunishere both have someone in common, Yuri. Come, Hassan should be in his room by now."

Fatinah looked at Jameel, "I want to visit Yuri."

"Emunishere, I will escort you to Hassan's room." Sabir offered her his arm.

"Fatinah and I are visiting Yuri first, and will join you shortly."

Jameel and Fatinah went to the recovery room and walked over to Yuri who was just coming out of the anesthesia.

Yuri looked up and saw Fatinah, "Cassandra, what are you doing here? I heard you married." His voice was gravely and he slurred some of his words.

"Cassandra is married; she is my wife," Jameel interrupted.

Fatinah felt pity more than sympathy for the broken man lying on the bed, his leg and shoulder bandaged. Yuri had gotten what he deserved and would no longer be a threat left to prey on unsuspecting women. Fatinah felt vindicated.

"Yuri, you look terrible. I met the woman that broke your nose. I do not like the way you turned me into a commodity, but if you had not kidnapped me and sold me to Jameel, I would never have met him. Thank you. I have never been so happy."

"I always liked you Cassandra. If your father had not objected to me so strongly, I would have asked you to marry me. Jameel is a kind man; he would never hurt you. Not at any time would I have sold you to a man who was brutal in nature. You are one of very few women with whom I had any emotional feelings."

Cassandra looked at Yuri and kissed him on the forehead. "Good luck Yuri and thank you for introducing us."

"I will make sure you are taken care of Yuri. You are responsible for me being the most jubilant man in the world." Jameel added.

"Maybe you could put in a good word for me. I think they are going to lock me away forever."

"Hopefully someone will put in a good word for me. You may have been a seller, but I was the buyer. We both knew what we were doing was wrong. Allah has given us both another day. It is up to us to decide what we will do with it. I will see what I can do."

Fatinah and Jameel left and went to see Hassan.

When they entered Hassan's room, Emunishere was sitting on the bed next to him in tears. An agitated Rafiq was scolding his brother.

"Hassan, I told you not to get involved. Now look at you. I need you to help with the hotels. You have always had the better feel for business than me."

"Rafiq, as soon as I recover and am able I will move my office back to Cairo. I am sorry that I have not been more help."

"Yes, but now you are getting married; I suppose you want another couple of weeks for a honeymoon?"

"Now that you mention it, Rafiq, yes, two more weeks would be good."

"Brother, I love you, but you can be a problem," he laughed and winked at their father who was standing near the window.

"Rafiq, you once told me that I had to move on with my life. I never thought I could be content again until I met Emunishere. I have asked her to marry me, and she said yes."

"Congratulations." Jameel interrupted as he led Fatinah into Hassan's room.

"Hassan, how are you feeling? It appears you are already getting back to normal."

"Rafiq and I were just having a discussion about the business."

"I would like you to meet my wife, Fatinah. If it had not been for Yuri, we never would have met. We were just checking on him. I understand he rescued a pregnant woman from the slavers. It is a strange world that has brought us all together. Yuri is not as bad a man as he pretends to be. Underneath his bluster, there is a descent man."

Hassan was starting to feel tired but wanted to respond to Jameel.

"I met the woman Yuri allegedly rescued, Magdalena, at the cave. She was upset that Alex shot Yuri. Despite his act of kindness, he will have to face a court for what he did.

On a brighter note, you and Fatinah will be back in time for our wedding?"

"We will plan on it." Jameel replied. "If you like, you and Emunishere are welcome to spend your honeymoon aboard my yacht. I have an excellent crew and it is perfect get-away. Fatinah and I are leaving in the morning to cruise the Mediterranean."

"We may take you up on that offer. Fatinah, you and Jameel make a perfect couple. May you always be this much in love. *Fi Amanullah* (May Allah watch over you)."

Hassan was starting to nod off, exhausted from his ordeal.

Jameel motioned to the others that it was time to leave so that Hassan could get some rest.

"Thank you. We must get together when we return. It seems we have a lot in common."

Hassan had fallen asleep and did not reply.

Quietly they left the room closing the door behind them.

Standing in the hall, Rafiq spoke to Jameel. "I do not understand. You and my brother meet these glamorous, talented, foreign women, and in less than two weeks marry or plan to marry them. I will have to pay more attention to foreign women traveling alone. I hope someday I will be as fortunate as my older brother and his doctor."

Jameel smiled at him, "You are only twenty-four. You have plenty of time to find the perfect wife. Hassan and I are very fortunate men."

Jameel and Fatinah said their good-byes and left for home.

Alex was waiting when Magdalena emerged from the examination room.

"Alex, I am so glad you are here."

"Magdalena, I talked with the doctor. He said that you and the baby are all right."

Magdalena smiled and placed her hand on her swollen belly.

"We are fortunate that Yuri picked me out of the group. I saw what they did to the other women."

"They were not so fortunate; Yuri took a big risk by protecting you from his associates. They could have killed him for what he did."

"What will become of me now? I have no money and my identity papers were burned."

"All your hospital expenses are paid and new identity papers are in progress. Would you consider immigrating to Scotland? You are welcome to stay there with me in my castle until you get back on your feet and decide what you want to do."

"You have a castle?"

"Yes, I do, a very ancient one."

"I'd love to if it is not too much trouble."

"Then it is settled. I have arranged for you to stay with Dr. Gaafar and his wife for a couple of weeks while your paperwork is processed. That will give me enough time to complete my assignment and track down the men who kidnapped you and the other women. As early as tomorrow, I will have to leave. Wait for me to return; I do not want to lose you."

"I have nowhere to go. My parents passed away and my uncle is angry that I was raped and pregnant. He threw me out of the house. I applied for that job out of desperation. I will wait for you for as long as it takes." She began to cry.

Alex put his arm around her and kissed her on the cheek. "I was hoping you would say that. Perhaps, we may have a future together."

"I would like that."

"May I visit Yuri before I leave the hospital? I want to thank him for what he did for me."

"I will take you to see him. The doctor said you are well enough to leave the hospital. Do you have any clothes?"

"Only what I am wearing."

"After we see Yuri, I will take you out to pick up a few things you will need before dropping you at Dr. Gaafar's home. His wife is expecting you."

"If it is permitted, may Yuri and I speak in private?"

Alex assured her, "It will be arranged. They have moved him to a secure detention area of the hospital. I will take you to see him."

Alex spoke with the guard and explained that the young women wanted to be left alone with Yuri.

"You have ten minutes," he told her. "No more."

"I understand."

The two men left them alone and closed the door.

Yuri was still woozy from the anesthetic when Magdalena arrived.

"Magdalena, it is good to see you. I wish I could get up and greet you, but I am not able."

Yuri spoke in a drug-induced voice.

Magdalena stood next to the bed and held his hand.

"I wanted to thank you again; I owe you my life. You could have allowed them to rape and beat me like the others, but you chose to risk you own life and protect my baby and me. I will never forget your kindness. Jameel and Alex promised me that they would try to get you off with a light sentence."

Magdalena was crying, when she bent over Yuri and kissed him on the lips.

"If they tell me where they are taking you, I will try to visit you when my baby is born."

"I look forward to that. Alex said he would take you to Scotland with him. He seems like honest man even though he shot me twice."

"Good-bye Yuri. I will pray for you."

"Good-bye Magdalena, you are the only good thing that has happened to me recently. If it was possible, I would take care of you myself."

Magdalena left his room in tears and Alex held her in his arms.

"Will he be in jail for a long time?"

"The more he tells us, the shorter his sentence."

"I know he will cooperate."

"I may have to leave tonight Magdalena. I have things to do this afternoon; it may be as early as a seven o'clock flight for Moscow. Trust me, I will return and take you to Scotland. My boss, Henry Ewing, works for the government, and is seeing that your paperwork is processed quickly. A friend, Lord Cavendish will be contacting you at Dr. Gaafar's home. He is going to expedite your visa to Scotland. In two weeks when I return you will be able to fly home with me."

"Please be careful Alex. I have only met you, but I trust you and want to know you better."

Alex kissed her and hugged her close to him.

"I will walk you to Dr. Gaafar's office. He will drive you to his home."

Alex went directly to Yuri's room after leaving Magdalena with Dr. Gaafar.

"Yuri, Magdalena is a compassionate woman. She and her baby are all right thanks to you."

"I am glad to hear that."

"We are taking you to a special location after you have recovered. No one will know where you are except some very good interrogators. You will tell them all you know."

"Fuck you. The Russian mob kills me or you kill me. I lose either way."

"What if we guarantee you a new life?"

"They will find me."

"We can be very persuasive. We know your orders come from either Moscow or Tel Aviv. Your friend, Aleksandr told us something of your operation and that you know everything. Might I remind you, you are still a whole man."

"*Mudak* (bastard). That is illegal."

Yuri strained against his restraints and wanted to hit Alex despite the pain in his shoulder.

"So is trafficking in women and contributing to the death of one of them. You have a choice. I can arrange for you to be out in as little as five to ten years or tell us nothing and become a dead man walking. You are just twenty five; I am offering you a life."

Yuri starred at the wall and did not answer. Back on the street, the mob would put out a hit on him believing that he had given them names. Alex was not his problem.

"Let me tell you what will happen next. Listed as an enemy combatant, you will be taken to a secure facility where freedom will never be an option, given three meals a day, no communication with anyone, and locked in a cell with no sunlight. Most commit suicide within six months. Make your choice. You have two hours to tell me what you know."

Yuri glared at Alex. "If I tell, how will I be protected?"

Alex continued to explain. "That is easily arranged. Officially, you will be dead. My government will issue a statement to the media that you died from your injuries shortly after being transported to hospital. You will serve your time at a facility the government of England sanctions for prisoners such as yourself. After five, maximum ten years or maybe less, a new identity awaits you."

What will it be? I am not known for my patience."

"Can I trust you?"

"Yuri, I am your only chance. I heard why you hate women. Magdalena told me what happened to you. My first wife almost destroyed me. I hated her. I hated myself. Not all women are like the one you met in Singapore. You were eighteen. You were angry, hurt, abandoned by your father. That did not give you an excuse to dedicate your life to brutalizing women. How many women have you killed?"

"I have never killed a woman. The woman I shot yesterday was already dead. She fell and hit her head. I had reached my breaking point. That American woman on the beach in El Arish broke my nose and got better of me. It has never happened before. Who would have suspected that appealing woman, wearing bathing suit, was martial arts expert? If I had known she was into martial arts, I would have been prepared. She would not have stood a chance. If my nose and groin had not hurt so badly, I might have beaten you in our fight. I am still recovering from an operation done in this same hospital by doctor Jameel. You are very strong and got better of me. On an equal footing, the fight may have ended differently." Yuri winked.

"The outcome would have been the same. I still would have shot you. You are lucky I have a good aim or it might have been your head or your heart with a hole in it. Did you really think you got lucky?"

"Cassandra's father convinced her I was not to be trusted. I was beginning to fall in love with her."

"You had a strange way of showing it."

"The Egyptian I do business with ripped me off. When the men I was working with discovered what I had been doing they threatened to send me back to Singapore to be jailed for life, and caned twenty-four times. I could not stand that again. Yes, I confess. I have raped, sodomized, and whipped women's bottoms, but never killed. Only reason she fell is that she pulled away while I was whipping her, ran, fell, and hit her head on a sharp pointed rock. It was accident; I may have contributed to her death, but I did not kill her."

"Raping, sodimizing, and whipping defenseless women hardly qualify you as innocent, but killing someone out of rage is something I understand. My ex wife died tragically as the result of an accident because of my anger. Tell me what you know. If I can get you free in five years or less, I will. Trust me."

Yuri was on the verge of a complete breakdown and was trying to hold back his emotions as his eyes filled with tears.

"Sounds like you and I have a lot in common. We have both caused the death of a person because of anger. We are the same."

Alex pulled back, revolted at the thought of being compared to the likes of Yuri.

"We are not the same. I do not kidnap and rape. I would never hurt a woman." His voice cracked as he thought of Catherine lying in a pool of blood next to the fireplace.

"Let me be clear, if I had it to do over we would be having a one sided conversation in the morgue. You are not my favorite person. The only reason I will try to help you is because of what you did for Magdalena. I will make the arrangements. I want names, telephone numbers and descriptions of everyone you met; is that clear?"

Yuri's voice quivered as he continued to explain. "I do not hurt pregnant women. I wanted to comfort her; I feel sorry that I threatened her before she told me of her condition. Later she offered herself to me out of gratitude. I could only hug and hold her close."

"Why did you single her out in the first place?"

"There is an easy explanation, a woman with red hair broke my nose; it was payback. If that woman had not broken my nose and kicked me in the groin, Magdalena would have suffered along with the rest. Those other men would not have cared if she were pregnant. They would not have told me of her condition. If the beating did not kill the baby, she would have been forced to have abortion as soon as she arrived in Tel Aviv."

"Interesting how things work out sometimes," Alex thought to himself.

"Yuri, you never cease to surprise me. I will be back shortly. I have to visit Hassan. You may remember you met him at the cave. He flew with you to Cairo in the same helicopter."

Alex went to Hassan's room.

Hassan was awake and sitting up refreshed from his recent nap. The two men greeted each other as brothers in arms.

"How are you? I knew you lost a lot of blood."

"I am going to be fine. The doctors are giving me antibiotics for a possible infection. Have you met my fiancée, Emunishere? We are going to be married in a couple of weeks; please come to the celebration of our marriage."

Alex turned to Emunishere. "I would love to come to your wedding; my assignment should be finished by then. You may not know it, but by breaking Yuri's nose, you saved Magdalena's life. Yuri was going to abuse her in revenge for you breaking his nose because she was a red head. When he found out she was pregnant, his alter personality took over. By telling them that he had bought her for himself, he was able to protect her from the others. They hated him but were afraid to confront him." Alex continued. "Right now, I must speak with Dr. Gaafar."

Alex walked to Sabir's office.

Sabir greeted him, "Come in Alex, what is happening with Berezovsky?"

"Berezovsky and I have come to an agreement. He is going to tell me what he knows. I do not like him, but I understand him. When I left, there were tears in his eyes. He has had a miserable life and finally reached his breaking point. I guess we all hit the wall at some time in our lives. Some of us manage to control it better. He actually saved that woman Magdalena from harm while putting his own life at risk. His Egyptian contact was not pleased that he kept the girl for himself. His Russian bosses would have had him shot if they found out. His compassion saved her life."

Sabir agreed. "I saw the disconsolate look in his eyes at the cave."

"If he tells me what I need to know; we can break the back of the organization. I know other groups will continue, but at least we will bring this group down. Please take care of Magdalena for me. I need her more than you could understand."

"I know something terrible happened to you in the past. Someday I would like to hear about it. Henry Ewing, my close friend, mentioned you were also at the breaking point at one time."

"Perhaps I will tell you, but not yet. I still have nightmares and cold sweats over what happened. I do not think I will ever forget what I did. Right now, my focus is on one thing. We can break this organization. I will interrogate Yuri before leaving tonight then move him to a secret holding area similar to the American's Guantanamo Bay. Unlike the Americans, we British do not disclose where our facility is located."

"Get back to me with the details. The information will help us track them down in Egypt."

"I will give it to you as soon as I get it myself. This sex slavery has to stop. Yuri mentioned he is angry with an Egyptian. Perhaps we can start here in Cairo. We need the public to be aware of how bad it has become. Leak a story to the media about what happened at the cave. The public needs to know that the governments of Israel and Russia chose to look the other way and are in denial despite strong evidence to the contrary. The world needs to know the atrocities that are being committed against these women and that Israel is one of the worst countries in the world for human trafficking and has done nothing to shut down the Russian mobs that run it."

"Be careful Alex. I would go with you, but my place is here in Egypt. My sons and soon to be daughter-in-law need me. May Allah watch over you. When you return, talk to me. I am willing to counsel you with what happened in your past; I am a good listener."

"I will keep that in mind. It depends on what Yuri tells me."

"Can you trust him?" Sabir asked.

"Yes. I think he will tell me all he knows. His accomplice, Aleksandr, already told us some of what we need to know. The Russians will think he has betrayed them. We have officially declared Berezovsky dead. It is in the newscast tonight that he died from his wounds. It will also be in this evening's paper."

"I hope he tells us what we need to know."

"He will or I promised him his voice will go up two octaves."

"MI 6 has agreed to give Berezovsky a new identity. You, one nurse, and I will be the only ones that know Yuri Berezovsky is still alive. He will become an arms dealer with a British passport."

"That suits him well. No one will ever suspect. What name should I use for the hospital records? Now that Yuri Berezovsky is dead, we will need to admit him as a British citizen with a gunshot wound he received during his capture."

"We have chosen the name Asad ibn Abi Fanan al Katib or Asad al Katib. With his dark hair and olive complexion, he will pass for an Arab. His identity will add two years to his age. This is for his protection. Yuri Berezovsky would not last a day once the Israeli government and Russian mobs discovered he had talked. They would hunt him down if they knew he was alive. Were you aware of his language skills?"

"He speaks flawless Arabic." Sabir acknowledged. "Most Russian speaking people speak Arabic with a terrible accent, and his English is very good."

Alex pulled out a manila folder stamped "CLASSIFIED" and began to read.

"His mother was a blue-eyed blonde from Romania. He was bi-lingual as a child speaking Russian and Romanian. He studied English in school and because his father was Jewish, he spoke Hebrew. In Singapore, his cellmate was Arab speaking. He speaks fluent Arabic and enough Greek to get by. If he is cooperative, MI 6 could give him a job working with us. He knows the sex trade and his language skills would be invaluable."

"The question is can he be trusted?"

"We will see how cooperative he is. I am going to his room when I leave your office. He should be fully out of the effects of the anesthesia by now."

Chapter 19

Alex walked into Yuri's room and found him asleep. He touched his arm to wake him. Instinctively Yuri sat up ready to defend himself.

"I had the nurse remove your restraints. Behave yourself and I will leave them off."

"Thank you for helping Magdalena. She told me everything you did for her." Alex said in a soft tone of voice.

"I do not abuse pregnant women."

"Yuri, we have gone to a lot of trouble for you. Officially, Yuri Berezovsky is dead. You died of your wounds. We have given you a new identity. You are now Asad ibn Abi Fanan al Katib or Asad al-Katib, a British citizen, born May 15, 1983."

"I aged two years? Why British and why an Arabic name?"

"I have connections through MI 6 and Lord Cavendish is helping me. We thought giving you an Arabic name would hide any of your Russian background. No one will suspect. You speak fluent and flawless Arabic according to Sabir, your surgeon. There are many Arabic speaking people living in London."

"Lord Cavendish has agreed to help me?" Yuri shook his head in disbelief. "Cavendish hates me."

"You are officially a British citizen. He knows nothing of your kidnapping Cassandra, and she promised not to tell him."

"What crime did I commit?"

"We are holding you on suspected arms smuggling."

"It sounds better than human trafficking."

"Now tell me everything you know. If you do not, we have ways to make you tell the truth. We can add something special to that drip in your arm. I must warn you, these drugs have been known to cause severe brain damage leading to delusions and paralysis in extreme cases. Your choice, Yuri, I mean Asad."

Asad took a deep breath before he spoke. "I tell you what I know."

"Begin with the Egyptian you were angry with in Cairo, who is he, what does he do, where can he be found?"

Asad began. "His name is Kahlil. He rents the organization I represent space for forty-eight hours when we have shipment. Other slave merchants rent from him as well."

"Why are you angry with him?"

"He cut our pay to twenty-five percent and five or more women each time we have a shipment. Kahlil chooses any five women, arranges an auction, and receives sixty percent of the profit from their sale. My organization is supposed to receive forty percent, but he said his costs have increased. When I purchased Magdalena, he was angry because he has a thing for redheads. It was his way of getting me to pay double. Kahlil knew I would have to personally make up the fifteen percent the mob lost on the transaction."

"How many other groups use his facility?"

"He has never said. Our group usually has a shipment of women twice each month."

"Where is this facility?"

"It is in a warehouse district in Heliopolis near Cairo International Airport."

"Give me the address. I will check this out and then decide what to do with you. If there is no Kahlil, we will find the information by using drugs."

"I do not lie. He has a shipment of women from another trafficker in four days."

"The guard will stay at your door. If this information is true, we will move you to a secure location for your safety and continue to interrogate you as soon as the doctor releases you. Try to escape; these men have orders to shoot you. This time, you will never walk again. I shot you in the arm to make you drop the gun and in the thigh to stop you from running; we did not want you dead. They have orders to permanently maim you, understood?"

"Yes."

Alex knocked on the door and the guards opened it for him. "I want this man guarded closely. If he tries to escape, shoot to maim him. If he cannot walk, he cannot escape. I do not want him killed. We need the information he has. No visitors are allowed except medical staff approved by Dr. Gaafar or myself."

Alex walked into Gaafar's office.

"I do not know if this information is correct or not. Yuri gave me the name of a man in Heliopolis that rents space to traffickers. His name is Kahlil."

"You must not refer to him as Yuri. Yuri is officially dead."

"Thank you for reminding me, a slip like that could get him killed."

Alex continued, "Here is Kahlil's address in Heliopolis. Asad said he deals with many traffickers. He also said a shipment is due in four days; we will lay a trap."

"I recognize this address and this name. It is in a warehouse area near the airport. Stay in town for a few days Alex. I have room at my house. Magdalena needs you. If this information is accurate, Asad will have proved himself."

"I have arranged for one of my best nurses, Helen, to care for him every day from eight in the morning until six in the evening five days a week. She works with the Cairo police to interrogate and eavesdrop on prisoners. Perhaps she can convince Asad to talk. The two other shift nurses have been here for some time, both are older women, only speak Arabic, and will only know his name is Asad al-Katib, a British citizen. There is a toilet in his room, and no need for him to leave unless he requires additional medical attention or tests. In a couple of days, he should be able to walk with the aid of a walker. The bullet caused some major damage to his muscle. He will walk with a pronounced limp for some time. The windows are barred and I have posted two guards at the door. He is secure here."

"Is Helen to know his true identity?"

"Helen is the only staff member other than me to know his true identity, the other staff, including the doctors will know him as Asad al-Katib."

"Helen has already been given all his information. She also knows the confidentiality that is required to shield his identity." Sabir cleared his throat. "We do not need some Israeli or Russian gunmen stalking him in the hospital."

"You are sure we can trust this nurse?"

"Helen has been with the Cairo police department working undercover for three years. She also speaks Russian fluently. Her father is Russian and Jewish; her mother is Egyptian and a Coptic Christian."

"Have her report daily to you on everything Asad says to her."

Alex thought a moment. "Put a listening device into his room. We will know everything that they say. Do not inform Helen the room is bugged."

"It will be done. Helen will be here in the morning, I will personally brief her."

"Sabir, I am going to stay in Cairo until we resolve this Kahlil warehouse situation. I plan to canvas the area around the warehouse today, and I will ask your men to maintain constant surveillance of the warehouse. If Asad's information is correct, in four days we could rescue a group of women from a different group of traffickers. Henry Ewing has spoken with the Egyptian authorities and my mission is sanctioned by both the British and Egyptian government."

Sabir continued. "Keep talking with Asad. We need to know his contacts in Moscow and Tel Aviv. Once we know who arranges the travel documents and makes the travel arrangements and where they are located we can bring about an official government response to stop this group."

"I will see Asad tomorrow afternoon."

Alex left Dr. Gaafar's office and drove to Heliopolis to join Magdalena at his home.

Chapter 20

Helen arrived at Asad's room at eight o'clock the next morning and the guards admitted her. He had not received his breakfast.

Helen was an attractive twenty-four year old woman, about 170 centimeters, medium build, buxom, long black hair pulled back in a ponytail, and green eyes. She had a soft caressing voice that was soothing to the ear, a perfect voice for a nurse. She was wearing a crisp white two-piece nurse's uniform.

Asad was in bed, a morphine drip attached to his arm. His wounded leg, and nose bandaged. There was bruising around his eyes from where they had to break his nose to set it properly. The shot to his arm was a flesh wound and no bandage was necessary. Attached to his good leg was a leather cuff that shackled him to the frame of the bed. A precautionary measure insisted upon by hospital security.

"Dobroy e utro, (good morning) Asad. *Kak vashi dela? (How are you?)*" I know your real identity. My name is Helen," She whispered. "I am the only nurse that has that information. I also know that you speak flawless Arabic. It will be best if you speak in Arabic and English, no Russian. With your new identity, speaking in Russian is dangerous. I will be shaving you and giving you a bath this morning after your breakfast arrives. In a couple of days, you will be able to do this for yourself."

Asad, smiled at her, "Dobroy e utro." He continued to speak quietly to her in Russian. "I am glad they sent a nurse that speaks Russian. The other shifts only speak Arabic. Helen is not an Arabic name, where were you born?"

"I am from Cairo, my mother is a Coptic Christian, and my father is Russian and Jewish. I do not go to church or synagogue. My English is not so good, but I understand."

"Not many people in Egypt speak Russian." Asad shifted to Arabic.

The guard opened the door and a nurse's aide delivered a breakfast tray. Helen had to help him with the food, his wounded arm was weak, and his good arm was strapped down with a morphine drip.

After finishing breakfast, she knocked on the door and the guard took the tray. Helen went into the bathroom and brought back a bowl of warm water and a towel, elevated his bed to a reclining position, wiped his face with a warm cloth, applied shaving cream to his three-day beard, and commenced to shave him.

"I do not understand why they did not shave you before this. You have a very heavy beard."

"Leave me with a mustache; it will give me a new look to go with my new identity."

Helen smiled at him. Despite his bandaged nose, and bruises around his eyes, Asad was a very handsome man. When she finished, she slid her hand gently across his face, "I shaved you close."

When she moved him to change his hospital gown, Asad winced in pain. She washed his body with warm soapy water, and noticed that he was aroused at her gentle touch.

"Sorry if I hurt you when I removed that gown; I will have an orderly help me change the bedding." She giggled, "You have a very hairy chest."

"Keeps me warm on cold winter nights in Moscow." Yuri could not suppress a snicker.

Helen laughed. "Could you lean forward so I can wash your back or do you want to wait until they remove the ankle cuff?"

"I will wait if you do not mind; moving my injured leg is painful."

Helen knocked on the door and the guards opened it. "Please let the orderly I requested enter when he arrives."

"How much longer will you be with him?"

"I need to change the bedding, his hospital gown, and take care of his personal hygiene. I should be finished in half an hour after the bed is changed."

The orderly arrived and the bedding was changed. Asad moaned in pain when they moved him to change the sheets. Helen helped him put on a clean hospital gown.

"Is there anything I can do for you?"

"You can promise to check back every hour. I need company." Asad smiled and changed to Russian. "*Ti takAya KrasTvaya.*"

After telling Helen how lovely she was, Helen combed his hair, washed his legs, and stared into his intense blue eyes.

"You have the most incredible blue eyes."

"I have been looking at your green eyes with flecks of gold in them; they are amazing." Asad asked her in a concerned tone of voice, "Are you afraid of me?"

"You are polite, which I did not expect, considering they told me you killed a woman, whipped other women into submission, and trafficked in women for the sex trade for several years . . . not exactly a great recommendation. You are heavily sedated with a morphine drip, what is there for me to fear given your present condition?"

"I did not kill anyone, nor am I extremely cruel wicked person. It was an accident; the woman ran from me, tripped, fell several meters off a mountain trail, hit her head on a rock, and died. I am guilty of all the other charges. My trafficking days are over. You may not believe this, but I was planning to quit the whole business." Asad changed to a concerned tone of voice, "When that woman died, I threw up. Helen, I will never hurt you. *DovEr' sya mne.*"

"Trust you. We will see. You do not fit the description of the man in the dossier I was given."

Asad reached for her with his injured arm and his manner was gentle and kind; he held her hand and raised it to his lips, kissed the back of her hand, squeezed it gently, and looked right into her eyes, "I am a gentleman with a lovely woman. DovEr' sya mne." He whispered to her again.

Helen smiled at him and squeezed his hand in return. "I must get to know you first. You do not seem the scoundrel they say you are." She smiled and cautioned him. "You must stop speaking Russian; someone may overhear you."

Helen lowered the bed and turned to leave.

Asad could tell she was concerned, more than frightened. Women always found him attractive. Helen was definitely his preferred nurse. He thought to himself, "I meet two drop-dead gorgeous women in as many days, get shot, and shackled to a bed and unable to pee by myself. Life is not fair."

Helen straightened her uniform and knocked on the door. "I will be back in an hour or so to check on Mr. al Katib." She turned to the guard after closing the door. "I will be bringing him his lunch and dinner today."

Helen left and Asad lay back on the bed deliberating about his future, "I do not want to die alone in a solitary cell never seeing the light of day again. Helen treats me like a human being even though she knows everything I have done to women recently." Unable to stay awake, he finally surrendered to the morphine and fell into a drug-induced, restless sleep.

Three hours later, Helen brought his lunch and woke him by gently stroking his arm. He was unable to feed himself and needed her assistance.

"You should be able to go to the bathroom with a helping hand once they remove the ankle cuff. I will bring a walker to your room to use over the weekend. With the aid of a nurse, you will be able to get to the bathroom, but do not attempt to do that on your own. Would you like a magazine or book to read? Television, radio, and telephones are not allowed in this section of the hospital."

"A newspaper in Russian would be nice and maybe a book to read. I read English quite well. Russian books are not popular in Egypt, and reading Arabic, except for street signs and numbers has proved difficult."

"What kind of book would you like?"

"Mysteries, adventure, winter sports, choose for me."

Helen smiled at him, and her lips brushed his cheek as she whispered in his ear. "I will be back shortly."

Asad held her hand in his and kissed it again.

"I look forward to your return. Because of my past, I do not deserve your accommodating demeanor. Thank you for being so amiable. A man named Alex MacKay is to see me shortly, and does not like me very much. If he tells you anything bad about me, do not believe what he says."

"I form my own opinion of my patients. See you later."

Alex was arriving at Asad's room as Helen was leaving with his empty lunch tray.

"You must be Helen. I am Alex MacKay, an agent with MI6 working with Dr. Sabir Gaafar. Did our prisoner he give you any trouble?"

"No sir, he is a wounded man and unable to do much of anything, including feed himself; they shackled his leg to the bed. What kind of trouble could he possibly cause? When will you be removing the cuff?"

"Be careful around him. Before I leave, I will remove the cuff. He is a cunning man, and may charm you into helping him escape."

"I will keep that in mind."

Helen hurried to her next patient and Alex entered the room.

"You have a very attractive nurse. I do not want to hear you have coerced her into helping you escape. If you do, I will see you have to stay in the hospital longer under the care of a large, ugly mail nurse who enjoys inflicting pain."

Asad articulated, "She treats me like human being. I am not a heartless unprincipled person."

"How did that woman die?"

Asad elaborated, "That woman died while running away from me; it was my fault she ran. I am used to being in control at all times. Her dying was never my intention; she was frightened. Whipping, spanking, and having sex with women is enjoyable for me, but I never had any woman die in my care before that incident. Women punished by me never had as much as a scratch, only marks from a whip or red bottom from spanking that faded in an hour or two. Believe me; I am no killer. When I spank women's bottoms with my hand, I find it arousing."

Alex reflected on his past as he answered, "The memory of that death, although unintentional, still haunts me. I cannot forget it."

"Alex, you must tell me someday. It is in your eyes; you are like me."

"I am nothing like you, a person died by mistake when rage took over. I know what drives you and I can say with certainty we are nothing alike."

"We will compare the death we caused to woman." Asad quipped. "It was woman you killed?"

Alex's voice cracked, "Yes, it was a woman. I still have nightmares and wake up screaming." Alex took a deep breath.

"The warehouse you mentioned checked out. Dr. Gaafar has heard of Kahlil and he is rumored to be very successful and quite wealthy. He loves expensive cars and lives well beyond the means of a man in the business of managing warehouses. We are keeping an eye on his operation and will have a little surprise in store if he has a shipment of women arriving."

"A new shipment of women will arrive at his warehouse." Asad assured Alex.

"I want to know how these women get their travel documents. Who arranges their travel? Who pays for their travel?"

Asad gave an answer to the questions posed by Alex. "The mob has travel agencies in Romania, the Czech republic, Athens, Israel, and South East Asia. There are also agencies in Russia. I have heard of others, but have no firsthand knowledge of them. In this business you learn to recognize them for what they are."

"Give me the addresses you know. Are these legitimate pay for service businesses or is this all they do?"

"One of the agencies in Athens is owned by Russian mob. It is not open to public; they are by referral only. The other two are legitimate agencies, like Kahlil; we pay them well for their special services."

"I will check them out personally after we finish with Kahlil here in Cairo." Alex continued by changing the topic, "The doctor said you should not try to get out of bed unless a nurse is here to help you with a walker. Dr al-Saqr will see you after I leave."

"Alex, believe me. I want to see this through. There is no future for me once they learn what I have already confessed. They would probably have contract on me already if you had not reported me officially dead and provided a new identity."

Alex assured him. "You are safe here. We are not moving you from the hospital for some time."

Alex unlocked the leg cuff and knocked on the door for the guards. As he was leaving the room,

Dr. al-Saqr, a young intern, entered the room accompanied by Helen.

"Mr. al-Katib, we are going to change your dressings. This may hurt a little."

Asad moaned quietly and grimaced as the doctor and Helen changed the heavy dressing on his thigh.

"I want you to try to get out of bed. We brought a walker that will give you support. That drip is on a trolley and will glide with you." Dr. al-Saqr explained.

Asad pulled himself to the edge of the bed with his wounded arm and swung his legs over the side. He felt weak and dizzy when he sat on the edge of the bed. Helen and the doctor helped him stand, but Asad started to fall, his leg was weak and started to give out. Asad clutched the walker with his good hand and regained his balance. Slowly, he shuffled to the bathroom with Helen's help and one hand on the walker.

The trip back to his bed went a little easier, but not without pain. Yuri was no stranger to pain but the loss of his mobility added an unfamiliar layer to his discomfort.

"Fuck, it hurts like hell," Yuri exclaimed.

"It will take a couple of days until you are able to do this without help. The morphine drip and IV will be gone on Monday. Try to keep as much weight off your leg as possible."

The doctor's words were less than reassuring. Until now, the morphine had helped him endure the pain. His leg still ached even with the drug, weight or not, he just did not mind as much.

"Your shoulder wound is healing nicely. Helen will bring you a ball that I want you to grip with your hand. Squeeze it several times and then rest. Then do it again. This will help you get strength back into your arm.

Keep the bandage on your nose another few days. They had to re-break your nose before setting at the same time they operated on your other wounds."

The doctor left and Nurse Helen got him settled. Despite his macho attitude, Asad was tired and being in bed felt comforting as he sunk into the freshly fluffed pillows. Helen handed him a Russian newspaper.

"I also bought you a book, *Hank'sMountain* by a new American author, Barbara Vaka; it is a mix of mystery, revenge, romance, skiing, and mayhem in the Rocky Mountains according to the cover."

"I think you found the perfect book." Asad smiled at her. "Skiing is my favorite winter sport; I hope my leg allows me to ski again."

"It will take time, but you will ski again." Nurse Helen's voice was reassuring.

"*Spasiba, Tymne be bezrazlichna.*" He reached for her and kissed her gently on her cheek.

"I care for you also. *Ty mne ne bezraclichen.*" Helen kissed him on the cheek and smiled. "Only speak Russian to me. Speak Arabic to everyone else. It is not often I hear someone speak Russian, other than my father."

"Where did you find Russian newspaper?" Asad shifted back to Arabic.

"My father buys them. There is a newsstand near the hospital. If someone notices the paper, tell them I left it in your room; they know I speak Russian."

"My next shift begins Monday. Tonight I will bring your dinner, but someone else will take your tray. You are doing well."

She ran her fingers through his thick hair and Asad touched her arm lightly with his hand.

Helen left the room and hurried to the women's restroom. She was in tears and thought to herself, "What is wrong with me? I never get emotional over patients. If a patient gets forward, I usually dump juice or throw water on them."

Helen rinsed her face with cold water starring into the mirror and wondered whom the women staring back was.

"Looking at him, all I want is to hold him in my arms and comfort him. It is difficult to believe that man did all those horrible things mentioned in his dossier. When he gently kissed my hand, a warm feeling enveloped me."

When she took the job at the hospital, she had prided herself on maintaining her professionalism, keeping her private life separate from her job. Unable to predict how she would respond if Asad went further was both troubling and exciting. Regaining her composure, she went about her duties checking in on her other patients in the secure wing of the hospital. Later that day she brought Asad his dinner tray last and stayed with him while he began to eat. He was pleased to see her and could not keep his eyes off her. Nervous and flustered, she checked her watch, "Time to go; my shift is over. Have a good weekend. See you Monday."

"Could you do something for me over the weekend? Check my email. I will give you the address and password. I am looking for a message from a young Romanian girl to tell me she is okay. I promised I would let her parents know. It is very complicated."

Helen carefully wrote the address and password.

"I will check it before I come to work on Monday morning."

She threw him a kiss as she knocked on the door.

Asad smiled, "Good night Helen. Thank you. I will think of you until Monday."

When Helen left his room, she went directly to Dr. Gaafar's office to report. She knocked and walked in without waiting for a response. Dr. Gaafar looked up from his desk and rose to greet her.

"Well, how is our patient. Has he tried to ask any favors of you?"

"His only request was for a newspaper and a book to read. He is kind and gentle and not at all like the criminal described in his dossier. He gave me his email address and asked me to check for messages; he is expecting a message from a young girl and said it was complicated."

"He must trust you. Let me know what messages he receives. It may be true he did not kill that woman, but she was terrified and running for her life when she fell and hit her head. Indirectly, he is responsible for her death. Human traffickers that deal in women are not nice people. Do not trust him. Did he ask you about anything else?"

"Nothing, he is like any other patient in the hospital. He is still in some pain and unable to get around without help."

"We will leave the morphine drip over the weekend, but cut the dosage. If he speaks to you about anything other than patient to nurse subjects, you must notify me immediately."

"Dr. Gaafar, I was surprised when asked what he did to warrant two guards; he gave me an immediate and honest answer. From what you told me earlier, he might have made up a lie. One of the women was pregnant and Asad saved her from being brutalized."

"That woman is staying with my wife and me. He protected her. Maybe there is a good side to his personality. Did he mention Alex MacKay?"

"He said Alex did not like him and I was not to believe everything bad that Alex told me about him."

"Keep your ears open. Let me know what happens on Monday when you read his messages. I want to know if there is a change in his attitude toward you after the weekend. He will be gaining strength on a daily basis and will be off pain medication. If he plans to escape or asks for your help, report to me immediately. Report anything suspicious directly to me before contacting the police."

"I will do that. So far he seems no different than other patients I have treated, and not as forward as some."

Helen knew that Asad was not like any other patient she had treated. His charming demeanor and helpless puppy act was causing her to doubt her rational sensibilities. The danger was real but she had chosen to ignore it.

"Have a nice weekend. He will be here all of next week. Gain his confidence. It sounds like he trusts you enough to check his messages. Be careful. Working undercover like this is dangerous. The wound in his leg has caused some damage to his muscle. Good that Alex had a 9mm instead of a large caliber gun; Asad suffered no broken bones and no damage to the femoral artery. He will need rehabilitation before he can walk without a limp. When the time comes to move him from the hospital, I may ask you to travel with him for a while. Those leg muscles need to be massaged daily or he will develop leg cramps."

"I have done this before. I am trained as a physical therapist."

Gafaar sensed that Helen was not being very honest with him.

"Asad is a cunning criminal. Do not forget for a moment the kind of person he is. If you got in his way while he was attempting to escape, he could become dangerous. He is a strong man, an expert in martial arts, and towers over you. Be careful."

Helen nodded at Dr. Gaafar, "I will always be alert. Over the last three years, informing on patients to the police has been part of my job. Asad is no different."

Chapter 21

Monday was the day that the shipment was due at Kahlil's warehouse. Alex situated himself across the street in another building watching the warehouse through a pair of binoculars with night vision lenses. Sabir had stationed men in close proximity to the warehouse. The Egyptian police were on standby and all had orders not to make a move until all the women had arrived. From the information Asad gave them, the women his group were bringing in were on three different flights, which was typical. Asad could not hazard a guess as to how many women would be in the shipment.

Alex confirmed there was a flight from the Ukraine into Cairo International at four in the afternoon. One of Sabir's men was at the airport when the passengers disembarked and called Alex to report that a group of ten women had arrived and that they were met by an Egyptian man who helped them to clear customs. The women were loaded into a small bus along with their luggage. Another man, disguised as a taxi driver, followed the bus and slowed to watch as it pulled into the warehouse before driving off. Alex observed as the ten women walked into the building with their escort. They would wait to see if more women were coming before making a move. There was a flight from Romania due at six. Sabir's men continued their surveillance of the warehouse and at five-thirty three men got into the bus. They followed the bus directly to the airport in an unmarked car staying back. Shortly after the plane landed, a dozen women disembarked, cleared through customs, and walked onto the bus. The bus went directly to the warehouse.

Alex counted twenty-two women had gone into the warehouse along with six guards. The armed guards appeared to be Israeli or Arab; it was hard to tell. Once again, the bus left headed for the airport. Alex knew there was a flight due in from Athens at seven in the evening. It was the only international flight due in at that time. No one had left the warehouse.

The last flight landed, and another eight women disembarked and were taken to the warehouse. Everyone held their positions. At one o'clock in the morning, four Mercedes Benz automobiles arrived along with a black limousine with diplomatic plates. They watched seven men emerge from the cars. One of the men made a call on a cell phone, and the door of the warehouse opened and they entered the building.

"It is time we looked in on this little gathering. Is everyone ready to go?" Alex called on his two-way radio system.

He got an affirmative from all operatives. "All the entrances and exits from the warehouse are covered."

One of Dr. Gaafar's men named Ghazi, went to the warehouse door and rang the bell. He was driving a small panel delivery truck.

The door opened and a tall man carrying an AK47 spoke in Arabic, "What do you want? The warehouse is closed."

Ghazi was dressed as a linen delivery service man. "I have a delivery for 47659."

"You have the wrong building. It is two buildings over."

Ghazi fumbled with his paperwork pointing to the address.

"Look for yourself. It is for this building,"

The distraction gave Ghazi time to draw his silenced nine-millimeter. A single tap to the head and the man fell to the ground without making a sound. Ghazi checked the man's body and picked his cell phone from his pocket. He stepped over the body and entered the building followed by ten men including Alex. Asad had given them directions to the stairway leading to the basement. In preparation, they had studied the plans to the warehouse and knew exactly where to go. Stealthily they made their way to the stairway. Suddenly the dead man's cell phone began to ring. Ghazi answered. They were checking on their friend.

"Who was at the door?" a gruff voice speaking Arabic came onto the phone.

Ghazi answered attempting to mask his voice so as not to raise suspicion. "Wrong address, deliveryman; I am watching to make sure he leaves."

The phone went dead. Would they notice the change in the man's voice? They waited but no one came up the stairs and they decided to go forward.

They could hear sounds coming from the basement of men laughing and a woman shrieking, "Don't touch me, you filthy beast," more laughter.

From the stairs, they could not see who was in the room and where they were standing. Alex signaled the other men to begin their attack. He was the first to rush down the stairs into the basement. Seven men sat on sofas watching a woman dance in the center of the floor while armed gunmen patrolled the perimeter. When they saw Alex, the armed men opened fire. The seven men on the couches dove to the floor. Kahlil ran for a back door. Alex dropped and rolled as he fired taking out two of the gunmen. Faced with overwhelming force, the others dropped their weapons and held up their hands. The woman who had been dancing a moment earlier ran to one of the doors on the side of the room screaming as she ran, "Help us, help us. These men are traffickers, pulled it open, and slammed it behind her."

The gun battle was over in a matter of minutes. Kahlil was exiting the building when an armed man shouted for him to stop. Kahlil went for his gun; his head exploded as the shell slammed into it just above his ear.

Alex and the others rounded up the gunman. Two were dead, but the others were uninjured having thrown down their weapons.

The Egyptian police escorted seven men that were there to buy the women to an undisclosed destination for interrogation. Trafficking of women was against the law in Cairo and these men faced prison and a large fine.

Moving from room to room, they released the naked women and gave them caftans to cover their bodies. The Egyptian police then escorted them onto a bus, and drove them to hospital for examination and treatment of their injuries. The police found a stack of identity papers and wallets on a desk in the corner and took them back to the station. At police headquarters, Cairo's finest would interrogate the prisoners to find out what they knew about the operation.

Alex and Sabir left and drove to Dr. Gaafar's home to give him the good news.

When they arrived, Gaafar answered the door and invited them in anxious to learn how it had gone.

"Welcome my friends; it is good to see you are safe and well. How did it go?"

Alex spoke up, "We rescued a lot of women tonight; our new informer, Asad told the truth. It is too bad that Kahlil went for a gun. We will search the building tomorrow and see if he kept any records."

Sabir answered, "Sometimes these operations keep better records than legitimate businesses do."

"My next destination is Athens." Alex continued, "I have some operatives from MI6 meeting me there, and the Greek officials are going to run the operation. The travel agency in Athens is the one that the Russians own privately."

"What about the agency in Romania and the Czech Republic?"

"Simultaneously, agents will be knocking on their doors. We have made arrangements in Romania and the Czech Republic."

"Has Asad given you any information on the head of this group either in Moscow or Tel Aviv?"

Sabir asked.

"I do not know how much information Asad has that could lead us to the top. Despite being a top operative, he preferred to work independently profiting from his side deals. His bosses knew what he was doing but were willing to overlook it provided he continued to deliver. What I don't know is how far up the chain of command he goes."

Sabir continued to ask questions, "When are you investigating the travel agencies?"

"We plan to strike them first thing tomorrow morning before they learn about today's raid. Our hope is that Kahlil was not working as an independent and the information we get will lead us to the heads of the organization."

"When are you speaking with Asad again?"

"I am going to fly to Athens tonight and will not be back in Cairo until Thursday night or Friday morning. I will see him on Friday. Is that nurse Helen keeping tabs on him?"

"Yes she is." Sabir answered. "She has worked with the Cairo police in this capacity for three years and is reliable and very trustworthy. Asad asked her to check for email and gave her the address and password. She promised to bring the messages with her on Monday."

"Any email in particular?"

"Helen said it would be from a young girl and he would contact her parents."

"Have her check with you every day after her shift ends. I want to know the instant Asad tries to solicit her help to escape. If he does try to escape, do we let him go, and track him, or do we stop him. Do not access that email again; someone might notice and suspect Yuri is alive."

"You make the call on that. While he was in surgery, I personally installed a locater devise subcutaneously under his skin near the wound in his thigh that the police gave me. We know where he is at every moment, even the time he goes to the bathroom."

"I will think this over."

Sabir asked. "Do you think he will try to escape and use Helen?"

"Anything is possible." Alex answered. "We need to let her know how she should play this. Asad is a very strong man; I know from personal experience. If not for his injuries, our hand-to-hand combat might have ended differently. Once cornered; he might kill to escape."

"Helen is aware of the danger and she has never quit on us before." Sabir assured Alex. "She will see this through. Have a good trip to Athens. We will let you know what those men we captured are willing to tell us. Four of them threw down their guns. Maybe they can be persuaded to tell all."

"I will call you from Athens. Let me know about any messages he received. How is Magdalena doing? May I see her?"

"Certainly, I will have my wife tell her you are here." Moments later Magdalena entered the room.

"I'd like to have a few moments to speak with her alone."

"Use my study. It is the second door on the left."

Alex closed the door behind him. Magdelena looked even more radiant than he had remembered. Her breasts were swollen and it was very evident that she was pregnant.

"Oh, Alex, thank you so much for helping me. I overheard that you are leaving. Must you go away?"

"Yes, it is what my job requires. I return either Thursday or Friday night at the latest." He took her in his strong arms and kissed her passionately. She returned his embrace and kisses.

Tears welled up in her eyes. "We miss you already; return safely,"

Alex leaned over and kissed her belly.

"Back soon, do not worry; you are safe with Dr. Sabir. I will miss you too."

They returned to the living room where Dr Gaafar and his wife joined them along with Sabir.

"Thank you for taking care of Magdalena."

"She has been a joy," Gaafar's wife said. "We will miss her when she leaves."

Chapter 22

Monday morning, Helen arrived at exactly eight o'clock wearing a white uniform skirt and blouse open one button more than usual revealing her ample bosom; she went directly to Asad's room. The color was back in his cheeks and he seemed to brighten when she entered the room.

"Did you have a good weekend?" She asked with a smile after reading his chart. "I am removing the morphine drip and the IV. Oral painkillers should be sufficient. If the pain creeps up on you, let me know. Do not let the pain get ahead of you. It is difficult to play catch-up."

"I am so glad to see you. It was boring weekend. I feel stronger. Great book, I have read over half of it. Did you check for my messages?"

"Glad you liked the book; I may borrow it back and read it myself when you finish."

Helen handed him a print out of his recent messages.

"She has not emailed me. Please check every day. It is important to me."

"We should not use your email again. Someone will notice and know you are alive. I checked your email from a cyber café; it should never be used again." Helen told him in a concerned tone of voice.

"You are right. Sorry I asked you."

Helen removed the IV, swabbed his arm, and put a bandage where the needle had been.

"Did you enjoy what you did to those women?"

Asad did not expect such a question from Helen. Was she jealous or had Alex been telling her tales about his past?

"I chose what I did, but only out of revenge for what happened to me in Singapore and for the money. I prefer to love, not abuse a woman."

Helen approached him with a look of confusion and concern on her face.

"You do not seem like a person that abuses women. How many women have you brutalized?"

Asad was becoming uncomfortable with Helen's line of questioning and did not want to confront her.

"Let's change the subject. That part of my life is over." Asad assured her.

"Can I help you to the bathroom?"

"Yes, I am still a little shaky. I needed help all weekend with the walker."

Helen helped him out of the bed and steadied the walker. She walked with him into the bathroom and before she could do anything, he pushed the door close with his foot, took her in his arms, and held her next to his body. Helen did not resist. He lifted her chin, cupped her face in his hands, kissed her passionately on the mouth, and whispered, "You are an exciting woman."

Fearing what he might do next, she pulled away and he immediately released her.

"*Presti menya*. (Forgive me), sorry, I should not have done that. I have wanted to kiss and hold you in my arms since you entered my room. It will not happen again," Asad paused, "if you object."

Helen looked at him and smiled. "You are forgiven." She stood on her tiptoes, kissed him on the mouth while looking into his blue eyes that seemed to cast a spell over her. He kissed her fervently and held her close; she kissed him with heartfelt emotion in return.

"Thank you. Your hug and kiss were better than any medicine to help me feel better." Asad whispered as his lips brushed her ear as he spoke.

It was a risk that could cost Helen her life; a risk she was willing to take. Pent-up emotion released by a kiss, all reason abandoned she proclaimed, "I thought of you all weekend. You have captivated me and hold me under your spell." Helen wiped a tear from her eye. "Are you able to take a shower or should I stay until you finish?"

"I should be okay, I will scream for help if I fall." He laughed.

"No need to scream, pull that cord and I will return immediately. Take your shower; I will give you a backrub when I return after checking my other patients."

Before Asad limped into the shower, Helen kissed him again, left the bathroom after straightening her uniform, finger combing her hair, and knocking for the guard to open the door.

Helen met Dr. Gaafar in the corridor on her way to another patient's room and told him about the email.

"Do you have a print out of his messages?

"Here is the print out. Asad said she had not sent a message and asked me to check every day. I told him we should never access the email address again. Originally, I thought his email might have information we could use."

"You probably should never have checked his email in the first place," Alex agreed. "Someone might suspect that Yuri is alive. Did he ask you to help him check anything else?"

"No, he said he was glad to see me. I am giving him a backrub later. Maybe he will talk to me then."

"Let me know. Be careful." Sabir cautioned Helen.

"I will. Remember, I have eavesdropped on other patients. Along with being a good nurse, I am a respected police officer. Asad has never been anything but courteous with me."

Helen went about her duties with the other patients and returned to Asad's room. He was lying on his stomach on the bed, completely nude except for a towel that covered his buttocks.

"I am ready for that backrub," he smirked.

"I see you are feeling better."

Helen opened a bottle of lotion and removed the towel.

"You are ready." She laughed. She was going to smack his backside lightly and gasped when she saw the scars.

"I read what happened to you. Those scars are terrible. They are deep."

"I asked a woman to my hotel room in Singapore and they sent me to prison for attempted rape when I was eighteen. I have had those scars for seven years."

"You must have been in terrible pain when they did that to you. You never raped her and they did this. Caning is a brutal punishment, but until I saw your scars, I had no idea."

"If I had raped her, it would have been twenty-four. The pain was excruciating. It made me scream." He paused, looked right into her eyes, and asked, "Why is a lovely woman like you single?"

"Being half Russian Jew and half Coptic is not popular with Egyptians, Muslims, or Coptics. I find it difficult to fit in with either group."

"I do not care about your religion; you are important to me."

Helen rubbed her hands together to get them warm and applied the lotion to his back and shoulders. She massaged his powerful shoulder muscles and her fingers worked down his spine.

"You must work out regularly, you have very well-developed muscles."

"I live on my boat when not traveling and exercise every day. Doing what I did, being physically fit was a requirement."

Helen's hands were strong and Asad let out a long deep sigh as she massaged his body. She applied lotion to his backside.

"I am removing the bandage on your leg. The wound has healed nicely."

Asad winced a little when she removed the tape and Helen massaged his legs and kissed the back of his neck. He turned, pulled her to him, and kissed her again.

"Can you lock the door from the inside for a little while?"

"No, but I can tell the guards you require an enema and not to disturb us for twenty-five minutes," she laughed.

"Tell them. I want to feel your body against mine. Allow me to make love to you before they send me away. It is all I will ever ask of you; it is against the rules, but please, just this once." He pleaded with her.

Helen kissed him as tears filled her eyes. She wiped the tears away, went to the door, and knocked. The guard opened the door.

"I have to get some supplies; he is constipated and needs an enema. If you hear him complain, do not pay any attention. I never had a patient that liked having an enema. They always protest." She laughed.

The guard laughed and promised not to open the door even if he heard yelling.

"Make it a strong enema. At least three quarts should be good for that rogue."

"OK, I will take care of it."

Helen returned to Asad's room with a small trolley with apparatus for an enema. The guard laughed and gave her a knowing nod.

"I am glad you are not sticking that up my ass."

Helen laughed. "Give me twenty-five or thirty minutes. Maybe you would like it."

"I doubt that Helen."

Helen went into the room and closed the door. The guard locked the door.

Helen sat on the bed next to Asad and he stopped her when she went to unbutton her blouse.

"Let me. I want to undress you."

He slowly unbuttoned her blouse, and kissed her breasts and her body as he removed her blouse and bra.

"You have done this before," she giggled.

Asad cupped her breasts and kissed her body. He slid her skirt down and took off her panties as she lifted her hips. He pulled her to him, kissed her, and his fingers found her sweetness; she was wet with desire.

"You shave your body the same as Muslim women."

"Growing up with Muslim girls, I have always shaved my body."

"You are lovely. Never change." Asad's voice was gentle as he whispered words of endearment in Russian.

Helen lay on the bed next to him and he kissed each breast and sucked her nipples until they were erect and hard to the touch. He rolled on top of her, entered her slowly, and moved in and out until he could hold back no longer and his movements became intense. He entered into her as far as possible, their bodies entwined, as he held her close and released his essence as she sighed. They were both breathing quickly and their bodies were wet from their vigorous love making. His leg throbbed from the physical activity, but he dismissed it as he kissed her again and his tongue explored her mouth.

"I know you must leave, before someone suspects there is a problem. I need to shower and so do you."

Helen helped him into the bathroom.

"What about my hair. I cannot leave here looking as if I took a shower."

"That is why they put these in here." He laughed and kissed her on the lips as he pulled a plastic shower cap over her hair and carefully tucked in all the ends so her hair would stay dry.

"You think of everything."

They showered together and he held her close to him.

"You have an exquisite body. Hold me a minute longer before you go. Please, please do not report me for taking advantage of you. Alex would send you away and castrate me. Making love to you is all I desired from the moment you entered my room." His voice changed to a concerned tone, "I need you; and I have never needed anyone before in my life."

The tears returned, "I dreamed of our making love. You have enchanted me, and hold me under your spell."

Helen looked at her watch, "They might get suspicious if I do not return to my other duties."

Asad kissed her once more, toweled her dry, and helped her get dressed. He limped back to bed.

"Do you need something for the pain in your leg?"

"I hardly notice it after making love to you, but a pain pill might be a good idea, thank you."

Helen got him a pill for pain, marked his chart, emptied the enema contents down the drain, and put the apparatus back onto the trolley.

"I will see you later, Asad. You have captured my heart and mind. Can I do anything for you or get you anything?"

"Come back to my room as soon as possible. You are the only person that makes my life bearable."

Helen knocked on the door and before the guard opened it, she threw him a kiss.

"See you later."

The guard winked, "Did he enjoy his enema?"

"He was not real pleased. Tomorrow he may need another, maybe two. He is really constipated, cannot shit on his own."

The guards both broke down laughing and talked about Asad having a couple more enemas the next day.

"I do not care how pretty that nurse is, she would not be shoving that tube up my ass."

"Mine either. Almost makes you feel sorry for the poor scoundrel."

Helen went about her duties and marked Asad's chart that she gave him an enema and scheduled one for the next day.

She thought to herself. "I find his seductiveness irresistible. He is passionate when he makes love to me. The touch of his hands on my body; his kiss ignites my emotions makes me want to make love to him. They cannot lock him away for years. If they do, it will be painful being away from him, but I will wait. I love him."

Helen visited Asad once more that day for a parting kiss before leaving for the day. On her way out she by Dr. Gaafar's office, but he was not there, only a note.

"Helen, see me tomorrow morning. I cannot make our meeting today. If you have an emergency, call my cell. The doctor said he would be ready to travel Saturday. Can you go with him? He will still need nursing care. It may be dangerous."

Asad was alone with his thoughts. His feelings for Helen were growing and he had to be sure that he could trust her.

"Helen is an unusual woman. I know they told her everything I have done, and still she responds to me. Can I trust her? She asks many questions and I suspect she is more than a nurse; perhaps she is undercover for the police. If she is, she certainly takes her job seriously. I will never forgive her, if she is playing with my emotions. Falling in love with this woman was not in my plans."

Chapter 23

Alex arrived in Athens and went directly to his hotel, the King George, at Syntagma Square. Two British MI6 operatives checked into the hotel earlier and were waiting for him. Jonathan Bridgeway was in his mid thirties, a little shorter than Alex was with sandy blonde hair and brown eyes. Albert Cunningham was the same height as Alex and powerfully built with brown hair and eyes.

"I am Jonathan Bridgeway and this is Albert Cunningham. We are glad you arrived a little ahead of time. Henry Ewing has approved the operation and it is officially sanctioned with the cooperation of the Athens police Department.

The locals have two undercover police officers meeting us in about fifteen minutes in our room. A representative of the Egyptian government will be there as well."

The two undercover police officers and the Egyptian operative got there at the same time and knocked on the door.

"This is Yanni Vires and I am Anastas Kirapolis."

"I am Mohamed Zamalek"

Yanni, 180 centimeters in height with black hair and dark brown eyes wearing black slacks and a white shirt, did most of the talking and reported what they had found in their investigation of the travel agencies.

"This is a private agency and does no business with the general public. They have no listing in the telephone directory, but are a licensed travel bureau and do nothing but charters. They have a very small store front near the Omonia Square Metro."

Anastas, about the same build as Yanni, added, "They are owned by a corporation with headquarters in Moscow, but they are licensed in Greece. We have not been able to find a direct connection to the actual owner."

Alex interrupted them, "That information agrees with what a Russian operative we have in custody has told us. Tracing this agency to the actual owner may be difficult. We would have had more information, but the owner of the warehouse in Cairo was shot and killed during a recent raid. We had hoped he could give us information."

"Athens, like Cairo, sees too much trafficking of women. We raid the brothels, but these women are so frightened they tell us nothing. They fear for their families and reprisal by the Russian mobs. The only thing we can do is attempt to repatriate them."

"The travel agency has been under surveillance; in the last two days only one person has entered the establishment."

"Alex, how to you wish to proceed. We have agreed to work with MI6 and fully cooperate with you."

"We will give them the name of Yuri Berezovsky. Tell them we spoke to him two months ago. Lead them to believe that we have twenty women in need of travel documents for Egypt."

"That will be very expensive according to our sources," Yanni added.

"We have several thousand dollars US with us to cover that contingency and are prepared to pay up to $3000 per woman to cover the cost of identity papers, visas, and airfare to Cairo. Our cover is that they are a dance troop" Jonathan interrupted.

"Won't they be suspicious?" Anastas asked.

"If we have the money, these people ask very few questions. They will not turn down $60,000 or more."

"Their posted hours are eleven to five."

"We will plan to be at their door when they open tomorrow morning."

Jonathan put a case on the table.

"One of us will be wired and record the entire conversation. The equipment we use is very high tech. If they search for electronics, our equipment will go undetected. Our Greek friends will do all the talking for us. Alex, we have a special miniaturized camera for you to wear. It will send a direct feed to a police van parked a couple of blocks away."

"We need proof that they can handle this operation and provide bogus travel documents that will pass inspection. We can take no action until we have proof."

"I suggest that you demand to deal with the owner. This operation involves a great deal of money. We have the right to meet the owner or person in charge; we do not want to deal with underlings."

Alex was confident the plan would work unless the staff became suspicious and decided to check with their superiors. If word of the raid that killed Kahlil had reached them, it would not be long before they made the connection. In that case, they would be walking into a deadly trap.

"If this agency operates the same way as the warehouse operation in Cairo, they will probably demand at least five women as part of the payment. If that is the case, we will of course agree. We will then follow them to a local brothel and make a larger sweep."

Anastas interrupted, "You do not plan to arrest them immediately."

"No, we want to see the identity papers and false visas. We need to know how long it takes them to produce twenty sets of papers and arrange a charter. Once we have a timeline and a date to pick up the paperwork, then we make the arrest."

"How long will it take?"

"According to the Russian we are holding, this group can have identity papers for up to thirty women in two to three days. We will offer them half of the money as a down payment and the balance on delivery."

"Tomorrow is Tuesday; I am hoping we can wind up this operation by Thursday afternoon or Friday morning at the latest."

"Until tomorrow gentlemen."

The two Greek police officers, Mohamed, and the two MI6 operatives went to dinner at the hotel. Alex ordered room service and stayed back to make his plans. He was expecting a call from Henry Ewing at any time.

Chapter 24

Asad got stronger every day and he and Helen spent as much time together as they could with no one noticing. One morning Helen arrived a little after eight o'clock and she was carrying a shopping bag. Asad was asleep and muttering the name Cassandra. She kissed him on the cheek and whispered in his ear, her lips brushing against his neck, "Time to wake up good looking. They have granted permission for a walk outside the hospital. Get dressed; here is a pair of pajamas and a pair of shoes and socks in your size. You do not want to walk around with your butt hanging out in that awful hospital gown. Who is Cassandra, you were calling her name in your sleep?"

Asad rolled over and put his arms around her.

"Thank you for the pajamas and shoes. Cassandra was a woman friend from London; I kidnapped her because she made me angry. I sold her as a sex slave to Dr. Jameel al Basara at this hospital; he married her. They came to visit me the day I arrived at the hospital. They are very compatible and thanked me for introducing them."

"I met Jameel's wife that day you arrived at the hospital, but her name was Fatinah, not Cassandra. You sold her as a sex slave, and he married her. I didn't know that."

"I have had some very interesting things take place in my life when dealing with women. Not all my victims were unhappy. Some, like Cassandra, marry the men that bought them and live very happy lives. Fatinah is an Arabic name that Jameel gave her."

"You will have to tell me more someday. I cannot believe Dr. Jameel bought a slave. There are things we need to talk about, but not in this room," she continued to whisper. "I think it may be bugged."

Asad looked fixedly at her while changing into the pajamas and shoes. "When we go for our walk, are the guards joining us?"

Helen noticed a change in his usually passionate voice.

Uncertain as to what Asad might have in mind she answered, "They will be tagging along behind us."

"I am feeling stronger. There are things I need to know. This walk has come at opportune time."

Before he could continue, she grabbed his shoulders and gently motioned him to sit on the edge of the bed.

"I am going to remove the bandage on your nose before we leave for your walk. Sit still."

Carefully she removed the bandage and smiled, "Your nose is straight and does not look like it was ever broken." Helen paused. "You are handsome." She kissed his nose gently.

"I was not handsome before?" he laughed.

"You are more handsome."

Helen walked to the door and knocked. The guard opened the door.

"Please grab that wheelchair by the wall. Mr. al-Katib may not be strong enough to walk back on his own."

The guard got the wheelchair and told the other guard, "I think I can handle this on my own. Why don't you take a break and get a cup of coffee."

"He looks a little unsteady on his feet. I have my cell; call me if I am needed."

The one guard left, Asad and Helen began to walk slowly. The guard gave them some space and sauntered along behind them by a good ten paces pushing the empty wheelchair and smoking a cigarette.

"What did you mean by opportune time?" Helen asked.

"Helen," Asad turned to her and asked in an inquisitive tone of voice. "Who are you? Tell me the truth. You are more than my nurse, yes." He stopped and faced her.

Helen knew she could no longer continue to pretend. Asad would figure out what she was doing even if she denied being anything but his nurse. Weighing her options and knowing that if something went wrong the guard would come to her rescue, Helen took a calculated risk that this man really did have feelings for her and would understand. If, as Alex had warned, he was simply using her to escape, Asad's response to the news would betray him.

"You deserve the truth. I am a member of the Cairo police department along with being a nurse. They use me to give them information from wounded or sick prisoners. I report to Alex MacKay and Dr. Gaafar every day concerning what we talk about."

Asad felt betrayed. He had trusted this woman despite his suspicions. What else had she failed to tell him? What intimate details of what they were doing behind closed doors had she shared?

"Why are you playing with my emotions?" A stern expression came over his face replacing the usual playful boyish demeanor he displayed when speaking with her. "I have passionate amorous feelings for you; do not trifle with my affection. I took you into my confidence and into my bed. You betrayed me. You are no different from the bitch in Singapore that turned me into the police for a crime I did not commit. No, worse, you are the police. I have been having sex with a member of the Egyptian police."

"No, please. I love you," pleaded a tearful Helen.

"I have never felt this way before with someone in my charge. It began that first day I walked into your room. You were helpless, shackled to the bed and you had the strength to take my hand in yours and kiss it. When your lips brushed across my hand, I felt a bolt of electricity surge through my body."

"Go on." His voice softened and the harshness faded.

"I have fallen in love with you. I know the crimes you have committed. I also know that you have a compassionate nature because you saved a pregnant woman from harm. The touch of your hands on my body, and your lips on mine when we kiss, my emotions are out of control."

By now the guard, watching from a distance was starting to pay attention. Helen started to walk along the path still supporting Asad looking straight ahead, as though nothing had happened.

"Are you having sex with me because you thought I would talk if you made love to me?"

"No, no, when I feel your body against mine, and we make love, there is only affection for you. I am smitten, moonstruck by you. When you kiss me, I feel wanted and loved. Believe me, Asad; I love you."

Asad turned and looked at her. Helen paused and searched his eyes for an answer before she asked, "Do you love me? I wanted you to make love to me. *Ya palyubIl tebyA s pErvava vzglyAda.*"

Asad reached for her hand and his smile returned. With passion in his voice he answered, "Helen, I fell in love the moment you entered my room. Seeing you every day makes life bearable. The fragrance of your freshly shampooed hair every morning, that fragrance you wear, your soft hand on my face when you touch me, when I make love to you, you are not like any other woman I have ever known; I have known many women. You respond to my embrace and I feel emotions new to me. I want to buy you jewelry, clothing, take you to dinner, take you dancing, I love to dance, but I am in a hospital room, no television, no radio, no telephone, bars on the window, and locked door. My love is all I can offer you. I cannot bear the thought that we will never see each other again. Losing you would make my life miserable and unendurable. *Ya tebyA lyublyU*. I love you, but I can do nothing about it. *Ti nuzhnA mne*. My life is not my own." Tears filled his eyes as he squeezed her hand gently.

"I need you too Asad."

Just then, his leg gave out and he started to fall. Helen grabbed his arm, called for help, and the guard quickly came to her aid. They helped him into the wheel chair.

"No marathon today," Asad quipped slipping back into Arabic.

"You did well for your first time walking. Massaging your legs when we get back to your room will help. Then after lunch, we will try to walk again."

She turned to the guard when they got back to the room and Asad was back in bed, "I do not understand why you are still guarding him so closely. He can barely walk."

"We have orders, Helen. Anyone can see that he is going nowhere on his own for some time."

The guard closed the door and Helen asked Asad, "Do you need me to help you take your shoes off.?"

"No, I can do it myself."

"Slip off your pajama bottoms."

"What do you have in mind?" Asad laughed.

"Not what you have in mind. Your legs need to be massaged to prevent any cramping,"

Asad removed the pajama pants and turned on his stomach; Helen massaged his leg muscles.

"Ouch, that hurts." He complained.

"I can feel your muscles are cramped. Walking at least three-times each day will get your strength back. It may be painful."

Asad turned and put his arms around her and pulled her close to him. He kissed her with intense emotion and held her so tight she had trouble breathing.

"You must know, if they ever give me my freedom, I want you to be my wife. There is money in Swiss bank. We can go anywhere in the world. They have given me new identity. I want you with me. Surviving ten years without you is impossible." Tears welled in his eyes as he kissed her once more; his body trembled.

Helen asked while tears streamed down her cheeks. "Do you know anything about the people who are behind this trafficking operation that might be worth your freedom?"

"Is that Helen the cop asking?"

"No, it is Helen the woman that loves you and could not live without you." She kissed him and held him close.

Asad answered her with a tone of optimism. "There is only rumor of who is at the top of this trafficking business in Israel. They are not made-up stories, and I can prove those rumors are true. It will shock the world when they learn how high this goes in the Israeli government. It is also high up the chain of command in the Russian government." Asad paused before continuing in a low voice so as not to be heard by anyone listening in. "I have seen documents. I do not think they know I saw them. I took pictures of them with my digital camera, and some women I know, despite the risk, used a miniature camera to film important men doing things with their clothes off they would never want to share with anyone. I was planning to retire in a month and tell them I about the documents and photographs in my possession. My plan was to warn them that if anything happened to me, a friend would release them to the media."

"Why not turn the evidence over to the authorities?"

"There are men inside Mossad, dangerous men, who are deeply involved. I wanted to quit but if they got wind of what I have, it would mean my death. These photos were supposed to be my ticket to freedom from the Russian mob. No one retires from mob. They own you until you die, or they kill you. I had never planned to work for them more than five years when this all started. After four years, I was disgusted at some things I saw and participated in, but there was no escape."

"Where are the pictures now?"

"They are in as safe place where they cannot be found."

Helen pleaded, "When Alex returns, tell him."

Asad shook his head but Helen continued.

"I will be with you when Alex comes. If it is possible, Alex will trade your freedom for this information. He has influence with MI6. Tomorrow is Friday. If all goes well in Athens, Alex will be back in Cairo late tomorrow night. I will leave word for him and Dr. Gaafar that I have important information. When they call, I will come to the hospital and we will see what can be arranged."

"If the source of this information was ever discovered, I am a dead man. I need assurances that my new identity is faultless. Both our lives depend on this. Part of any deal is that you and I be allowed to go away together. I can think of nothing else I want more in this world than spending my life with you."

"Oh Asad, I do love you."

A knock came at the door; it was Dr. Gaafar.

Helen smoothed her uniform, wiped her eyes, and opened the door. Dr. Gaafar entered.

"How is our patient doing?"

"He walked for awhile, but his leg gave out. I massaged his muscles and we will go for a walk after lunch."

"Good, exercise is the only thing that will get him back on his feet."

"Helen, I need to speak with you in my office. Are you finished with Asad?" Dr. Gaafar asked in a somewhat irritated tone of voice.

"Yes, I am."

Helen and Dr. Gaafar left Asad's room and went to his office.

"Please, sit down. I have been watching you interact with Asad; I have overheard your conversations with him. It is obvious there is more than a nurse to patient relationship. What is this man to you?" He demanded in a stern voice.

Helen broke down. "This has never happened to me before. Many patients have made sexual advances to me; I felt nothing but repulsion. Asad and I are in love. He has a tender decent loving side. Don't let them send him away to prison."

"That is not my decision. Has he told you anything we can use to stop this trafficking?"

"Believe it or not, he kidnapped this woman named Cassandra Cavendish, who he was dating, sold her as a sex slave to our own Dr. Jameel al-Basara. He introduced her to me as his wife; her name is now Fatinah."

"I met her. Jameel told me everything; it will be our little secret. His first marriage had ended in a divorce. Hard to believe one of our staff was involved with buying a sex slave." Dr. Gaafar cleared his throat. "Anything else?"

"He has digital pictures of some documents that lead to the top of the Israeli and Russian governments; he also has photographs of officials having sexual affairs with prostitutes. The pictures show fetching young women dominatrix whipping influential men they have bound and gagged. Inside Mossad, a secret group operates in the background controlling everything.

The Mossad leadership is not aware of their existence. Asad said he was planning to retire from the Russian mob and disappear, using the threat to release the pictures if he was ever harmed."

Gaafar sat back in his chair planning his next move given this new information.

"Alex might return tonight, but no later than Friday. As soon as he returns, we will discuss this with Asad. If it is as important as he told you, MI6 may deal."

"Are you going to tell my department head about my affair with Asad? If you do I will lose my job."

"No. I think it is better we say as little as possible until we have a chance to find the people behind this."

"May I continue to see him? I love him." Helen was sobbing.

"As long as you are honest with me and Alex, you may continue. The last thing we need is an investigation by your department into the matter. When we move him on Saturday, you will come along to take care of him until he is fully recovered."

"Is there any way to trade his information for his freedom?"

"That is up to MI6. I will speak with Alex. If his information is as vital as you say, you two might have to disappear. We reported him as officially killed, but it might not be enough. The Mossad never gives up."

"I am prepared to do that as long as I can be with him. He said he has sufficient money that we could live and not need to work."

"We will discuss this with Alex. I have always admired you Helen but never imagined this man would affect you the way he has. You have always been the consummate professional, until now. I hope you have thought this through and he is not using you. Does he know you are with the police?"

"Yes, I told him."

"You must be in love. Does he love you as much in return?"

"I am sure he does."

"As soon as Alex returns, we will discuss the next step."

"Thank you."

"Do not thank me yet. A great deal rides on who believes what Asad has is damaging enough to have him killed."

Helen left Dr. Gaafar's office for the woman's room to wash her face and regain her composure before attending to her other patients. She looked forward to bringing Asad his lunch before they would try another walk.

Chapter 25

As soon as Alex returned to Cairo, he called Dr. Gaafar on his encrypted satellite phone.

Gaafar answered immediately. "Doctor I am back in Cairo. What has happened with our patient?"

"Alex, I am glad you called as soon as you arrived. Helen has told me that Asad has highly confidential information and that he has incriminating digital photos of prominent government officials with known prostitutes. He wants to trade his information for his freedom. My nurse Helen informed me that she has fallen in love with him and assures me that he loves her as well."

"That is a twist I did not expect. I always thought he might try to win her over and use her to escape. I will come directly from the airport to the hospital. I want to meet with you first and then bring Helen into the conversation before you see Asad. So far his information has been accurate."

"It is nine o'clock. I will order a late dinner for the three of us," Gafaar said. "Did you eat on the plane?"

"If you call a package of crackers dinner, the answer is yes."

Helen was at home watching a movie on television when the phone rang, "Hello."

"Alex is back from Athens. He is coming directly from the airport to the hospital. He wants to meet with us tonight before we speak with Asad. I have ordered a late supper."

Helen got dressed and immediately drove to the hospital. Before going to Dr. Gaafar's office, she went to Asad's room.

The guard on duty stopped her, "I am sorry Helen; Dr. Gaafar has ordered no visitors tonight unless he escorts them personally or gives me his approval. Do you want me to call?"

"No, thank you."

Helen glared at the guard and got back on the elevator to the second floor where Dr. Gaafar's office was located.

Alex had already arrived and he and Dr. Gaafar were in the middle of a conversation.

"Helen, I will be free in half an hour. Get a cup of coffee," he called out when she knocked on his door.

Alex continued to give information to Sabir. "I cannot believe the number of brothels in Athens. The main area is near the travel agency. You go one stop past Omonia square and there dozens of unlicensed, so-called 'white bulb' houses. Many of the women in these brothels are from Romania, Ukraine, Bulgaria, and Moldavia. I can assure you that after we are done this travel agency will not be doing business for a long time. We found the price at these brothels to be anywhere from thirty up to 150 Euros for 20 minutes. They advertise in a newspaper called 'Gnorimies'."

"Are all these brothels filled with illegals?"

"Surprising, most of the brothels are licensed by the Greek government and the girls have regular medical checkups, but there are a great many women, we suspect, are victims of trafficking and are being held against their will. Most will not speak to us for fear of reprisals on their families. Outside of the licensed brothels, there are thousands of full and part time hookers. In Greece, participating in sex with a victim of trafficking is considered rape and punishable by law."

"How helpful were the Greeks?"

"They were very forthcoming. Our sting operation worked. The travel agency produced the forged documents for twenty women in less than forty-eight hours. They provided us with identification, visas, and passports all of high quality and difficult to detect. The cost was $3000 American money for each woman payable in cash."

"What happened to the agency?"

"We demanded to see the owner given the large amount of money involved. He flew in direct from Moscow to meet with us. We learned that he operates in Solntsevskaya and is a member of one of the largest Mafia groups in Russia. That group is usually associated with guns and drug smuggling, but they profit from sex slavery as well. The travel agency in Athens was one of their key locations. The Greek authorities placed everyone at the agency under arrest; including our Russian kingpin and are conducting their own investigation. In the back, they found drugs, $200,000 Euros and records with telephone numbers and emails for their regular customers. The Athens case is completely in the hands of the Greek authorities. They are working diligently on getting to the top of the organization. When I left, they were in the process of contacting the Russian authorities."

"What do you want to do about Asad? I forbid any visitors to his room as soon as you called, including Helen. I was told she went to visit him before coming here."

"Can we still trust her to report to us?"

"Helen is thinking with her heart not her head. Any information should be suspect until verified. There is no doubt in my mind she is in love with him. I also suspect Asad has strong feelings for her. I have overheard some of their conversations. He was in a vulnerable emotional state when he arrived."

"I want to speak with Asad alone. When Helen comes back to your office, have her eat her dinner then wait an hour before sending her to Asad's room."

Alex finished his food and left to interrogate Asad. Dr. Gaafar notified the guard that Alex was coming and to let him pass.

Alex found Asad sound asleep with the lights off when he entered the room. He flipped on the lights waking Asad immediately.

"Wake up."

"You are back. Did the information on Athens prove worthy of your time?" He sat up and elevated the hospital bed.

"It was very accurate. We even took down one of the leaders from the Solntsevskaya Mafia organization. I was surprised to find them involved in the slave trade instead of their usual, guns and drugs. I left the Greek authorities in charge of the investigation."

Alex pulled up a chair alongside Asad's bed and sat down.

"Russians will do anything for money." Asad answered.

"Helen told us you have verifiable proof of ties to the Israeli and Russian governments."

"News travels fast."

"Where are these pictures you told Helen about?"

"They are safely deposited in Swiss bank. It is same bank where I have my money for retirement."

"How important to you is Helen?"

Asad explained in a concerned tone of voice. "When you met me, I was at breaking point. Magdalena says I saved her; that is inaccurate, she rescued me. She caused me to see what I had become, and I did not like myself. I have always preferred loving women to brutalizing them. I saw chance to do something good. To save a woman from the hell I helped to create."

"You behaved decently Asad. Magdalena will never forget you." Alex reassured him.

Asad continued. "This is an impossible business just to walk away from. I thought I could threaten them but I do not think that would have been possible. My plan was to send Magdalena to old friend of mine in Moscow. It was too dangerous to bring her with me. She had no identity papers as I personally destroyed them. The only way to get her into Russia was through one of our travel agencies in Cairo. I will give you their information." Asad paused and looked directly at Alex. "Escaping from this hospital did cross my mind, but it meant I would never see Helen again. Life without her would be unbearable. She is my reason for living."

"Escape was never an option. Without a new identity, they would have tracked you down, and most likely killed you. You are officially dead, and should be off their hit list."

"I seldom have real emotions for any woman. I enjoy sex and company of elegant women, but never for any length of time. I was always afraid to get involved. Helen is different; I am in love with her. I have asked her to be my wife. You are only person that can make that possible." Asad continued and asked in a concerned tone. "What can you do for us? My life and future are in your hands."

Alex articulated his response carefully. "I think we have room to maneuver. You have language skills I could put to use and insider information on this trade from the back alleys of Moscow to the slums of Tel Aviv. It would involve going undercover and the chance that someone from your past might recognize you. Do you think we can work together without trying to kill each other?"

In a conciliatory tone of voice, Asad responded. "In exchange for my freedom and a chance for a life with Helen, I would work with Lucifer. You are not my enemy Alex; it would be honor to work with you."

"Dr. Gaafar and Helen are on their way. The doctor left word that extensive rehabilitation by walking and exercise is necessary. Helen has the training and with her help you should be able to walk on your own in a month with only a slight limp." Alex continued with an apologetic tone, "It seems the bullet I fired into your leg created some damage to the muscle. The limp may be permanent. It was not my intention to maim you, only stop you."

Asad offered his hand to Alex. "At least I will be able to walk. You have helped bring me to my senses. Trust me Alex, I have never felt about anyone as I feel for Helen. If not for her, I would have nothing to live for. My emotions were dead. I felt despondent, until I met her. She has given me a desire to survive."

The two former enemies shook hands, perhaps the beginning of a friendship.

"First we try, then we trust."

Alex reached in his pocket, took out five hundred British pounds, and handed it to Asad. "You will need some cash, consider it a gift from Magdalena and me."

"I do not know what to say," Asad's voice cracked. "No one has ever done anything for me before, thank you. This means more than I can express in words."

The guard opened the door; Helen and Dr. Gaafar walked into the room.

Helen hurried to Asad's bedside and there were tears in her eyes. Asad reached up and pulled her to him. "I love you so much. Alex is giving us a chance for a life together. We will be working side by side as partners."

Helen turned to Alex, gave him a big hug, and kissed him, "Thank you. Thank you. Asad will not let you down. If I can help, please let me know what I can do."

"Get our boy back on his feet. He needs to be able to walk without falling down."

Sabir interrupted. "How long will it take Helen?"

Helen immediately responded. "It has already been two weeks. If Asad works through the pain, he will be able to walk longer distances with the aid of a cane in another week. In a maximum of two weeks, he will walk without a cane. He needs to stay at the hospital. This hospital has one of the best rehabilitation centers in Cairo."

Alex continued to explain. "The arrangements will be made. I will take care of the paperwork. Officially you are a contract informant and are on the payroll of MI6 as of today."

"If I am free and able to marry Helen, I will do anything you ask. This is my only chance for my future." Asad looked to Helen and then to Alex, "Take care of Magdalena for me; she needs a man to care for her."

Alex replied, "I hope we can get to know each other. I need Magdalena as much as you need Helen. Someday, I will tell you the whole story of what happened to me and why I understand you."

"I will regain full use of my leg. There is now reason for me to live. Helen needs someone with two good legs. Alex, you and I will make unusual team."

"Yes, we will. While you are recovering, I am going to rent an apartment here in Cairo so that Magdalena and I can get to know each other. One thing, to pass as an English man you must begin speaking better English. You sound Russian."

"When I arrived you made me an Arab and told me to speak only Arabic. You gave me an Arabic name. I was happy being Russian. Now you want me to be English. I will work on it." Asad laughed.

"Sabir interrupted, "Do not forget, in a week my son and Emunishere are getting married. Jameel and Fatinah called. They are leaving tonight from Athens to fly to London. They will return to Alexandria on his yacht in time for their wedding. I have never seen a couple more in love. The irony is that we came together, not by divine providence, but by time, *dahr, zamān*. Time is the most malicious of companions, *Al-Mutanabbi*. If it had not been for the misdeeds and suffering of one man, we may never have crossed paths. As an Arab, I do not believe in fate, only Time. Asad seems to have brought us all together."

Alex laughed, "We certainly did. You are so right. Without Asad, we may never have met."

Helen turned to Alex, "Thank you for not killing him or wounding him any worse than you did."

"In battle it is more instinct born of training that dictates what we do. It was not my intention to hurt him as much as I did. I only meant to stop him from running. We have all led interesting lives lately. When this operation is over, perhaps our lives will return to the new normal."

Sabir Gaafar spoke to Asad, "Tomorrow morning you will begin a major rehabilitation schedule. Right now, we will leave you to get some sleep. You look exhausted. Helen will be back at eight in the morning."

Alex and Sabir left the room while Helen said goodnight in private.

"Asad, I love you so much. Alex is a good man and we owe him a lot for giving us a chance. You will be free when this is over."

"I will not disappoint you. As soon as I am walking better, my first assignment with Alex will be in Switzerland. I will then have money to buy you extravagant gifts."

"You do not have to buy me anything; your love is enough."

Asad handed Helen the five hundred pounds, "Alex gave this to me, buy yourself something nice."

Helen kissed Asad; they held each other close.

"We will go shopping together when you are out of the hospital. I have to go, it is late, wish we could sleep together, but it is against the hospital rules."

She joined Alex and Sabir in the hall.

"Asad and I cannot thank you enough for helping us. He really is a very passionate man and when he said he will work with you, he meant it."

Alex gave her a hug, "He is a lucky man to have you Helen. You saved him from having no future to a man with a purpose and a goal. We will work well together; I understand him because I have been there myself."

Chapter 26

Jameel and Fatimah's flight landed at Heathrow Airport. Fatinah went to walk through the resident's entry when Jameel pulled her aside.

"Remember, you now have an Egyptian passport that is the wrong gate."

"I forgot. I am so used to coming through the British citizen's gate when I return to London. My father is waiting in baggage claim for us. I hope this goes well. He was very upset with me when we spoke."

"Remember Fatinah, the two most important people right now are you and me. Your father is welcome to join us on our cruise aboard *El Jumanah* from Athens to Alexandria. It would make me very happy and give us a chance to get to know each other."

"What if he won't come?" Fatinah asked.

"Then that is his problem, not ours. Your father is overly protective and must understand that you are now my wife and that we love each other. I know your father is important to you, but he cannot live your life for you. You do love me?" Jameel questioned.

Fatinah looked into his eyes, "I love you more than life itself. I did not know I could be this enraptured. These last ten days with you have been entrancing. If my father refuses to give his consent, that is his choice. We will know shortly, we are next in line."

As Jameel stepped to the entry gate, the immigration officer read his name and signaled for an official to come over.

"May I see your passport and identity papers, please? Is this woman traveling with you an Egyptian, her accent sounds British."

"She is on my passport; we are both Egyptian. Is there a problem?"

"One moment please. You and your wife must wait here. Thank you."

The official left and went into the main terminal and paged Robert Cavendish.

Robert appeared, "Well, did you deny him entry as I requested?"

"Your daughter is married to an Egyptian citizen. Both their names are on the same passport. She is no longer a British subject. I cannot deny entry to him without denying her entry. Is this what you want?"

"No, very well, admit them. I cannot understand why my daughter married an Egyptian." Robert Cavendish had a disgusted look on his face.

The official returned to the gate and found Jameel and Fatinah having a discussion. They stopped as soon as the official approached.

"I am so sorry sir; there was a problem of mistaken identity. Your name is similar to someone on our watch list. Welcome to London and enjoy your visit." He turned to Fatinah, "Your father is most anxious to see you. He is waiting in baggage claim. We will expedite your luggage. Sorry for the delay."

"Thank you sir," Jameel looked at Fatinah. "I am willing to wager, and I am not a gambling man, your father had a plan to send me packing on the next flight back to Egypt and get his daughter back."

"If he did, we are on a fight to Athens tomorrow. I cannot believe he would go this far."

Fatinah realized that in her absence nothing had changed.

"I do. I know why the official welcomed us. We are on the same passport. He could not send me out of the country unless you went with me. I believe your father would go to any extreme to get his daughter back. I question we are doing the right thing by visiting with him at all. We could avoid him and stay at the Dorchester tonight."

"We should try, but if he has done this, we will leave on the next flight to Athens. My father has meddled in my life long enough. He must accept the fact that I am a grown woman."

Fatinah was crying. "I love you Jameel. Do not abandon me because of my father."

"The last thing I would do is desert you. I love you and we will make a life together. If your father cannot accept that, he is going to not only lose his daughter, but he might never see you again."

Jameel and Fatinah walked toward the luggage claim; he held her hand and squeezed it lightly.

"Do not worry. I am with you. I will not let you down."

As they approached the baggage carousel, an official asked for their baggage claim and said he would get it for them.

"Thank you." Jameel gave the man a five-pound note.

Robert Cavendish saw them and walked quickly to where they were standing.

"You are wearing an abaya and hijab. I hardly recognized you."

He wrapped his arms around Fatinah and hugged her tightly. "Cassandra, I have been so worried about you. I am so glad you are back in London."

"Father, I told you my name is Fatinah. This is my husband Jameel."

"To me you will always be Cassandra. I will not call you that other name. I disapprove of your being covered head to toe. At least you are not veiled."

Robert did not acknowledge that Jameel was standing there.

Jameel released Fatimah's hand and extended his hand toward Robert Cavendish, "I am your daughter's husband, Jameel al-Basara. I had hoped we could meet civilly. Apparently, you do not wish to acknowledge I am standing here with my hand outstretched. Is this the way you plan to treat me during our visit?"

"I do not know you sir. I wish to visit with my daughter for a while in private."

Fatinah glared at her father, "If this is the way you feel, Father, Jameel and I are claiming our luggage and spending the night at the Dorchester. We will fly to Athens on the first flight out in the morning. I cannot believe the way you are acting. I love Jameel. He is my husband. You do not own me. I am a slave to no one," she shouted in an angry tone of voice.

Jameel smiled at her reference to being a slave and watched without saying a word.

Robert Cavendish was not prepared for his daughter's reaction.

"You should be ashamed of speaking that way to your father." Robert, his voice strained, shouted in reply.

Fatinah was furious and replied, "You should be ashamed of yourself. I do not know you. I have not seen you for weeks and this is the way you act. What is wrong with you? You should rejoice that I am in love with a wonderful man and we are so happy. Celebrate with us. If you do not acknowledge my husband, I will tell him that my father is dead; I do not know the man standing in front of me. As for my dress, I wear this in public only out of respect for my husband's wishes. On occasion, I also wear a veil."

Fatinah continued and was becoming more vexed by the minute. "Did you try to hinder Jameel from entering the country just now? I want the truth; no lying to me; I would know."

Tears rolled down her father's cheeks. "I did. I wanted my little girl back so badly. I did not realize you were that much in love. Give me another opportunity to make things right. I could not live if I lost you forever. I am an unthinking overly protective boorish man. I am an old fool." He turned to Jameel, "I am Robert Cavendish, Fatinah's father."

He extended his hand and Jameel grasped it firmly.

"I wanted to meet you sir, believe me; your daughter is my life. I could not live without her either. Let us forget our first greeting and start to know each other from this point onward."

"Thank you. You are most compassionate. I do not deserve it."

Fatinah hugged her father. She looked from her father to Jameel, You two will have to share me. I love you both."

A porter collected their luggage and they got into Robert Cavendish's limousine and drove to his home in the country. "We are not going to London?"

"I thought you would enjoy riding Humam when you returned."

"Yes, I would. Did I tell you that Jameel raises Arabian horses? They are known all over the Middle East as some of the finest."

"No, you did not mention that." He turned to Jameel. "We will have to talk about horses when we get there. I will show you their papers. They are from Egyptian stock."

"I am sure I will recognize the sire or dam. My family has raised horses for over a hundred years. We are one of the oldest breeders of record. You should return to Egypt with us; the National Horse Show is in October. You would find it interesting. My horses are 'Straight Arabian'."

"Do you export your horses?"

"No, I believe that moving an Arabian horse from the dry climate of Egypt to the cold and damp of Great Britain causes problems and would eventually lead to a genetic change. For centuries, we have raised Arabian horses in the harsh climate of Egypt. It is not easy to move them elsewhere. That is why I only sell sperm."

"I have heard of that show. Humam, Cassa . . . Fatinah's horse is pure Egyptian. His line goes back to the state stud farm El Zah-raa."

"That is a good line."

Fatinah interrupted, "You have found a common interest. I am so glad to hear you discussing something you can both agree on without any nasty innuendos."

"Horses have always been of interest to me. I am sure Jameel will enjoy seeing my small herd. I have two stallions and four brood mares. They are all from Straight Arabian stock."

"I am anxious to meet them. My horses are part of my family. I am most proud of my stallion Altair."

"He is an exceptional horse Father. Jameel and I rode several times the first week we met."

The car slowed and pulled into a gated entrance. The gate opened and they drove to a huge house surrounded by the magnificent rolling English countryside. Long fences along both sides of the lane enclosed lush-green paddocks. Several horses were grazing on the tall grass.

"After lunch, I will have the stable boys saddle three of my horses and we will go for a long ride."

"I have missed Humam. Could we take him to Egypt with us?" Fatinah asked Jameel.

"We could do that, but I would not use him for breeding. I do not know how he would acclimate to the harsh Egyptian climate. He is used to moist and cool conditions. I know you are fond of your horse, but it may be best if he stays in England where he was raised. Many horses do not do well when imported into Egypt."

"I think Jameel is right. He is fifteen years old and a change like that might make him ill or even kill him. I am sure Jameel will give you a horse to ride."

"He already has. Her name is Badra. She is marvelous and will drop a foal in the spring. Jameel told me I could name it."

The car pulled to the front of the house and a servant came out to carry in the luggage.

"Lunch will be served in an hour my Lord."

"Thank you Geoffrey."

"Geoffrey will show you to your room. I have put you in the large guest room overlooking the meadow."

"Oh Father, I have always loved that room. Come Jameel. I will show you the way."

Jameel and Fatinah went upstairs and freshened before going to lunch.

"Your father's home is quite impressive."

"It is part of a much larger estate. We have only five hectares. The barn is big enough for twelve horses. The house has six bedrooms. The main estate is owned by someone else and is being restored. I think you and my father will get along. He loves horses and is very proud of their lineage. If moving Humam might make him ill, he should stay in England. Wait until you meet him; I have owned him since he was a three-year old."

"It is helpful that your father and I have a common interest. When I first met him, I thought we would be at the Dorchester by now planning to fly to Athens in the morning. I am glad we are staying for your sake. Despite incident at the airport, he is still your father and you would regret leaving him. He is welcome to return with us to attend The National Show in October."

Fatinah changed into her riding clothes. Jameel had not planned to ride and had nothing to wear. "I did not plan on riding, is there a pair of boots I can borrow?"

"I am sure we can find a pair to fit you. My father's head stable man is about your size."

After lunch, they walked to the stables and Fatinah was right; Henry's boots fit perfectly.

Fatinah walked over to her horse and he nuzzled her as she blew gently over his nose.

"This is Humam."

Jameel surveyed the horse as if he was going to purchase it.

"He has beautiful lines. He is pure Arabian. Would it be possible to see his papers before we leave? I recognize his breeding."

They mounted up and rode. Jameel was impressed that Robert Cavendish was such an excellent rider.

"You must have ridden competitively at one time, sir."

"Yes, I did. Please call me Robert. When I was younger, I won many competitions. In 1988, I rode in the Summer Olympics after qualifying for the Equestrian team, took a Bronze Medal. It was one of the best memories of my life. Fatinah was just a little girl and her mother was still alive."

They returned to the house and planned for the return trip to Egypt. Fatinah found her father sitting in his favorite chair smoking a cigar.

"Father, Jameel and I will fly to Athens, to board Jameel's yacht and cruise to Alexandria. He lives in Cairo, about a three-hour ride by car. When we arrive, we will be celebrating our marriage at the wedding of friends of ours."

"You told me you were married."

"We are, but we had no reception with our friends. We had a signing of contracts and a private ceremony at Jameel's home. Hassan and his wife Emunishere who is an American are close friends. Hassan and his brother own several hotels and Hassan's father is a surgeon at the same hospital as Jameel. I'm sure you will like them."

"Will it be a Muslim ceremony?"

"I am a Muslim, Father."

"How could you? You were raised a very Christian woman? I thought the abaya was for public show; I did not realize you were now a Muslim." Trying desperately to comprehend what was happening her father reacted in anger.

"Father, you have not been in a church since mother died when I was six. We only went to church on Christmas and since I was eighteen, I have not done that. Do not be a hypocrite. I have become a Muslim, not just because of Jameel, but I believe as they do. I share their morality. The main difference between Christianity and Islam is that they do not believe Jesus is the son of God, but he was a messenger, a prophet. In the QURAN, it states all the prophets were messengers of God and Mohammed was the last messenger of God. To marry Jameel, I became a Muslim. You will never have need to worry when you grow old. Muslims treat elderly family members with honor and kindness. There are no old people's homes in Muslim society. Family is the foundation of Islam. Jameel has taught me about Islam and I became Muslim, Father. It was my choice. Allah is the Arabic word for God."

"I am displeased, but there is nothing that can be done now. It is clear you have made up your mind. No more talk of religion, my beliefs are set." Robert Cavendish shook his head and was annoyed with her decision, but reluctantly accepted it.

"Have you made a decision about going back to Egypt with us?" Fatinah asked.

"It appears that this may be the only opportunity I have to spend time with my daughter. Of course I will come, what choice do I have?"

"Thank you Father you will not regret it." She kissed him on the cheek.

Jameel entered the room and asked what they had discussed.

"Wonderful news, Father has decided to join us."

Her father spoke to Jameel.

"I am looking forward to learning more about your family. Will we have time to visit your stud farm and ride?"

"My parents will arrange everything. My horse farm is some distance from my home in the city. I will ask them to get tickets for the National Horse Show. You will stay at my home in Cairo which has a very large guest suite where you will be comfortable."

The trip went smoothly and the three arrived in Cairo three days before the wedding.

Chapter 27

Dr. Gaafar entered Hassan's hospital room. Emunishere was sitting at his bedside.

"The wound is finally healed and you are strong enough to go home. You would be home by now if it had not been for the severe bacterial infection you developed. I heard from Jameel. Fatinah's father is coming to Egypt and we will all be attending the National Show in October. It seems Cavendish is also a horse breeder and a former Olympian. He won a Bronze Medal for the British Equestrian team in 1988. He will be anxious to see our stud farm along with Jameel's."

"It sounds like he has accepted Jameel."

"He attempted to keep Jameel out of the country but gave in when he discovered she was now an Egyptian citizen and on the same passport as Jameel. He seems to have accepted their marriage and the fact that his daughter is now a Muslim. I will arrange for a car to take you home. Emunishere, you look more radiant every day."

"Thank you." She reached down and picked up two large packages she had brought with her to the hospital. "This is for you and the other package," she handed Hassan a package, "is for you. I finally finished, I hope you like them."

The two men opened their gifts.

"I love it," Hassan grabbed her, pulled her to him, and kissed her. "It looks just like Baraka. I could reach out and stroke her silky mane. Thank you."

Dr. Gaafar opened his, and it was a portrait of Hassan done in oil and placed in an exquisite frame.

"My wife and I will treasure this always. You have a wonderful talent."

"Thank you. I want to paint portraits of all your horses. They are exceptional. I had one of your servants drive to the horse farm and photograph Nabil."

She turned to Hassan, "I am painting a portrait of him for a wedding gift. I am almost finished."

"I shall treasure it always." Hassan took her in his arms and kissed her.

"We will see you for dinner at eight."

Hassan and Emunishere drove to his home. Emunishere had been staying with his parents and her luggage was in the car.

"It will be nice to get back to my own home. I have not been here for over a month. I called from the hospital and my staff has everything ready."

"I am anxious to see where you live. Your father said he thought you should have the pleasure of introducing me to your home."

"I am looking forward to it. It has been so empty for the last year. There were days I stayed at the hotel rather than face the emptiness."

"I understand; hopefully your life will be full again. I love you so much and worry when you get that distant look in your eyes. I know what is going through your mind; you will never forget them. You should not, but try to remember the good things. I hope I can make you contented and untroubled again. Your mother is so worried."

Entering a hidden part of the city one building towered above the rest. The narrow street was in the Garden district near the Arabian Embassy. They passed a long line of men waiting patiently to get visas.

"See that tall apartment building. Our home encompasses the top two floors. We have five bedrooms, five bathrooms, and servant quarters."

"It is a very modern building. Have you lived there long?"

"I moved there just before my marriage. I will introduce you to my driver and his wife. They live in the apartment and she is a wonderful cook. There are other staff members, but they do not live in my building."

"I am anxious to meet them."

The sedan pulled into the underground garage and the driver parked the car.

"Go on Hassan. I will bring the luggage. Karimah and Abu will be glad to see you. They did a lot of cleaning while you were gone and Abu repainted two of the bedrooms."

Hassan ushered Emunishere onto the elevator, inserted his personal key, and they began to climb to the penthouse.

"Only Abu, you, and I will have a key to the elevator. I will have one made for you. This part of the city is safe but limiting access gives us security knowing that no one else can get to the penthouse."

"What about the stairs?" Emunishere asked.

"All the doors leading to the stairs open from the inside but lock automatically when they are closed. A locked wire gate, which can only be opened with a key from the outside, blocks access to the top two floors. In case of an emergency, it pushes open from the inside."

"You certainly take security seriously, everywhere in Egypt."

"Egyptians are good hearted people but this is a very poor country. Desperate people do desperate things. They steal to eat and feed their families. Unlike the British and Americans, we prefer to take precautions to deter potential threats rather than waiting until something happens.

Do not go out alone. Abu or Karimah will accompany you whenever you go out of the apartment. Abu is an experienced driver and Karimah will help you with shopping until your ability to read Arabic is better. The big mall in Heliopolis has everything including signs in both English and Arabic."

Abu opened the door, embraced Hassan, and kissed him on both cheeks.

"It has been an empty home without you. Karimah is anxious to meet your future wife."

"Abu, this is Emunishere. We will be married in a few days. She is a wonderful woman and very talented." He handed Abu the painting. "Hang this in the living room. It is a painting of Baraka, my brood mare. She is currently painting a portrait of Nabil."

Abu unrolled the canvas and smiled with approval.

"You have captured her in paint. You are a very talented artist."

Hearing the commotion Karimah left the kitchen and came hurriedly to the front room. Seeing Hassan, she threw her hands into the air and exclaimed:

"Hassan you are fully recovered, but you look so pale. Have you lost weight? I will see you gain it back quickly. Does your shoulder still hurt? Is the infection gone?"

Hassan attempted to respond but could not get a single word into the conversation.

"I am fine Karimah. This is my future wife, Emunishere."

Karimah hugged Emunishere and kissed her on both cheeks.

"You are almost as tall as Hassan. You will have very tall children."

"I think you are right." Emunishere responded in Arabic.

"Your Arabic is excellent. I will help you learn to read and write."

"Thank you."

Hassan took her by the arm; let me show you my home. He walked with her to the large windows that opened onto a balcony.

"The view of the city of Cairo from here is breathtaking. You can see the Nile and watch the feluccas sail up and down the river. It feels more like my home used to feel just by having you with me. Come let me show you the dining room and kitchen. I have a computer room on the first floor and a library."

The windows of the sitting room were tall and narrow; each covered in translucent white and gold embroidered fabric. The ceiling and the cap around the top consisted of intricately carved wood paneling. Ornate brass fixtures hung on long gold chains. The furniture upholstery was light blue and gold brocade. Several large cushions covered with the same material littered the floor. Low tables inlaid with Mother of Pearl held fresh flower arrangements, their fragrance filling the room.

Emunishere found herself drawn to the sculpted figures that stood upon pedestals placed to capture best the diffuse natural light provided by the windows. The alabaster figure of a woman with her arms outstretched holding a shawl was perfect in every detail, smooth polished stone revealing every anatomical detail as if frozen in time for all eternity. She caressed the smooth surface.

"It is beautiful, so lifelike. Who is the artist?"

"They are contemporary pieces sculpted by a local Egyptian artist. I do not know his name."

A flash of color caught her eye as she glanced around the room. "Those glazed tiles on that wall look much older than this apartment."

"Yes, they are, much older. Those tiles once adorned the walls of a Sultan's palace. I bought them at an art auction."

"You have a fine eye for art. Those abstracts, are they by Hisham Zrake?"

"Yes they are. They are from the 1950's. Do you recognize that large painting over the sofa?"

Emunishere carefully examined the large oil tracing the brush strokes with her hand as though she was painting.

"This one is by Gizam Sagar and the one on the other wall is another Hisham Zrake."

"I did not know you were such an art connoisseur."

"There are many things you will learn about me over time."

"I hope to. You never cease to amaze me. Come with me I have the yet to show you the best parts of the house."

They walked up the stairs and down a long corridor with two doorways on each side. At the far end was another doorway leading to the master suite.

"Where does that door lead to?" Emunishere asked pointing to the end of the hall.

"That my dear Emunishere is our master suite. It has an awe-inspiring view and its own balcony. Each of the other bedrooms has its own bathroom. The servant's quarters are on the first floor behind the kitchen."

Sunlight reflected off the cream white walls gave a warm glow to the entire room. The French doors opened onto the balcony. Emunishere looked around the master bedroom. The bed had a magnificent silk throw with a gold embroidered design. The floor was wood parquet and covered by silk carpets in intricate designs. A painting called *Oriental Dancers* hung on one wall of the bedroom"

"I know that painting. It is by Paul-Louis Bouchard and that other painting is *Harem Bath* by Rudolph Ernst. Are they originals?"

"They were a wedding gift from my parents. They are reproductions in oil by a modern artist."

"They are exquisite."

Curious to see everything Emunishere walked into the bath. Sculpted marble sinks adorned with gold fixtures and an etched glass shower large enough to hold three stood in one corner.

Hassan called for her to join him on the balcony.

"It is just as beautiful as you described," Emunishere remarked drinking in with her eyes the vista of the city below spread out below like the finest oriental carpet in muted shades of tan punctuated by spots of bright color and green vegetation. She turned to Hassan.

"I look forward to the wedding and having Jameel and Fatinah celebrate with us. Is her father coming to the wedding?"

"I'm told he is coming with them, but is not very pleased that Fatinah is now a Muslim."

"I will talk to him. Remember I have lived with a mixed religious household all my life. My mother was Muslim; my father never converted, but never objected to her religion. My uncle was most unhappy with my father's marriage, but he never pushed that I join he and his wife at church on Sundays. Some people will not change and it is best not to try. Perhaps in time he will come to accept her beliefs. Personally, I was always confused with Christianity, too many interpretations of the *Bible*; there were always unanswered questions."

"It is important that a father attend his daughter's formal celebration of marriage. It is a special day. Robert should be happy his daughter is in love and not dwell on the faith she has chosen." Hassan looked at her and smiled, "I love you so much, and that is what is important."

He took her in his arms and kissed her affectionately on the mouth. "I love you from the inmost recesses of my heart. It has been very difficult for me not to make love to you." He held her close and looked into her amazing green eyes.

"I too want to make love to you. Once we are married, we have a lifetime to discover each other, explore our passion."

Hassan pulled her closer pressing his body into hers.

"Let me hold you close. The feel of your body next to mine feels so right. We have not known each other that long, but I feel I have known you forever. You are soft yet strong, sensual but discreet, intellectual and kind, an extraordinary woman."

Hassan was becoming aroused and kissed her before returning to the bedroom. Emunishere sat on the edge of the bed.

"It will be nice to see Alex and Magdalena again. What has happened to Yuri?"

"That is a long story. Officially, Yuri Berezovsky died from his wounds. We had to change his identity and made him a British subject. We are sure that the Mossad will be looking for him or an assassin hired by the Russian Mafia. His new name is Asad al-Katib and the information he has given us has already proved useful and allowed us to take down a major operation in Athens while capturing one of the leaders. We will never stop the slave trade, but we can slow it down. Every life saved is a victory. His cooperation comes with great risk to his personal safety. You must not reveal his identity to anyone at the wedding. One slip of the tongue could cost him his life. Asad is a very common name for men with an Egyptian background. He speaks fluent Arabic and will only speak Arabic and some broken English while he is here. As part of his cover, we gave him a Russian/Romanian mother with an Egyptian father. He has a moustache, and wears brown contacts. You will not recognize him. He looks and sounds like a very different person. Because of his leg wound, he walks with a limp and requires a cane. Since you last saw him, he has fallen in love with his nurse at the hospital."

"Why is he invited? That Russian bastard tried to abduct me. I could have ended up like Fatinah, sold as a sex slave. I will let you know how effective his disguise is. I will never forget those blue eyes, but with contacts and a mustache, he will look different."

"We need to know if his disguise is sufficient to fool people, even those who know him. His life and that of anyone working with him will depend on it. You, my father, Jameel and Fatinah along with Alex are the only people who know his real identity. The first time I saw him at the hospital, I failed to recognize him. He and the nurse stopped by to visit. His disguise is perfect. When he speaks English, the Russian accent is barely noticeable."

"Can he be trusted?"

"Alex says he trusts him and that is a good enough recommendation for me."

Chapter 28

Under the direction of Boris Schochat, head of a powerful Mafia group based in a small town near Moscow, the small covert group inside of Mossad tried to determine who had compromised their human trafficking operation.

The five men gathered in a room located in one of the sub-basements hidden in the middle of a large government building. It was a room marked 'Private'. These very special members of Mossad sat at a table with Boris Schochat a known criminal to discuss their plan to discover the traitor that had leaked information that led to the takedown in Athens. Ironically the sign above the table printed in English, Russian, and Hebrew read.

> *"Where no counsel is, the people fall, but in the multitude of counselors, there is safety."*
> *Proverbs XI/14.*

Boris was a heavyset man standing 190 centimeters with dark brown eyes and hair wearing black slacks and a long sleeved blue shirt. Bushy eyebrows that met in the middle of his brow topped his heavy framed dark tinted glasses hiding the fierceness in his eyes. Approaching fifty, this middle-aged man had developed a paunch that overhung his trousers. His arms were muscular and he had the grip of a bear. A cigar was clenched in his teeth, stained brown from too much smoking.

The four other men were in their early thirties, Ofer Inbar, Dror Caspit, Dov Zahavi, and Amir Harari; sat along both sides of the large table with Boris at the head. They were Israelis, trusted members of one of the world's elite intelligence agencies. Unknown to Mossad, they had developed strong ties to the Russian Mafia. The men sat smoking Cuban cigars while drinking from a bottle of Russian Vodka that sat in the middle of the table.

Each man had a shot glass in front of him. They all clinked glasses, drank a shot of the fiery liquor, and poured a second round. Cigar smoke hung in the air drifting over the table to form a cloud. The scene was reminiscent of a back room political meeting in the American segregated south.

"Comrades, we have a major problem. Our warehouse in Cairo, Egypt is shutdown, and out of business. Two shipments of women were lost and are irretrievable. The first group consisted of twenty women under Yuri Berezovsky's control and the second was a group of thirty women that were Ivan Sternovsky's responsibility. Last week, the travel agency in Athens, Greece was closed permanently by the Greek authorities."

Boris slammed his fist onto the table.

"We have a mole, a leak, a traitor in our midst. This cannot go on. Others are beginning to notice. If we cannot hold our organization together, we will fail. We have too much invested to let this happen."

Boris turned to one of the men seated at the table. "Amir, we depend on this business. The informant must be found, and identified soon."

"Boris, we have at least three possibilities and all three of them are dead. Yuri Berezovsky was shot and killed in the Sinai Mountains when we lost that shipment of twenty women. Dobrashin died at the warehouse in Cairo and Ivan Sternovsky was also killed in Cairo."

"One of the guards with Yuri was shot and is being held in an undisclosed prison by MI6." Dror added. "I did not think he knew enough information to be a danger to our operation, but perhaps I was mistaken."

Dov entered the conversation. "Are we sure that Yuri, Ivan, and Dobrashin are dead?"

"One of the Bedouins we contacted said Yuri was still alive when they airlifted him to hospital in Cairo," Caspit added, "He had a shoulder and leg wound and overheard the doctor say he had lost a lot of blood. Later that night, the hospital released a statement that he died on the operating table. We checked out the information using an operative in Moscow who reported that his remains arrived there and claimed by his uncle. Yuri had requested cremation, and that his ashes be scattered over the Caucasus Mountains."

Boris shook his head in agreement.

"I know his uncle, Petrov. He is very close to us and personally attended to everything. Petrov would never have gone along with a plot to cover up anything especially if it concerned Yuri. He is the one who convinced Yuri to join us after that problem he had in Singapore. Yuri's bank account is closed and his uncle received a letter from the bank giving him access to the funds." "What about Dobrashin and Ivan?" Amir asked.

"Their bodies were flown to Moscow and I took care of the arrangements personally. I identified both men." Boris continued. "That leaves us with the guard, Aleksandr Zahavisky, who was not killed, but wounded. We need to find where MI6 is keeping him and put an end to his betrayal."

"He is costing us a lot of money," added Ofer.

"Let us begin with the Zahavisky family. See if they have had any correspondence with their son," said Boris in a threatening tone.

Ofer answered. "Only his mother is alive. His father died in Chechnya."

"Where is his mother?" Boris asked.

"She will be of little help because she suffers from dementia. The shock of her husband being killed along with the news three weeks ago that her son Aleksandr was wounded and captured by MI6 was more than she could bear. She withdrew into her own mind and had to be hospitalized."

Amir interrupted. "See if MI6 is open to an exchange. We hold a few British subjects they would like to see returned. We need to free Aleksandr and interrogate him and to find out who he has been giving information to and why."

Boris responded, "The wheels are in motion. Remember, only the members of our small group can get involved with this kind of business. If this were to leak, they would arrest all of us and we would disappear. The current PM would not help us. Our friend, the former PM is long dead. Mossad would order all our deaths."

Boris continued to outline their strategy. "For this operation the following will be your code names. Amir, you will be STRONG; Dov, you will be BEAR; Dror, you will be BIRD; Ofer, you will be DEER; and as always, I will be BUTCHER. You will each have an encrypted satellite phone for communication. You will receive directions on where to pick up your weapons and gear once you have checked into your respective hotels. Use one of your cover identities and use only code names between each other."

Dov asked. "What are our assignments, Boris?"

"Bear, you will fly to Athens tonight and check into the King George hotel. Your contact will be a block from the Omonia Metro stop. It is near the red light district in Athens. Check with the brothel owners. They may have heard something prior to the government raid on our travel agency. Keep a low profile so as not to attract any attention during your visit. Keep your identity a secret. Do not identify yourself as Mossad."

Dov took his phone, stretched his 185-centimeter lean muscular frame out of the chair, brushed back his shoulder length blonde hair, and left the meeting.

"Deer, you will fly to Cairo and make arrangements for another warehouse to replace Kahlil's operation. Be careful, once the government gets involved, these people become wary. It will probably cost us more."

Ofer, a bit shorter than Dov, but with sandy brown hair, grey eyes, heavy three day beard on his face, reached across the table, took his phone, poured himself one more shot of vodka, and drank it before he left.

"Bird, you will fly to Cairo and then onto El-Arish by bus, a port city east of Suez, not far from the border with Israel. I will arrange for you to meet a Bedouin by the name of 'Adey. He worked closely with Yuri and witnessed the battle in the mountains. Find a new base where we can hide the women until the Bedouin's can smuggle them into Israel. It should be more accessible but hidden. They know every inch of that country."

"Can this Bedouin be trusted?"

"He owes us. Yuri arranged circumcision for his daughter and two of his nieces by a doctor from Cairo. He has been working with us for three years and is our main contact with the Bedouins. They like the money and the freedom to have their way with the women before they are smuggled over the border. He is always eager to have more women and more money."

Dror, the tallest of the five men, almost two meters in height, leaned down and kissed Boris on both cheeks, picked up his gear and left the meeting.

"Strong, I have saved you for the most important mission. You will fly to London and try to pick up Yuri's trail. If he did survive the attack, MI6 has most likely turned him and given him a new identity. I understand he kidnapped a British Lord's daughter Cassandra Cavendish. Her father is a member of the House of Lords. She seems to have disappeared. The Bedouin's say they never saw her and that Yuri did not bring her to the mountains. I want to know what happened to this woman."

"What are your plans?" Amir asked.

"I will return to Moscow and use my influence with some members of the Duma who owe me for favors I have done. Many of these men are my best customers. I want to offer MI6 a trade to free Aleksandr. He is the key to this mystery. Once we get him back from the British he will tell us everything"

Barely 25, Amir was already going bald and no taller than Boris. A full beard hid his features. Lean and muscular Amir was agile and highly skilled. He embraced Boris, poured himself another shot of vodka, drank it, smashed the glass into the wall, took his phone and left.

Boris, now alone at the table, drank another two shots of vodka, and finished his cigar. He took the time to call his brother Mikhail on the island of Cyprus and bring him up to date on the situation.

"Mikhail, you are needed on this mission. Fly to Cairo and find a new warehouse we can use as a retraining center for the women when they arrive. Your code name will be Fox."

A gravelly voice answered, "This must pay well or I am not interested."

"Pays very well, comrade. Call me when you arrive."

Boris turned off the lights and locked the door of the private chamber. He left the building and had a taxi drive him to the airport.

Chapter 29

The big day had come, but before the gathering at Jameel's house, Hassan drove Emunishere to the mosque in Cairo. When they arrived, the imam who was waiting for them escorted the couple to separate wing of the mosque. The ceremony, referred to as the "two testimonies" was brief. First was the confession: "I bear witness that nothing deserves to be worshipped except Allah, and I bear witness that Muhammad is the Messenger of Allah."

Emunishere then recited the second part.

"Ashadu an La Ilaha illa-llah, wa Ashhadu anna Muhammadan Rasulullah."

With the profession of the *shahadah*, Emunishere became a Muslim, submitter to God;, an adherent to the religion of Islam. They returned to the house to meet the arriving guests.

Jameel and Fatinah along with her father arrived the day before the wedding and were staying at Jameel's house.

The day of the wedding, all of Jameel's and Hassan's friends and families gathered to the beating of drums to announce their marriages. Hassan and Emunishere met separately with the Imam and signed the *nikaah*, the marriage contract. Emunishere already knew what to expect. Unlike Jameel, Hassan did not require Emunishere to wear an abaya, but in public, she wore a hijab, long sleeves and skirts or dresses that covered to her ankles. Before announcing the marriage of his brother to Emunishere and the marriage of Jameel to Fatina, Rafiq delivered an oration. When he finished, their marriages were proclaimed. Friends and family that had gathered, raised their hands, and prayed for the blessings of God on the two beaming couples. *barak-Allahubaraka Feekum*(May Allah shower you with his blessings. Words of a poem Fatinah loved went through her mind, and she whispered them to Jameel, "*I wish I could be your teardrops, for* what more could anyone ask for them to be conceived in your heart, born in your eyes, live on your cheeks, and die on your lips."

"That is inspiring, who wrote it?" asked Jameel.

"No one knows. It is in a collection of poems and the author is Anonymous."

Fatinah and Emunishere discovered that the most important of the restrictive regulations of Islam were those pertaining to marriage. Marriage in Islam is a sacred contract; expected of every Muslim. Love is not as a momentary passion, but a lifelong connection.

Emunishere and Fatinah got together after the ceremony and Emunishere said, "The young people in the United States could benefit from that one belief alone. Free love seems to be replacing marriage in the United States."

"The same applies to Great Britain. Many young people do not bother to get married. They move in together and when they tire of each other, they move on to a different partner. Jameel has taught me about Islam. How do you know so much?"

"My mother was Egyptian and a Muslim. I practiced her religion until I was thirteen. When I met Hassan, one of the first things I did was promise to declare myself as a Muslim; I learned all the prayers as a child from my mother. Hassan drove me to the mosque earlier today. We are both fortunate women to have found such wonderful men."

Alex and Magdalena approached the newlyweds.

"Congratulations to all of you. You will be glad to know that Magdalena's paperwork is completed. We plan to marry the moment we arrive in Scotland. The Bishop of Fettercairn, an old friend of my family, has agreed to perform the ceremony. I would not be married by anyone else."

"I am pleased for you. Fatinah and I will visit when the baby is born."

"We will look forward to that," Magdalena said.

Emunishere put her arms around Magdalena and hugged her. "You look wonderful, and are really beginning to show. Alex is a good man. I wish this slavery problem would end. I worry there may be more violence. You must have been worried when you got the news that Hassan was wounded. May they both be safe."

"I too, wish this slavery business was over. I know Alex is dedicated to closing down this operation. I pray no one is injured. I do not know what I would do if he were killed." She began to cry.

Jameel watched as Helen and Asad had entered the room. Asad was walking, with a pronounced limp, but with no cane. Helen held his arm as they walked over to Hassan and Emunishere.

"Hassan, I want to wish you the best of everything for you and Emunishere. May I introduce Helen. She has is one of the best nurses in the hospital." Asad spoke in Arabic.

Emunishere looked at Asad and smiled. "I am very pleased to meet you both. I understand you are working with Alex and are from England."

Yuri, now known as Asad, answered her in Arabic. "It is good to meet you. Hassan owns a hotel where I stay frequently when I am in El-Arish. I feel I have met you before." He touched his nose and winked. "You are very lovely and make an extraordinary bride."

"Thank you." She smiled in return.

Emunishere turned to Hassan, "If I had not been told, I would never have recognized Yuri. His Arabic is flawless. The real test will be if Fatinah's father recognizes him. He is walking over there now."

"Lord Cavendish, I would like to introduce you to Helen and her fiancée Asad." Hassan made the introduction.

"Pleasure to meet you; my daughter said she met you when she visited Jameel at the hospital. I believe Asad was one of his patients."

"Yes, I helped him with his rehabilitation. When we started, he could not walk without the aid of a cane or walker."

"Helen is a specialist in rehabilitation," Asad added.

"How did you injure your leg?" Robert Cavendish asked.

"It was a riding accident. I fell off a horse." Asad spoke in perfect English. Having practiced, he no longer sounded Russian, but British.

"I suffered a bad fall from my horse in competition and broke my leg," Robert added. "I was fortunate that over the years the limp went away, but on cool damp days, it still pains me. It has been over twenty years."

"With Helen's help and therapy I hope to walk long distances shortly and eventually without this limp."

"Best of luck to you both."

Asad and Helen moved among the other guests.

"He seems like a nice young man. He looks familiar, but I cannot place him."

Fatinah smiled, "Father, come, I want you to meet Jameel's parents. His father is retired from banking and spends his time raising horses. He has made all the arrangements for us to attend the National Horse Show next week."

Her father looked surprised.

"I had not planned to be here that long."

"Please Father. It will mean so much to me and Jameel."

"One more week, then I must return to London. There is some abominable issue coming up in Parliament and I must be there."

"I understand Father."

Alex and Magdalena joined Helen and Asad.

"It seems your new disguise is good enough to fool Lord Cavendish. He did not recognize you and Emunishere told me she would have never known you as the same man that tried to kidnap her off the beach. Your English has improved so much, you sound British."

"Having an Egyptian name and speaking Arabic, no one thinks of my being Russian. The contacts also hide my distinctive eye color. I hope Emunishere will forgive me for attacking her."

Alex laughed, "Emunishere told me you scared her to death and if you had suspected she knew martial arts, you would have won. She forgives you, but will never forget you."

"I am optimistic that in the months to come, we will all be friends." Asad replied.

"Magdalena and I leave for Scotland tomorrow for a week to get married. On our return to Cairo we plan to stop off in Switzerland to retrieve that evidence you mentioned."

"I will be ready. Helen and I will be waiting for your return. Trust me Alex; I am a different man. Helen and I were married secretly at the hospital by a local magistrate."

"Congratulations. I did not know."

"No one knows. We will be telling everyone later today. Is it permissible to move into Helen's apartment? It is walking distance from the hospital. I will be at the hospital everyday for rehabilitation."

"The arrangements will be made. Know this; however, if you do run; I will find you."

"I know that Alex. You will not be disappointed; we are partners."

Helen looked at Alex and gave him a hug. "He is a man worthy of your trust. I will keep him on the right path. He has responsibilities; a little one is one the way."

"I thought you were beaming. You have that same glow as Magdalena. Pregnancy brings out the best in a woman."

"Thank you."

The celebration went on for another two hours and Emunishere and Hassan got into a car with Jameel and Fatinah and drove to Alexandria.

"Thank you for the use your luxurious yacht. It is spectacular." Hassan exclaimed.

"My crew will give you privacy and take you wherever you wish. Enjoy. You are a great couple. See you soon."

Emunishere and Hassan went on board and two of Jameel's crew carried their luggage.

"Take care of my friends."

The yacht pulled away from the dock and Jameel and Fatinah drove back to Cairo. The next day they drove Alex to the airport and he and Magdalena left for Aberdeen where they took a private car to Fettercairn and Alex's castle.

Asad and Helen went home to her apartment. As soon as the door closed, he picked her up in his arms and carried her to the bedroom.

"Tonight I will make love to you in a way that was impossible in the hospital."

Asad undressed Helen slowly kissing her body as he went.

"Lay face down on the bed, I will massage your body for a change. He took a jar of fragrant oil and opened it carefully. The smell of fresh roses filled the air as he rubbed his hands together to warm the oil. He massaged her shoulders and kissed the back of her neck then running his hands along her body pressing his fingers into her muscles.

"If I press too hard, tell me."

Continuing to work his way down her body, he grasped her breasts, and squeezed them softly, then caressed the lower part of her back with kisses. His hands fondled her bottom, stroked her legs, and he kissed the innermost part of her thighs. Helen let out a sigh. Asad massaged her feet and kissed her toes.

"Turn over on your back; I have only begun to savor your body. In the hospital, everything was too much in a hurry. We have all night."

He kissed her Venus mount and gently spread her lips covering as much as possible with his mouth flicking his tongue inside of her eliciting a long sigh as he kissed her deeply. Pressing his erect manhood against her, he moved his hips slowly. Gradually he let himself enter her warm moist beckoning body then withdrew himself and slowly entered her again. Her body was hot to the touch, he could hold back no longer, and his thrusts became faster and closer together.

"Put your legs around me, I want to make love to your innermost parts."

Helen pushed down, her vaginal muscles seemed to grasp him and hold him as their bodies moved in harmony, and he could wait no longer. His muscles tightened and he drove himself into her as he exploded. Their mouths sought each other and they kissed until the necessity to breath overcame their lust. They lay exhausted in each other's arms.

"Helen, I have never made love to another woman until tonight. Having sex with a woman is not love. My love for you is endless and I will always cherish this moment."

"Asad, I have never been loved before." She cried and he held her close to him and kissed away her tears.

They fell asleep holding each other.

Chapter 30

Dov arrived at Athens International Airport wearing jeans and a dark blue shirt, hurried outside the terminal, took a taxi to the King George Hotel, and checked in at the reception desk using his false identity. The man at the desk handed him a package.

"This arrived early this morning for you Mr. Dmitriev. Is there anything you require during your visit? Do you have plans to tour our city?"

"No, thank you. I have been here many times and seen all the sights. Where is the Metro Station from the hotel?"

The man gave him the directions along with a small map. Dov took the lift and went to his room. After carefully unpacking and reading the contents of the package, he left the hotel and walked to the Metro Station. He got off the train at the Omonia Square Station and walked two blocks to his destination in front of an old hotel that looked as though it had seen better days. On each side of the main entrance were two large windows. An alluring woman sat in each window. Both blondes were dressed seductively and flashed beaming smiles at him but Dov paid no attention as he entered the hotel. An older woman met him at the reception desk. A tall heavyset muscular man stood behind her.

"I am Bear, you are expecting me."

"Yanni, take this man to the office in the back. We have been expecting you."

Yanni led Dov to a locked door at the end of the corridor. He knocked twice, waited about ten seconds and knocked two more times. Then the sound of an electronic lock releasing and the door slid into the wall as it opened. As soon as Dov entered, the door closed behind him and an electronic bolt dropped into place.

A heavyset man, obviously Russian sat behind a desk littered with stacks of paper and a bottle of vodka and several shot glasses. Various computers, resembling sentinels, sat in a row on desks along one side of the room where men were busy at each terminal. Anatoly Vorobyov poured two shot glasses of vodka and shoved one in front of Dov. "Sit down. It is good to see you again, Dov. Your gear is here."

Dov drank the vodka in one gulp and asked, "Anatoly, have you been able to find out anything about the attack on our agency? Were there any unusual customers before the raid?"

"There were three Brits that visited two days before the raid. They each paid for a woman, but not one of them had sexual intercourse with the whores. They hugged, kissed, and within twenty-five minutes, the three of them left. I thought it was odd at the time. That is a lot of money for a hug and a kiss."

"Did you find out their names?"

"Our customers rarely want to identify themselves. It has happened before; men just want to hold a woman. Stodgy Brits, what can I tell you. We questioned the women when they left and one of them mentioned the men were staying at the King George Hotel."

"I will inquire when I return to the hotel. We will need to find a cooperative agency already established or set up a new agency. It is too soon after the raid to set up a new business. Do you have any friends in the travel business that owe you a favor?"

"There is my cousin. He is always trying to make some extra money. He might be willing. He works for his parents who own their own agency. They would not do anything, but my cousin, he could be tempted for the right price."

"Look into it. I am returning to the hotel. My gear; what weapon do I have and is there a silencer?"

Anatoly placed a large duffle bag on the table and opened it up.

"Everything is here. A Glock 9 mm with several fully-loaded magazines, full metal jackets."

One by one, he removed the items placing them in front of Dov.

"You have night vision and a sniper rifle, clothes, extra cash, and a new set of identity papers. I checked everything personally. Good luck, we will speak again tomorrow. Return the gear before you leave Athens."

Dov carefully inspected the items before placing them back in the bag.

He returned to the hotel and sat in the lobby watching the porters and the concierge carefully. He noticed one of the porters, a man in his late thirties, was wearing a very expensive watch. The man singled out male tourists traveling alone that appeared to be wealthy. Money changed hands several times during the afternoon. Dov thought to himself, "This is a man who would be willing to help me for a price."

Dov approached the porter and took him aside. "I need some special services while staying at the hotel. Could you help me?"

"I am always ready to serve our clientele. What did you need?"

"I am interested in three men from London who stayed here a few weeks ago. One of them mentioned to me you provided him with an address of some interesting women."

"Yes, I remember those three. One of them, Alex, asked a lot of questions about where he could have a pleasurable evening."

"That sounds like Alex. I would like to check on them. I am working undercover and they are suspected of drug trafficking."

"They did not strike me as drug dealers."

"Could you take me to a computer terminal where I could research their reservations?"

"Not while I am on duty. Meet me across the street at the open-air café. I get off in an hour. We will come back to the hotel around midnight when it is quieter. This of course will be expensive. I could lose my job for doing anything like this."

"Understood, I will see you in an hour."

An hour later at 2300, Anastas, met Dov at the café. They ate some pastries and drank Turkish coffee until midnight.

"Come, I know a back way into the hotel where we can get in unnoticed. There is a computer terminal in a back office you can use, but I do not know how to access anything on the computer."

"I am an expert. Do not concern yourself. I read Greek."

Dov followed him into the hotel and as they were walking to the office one of the other porters called to them.

"Anastas, what are you doing back at work. Your shift was over a couple of hours ago?"

"I forgot something, Stamos. This is a friend of mine from Tel Aviv."

"See you tomorrow." Stamos went back to work.

Dov and Anastas entered the office and Dov quickly worked around the computer and brought up the registration records from three weeks ago.

"I do not see any men with the first name Alex."

"I remember. The other men had rooms in their names. Alex shared a room with one of them. Let me look."

Anastas looked through the reservations.

"There they are. The older man was Jonathan Bridgeway and his traveling companion was this man, Albert Cunningham. The third man, Alex, shared a room with Albert Cuningham. There is no record of his last name anywhere."

"Describe this man Alex."

"He was tall, muscular, dark hair, and had a scar that ran from his left eyebrow to his chin. The scar is probably from a knife fight; my brother has a similar scar."

"The other two men, I will need a print out of their information. It is fortunate you also have their passport numbers."

Anastas printed the information for him.

"You said you would pay me for this information."

"Yes, let us go to your apartment. I want to talk more about these men and find out anything else you may have noticed."

"My apartment is close."

The men walked about five blocks to a walk up apartment in a shabby building near an area filled with Tavernas.

"Describe the other two men for me."

"I want to see your money first. I have taken a risk to get you onto the computer. No money, no more information."

"Do you have a bathroom?"

"Yes, down the hall. My money?"

"In a few minutes, I have to pee."

Dov walked into the bathroom and carefully secured the silencer to his gun, put it back in his waistband under his shirt, flushed the toilet and walked back into the front room where Anastas was pacing back and forth.

The words, 'My money' had barely been spoken when Dov shot Anastas in the forehead. His head opened like a blooming flower and blood and yellow custard colored brain matter sprayed into the air and down the wall of the apartment. Anastas fell back on the floor. Dov wiped some blood off his shoe and left the apartment being careful not to leave fingerprints. He locked the door behind him and walked back to the hotel.

Dov went to his room and contacted Boris.

"I have the names of two Brits that were here three weeks ago. They were very interested in where to find women. I suspect they were with MI6. It seems that only local Greek authorities and an Egyptian made contact with the agency. I have no information on the Greeks or the Egyptian. It was very confused during the raid. I have the names and passport numbers on two of them. They are traceable. There was a third man, but we only have a first name and a description."

"Send me the information. Are there any loose ends?"

"I took care of the porter who helped me, but there is another man who saw me with him. He told his friend I was from Tel Aviv. I will take care of it and check out of the hotel tonight to fly to Cairo."

"Be careful. Do not kill anyone else. Two bodies from the same hotel will be sufficiently suspicious."

"I will take care of it."

Dov checked out at the desk and spotted the porter. He left his bags by the door, motioned to the porter, and took him aside.

"Your friend Anastas is off duty. He said you could give me information on some ladies of the night."

"Yes sir," he whispered.

"Good, come with me outside. Pretend you are going to have a cigarette. I do not want anyone to notice my paying a porter for information. I have friends at the hotel who might tell my wife."

"I understand sir; I have done this many times."

The porter walked outside and Dov directed him around the side of the hotel. It was two in the morning and no one was around. Dov was walking behind the porter and before they had gone ten steps into the alley, Dov shot him in the back of the head with his silenced gun. No one was in the alley and Dov walked back to the desk, retrieved his bag, walked ten blocks, got into a taxi at another hotel, went directly to the same Russian to return his gear before returning to the airport to catch his flight to Cairo arriving around noon the next day.

Chapter 31

Dror arrived at Cairo International Airport carrying a duffle bag, took a taxi to the bus station, and got on a bus headed for El-Arish. He arrived and checked into a five star hotel, Sinai El-Arish owned by Hassan and Rafiq. After clearing the security scanners, he approached the desk.

A young desk clerk greeted him, "Good afternoon Mr. Gerasimova. You have reservations for tonight and tomorrow yes. May I say, it is too short a stay? Our beaches beckon travelers to enjoy the sun and rest for at least a week."

"I am tempted, but I am on official business and have only two days to relax."

"This letter arrived for you this morning."

"Thank you."

Dror took the envelope and went to his room. He was traveling light and did not need a porter to help with his duffle. He read the note and took a taxi to the address on the waterfront. The building smelled of fish and the sea.

"Bird, I was expecting you. We are less than an hour from the border. It is almost like being home. Boris contacted me. You want to know if any Brits stayed at the local hotels recently."

"Yes, I have the names of two men from Athens, both operatives with MI 6. We only have a description and a first name of a third man. We need to know if these three men stayed in El-Arish. Begin with your hotel and see if the concierge remembers three Brits. They may have inquired about hiring local prostitutes for a pleasurable night. That was their cover in Athens.

Supposedly, Yuri tried to kidnap a woman off the beach near the hotel where I am staying."

"I did my own investigation asking several workers at the hotel what they may have seen around that time. The woman was a martial arts expert, broke Yuri's nose and got away from him. She was in the company of the hotel owner while she was staying here, but left for Cairo and the airport with another man."

"I cannot believe a woman broke Yuri's nose. That would piss him off."

My information says he left the area on his boat headed up the coast to another marina about three hours from here. Now that Yuri is dead, I assume the boat will go to his uncle. Right now, it is tied to a mooring."

"I am only here two days. The only gear I need is a handgun."

"It is a Glock and there are five magazines with it. Good luck."

Dror returned to the hotel and spoke with the concierge, "I am trying to discover if three men traveling together from London stayed at this hotel."

"When would they have been guests of the hotel?"

"About three weeks ago. Their names were Bridgeway and Cunningham. A third man named Alex was traveling with them."

"The names do not sound familiar, but we have many guests. Can you describe them?"

Dorr described the three men.

"I would have to check the hotel registry. I do not recognize anyone from those descriptions, I will see if the records are still here, while you have dinner."

"Records, still here?"

"Yes, we are one of a chain of several hotels with the same owners. Our records are in Cairo. We send them our registration records periodically twice a month."

"I will check back."

Dror went to the restaurant and Mohamed, the man Hassan put in charge when he was not at the hotel, immediately called Hassan on the satellite phone.

"There is a man asking a lot of questions about three Brits who may have stayed here. He had Alex's first name only. I did not recognize the two other names. He did not ask about Robert Cavendish."

"Alex said he suspected either the Israelis or the Russians would be snooping around. Who is this man?"

"His accent is Israeli, but the name on a Russian passport is Anikey Gerasimova. He is very tall, maybe two meters. His reservation is pre-paid for two nights. I will wire you his information. The passport is an excellent forgery; most likely supplied by Mossad."

"Tell him the registration records have been sent to Cairo. Give him the name of the Pharaoh's Pyramid Hotel. Contact my father and send word to Alex in Scotland."

"He is coming back to the desk. I will tell him."

"I am sorry sir; our records were shipped two days ago."

"What is the hotel where the records can be found?"

"Why is this of interest to you, you never said?"

"I am working on a rumor that three men from London are smuggling drugs into Israel from Egypt." He flashed a false government identification badge at Mohamed. "They may have been staying in El-Arish."

"There are many hotels in El-Arish. Have you checked with them?"

"I will check with the other hotels tomorrow."

"What is the name of your hotel in Cairo?"

"It is Pharaoh's Pyramid Hotel located on the Cornish. Will you need a reservation? I could call ahead and see if they have a room available."

"I also heard a woman was almost kidnapped off the beach near your hotel."

"Yes, she escaped injury, and the man disappeared. He escaped by boat."

"When something like that happens, it must be bad for business."

"Yes sir, but it received no public notice. The hotel manager handled it discretely and the woman's hotel room was at no charge. She was an American. Do you want me to phone ahead on that reservation?"

"Yes, do that. Thank you. The Russian government thanks you. Please keep this conversation off the record."

"But of course."

Dror went to his room and contacted Boris on his satellite phone.

"This hotel admitted there was an attempted kidnapping of one of their female guests, but they did not recognize any of the Brits. I thought I noticed a glint of recognition in his eyes when I described the man named Alex, but he said he did not know anything."

"Can you check their registration records?"

"There records are in Cairo. They retain no records at the hotel; it is part of a chain. I plan to investigate the other hotels in the area and if I find nothing, I will fly to Cairo and check with the main hotel."

"No, do not fly; go by bus. We had a problem in Athens; Dov killed two hotel porters. The story made the headlines and created some problems for us. Do you feel anyone should be eliminated in El-Arish?"

"No, the concierge was helpful and seemed to know nothing. I asked other hotel personnel and they remembered the tall American red head, but did not know of three Brits traveling together."

"Deer is already in Cairo and Bear should be there shortly. They are at the Nile Hilton. Contact them as soon as you arrive."

Chapter 32

Ofer arrived in Cairo and took a taxi to the Nile Hilton. Ofer was carrying a duffle bag and passed through security without a problem.

"Good afternoon Mr. Bagration. We have only one night reserved for you. Will you be staying longer? We are quite busy, but can reserve a room for you for three additional nights if you wish."

"Yes, make the reservation for at least two more nights. I did not realize you would be so busy."

"This letter came for you. You missed the messenger by only a few minutes."

"Thank you."

Ofer went to his room and called the contact number from his satellite phone.

Mikhail, Boris's brother answered the phone in a gravelly voice.

"Meet me at the pyramids. Take a taxi. I will be at the Kentucky Fried Chicken across from the entrance."

"I hate American food."

"I like it. You do not have to eat."

Ofer called Deer and Bear, they did not answer. He left a message that he was meeting someone and would return soon. He called for a taxi from his room and went into the lobby.

"Your taxi is out front sir,"

Ofer tipped the concierge and went to the KFC opposite the entrance to the pyramids.

"How have you been Mikhail, you look just like your brother?"

"I haven't seen Boris in six months, he is always in Russia."

"Boris is a wise man and a great leader."

"And you are a wise man to say that. What have you found concerning the raid on Kahlil's warehouse? Have you found a replacement?"

"The authorities are all over the warehouse district." Mikhail answered while eating chicken. "There is a group in Cairo driving this anti slavery movement. It is headed by a doctor from one of the local hospitals."

"Can he be eliminated?"

"He is only one man and there are at least thirty others. They are all capable of operating individually. Cutting down one man, will not eliminate the problem, but bring unwanted attention. We will have to work around them. A new warehouse is out of the question."

"What do you suggest?"

"I have made an acquaintance during my visit. This man is always looking for money. He knows of a Coptic Church in Cairo that has an empty basement. It was flooded several years ago and not being a wealthy church, they boarded it up and do not use it. It is not far from the airport and my friend says the director would love to make some money for his congregation."

"We need to meet your friend."

"His name is Yusef al Karim, a member of the church."

"Can we trust him?"

"We need him to show us the location. He said without money up front, he would show us nothing."

"I like this man already. He is greedy and willing to do anything. Call him."

Mikhail took out his cell phone and placed the call. "Yusef, it is Mikhail."

Ofer could hear the man on the other end of the phone.

"You are ready to see the property?"

"Yes, my man with the money has arrived."

"Good, I will meet you at the Hilton."

Yusef drove up to the hotel in an old Saab and the two men got into the car.

"My money."

Ofer handed Yusef an envelope with $500 American dollars. "Take us to the location. It had better be worth the money I paid you."

"Yes, yes. It will be a perfect location for your warehouse." Yusef laughed.

The car zigzagged through the confused traffic and they finally arrived at a Coptic Church in an area of Cairo surrounded by six—story high apartment houses. The only clean thing in the area was the laundry hanging from the balconies of the apartment houses. Everything else was dark and dirty.

Yusef parked the car and guided them to the back of the church. "See that door that is boarded. It is an outside entrance to the basement. The entrance from the church is blocked. This is the only way in."

"I do not like it. We need another way out of the building. One entrance will never do." Mikhail said in an irritated voice.

"You could tunnel out through one of the walls and come up near that old abandoned apartment house about fifty meters away. Come, let me show you."

Henry pulled back the boards and the three men went into the basement of the church. Henry flipped a switch on the wall; three bare bulbs suspended from the ceiling cast an eerie light over the dark, damp, dreary basement that smelled of mold and rodent excrement. The only sound was the scurrying of a rat.

"The smell is terrible. It is so dark. It will cost a lot to refurbish this hellhole. Stinks like a Russian prison." Mikhail grumbled.

"The director said he would consider a rental for six months. You fix the basement and he will allow you to hold your training sessions for the time of your lease. He will ask no questions about your business, but he wants $5,000 American dollars a month with three months paid upfront and the balance a month before the end of the lease."

"Did you tell him what our business is?"

"No, of course not. I said you were Jewish and needed to train some business men in the ways of dealing with Muslim Egyptian Arabs."

"He said a Jew doing business in Cairo might have difficulty."

"I explained that was why you needed a sanctuary to hold our meetings and that the basement of a church would go unnoticed."

"It sounds like your director is a greedy man."

"No, no, he will do it for the benefit of the church. They are a poor congregation and cannot afford the repairs."

Ofer and Mikhail explored the basement.

"We would have lots of room. If we soundproof the ceiling and walls, it might work. We would bring the women in after midnight and leave early in the morning. We would need to schedule during the week when very little is going on in a Christian church. They only get busy on Sundays, Friday night and an occasional prayer meeting once a week. No one would notice unless the neighbors complained about our vehicles coming and going."

"The people in this neighborhood are too busy trying to make a living. I do not think they would care."

Ofer added to the conversation.

"Yusef, take us to the director. We will hire five or six men to do the work. Make sure they are men with no families and not from this part of Cairo."

"I am sure the members of the church would help."

"No, I want no members of this church working on the project. I have my reasons. Can you find five or six men? They do not need to be Christian." Mikhail was sounding irritated.

"I can arrange everything."

The men left the church and Yusef took them across the street to the director's office. The director excused his secretary and locked his office door.

Hamal Arouyb was a man in his fifties, graying hair, clean-shaven, over weight by twenty-five kilos, dressed in a black business suit with a white shirt and no tie.

"I understand you need a meeting place for six months. There is a lot of work to do before that basement is usable. That would have to count as part of the six months." He said with an ever-present smile on his face.

"We can have it up and running in two, maybe three weeks. Our main restriction is that no one, absolutely no one, including you visits the basement until the end of the six months."

The good father was becoming suspicious and like a good businessman saw an opportunity to up the price

"I do not like this secrecy. I demand you pay $1000 more per month. I think that would cover the effort I must make to keep people from asking questions."

"You are a wise man. The $5,000 will be paid to the church and a $1000 will be paid separately to you."

"I think we understand each other. When would you like to begin work?"

"I think we can begin tomorrow." Ofer took a large brown envelope from a brief case he was carrying and handed it to the director. "Here is the first three months rent."

"The extra?"

Ofer reached inside his suit jacket and handed the director $2,000 cash in American money.

"That is all the loose cash I have with me. I will give you the balance the beginning of the fourth month. Remember. No one is to enter the basement. The windows will remain painted black and we will reinforce the door. The entrance from the church will not be usable, but we will restore it before we leave. We demand privacy."

"I understand perfectly. I did not get your name."

"I did not give it to you. You are well paid. The workers will not be from this area of Cairo. Question them and we will destroy your church. I hear Christian churches in Cairo are a prime target for terrorists. Am I making myself clear?" Ofer snarled at the director in a gruff voice.

"I understand perfectly, sir. I will see you for the balance in four months."

Ofer and Mikhail got back into Yusef's car. "Find us a crew by tomorrow. We will explain what work they are to do. These men have just two weeks and will have to work long shifts to complete the renovation."

"I know nothing of building."

"Then you will learn. You are well paid. We meet here tomorrow morning at five a.m. All your supplies and materials will be delivered before seven. Make it clear to these men; they speak with no one outside the basement. It will be their world for the next two weeks. They will live here while they work. You will stay with them."

"I have a wife and daughter."

"If you wish to see them again, make the arrangements. We demand certain things from our employees. Do not force us to visit your family."

"You would not dare touch my family." Yusef pleaded.

"You have no idea who you are dealing with. You are part of our operation now. Pick men that will not mind being living in a basement for two weeks if they are well paid. Tell them they will have all the food they can eat and women to keep them company." Mikhail told him in a stern tone of voice, his Russian accent making his Arabic hard to understand.

"If I refuse?"

"Refuse and you will not leave this car alive. Mikhail will ride with you and help with the recruiting. He speaks fluent Arabic. Do not try anything. Your family will suffer first." Ofer continued in an angry tone of voice. "Mikhail knows where you live and what school your daughter attends. We are in the business of trafficking women. Your daughter is twelve, just about the right age to sell for a good price."

"I will do what you ask. Do not touch my daughter." Yusef was almost in tears.

"Do what we ask and you and your little family will have $5000 American money for two weeks work. We will pay your workers the same,

$5000 American money is more than these men and you would make in six months."

He drove Ofer to the Hilton and Mikhail and Yusef drove to the other side of Cairo to find some workers for the project.

Ofer contacted Boris on an encrypted sat-phone.

"The director, Hamal, is very greedy and with the added threat of his church being leveled during a Sunday service, he was most cooperative. Of course, he and the six men working for us must all go away when the job is finished. I am thinking a fishing trip on Yuri's old boat. We can sink the boat or weigh them down and drop them into the sea. Arrange everything through Yuri's uncle. He has not touched that fishing boat in three weeks. Petrov likes money."

"I will make the arrangements with Petrov. Dov is on his way to Cairo. Do you know the Pharaoh's Pyramid Hotel?" Boris asked.

"Yes, it is very new and if there were seven star hotels it would qualify. It is on the Cornish. Why?"

"Dror was in El-Arish and found nothing on our three Brits. He noticed a spark of recognition in the concierge's eye when he described Alex at one of the hotels. We are not sure if it was our man Alex or not, but it will not hurt to check. The hotel registration records from the hotel in El-Arish are kept in Cairo at that hotel."

Did you make reservations for Dror at the Pharaoh's Pyramid?"

"No, he is staying at the Hilton along with Dov. He will leave a message at the desk when he arrives sometime tomorrow."

Boris continued. "Keep me informed. If you can have this basement finished in less than two weeks, do it. Pay them more money. It does not matter. We will just take it back when they finish."

"I understand."

"I want you to find those registration records without raising suspicion. Dror is a wizard with computers, find a terminal at the Pharaoh's Pyramid, and see what you can find. I do not want anyone asking questions. Mikhail met you with no problems?"

"He had everything planned, most efficiently."

Dror took a shower and began making phone calls to arrange for the supplies he needed for the basement. It took him the rest of the afternoon, but the supplies would arrive the next day before seven.

Chapter 33

Alex and Magdalena arrived in Edinburgh and picked up a rental car for their drive to Fettercairn, Kincardineshire Scotland to his ancestral land where the rebuilt castle stood. The original town of Kincardine had ceased to exist back in the middle ages. The only thing left was the ruins of the castle from 1296 when King John Balliol wrote a letter of surrender to Edward I of England following a short war for Scottish independence.

It was Magdalena's first time in Scotland. They picked up the A90 North just outside the airport.

"It will take us the better part of two hours to go the 156 kilometers. My staff will have the castle ready when we get there. Only part of it is completed. The rest is under construction. If you close your eyes, you can almost hear knights from the middle ages practicing their swordsmanship in the courtyard. The old banquet hall is now my dining room. I swear that on a quiet night you can still hear the hearty sounds of men drinking and hounds barking."

"I am anxious to see your castle. It sounds wonderful."

"It is. The section where I live has four bedrooms, a large great room, huge kitchen, library, and dining room. The plumbing is modern and everything is working smoothly. I like to wander around the ancient parts of the castle. The original castle goes back to the 1300's. My father bought the castle some years ago and had it moved here. The land where it stands has been in the MacKay family for hundreds of years. The ancient home was gone years ago. My father was quite eccentric and thought that the family should have a castle. He carefully restored it block by block erecting the tower and walls first before building the rest of the castle. It is an exact replica as it stood back in the middle ages."

"I know I will love it. Does your father live there?"

"The sad part is he never got to enjoy it, he died of a massive coronary within a month of this part being finished."

After what seemed an eternity of twisting roads and roundabouts, the castle came into view. It stood atop a hill surrounded by a dry moat in full bloom with colorful fall flowers. Where a drawbridge would have crossed the moat, Alex had built a modern bridge. They drove under the portcullis that operated the same way as a garage door. Alex pushed a button on a small remote and the gate rose slowly and dropped down behind them once they had passed.

"I had that installed about five years ago. We had some problems with privacy. Tourists thought it was open to the public even though there are several signs marking it as private."

"It seems to be far away from any tourist attractions."

"Never underestimate the curiosity of a tourist, especially American and Japanese tourists. It is not even an historic castle from this part of Scotland. The original castle stood many miles from here."

"Do you plan to finish it someday?"

"The work is finished with the exception of completing additional bathrooms and bedrooms, building a stable inside the walls, and adding a study. My caretakers, Albert and his wife Samantha, have their own living quarters complete with living room, kitchen and dining room. I had the moat dug and planted it with flowers that are changed with the seasons. The portcullis was my idea. I think the original castle may have had one, but I am not sure. Father always said it had one and he wanted to erect the gate, but never got around to it."

"Here we are." Alex stopped the car and helped Magdalena who was obviously stiff from the long ride. As they walked to the front door along a gravel pathway, a tall, thin, gaunt man with grey hair, in his early seventies opened the front door.

"Lord Alex, I have been anxious to meet your lady."

"Magdalena, this is Albert. He has been with the family since I was a child. He helped my father plan the castle."

"Pleasure to meet you Albert. It is a magnificent castle. It looks like it has always been here."

"Welcome to MacKay Castle. Alex has not stopped talking about you for the last two weeks. Every other word is about this wonderful, woman he met in Egypt. He is right, you are very beautiful."

"Thank you." Magdalena blushed.

"Where is your lovely wife, Albert?"

"Samantha is shopping for groceries; she will return soon."

Albert removed their luggage from the boot and brought it inside. Alex could hardly wait to show Magdalena around.

"Come let me show you the part of the castle that has been finished and the plans to turn that huge pile of cut stones into the rest of it in the spring."

They walked into the great room that had paintings of old Scottish kings on the wall and the MacKay coat of arms hung over the ancient fireplace. In the dining room paintings of MacKay ancestors filled the walls.

"The fireplace has been carefully rebuilt and looks like it must have hundreds of years ago. The castle has been in ruins for over two hundred years, but my father found some old paintings and even a sketch of the interior in an old book. He wanted it to look authentic."

"It does look authentic. Did Albert address you as my Lord?"

"I inherited my father's title when he died. I do not use it very often, but Albert never fails to address me as my Lord. My father was not into titles but Albert always addressed him the same way." Alex laughed.

"What was your father's occupation?"

"My great-grandfather and my grandfather were in the business of distilling fine whiskeys, a Scottish tradition. He and his father sold their business to the current distillery in Fettercairn. My family has not been directly involved in the business since the late 1800's. My father worked for a time as a consultant with the current owners, but they had their own ideas. It is still the finest whiskey in the world in my opinion. I always travel with a bottle or two in my luggage."

"My Lord, I put the bags in your quarters. Is there anything else you require?"

"No, that will be all Albert. Thank you."

Albert excused himself. "Pleasure to meet you Mam."

"We will meet with the Vicar tomorrow and ask him to marry us at a small private ceremony. I want you to be content."

Alex placed his hands on her belly.

"I will treasure this child as if I was the natural father."

"There is a bookstore on Portobello Road in Notting Hill that carries old antique books. On a trip to London, I paid the shop a visit and purchased an old book that contains stories that my grandmother used to read to me. Now I will have a chance to read them to our child."

Magdalena has just arrived and Alex had already planned her life. Eternally grateful for everything he had done for her, she did not want to hurt his feelings but her first concern was providing for her new baby and a large part of that plan was a stable home and a husband that would be around to watch her child grow up.

"Must you hold such a dangerous job? What happens to me if you are shot? That scar is so close to your eye; you are lucky you did not lose it. When did that happen?"

"It happened years ago, a complicated story. I believe in what I do. If I were not involved with this, I would have never found you. I promise to be careful. Come; let me show you the master bedroom."

"Oh my, it doesn't look like a room from a medieval castle. It looks like a suite from a very expensive hotel."

The room painted in pale yellow reflected the sunlight streaming through the large windows giving everything a warm glow. Dark mahogany furniture filled the room and the duvet was a patchwork of multi-colored silk. The floor was beautifully matched parquet covered with a deep burgundy Oriental rug. Lace curtains covered the windows and a decorative bead and dental molding ran the circumference of the room.

"I disagreed with my father's passion for authenticity. When he died, I refurbished the room to suit my taste. I like a comfortable room with all modern conveniences."

"It is so spacious," Magdalena said as she ran around the room stopping in front of Alex.

"Hold me, please."

Alex folded his arms around her and pulled her close.

"Magdalena I love you. I know you suffered a great deal. If it were not for Yuri you would have been beaten and raped and possibly lost the baby."

"Yuri, I mean Asad, said I rescued him, but if he had not stepped in to help us I might have died at the hands of the traffickers. I will never forget what he did for us. At the wedding, I hardly recognized him. No one will ever suspect his identity. Do you have to go to Switzerland with him?"

"We have time to get to know each other before I go. Albert and his wife Samantha will take care of you and I hired another woman to help with the chores. You will want for nothing. Relax and enjoy the beautiful countryside and everything Scotland has to offer. This is the best time of the year. My castle is your castle. I will make sure you have the best care when the baby comes."

"When do you leave?"

"I will let you know. Right now, forget my leaving. Here we are sheltered from the rest of the world, alone and only for each other."

Alex took her in his strong arms, kissed her, and held her tightly. He carefully unbuttoned her blouse, kissed her body, and caressed her breasts. Gently he picked her up and laid her on the bed. He helped her out of her blouse and bra and slid off her skirt along with her panties. After removing his shirt and pants, he covered her breast with his mouth sucking the nipple until it was hard and erect. Then moved to her other breast, and did likewise. Her arms held him and her lips kissed his chest with its carpet like covering of dark black hair. His fingers entered her and he felt her grow moist at his touch. He kissed her and his tongue flicked at her warm moist vaginal lips as he stroked her with his tongue. Her hand grasped his swelling manhood. Alex moved his body over her and gradually entered her with slow strokes going further and further into her as she lifted her hips toward him so he could go deeper. His thrusts became fiercer and he kept thrusting and thrusting until he exploded shooting forth his very being into her.

Breathless they remained motionless, frozen in place as one.

"I love you Magdalena," he whispered in her ear.

He rolled off her and lay by her side holding her in his arms. "I must tell you something and explain why your child is so important to me. I never want secrets between us."

"I cannot believe you ever did anything wrong. Tell me someday, but not today. I do not like sad stories. Tell me after the baby arrives."

"Magdalena, I hate having to return to work. Every time you look at your wedding ring, think of me."

Magdalena pushed away from him with tears streaking her face and ran to the other side of the room and stood in front of a set of French doors that opened onto a balcony,

"What is wrong?"

"Alex, I cannot marry you now. There is something I must tell you."

"I love you, talk to me."

"I lied to you. I lied to Yuri . . . Asad." Magdalena was crying.

"Lied about what?"

"I was not raped. I had an affair with an American soldier who was on holiday. He promised to take me to America with him. We were lovers for two weeks. I woke up the morning of the fifteenth day; he was gone. No note, no good-bye, just gone."

"I forgive you."

"No, you do not understand. Let me finish. When I discovered I was two months pregnant, I told my family a man raped me. They did not believe me, threw me out of the house, and called me a whore. I was having an affair; I was a whore."

"Marry me. I do not care if you lied."

"I knew the job offer I applied for might be a trap for slavery. I had read about these offers, but I did not care. I had nowhere else to go. I want to wait until the baby is born. I have to know you better. Forgive me. I will cannot marry you now, throw me out, and order me away. I need time. Please understand."

Alex grabbed her by the shoulders, looked into her eyes, and shouted, "What are you not telling me. I know you are still lying or holding something back. I want the whole truth. Who is the American that fathered your child? What kind of a man was he? Do you still love him?"

"No, no, he was so different from any man I had ever met before. He was so suave, promised me a new life and said he loved me. I wanted to believe him. He used me like a whore by making me do things I had never done before. I made love to him in many ways; he was into bondage, bound and gagged me. Using a flogger, he whipped my bottom until it was red and then slapped me with his hands. Sometimes he whipped my whole body, sodomized me with a phallus, but it aroused me and I let him do it. He had other strange ways to make love. It was not love, only his lust. He never loved me. I have no feelings for him except hatred. He used me."

"You have told me nothing to change my mind. Why must we wait until the baby arrives? What are you not telling me about this man?"

Magdalena burst into tears and pushed Alex away. "He was in the army. I tried to find him when I knew about the baby, but the name he gave me must have been false." She sobbed uncontrollably. "I was so stupid; money was all I wanted. I was a whore, this man paid for me for two weeks; my uncle was right. I was a well paid whore."

"What if I told you it does not matter how you got pregnant? Marry me tomorrow. I love you. I will love your child."

"Thank you for offering. I will not. If you feel the same way and still want me after the child is born, I will consider it. Please try to understand me." Tears streamed down her cheeks, "It is too soon. I have had too much happen in the last four months. Asad rescued me and I cared for him, but he could not help me. You shot him and threatened to castrate him. Other people were shot; I was terrified. You say that you love me. You lead a dangerous life and could be shot or killed at any time. What would I do if something happened to you?"

"Asad could not do anything for you, he thought he was going to prison for life. I do not understand you. If something happens to me, I will make arrangements, you will be cared for as well as your child. Stay here at the castle until the child is born. We will talk more in the morning. Answer one question, Magdalena, do you love me?"

"I do not know. I am not sure I know what love is. I do care for you and feel safe when you hold me. When you make love to me, my emotions soar and I never want you to let go of me. I am confused. Please, please give me time." Magdalena pleaded with Alex.

Alex walked her to the bedroom and went down stairs by himself. He picked up the children's storybook he had bought for his lost child and stared at the cover. "Will I ever read these stories to a child of mine?" He asked himself.

The next morning, Albert found Alex asleep on the sofa and a half-empty bottle of whiskey on the table. A glass lay shattered on the floor in a small pool of whiskey.

"Lord Alex, Henry Ewing has arrived and the Vicar is due in two hours."

"Go away. There will be no wedding today."

"You must get up. What should I tell Henry?"

Henry Ewing of MI6 walked into the room and glared at Alex.

"What do you mean, no wedding. You told me Magdalena and you were special, so much in love, what happened?"

"Go away Henry. I do not understand women. I never will. She will not marry me until after the baby is born. She told me she needs time."

"She's had a difficult go of it, raped, kidnapped, thrown out of her own family, and people around her were shot. I know you love her but you need to give her some time. I would like to meet her."

"I will tell her."

"Before I meet her, we must talk."

"It will have to wait."

"This cannot wait."

"I have read your reports. What you do not know is that Rafiq called from Cairo. The Israelis are snooping around. They already have the names Bridgeway and Cunningham. They know your first name is Alex, but that is all. They are using Russian passports that are very good forgeries. Only the Mossad could produce such accurate documents."

"Where are they?"

"They found out about the three of you in Athens. You must have made an impression at one of the brothels. We have an insider feeding us information from Athens. They sent another operative to El-Arish, but got no information there. I understand the man in El-Arish took the bus to Cairo. I am sure the operative from Athens is in Cairo as we speak."

Alex stood up and started to pace trying to understand what was happening.

"I must return sooner than expected. Do they still believe that Yuri is dead?"

"I have not heard otherwise. We are watching the apartment where Asad is living with his new wife in Cairo. Cunningham and Bridgeway have families. As a precaution, we sent them with their wives and children to Australia on an extended assignment."

"I am not dropping this investigation. I want to see it through."

"I have made arrangements for you and Asad to fly to Switzerland next week."

"We are getting close Henry. I know we will be successful."

"We are tailing the four men in Cairo. They are staying at the Nile Hilton. One man is Russian and the other three are most likely Israeli, but traveling with Russian passports. They were speaking Hebrew and Russian in the dining room of the hotel. We followed them to a Coptic Church in one of the poorer sections of Cairo where they are doing a lot of work in the basement."

"What are they planning to do in the basement of a church?" Alex asked.

"We are not sure. There has been no activity in the warehouse district since we raided their operation. We have kept our distance. Six men dressed like construction workers entered the church a week ago, and have not come out since. Every night six or eight women enter the basement and leave early the next morning. Building supplies arrive and the three Israelis and a Russian visit the site every day. They take turns guarding the building twenty-four hours a day. They each have a six hour shift."

"What kind of supplies?"

"Wood, wall board, doors, ceiling tiles, and yesterday thirty single beds were delivered."

"It has to be a replacement for the warehouse. They are using a church. How did they convince a church to go along?"

"No one from the church has gone near the basement. We have seen a man that is the business director of the church walk by several times. He tips his hat to one of the guards and continues his walk. I believe he knows. We have not approached him. The guards have a clear view of the director's house. They have observed him walking into the main sanctuary every day following his walk. We attended services last Sunday to look around. There appears to be no access to the basement from the main church. One of our men asked and he was told the basement was flooded years ago, but the director was having it refurbished with his own money as a surprise to the congregation. He said the basement would be opened in six months as a recreation hall, but no one would say anything because they wanted the director to think his plan had not been discovered."

Alex was troubled by the new information. Despite two successful raids, both in Cairo and Athens, the mob was still able to conduct business as usual.

"I will be in Cairo before flying on to Zurich and will take a walk by myself."

"Be careful Alex. These men know about that scar. They might recognize you."

"I will go at night. In the dark, we all look like shadows."

Albert interrupted, "My Lord, the Vicar has arrived."

"Thank you Albert."

"Please send him away. There will be no wedding today."

Henry acted surprised.

"He still addresses you that way? Albert will never change."

"I wanted to tell Magdalena about Catherine. She bolted before I could say anything." Alex whispered to Henry.

"Why would you tell her? It happened over a year ago. Leave it where it belongs, in the past."

"I do not want any secrets between us."

"Wait. If you must share your past, do it later, not now."

"I love her. I wish she would believe me that her past is not important to me."

"It is important to her. I am anxious to meet this woman. Please, let me talk with her."

Magdalena entered the room where Henry and Alex were still talking.

"Sorry, I did not realize someone was here."

"No, Magdalena, come. Let me introduce you to Henry Ewing. He is the man responsible for my not losing my sanity over a year ago. I want you to meet him."

"Magdalena, you are as enchanting as Alex said you were. I understand there will be no wedding today."

"No, not today. It is too soon. I had too much happen to me. I care for Alex, but I must know him better to marry him."

"Alex is a good man. He will wait; he told me so."

"I do not want to lose him, yet I must have time. Excuse me; I need to be alone. It was nice to meet you."

Magdalena hurried from the room.

"I must go to her."

"No, Alex, leave her alone. She loves you. I saw it in her eyes. If you go after her now, she might leave permanently. Trust me Alex, she loves you."

"I must return to Cairo tonight."

"Good, Tell her you love her and will call every day. She will come around, maybe even before the baby is born. I am glad you did not have a chance to tell her about Catherine. She has too much on her mind. That would have pushed her away forever."

Alex left and went up stairs to pack. Magdalena was staring out the window. He put his arms around her and kissed her gently on the cheek.

"Something has come up and I must return to Cairo tonight. I love you. Please be here when I return and promise me you will not run away."

"Is it because of me?"

"No it has nothing to do with you."

"I promise to wait. I do care for you. Thank you for understanding. Call me from Cairo."

"Every day."

"Do not hate me for not marrying you today."

"I could never hate you. I do not care what happened in your past. You are my only love."

He put his arms around her and kissed her affectionately on the lips and she returned his embrace.

"She broke down crying, "Give me time and come back safe."

Alex closed the door quietly as he left to join Henry.

Albert entered the room.

"Take care of her Albert. She is special."

"Yes, my Lord. She will be safe with me. Perhaps Samantha may help. One of her virtues is that she is understanding and listens well. Be careful sir. We need you."

Chapter 34

Alex arrived in Cairo and called Asad on the phone.

"You are back. We have a spare room; spend the night. Is Henry with you?"

Asad was glad to hear Alex was back as he was tired of sitting on the sidelines and wondered if his old enemies were getting close to discovering his secret.

"No, he decided to return to London, but will arrive in Cairo tomorrow."

"I will pick you up shortly. The Israelis and Russians are in Cairo searching for me"

"I know. We will talk as soon as you get here."

"You are in time for dinner. Helen is a marvelous cook." Alex arrived at Helen and Asad's apartment building located in an upscale neighborhood in the north end of Cairo not far from the airport. The apartment was on the seventh floor with a view of the Nile from their balcony. Even before they entered the apartment, they could smell the aroma of Pelmeny, spiced meatballs and boiled cabbage. The table was set for three and bowls of borscht with dollops of sour cream were on the table.

Alex gave Helen a hug, "You look happier than I have ever seen you. Careful of all the Russian food, the neighbors might talk."

"They are used to it," Helen answered. "I cook Russian and Egyptian food. No one cares. My father and mother live one floor down and it always smells of Russian food. Now they are in their apartment in Alexandria. You must meet them sometime."

"You are looking different, married life agrees with you."

"It does, and what is even better, I am pregnant. In eight months, we will have a little one. How is Magdalena? I am so happy for you."

"We did not get married. She is confused over everything that has happened to her. She needs time. I pushed too hard."

"Do not blame yourself Alex, Magdalena loves you. Trust me. She told me so before you left for Scotland."

They sat down to dinner to break bread and catch up on what was happening. As soon the meal was finished, Helen cleaned up and excused herself. "I am so tired. It must be the baby."

"Magdalena goes to bed by nine and sometimes as early as eight. Goodnight."

Asad went into the kitchen and returned with a bottle of vodka and two glasses.

"It is difficult to buy good vodka in Egypt. When we fly to Switzerland, I will buy several bottles at the duty free. Sorry to hear Magdalena wanted to wait. She seemed so in love with you."

"Magdalena is a woman with many secrets about her past. I do not think she knows her own feelings. I do love her, but I will have to be patient."

Asad poured two glasses; they downed the shots in one swallow.

"You drink like a Russian."

"There is something going on in Cairo. Three members of Mossad are in the city and putting something together in the basement of a Coptic church along with a Russian. We think it is a replacement for the warehouse we raided."

"I have been so busy with rehab I have not been anywhere but the hospital, this apartment, and shopping with Helen. As soon as I get my finances under control, we plan to buy a house or at least a bigger apartment in Alexandria near the water. I need to speak with you about a personal matter."

"Personal matter?"

"I have never asked anyone to do anything for me since I was eighteen. Do I have your assurance that if anything happens to me, you will arrange to take care of Helen? I love her and with the baby, she will need someone. Will you do this for me?"

"Of course, I was about to ask you a similar question concerning Magdalena. Even though we are not married, I feel responsible for her."

"See, I told you we are the same." Asad laughed and poured a second shot of vodka.

"I would like to drive by that church tonight. They have a guard in front twenty-four hours a day. There are four men that rotate shifts throughout the night."

"I have a car but I hate driving in this city. Driving in Cairo is like a wild video game. Cars careen around corners and charge through intersections; it is more dangerous than working with the mob in Russia."

"I know what you mean. The most dangerous aspect of Cairo is the traffic."

"I will tell Helen that we are going out."

When Asad returned, Alex was looking at a book he found on their coffee table.

"Helen and I finished reading the book. It was an interesting read. I'll loan it to you. Part of the book deals with the Russian mafia and trafficking of women. Helen bought it for me when I was in the hospital."

"I never heard of Barbara Vaka."

"Helen said she is a new American author. Let me know how you like *Hank's Mountain.*"

"I'll read it when we fly to Switzerland." Alex put the book into a small black case he always carried.

The two drove to the church and as they arrived a woman was running from the building screaming. The guard tried to run after her, but he stopped chasing her when she ran in front of Asad's car. The guard hurried away and Alex jumped out of the car and picked up the woman who had fallen in the street.

"Are you okay?"

She spoke no English and Asad got out of the car and asked her in Romanian if she was hurt.

"No, no. they are killing a man in there."

"Did you call the police?"

"No, I have no papers they would put me in jail. A year ago I applied for a job, but it was a fraud; they made me a sex slave."

Asad held her and spoke in a quiet voice and got her to get into the car.

"She is like the women I used to handle. We will take her to the hospital and make sure she is okay."

"Tell me about the man they are killing."

"His name is Yusef. He tried to send a message to his wife and daughter through one of the women and one of the guards overheard them. They have him stripped naked and are whipping him with their belts. They said he was an example of what would happen if any of the workers tried the same thing."

"What is going on in that basement?"

"They are constructing small rooms with heavy doors, putting bars on the windows and digging a tunnel out of the building. They bring six or eight of us here each night for the pleasure of the workers and guards. Most of the men have sex with us, but Yusef was different. He was very unhappy and missed his family. The other men were rough with us and one woman had to go to the doctor. I could not stand it and ran away. If you had not driven by when you did, they would have caught me and killed me."

"You are safe now. We will make sure you get papers and a flight back to Romania."

"How does an Egyptian speak Romanian?"

Asad pulled his car into the emergency entrance and got out.

"I speak many languages. I know several of the doctors here; you will be treated well."

Alex and Asad walked the woman into the hospital and went to Dr. Gaafar's office and called him at home.

"Dr., this is Alex. I'm sorry to call you a home but we need your help. Can you come to the hospital? Asad and I were driving by the Coptic Church we have under surveillance when a young Romanian woman trying to escape, ran in front of our car and fell. She claims they forced her to have sex with the workers and the guards."

"I will be there directly."

Alex got some coffee while they waited for Sabir to arrive and called Henry on his phone.

"Henry, we have some inside information on the church. We rescued a woman who was forced to have sex with the workers every night. It seems they are whipping a man named Yusef for trying to send a message to his family. Do you want us to alert the authorities or see how it plays out?"

"I think it may be too late for the man inside the church from what you said. Keep watch and see what information the woman has on where she was imprisoned in the city. We can rescue those women and put her under protection. They will blame it on her and no one will know that you are involved. Keep me informed. This may be the break we have been expecting."

Asad was talking with the woman, discovered her name was Cami, and that she was from Botosani near the border with Moldova, but had recently moved to Bala Mare on the Ukrainian border. She had been visiting a friend, Antoaneta, in the Ukraine when she and her friend applied for a job as housekeepers in Egypt. The pay was good. They would live-in with all their meals provided. They arrived in Cairo over a year ago, were beaten into submission, and forced to work in the brothels of Cairo.

"I know the area," Asad said. "My friend grew up along the Prut River before she got married and moved to Moscow."

Asad turned to Alex. "My mother was from that area. She often spoke of playing along the banks of the Prut."

"Be careful Asad, you are a British citizen now. Talking about your Russian past could get us both killed."

"I told her I had a friend from that area and that we will find a way to send her home. She has two sisters and a brother that has not spoken with in over a year. The girls were separated when they arrived."

Sabir entered his office and with Asad translating, they got her to agree to a complete physical and arranged to keep her in the hospital for the night.

"Tell me Asad, "How do you know so many languages?"

"That is easy. My mother was Romanian, my father Russian and Jewish, I learned English in school, and my cell mate in Singapore for three years spoke Arabic."

"I wish I had your gift for languages."

"I also speak a little Greek and some French. Languages come easy for me."

"We will delay our flight to Switzerland for a few days. I want to watch that church and see what happens. If there are other women like Cami at the same brothel, we can rescue them."

"Do you think that is wise?" Dr Gaafar cautioned Alex. "I suggest you let the Egyptian Police handle it."

Alex agreed and suggested the hospital file the report.

"Helen will be glad to have me around a little longer. My leg is stronger every day and I can walk two kilometers without having to rest. She says I am doing better than most of her patients considering the extent of the muscle damage."

"Sorry about that. At least your shoulder wound was not serious."

"I think of you every time my leg hurts." Asad winked.

"Henry is flying into Cairo tomorrow. Things are really heating up. He has a meeting at Hassan's Pharaoh's Pyramid Hotel. Counting Henry, there will be eight operatives at the meeting. Dr. Gaafar will bring at least ten of his people if they are available. We should be able to close down the basement before it opens. What else could it be? They received thirty cots the other day."

"I agree. Kahlil's warehouse had thirty cots. The tunnel out the back is an emergency exit; I think it is definitely a new holding area." Asad interrupted. "We always had to have an emergency exit. Kahlil's place was perfect. It had two back entrances from each side on the ground level and a basement entrance in the back."

"Tell Cami that we will arrange new identity papers and she will be flown home as soon as possible."

Asad walked into the room where Cami sat crying. He walked over and put his hand on her shoulder but she withdrew from his touch never looking up.

"Do not cry, you will be going home very soon. You look so young. How old are you?"

"I am seventeen. I was just sixteen when they took me. It was a nightmare and I was afraid I would never wake up. After a while, you feel numb and wonder is there something wrong with me. I must have done something to deserve this."

"None of this is your fault. You must not blame yourself. It may take a few days, but you are free now. Someone will bring you clothes tomorrow."

Cami looked up at Asad with fear and pain in her eyes. It was a look he had never seen and never wanted to again.

Asad kissed her on the cheek and left.

The young girl's story touched him deeply. The consequences of human trafficking were reflected in her eyes.

Alex met Asad in the hall and sensed he was upset.

"Asad, what is wrong?"

"Alex, she is only seventeen. I never realized that what I was doing the last four years could cause such pain and suffering. I need a drink."

Alex smiled, "This time, let's have some whiskey. I have a bottle in my luggage. MacKay whiskey was originally my family's trademark. My family has been in the business for years."

"You keep such secrets from me." He laughed.

They drove to Asad's apartment to find Helen pacing the floor waiting for them.

"I was so worried. It has been hours."

Asad pulled her to him, held her close, and whispered to her in Russian, "*LyublyU tobyA vsem sErtsem, vsEy dush Oya, Ti nuzhnA mne.*"

Helen kissed him and broke into tears as he held her.

"What did you say to her?"

"I told her I love you with all my heart, with all my soul. I need you. Russian women are so emotional."

"I never pictured you saying such endearing words to a woman."

"I love women. You will learn to say that to Magdalena. She speaks Russian well. I will write it for you in English phonetically. Call her and see how she reacts."

Alex repeated it a couple of times with Asad's careful instructions.

"I look forward to calling her."

"It is late. I am exhausted. Good night."

Asad and Helen left Alex sitting on the sofa in their living room. He was calling Magdalena despite the late hour.

When she answered the phone, he read the words that Asad had taught him in Russian.

"Alex, Yuri, I mean Asad, must have told you to say that to me. Your pronunciation is good. Thank you. I will teach you when you return to me to say other things. I was so afraid you would not call me."

"I wanted to let you know that I will be in Cairo a few more days. Something came up. I will call you again before we fly to Switzerland. I will bring you back a music box and some chocolates."

"Be careful. *Miluju Te*. Forgive me for what I said before you left, I love you and miss you terribly," she began to cry and hung up the phone.

Alex hung up the phone, whipped a tear from his eye and went to bed in the guest room.

Chapter 35

Boris immediately drove to the area of Tverskaya Street to call on Petrov Berezovsky, Yuri's uncle and confidant. Petrov was surprised to see Boris when he opened the door.

"Petrov, my old friend we need to talk."

Petrov said nothing but motioned him to come in. He was as tall as Yuri was and towered over Boris, the same black hair, but dark brown eyes instead of blue.

"Well if it isn't my old friend Boris, better known as the Butcher; killed off another thousand Chechens or Afghans? Sex slaves giving you trouble. What is the problem Boris? You never call on me unless there is a major catastrophe."

"We have a leak in the organization. Kahlil's warehouse in Cairo was the first to go. We lost fifty-five women last month. The warehouse was attacked by the Egyptian police, and Kahlil was gunned down."

"My nephew was killed during that operation in the mountains. I feel so sad; I brought him into this business four years ago. He deserved better."

"That is one of the things I wanted to talk to you about. Are you sure that Yuri is dead?"

"I cremated his body as he requested and scattered his ashes. Why do you ask?"

"Yuri knew many things regarding our affairs. Did you look at his body?"

"It was bad enough he was killed, no. Cremation was immediate. I do not look on the dead. The mortuary would have seen the body."

"I need to verify that Yuri is dead. Someone told me some time ago that Yuri had proof against me and several others, including one member of the Duma."

Petrov looked genuinely surprised by what Boris was telling him. If Yuri was alive and cooperating with the authorities he would not be for long.

"That is the first I have heard of this. Yuri seemed to be making a lot of money and I know he did some side business, but it was all in the family. He shared his profits with me."

"I never knew he dealt women on the side."

"He would date them, find a buyer in the Middle East, and sell them privately. They were all exceptional women from good families. Yuri conditioned them personally. I even heard one sent him a thank you for introducing her to her husband. Yuri was very good at what he did. I resent the idea you think he is a traitor."

"Let us go to the mortuary."

"I will come with you, but I do not like the implication. Boris you have gone too far when you accuse my nephew. It is bad enough that he is dead."

"We will see about that."

The two men drove to the mortuary in silence and met with the owner.

"Vasilli, remember when you handled my nephew's cremation last month?"

"Yes, very sad. He was in his twenties and a very handsome young man."

Boris interrupted, "Did you examine the body?"

"I opened the coffin, and took care of the cremation personally. Why do you ask?"

"Are you certain it was Yuri Berezovsky?"

"The body was that of a tall man, very dark hair, and had been shot twice."

"Are you satisfied, Boris? This has been very painful for me. He was my brother's only son."

"Thank you Vasilli."

"How dare you suggest Yuri is a traitor? Let me tell you something Boris. Yuri was loyal for the four years he worked for us. I did hear he bought a woman from that last shipment, a pregnant red-head, but Yuri always did have a soft heart for a pregnant woman, especially red heads."

"What happened to the pregnant woman?"

"I do not know. Anton told me Yuri had asked him to take care of her, but then Yuri died. I guess the Egyptians sent her back to where ever she came from. Let us check on some of our nighttime butterflies on Tverskaya Street. I have just the woman in mind for you Boris. It will calm you down."

"I do not want some overworked street rat whore to entertain me. I guess it has been verified Yuri is really dead."

"My nephew is dead and you question me. Do you think I had anything to do with the leak? I have not been out of Russia in years. What else has happened?"

"We lost the travel agency in Athens."

Petrov raised his hands in disbelief and wondered what else Boris had not told him.

"Someone told me that a guard had been taken alive in the raid in the mountains. Where is he being held?"

"MI 6 has him in custody. We are holding a couple of Brits and are trying to arrange a trade."

The two men had returned to the car when Petrov had an idea.

"Let's drive to the Duma and see my friend Nickoli. Perhaps he can speed up this trade deal. What is the guard's name?"

"Aleksandr Zahavisky"

"I do not know the family. When we get him away from the Brits, I want to interrogate him personally. I am so angry; I could make a mute speak."

"Have your operatives in Mossad found anything?"

"We found the names of two MI 6 operatives, and they have disappeared from London. Strong reported they and their families are away. There is a third operative, but we have no last name and only a first name of Alex or Alexander. Strong is also trying to track down a woman that Yuri was seeing in London, she was the daughter of a British Lord, Lord Cavendish. Strong reported that Lord Cavendish was in Egypt attending his daughter's wedding. She ran away and married some Egyptian saw-bone."

"Nickoli can speed up the trade. That is our next stop."

Boris and Petrov went to the government building just past Novaya Ploshchad where the Central Committee of the Communist Party once sat, now headquarters for the Duma of the Moscow Region. They entered Nickoli's office.

"Petrov, I see you are keeping strange company these days. How can I help you?"

"We need to expedite the release of that guard captured by MI 6. Have you heard anything?"

"The Brits are working with us. They plan to have the paperwork finalized and the trade will take place shortly. They were most anxious to have the two British operatives returned that we have held for the last five years. Not to worry, we will have him soon and if he is the traitor, he will suffer greatly before we execute him. I hate a traitor. The many luxuries the profits from your filthy business provide are what make my otherwise miserable life bearable."

Boris spoke up.

"If this man is our leak, we must make an example of him."

"The exchange is set. We will bring him to our location in Saratov. The governor there is very pro legal prostitution. He will say nothing."

Boris and Petrov left the Duma after thanking Nickoli who promised to keep them informed as to when and where the exchange would take place.

Boris turned to Petrov in the car.

"Petrov, keep your ears open and keep me informed. I am flying to Cairo to check on the new warehouse. Three of our operatives Bear, Bird, and Deer are working there with Mikhail. Strong is still in London."

"I thought your brother Mikhail was in hiding in Cyprus in that Villa the two of you own."

"He was bored and decided to help me for a change. I gave him the code name Fox, the Russian government would order his death if they knew he was alive; no one knows he is in Egypt, but you and my operatives from Mossad."

"Stay the night Boris. I'll drive you to the airport in the morning."

Chapter 36

Amir Harari codename Strong, landed at Heathrow airport and immediately took the Underground to London's West Side near Hyde Park, and checked into a small hotel run by Germans. He dropped his luggage in the room, immediately left the hotel, and took the Underground to Parliament. When he arrived, he spoke to a receptionist behind the desk.

"I am looking for an old friend of mine, Lord Robert Cavendish. Is he in London at present? No one answered his phone."

"No sir, Lord Cavendish is attending his daughter's wedding in Cairo, Egypt and is staying to attend the National Horse Show. His Lordship raises horses you know."

"Yes, I knew that. When will he return?"

"He is expected next week. Would you like to leave him a message?"

"No, I was concerned when I heard his daughter was kidnapped."

"Yes, that was a rumor. Turns out she ran away and got married. His Lordship was not pleased, but young people these days do what they want and do not consult their parents. Can I take your name and a number where he can contact you?"

"No, that is all right. I was planning to surprise him. It has been a long time since we last met. I am only in London a few days and I will be gone before he returns."

Strong left Parliament and took a taxi into the city of London and to his friend's office in the heart of London's financial district off Fleet Street.

Strong arrived at the office and after pleasantries requested the use of a telephone. He closed the door and dialed his contact inside MI6. Being a member of Mossad had its advantages. A voice answered, "Hello"

"This is Amir. What is the news on the two men identified as MI6 that were in Egypt?" I understand they left England and were relocated to Australia on an extended assignment with their families."

"We have heard the same."

"I am searching for an operative that may have been on assignment with them."

"What is the name?"

"I have only the first name, Alex, short for Alexander."

"There are several operatives with that name. MI6 is a large organization. I need more."

"He was a big man, had a nasty scar on one side of his face."

"I think I know the chap. He was on leave for almost a year. His wife was murdered and he was having difficulty handling it. He has a residence in London, but his home is in Scotland. Give me a few minutes; I can give you an address and a phone number."

Amir carefully copied down the number over the phone the snitch gave him.

"I do not have an exact address just Fettercairn Castle where he is currently. No assignment found, but that does not mean anything. Many MI6 operatives do not leave their assignments on file. Sorry I cannot give you anything else."

"That is all I need. I assume the customary payment is acceptable?"

"A pleasure doing business with you as always, good hunting."

Strong returned to his hotel and rested awhile. He walked around the corner from his hotel and placed a call from a pay phone to the number the snitch had given him. A gravelly voice answered the phone.

"Castle Fettercairn, State your business," Albert growled into the phone.

"Is Alex at home?"

"Who wants to know? Do you realize it is one o'clock in the morning?"

"Sorry about the hour, I am calling from out of the country and did not realize the time difference in London. Alex and I worked together in the Agency."

"No, Lord MacKay is not here. He is away on holiday. He went to a wedding in Egypt."

"Was that Lord Cavendish's daughter's wedding in Cairo?" Amir asked.

"Yes, as a matter of fact it was. He should be returning shortly."

"Is his wife at home?"

Expecting to hear that Alex's wife was dead, he was not prepared for the answer he received.

"Magdalena is here, but she is not his wife. They never married. She is asleep. I will not wake her at this hour."

"Thank you. I will be leaving London, but will call Alex in a week or two. He will be home then?"

"His schedule varies. I can leave a message."

"No sir that will not be necessary."

Amir returned and phoned Boris on his encrypted phone.

"I have the name of the other operative. It is Alex MacKay. He and Lord Cavendish are in Egypt at his daughter's wedding. This man has a woman living with him."

"Kidnap this woman. Perhaps we can use her as a bargaining chip. If this agent had the information to break down our organization, perhaps some persuasion will convince him to tell us what he knows. Be careful. When you have the woman call me."

Albert placed a call to Alex.

"Sorry to bother you sir, but a stranger called and he had a heavy accent, could have been Israeli. He wanted to know your whereabouts. Asked about your wife."

"Very few people know I planned to remarry. I will call headquarters have them send some men to keep you company. Lock the portcullis and put your gun where you can get to it in a hurry. Keep Magdalena in the castle. Keep everyone in the concealed room off the master. If you hear anything at all, grab your gun and shoot first. If it is one of Boris's trained Mossad operatives he will be heavily armed"

"Want me to call the local police?"

"No Albert, I think we should keep this between us and Henry's men. If you see anyone before they arrive, lock yourself in the room with Samantha and Magdalena. I want you all safe. If the Israeli's are sniffing around, they will stop at nothing. They might try to kidnap Magdalena. Be careful. We will try and capture this man."

Alex placed a call and before he hung up, Henry had two operatives on their way to Fettercairn from Aberdeen.

Strong went to the hotel and rang British Airways for flight information.

"It is an hour and forty minute flight from London to Aberdeen. You can rent a car and be in Fettercairn in less than an hour."

"Is there a train?"

"The train will take about seven hour's sir."

"Book a round trip flight for me."

The next day Amir boarded the flight at Heathrow under the assumed name of Ivan Komarovski, with false Russian identity papers. When he arrived in Aberdeen, he rented a car under the same name and drove toward Fettercairn. The castle sat on top of a small hill surrounded by farmland. Amir surveyed the area through a pair of binoculars. There was no way to approach the castle unnoticed except on foot through a woods that came within a hundred meters of the building. Amir decided to wait until the cover of darkness before he made his move. He parked the car in the woods, covered it with some brush, and took a nap.

Henry's men who arrived before Amir were laying in wait. They had noticed a car drive into the woods from the castle tower. They ordered Albert, Samantha, and Magdalena into the secret room and waited.

Amir changed into black slacks and shirt and put on his night vision goggles turning the landscape a dull green. It was three in the morning, when he began to creep toward the castle. He had noticed the portcullis earlier and was surprised to see the gate not only lowered, but also securely locked. The only way into the castle was over the walls. He watched for sometime before he took a rope with a grabbling hook and tossed it up to the walls of the castle.

His throw missed and the hook clattered down the walls making an eerie sound. Amir raced back to the cover of the trees to watch for signs that the noise had wakened anyone. It had not. The castle remained dark and was silent. Unaware that two pair of binoculars was watching his every move, he waited an hour before approaching the wall a second time. This time his aim was more accurate and the hook grabbed fast. Hand over hand he quickly climbed the wall and paused at the top before dropping quietly onto the walkway below. Suddenly he felt a sharp pain as a dart punctured his neck. The tranquilizer acted so quickly he slumped to the walkway without a sound.

Henry's two men approached in a few minutes to make certain the intruder was unconscious, handcuffed him, and dragged him into the castle and secured Amir in the dungeon under the castle with stainless steel cuffs and chain. When he finally regained consciousness, he realized his sorry state, stripped naked and chained to a stonewall.

"Welcome to Fettercairn Castle. The identity papers from your rental car are very good, but not quite good enough. Who are you?"

"Fuck you. I will tell you nothing."

"We pride ourselves on our ability to interrogate prisoners. We find a couple of days chained to a wall in a dungeon without food or water seems to weaken the strongest spirit. Understand that there may be a few rats to keep you company. See you in two days."

"You cannot leave me here without food, water, and clothes in this cold and damp."

"That is our weather. It might interest you to know I saw skim ice this morning on a puddle. October can be chilly."

"Come back here you fucking limey cowards," Amir shouted.

"We will be back after you chill down a little. It can get bone chilling cold this time of year.

We will check on you later this evening. Perhaps the cold will loosen your tongue."

The two men closed the dungeon door, bolted it shut, and turned off the lights. It was cold, dark, damp, and silent in the dungeon except for the scurrying of rodent feet. A musty smell of mold hung in the stale air. It was difficult for Strong to realize he was chained securely to the wall of a dungeon with no way to escape. The steel cuffs fit tightly around his wrists almost cutting into his skin. The chains were short and gave him very little movement. The floor was cold and damp.

"You bastards, even in the old days they put straw on the floor." He shouted into the darkness and heard only the echo of his own voice in the depths of the dark dungeon.

It was not long before Amir began to shiver from the cold. Hypothermia was setting in and he knew if he did get warm soon he might pass out. Already his arms and legs were feeling numb when the lights came on and the door creaked open.

"Had a pleasant day?"

Amir had lost track of time in the darkness with no frame of reference. Eight hours had passed.

"I am freezing to death. Give me a blanket. I could die from hypothermia and you would find out nothing."

"Perhaps he is right."

One of Henry's men approached carrying a cup of hot tea. When he got within three feet of their captive, he tossed the hot tea over Strong's head and started to laugh."

"Did that warm you up a bit?"

"You scumbags, this is not legal. When I get free, I will complain to the Israeli Embassy. They won't standby and allow one of their citizens be treated this way."

"What makes you think you will live to see the Embassy? Why Israeli, your identity papers described you as Russian. Thank you for the correct information."

"We Scots do not take kindly to people sneaking up on our homes and trying to invade our privacy. We found inhalational anesthetic a substitute for chloroform that requires almost a lethal dose in your bag along with wrist, and ankle cuffs. We suspect you planned to kidnap the woman."

"I need a blanket. I'll die from the cold."

"We should care. Does anyone know that you are here? We returned your car to the airport and changed your return flight under your assumed name to London. One of our friends took that flight. He looks a lot like you. They will never search for you here. London is a large city. People sometimes disappear in a large city."

"I cannot tell you anything. My life would be over. They would kill me."

"They kill you or you die from the cold or starve to death. It is your choice. We really do not care. Our boss is not a patient man and hates anyone trying to bother his woman."

"He suspects you are in the business of kidnapping women for the sex trade. Either you are an agent of the Israeli, Mossad, or work for the Russian mob, maybe both. Are we close?"

"What gave you an outrageous idea like that?"

"The fact you have an encrypted phone and no real identity papers on your person. The equipment you carry is par excellence. Your gun is a model carried by most Mossad agents. We have interrogated your kind before. The forged identity papers gave you away."

"Then you know I will not talk."

"You have just told us you are with Mossad. Care to fill in the details."

"I am not going to say another word."

One of the men tossed a blanket over him. "We need more information from you and would not want to see you die of the cold before we get what we want. We will return to check on you about 0300."

The men left him shivering under the blanket, turned off the lights, and bolted the door leaving him in the cold damp darkness of the dungeon.

Alex received a call from one of the operatives at the house.

"Alex this is Tim Ferguson. We caught a visitor trying to scale the walls of your castle. He is not very talkative, but he has admitted he is with

Mossad. Albert gave us the keys to your dungeon. Nice area Alex, use it often?"

"Actually I had it built for the fun of it. What is a castle without a dungeon? I equipped it just in case I ever needed it. I guarantee our friend is going nowhere. Those cuffs are strong and embedded in solid stone a meter thick."

"We stripped him naked; he complains he is cold and being mistreated. There is no doubt he was on a mission to kidnap Magdalena. He had all the equipment. The Mossad provides the best for their operatives including the latest inhalational anesthetic."

"See if you can pry some information out of him. Things are happening here in Cairo and I cannot return right now. We have three Israeli's and one Russian under surveillance. There are not that many Israeli or Russian Jews visiting Cairo."

"Do you want us to keep this bastard alive? He is weak from the cold?"

"Keep him alive, but do not make him comfortable. I want to deal with him myself when I return. See that Magdalena, Albert, and his wife Samantha are safe. Make certain that this man was alone. There are enough provisions in that room for a month. I could not bear to see any harm come to them. Magdalena has suffered enough and she is pregnant. Keep a careful watch. She must be terrified."

"We are certain he was traveling alone."

"We will make sure he doesn't die, but I guarantee he will not visit Scotland again anytime soon. That dungeon of yours could use some heat."

"What and loose the atmosphere. In the summer, it is great. Always cool, but Scotland never suffers from much of a heat wave. Keep in touch."

The men returned to the dungeon.

"We do not want you dying on us. We brought you some more blankets and some bread with wild honey, and water. See you in the morning. If you want to chat, we can supply something a little more filling."

The men laughed and hand fed him the bread and held the water bottle to his lips.

"Could you bring me a bucket to go in?"

"We could, but sitting in your own excrement will keep you aware that you are not staying at the best of hotels. We may sweep it out tomorrow. You stink Israeli."

327

y left, turned out the lights and re-bolted the door.

Amir pulled against his chains and only succeeded in having the steel cuffs cut into his skin.

"Boris will come looking for me and when he finds you bastards; I personally will delight in killing you slowly," he shouted as the men left.

Angus Mac Todd called back, "Thank you for the other name you gave us. You are really becoming cooperative."

"Fuck you."

Chapter 37

Boris arrived in Cairo and ordered his three men back to the hotel and left Mikhail and the Bedouins that accompanied him to guard the workers at the basement.

"I have gotten some information concerning the Pharaoh's Pyramid Hotel. It appears that the father of the man who owns the hotel heads up a volunteer group working with the Egyptian Government to investigate our business and shut us down. That is the hotel where the records from El-Arish were sent."

"What do you want us to do?"

"I want you to lure the hotel owner away, kidnap him, and beat him senseless while we record his torture on video tape for his father. I am certain that seeing his son stripped naked and beaten within an inch of his life will make him back off."

"What about the man we beat at the basement that tried to send a message to his wife?"

"Keep him alive. We will dispose of him when the job is finished along with the rest of the workers."

"Once we kidnap the son and beat him, what do you want us to do with him?"

"Put him to work in the basement with the others so that he can share their fate. We will take the bodies, and dispose of them in the desert or use Yuri's old boat and drop them in the middle of the Mediterranean. Our Bedouin friends will see to it."

"How do you want to kidnap this hotel owner?"

"On second thought, leave that to me. The three of you return to Mikhail. See that the work is completed in the next three days."

The three men left and Boris ordered a taxi and went to the hotel. He flashed his passport, walked through the scanner without a problem, and approached the concierge's desk.

"I would like to speak with the owner; it is of utmost urgency."

That day Rafiq was in the office filling in for Hassan who was still on his honeymoon. He asked his secretary to send the man to his office.

"How can I be of service?" Rafiq asked.

Boris responded, "This is an urgent matter. I am trying to find some information on tourists that may have stayed in your hotel in El-Arish. They told me all hotel records were sent to this hotel in Cairo."

"What do you need to know?"

"About three weeks ago three British men traveling together checked into your hotel in El-Arish. I need their names."

"May I ask who you are and why you need this information? We zealously protect our guest's privacy. I cannot give you that information without a good reason."

"I am investigating a drug running operation that we believe is connected to these three men."

"I will try and find the records for you by checking the computer files. It will just be a moment."

Rafiq was looking at his computer screen, his hands were moving quickly across the keyboard and did not notice Boris take a small tube from his pocket and fire a tranquilizing dart into his neck. Rafiq rubbed his neck and slumped across his desk. Boris had planned his escape using a rear door to the office he noticed when he arrived. He looked at the screen and saw that Rafiq was sending an email to a Dr. Gaafar at the hospital, "A man is in my office asking questions about El-Arish. I suspect he is Russian. Contact . . . ."

The message was incomplete and Rafiq had not pressed the send button. Boris added a footnote to the email.

"We have your son and will send a video to confirm. We need to talk." He pressed the send button.

Boris carefully opened the door to a long corridor that led to the elevator. Carefully he picked up the unconscious Rafiq, put him over his shoulder, and walked quietly down the hall toward the elevator. He stepped in and pushed the garage level. The elevator stopped and the door opened. Boris waited a moment looking carefully for anyone in the area, then exited with the unconscious Rafig slung over his shoulder. Checking Rafiq's pockets he found a set of car keys, pushed the unlock button and the car closest to the elevator blinked its lights. He carried Rafiq to the car, laid him in the trunk, got behind the wheel, and left the garage.

Boris drove through the crowded streets narrowly avoiding an accident on his way to the church. He parked the car on the side of the building facing the alley where the recently dug tunnel exited. Boris gave the coded signal and Mikhail opened the door.

"Help me with the man in the trunk. He is the owner of the hotel. Set up a video camera then strip him beat him severely and send the tape to me. I am trying to convince his father to back off. He heads up the group that is responsible for our problems in Cairo."

Mikhail carried Rafiq into the basement. The workers were busy, but watched as the unconscious man was carried into the basement. Mikhail laid Rafiq on the floor and together with Dov; they stripped him and tied his wrists to the whipping post they had erected in the center of the room.

Rafiq was coming around when Boris shouted to his men, "Soften him up a little. Then, we will whip him. Make sure he is hurt and screams loudly."

Rafiq began to say something when Dov punched him hard in the stomach followed by three more hard hits to the face breaking his nose. The sound of the breaking cartilage brought the workers to a standstill.

"Back to work, this does not concern you," barked Boris. "Continue the beating."

Rafiq slumped against the wrist restraints.

"Bring him around. I want to see his back laid open."

They brought him around. His eyes were turning black and swelling shut. Blood still dripped from his broken nose.

Boris picked up a pair of pliers, "Pull a few teeth before you whip him." He tossed the pliers to Mikhail. Dov forced Rafiq's mouth open and Mikhail yanked out three teeth in rapid succession while he screamed and writhed in agony. Blood flowed from his mouth as he let out a piercing scream that seemed to last forever.

"Whip him. I want his father to know we mean business."

They began to whip Rafiq's back cutting through his skin until his back was raw flesh. The pain was excruciating and more than Rafiq could bear. Rafiq suddenly stopped screaming and his head slumped as he lost consciousness.

"Bring him around again."

Mikhail tried to revive him, but it was useless.

"I think this man is dead."

Boris screamed in disbelief. "You are fucking ass holes. I did not want this man dead."

He played the film back and watched the torture of Rafiq. At the end of the tape, the last thing heard were the words, "Bring him around again."

"I do not think they will know that he is dead. He passed out once before. Cut him down and lay the body in one of the rooms. We will keep it for now and dispose of it later."

Boris took the video tape and put it into a plain brown envelope. "Mikhail, take this to the hospital and leave it for Dr. Gaafar and return. We will call the doctor in two hours after the images of his son sink in. I am sure he will deal."

"What happens when he finds his son is dead?" Dov asked.

"He will not know his son is dead. We will tell him we will hold his son for six months as insurance. By the then we will no longer need the basement and be gone. He has no information about who we are. By the time they figure it out, you will be back in Tel Aviv, Mikhail will return to Cyprus, and I will be back in Moscow. There is nothing he can do but mourn his loss. These people do not know who they are dealing with."

"Before I leave," Boris asked, "Did Amir check in. He was on his way to Scotland to kidnap this man Alex's woman."

"No, he was due to check in an hour ago."

"Try to reach him on his phone. It is not like him not to check with us. Something is wrong."

Sabir exited the operating theatre and walked over to his secretary. "I think that went well. I plan to clean up and go home. There is an important meeting tonight and I may be late tomorrow."

Sabir went to his office, took a long shower and got dressed before noticing he had a new email. He glanced at the screen without noticing the sender's name and thought to himself, "That can wait until tomorrow" Sabir shut down the computer, turned off the lights, and locked his office.

Mikhail arrived at the hospital and went to the main desk.

"This package is for Dr. Gaafar."

"I believe he is gone for the day. I will leave it on his desk. He should be here sometime late tomorrow morning."

Mikhail shook his head, left the hospital, and went to his car. He noticed a tall man with graying hair getting into a car near where he parked. He called Boris.

"They told me that Dr. Gaafar is gone for the day. I recognized him from a picture you showed at out meeting; he is getting into his car in the parking garage. Do you want me to follow him?"

"No, he will get the news in the morning. His son is not going anywhere."

Chapter 38

Henry arrived in Cairo and drove to the Pharaoh's Pyramid Hotel. Alex had already checked in and Henry went to the reserved conference room. Dr. Gaafar and twenty of his men were already in the room having dinner.

Alex greeted him when he entered. "Good to see you Henry. We did not think we could wait any longer. According to the woman you rescued from the church, the refurbishing of the basement is nearly complete. When that happens, I cannot imagine they will allow any of those men to leave alive. We need to move tonight. Dr. Gaafar and twenty of his men are ready to go along with a small contingent of Egyptian military that helped with the Sinai mountains operation."

"How many suspected Mossad are here?" Henry asked.

Asad answered, "We think there are five of them. Two men appear to be Russian and the other three may be Israeli. Another Mossad member is a guest at Alex's castle dungeon in Fettercairn. He has refused to tell us anything, but we know we can break him given time."

Henry laughed. "You really finished the dungeon? Good to hear it is being put to good use. I hope that bastard enjoys his stay."

"He was prepared to kidnap Magdalena." Alex introduced Henry to the others. "The man with me is Henry Ewing my handler at MI 6. Along with several other operatives, we have the church under 24-hour surveillance. It is going to be a long night. MI6 is working with the Egyptian authorities. We cannot afford to put off our attack. They took another hostage into the basement through the escape tunnel earlier tonight."

"Any identification on the new hostage?" Sabir asked.

"It was hard to tell. The man carried in appeared to be unconscious, was dressed in a business suit, and had a mustache. We have not been able to identify him." Asad responded. "Must be an Egyptian businessman from the way he was dressed."

"How many men are we up against?" Henry asked.

"We suspect nine; maybe five of them are Mossad or Russian. They are heavily armed and very dangerous. The others are Bedouin and most likely carrying automatic weapons provided by the Mossad. Two of the men we know are Russian." Alex answered.

"What time do they bring in the women?"

"The women are delivered after midnight." Asad added to the conversation. "We must move before they arrive. It is 2000 hours. I suggest we move at 2200. That gives us two hours to surround the building."

Captain Hussein with the Egyptian military addressed the group. "The Mossad are deadly. We must shoot to kill. They will tell us nothing if captured. The Russian may talk but I doubt the Bedouins will know anything. Our attack must be swift with no warning. We will take out the lookout posted across the street as soon as he calls in and the guard in the back alley at the same time."

One of the soldiers continued with details. "They check in every half hour. At exactly 2200 hours, we will take them out. Use tranquilizer darts. We want no disturbance. Tie and gag the lookouts then put them both in the trunk of one of our cars. We can interrogate them later."

Alex turned to Sabir. "I want you to stay back. We may need your medical talents so bring a large medical kit. We may receive heavy fire. These are dangerous ruthless people."

Inside The Basement

"Any word from Amir?" Mikhail asked.

"No, he has not called in and is not answering his phone. I have to leave for a couple of hours. I need to contact Moscow and I would rather do it from my hotel." Boris answered.

"Do you want me to pick up the women at the airport?" Mikhail asked.

"Yes, bring the women. Everything is ready. Be sure they escort our hard working friends out of the building before the women arrive and give them what they deserve. I will return around midnight."

Outside The Church

One of the operatives spotted Boris getting into his car. Mikhail headed for the airport in a van after leaving instructions for his crew.

"Alex, two men just left the building, one in a car the other in a van. One of them is the same man that brought in the new hostage a while ago. Do you want me to follow them? I believe they are the Russians."

"Yes, follow the man in the car. The van is headed to the airport to pick up the shipment and will return. Tell the other agent where you are going. We plan to attack at just past 2200 hours. Get back as soon as possible. We need to know where he is going. As soon as he arrives at his destination, phone in the location and we will send someone there to report any movement and tail him when he leaves. When your relief gets there return to your post."

Alex checked his watch, thirty minutes to go.

"Get into position and be careful. They have two guards, both local thugs from Cairo, one in the back alley and one across the street." Sabir directed his men.

"Move out gentlemen. Once we are in position, I will signal our attack." The Captain left and the rest followed him out of the room, got into separate elevators and met again in the garage under the hotel.

"Sabir, Henry, Alex, you will ride in my car. We will park about three blocks away and go in on foot in small groups." Asad told them.

The group of thirty men under the orders of Captain Hussein and Asad drove quickly to the area of the church and left their parked their vehicles along the side streets and broke into small groups on foot walking to within a block of the church where they held their positions. They were set to move. The guard across the street phoned in his call at exactly 2200 hours and instantly went down with a tranquilizer dart as he hung up his phone. The guard in the back was a little late on his call and his phone rang.

"Everything all right?"

"Yeah, had to take a piss. Quiet as usual."

Another dart fired and the lookout slumped to the ground. The men moved in. Ten men were at each entrance to the basement and the remainder stayed concealed on the street in case anyone managed to escape.

Alex's group was at the tunnel entrance and the Captain's men and some of the others were at the front. The Captain ordered the door broken in and percussion grenades landed in the basement. The Mossad responded quickly and opened fire immediately.

"We have been found. Weapons, fire at anything that moves," Dov shouted.

Alex's group had penetrated the tunnel and crawled into the basement unseen. They shouted, "Workers, get down, get down."

The smell of cordite and gunpowder filled the basement and the sound of heavy weapons fire was deafening.

Asad recognized one of the Mossad and shot him in the shoulder.

"I'm hit, I'm hit," shouted Dov as he fell to the floor clutching his shoulder.

Ofer was aiming at an Egyptian soldier when his head burst open like an overripe melon, fell back, his gun clattering to the floor bouncing as it hit.

The Bedouins threw their guns away and laid flat on the floor putting up no fight as some of Captain Hussein's men held them at gunpoint.

Dror, the last Mossad agent grabbed one of the workers and shouted, "Let me go or I will kill this man."

As he went to slit the man's throat, Alex shot him in the middle of his forehead and he fell straight back to the floor releasing his grip on the hostage. The last of the Mossad were dead, except for Dov who was in handcuffs with a shoulder wound. The room fell silent.

Yusef staggered to his feet and walked toward Alex. "Do not shoot, do not shoot. We are captives of these men. Two of them left earlier, brothers Boris and Mikhail Schochat. Boris is the leader."

The Captain ordered his men to check for any survivors.

"Take the Bedouins into custody. Take that wounded man outside to Dr. Gaafar. I want him to talk. Check the rooms for anyone that may be hiding." Asad and Henry followed the guards as they hustled Dov out of the building.

Asad said in a quiet voice, "I know this man; he is a deadly assassin and is a member of Mossad, but works deals outside the organization."

"Captain, there is a seriously wounded man in this room. He is barely alive. He has been tortured and beaten. I am not sure he will make it."

"Get the doctor in here. We have a seriously injured man."

Sabir rushed into the building and went to the room.

"Oh no, Alex," he screamed, "I need you at once."

Alex rushed to the room.

"This is my son, Rafiq. He was the hostage they took today. Call Jameel and Helen to the hospital at once. Tell Yuri, I mean Asad we need him to interrogate our Mossad prisoner."

"He is with Henry; they are leaving the building with the injured man." Alex replied.

Rafiq's eyes opened slightly and he groaned in pain.

"We will get you help. Jameel will meet us at the hospital. I cannot give you anything for pain until we stabilize you. Hold on."

"Alex, this just got real personal. We have to stop these monsters."

"We will. Clear the way, clear the way. Is that ambulance here yet?"

"It is just arriving. Take Dr. Gaafar's son first. Let me talk with our hostage while we wait for another ambulance."

Sabir saw that Rafiq was carried into the waiting ambulance. "Start a saline drip. He is in shock."

Sabir wiped his son's face with a cool cloth and wept as the ambulance hurried to the hospital. As soon as they got there, Jameel had an operating room ready.

"Sabir, wait here. I will bring him through this. He has lost some blood and is in shock. Helen is scrubbing. She is the best surgical nurse I have."

Jameel checked Rafiq and found his main problem was shock. "We need to stabilize this man." He bent over Rafiq and whispered to him, "I need you to stay conscious. As soon as we get you stabilized and transfused, I will give you something for the pain. You are lucky; I did not find any indication of internal bleeding."

Rafiq groaned.

"Help me turn him on his side. I need those lacerations on his back cleaned and sutured. Use a local to ease the pain."

Helen entered the operating room. "Helen, glad you could make it. You know Hassan's brother. He had a run in with the slavers tonight. They are dead or in custody, except for two men that left earlier. We will get them all. Asad is going to interrogate the Mossad he shot; another Mossad member tried to kidnap Alex's lady Magdalena and is being held prisoner in Scotland at Alex's castle."

"Some of those cuts in his back are deep enough to expose the bone; they tried to whip him to death."

"They came close. Fortunately, Rafiq is a strong young man. He will survive this."

They worked carefully and after two hours were able to give him a morphine drip.

"I know a good oral dentist. We can fix his mouth without any trouble." Jameel added. "These men were brutal."

"When is Hassan due back from his honeymoon?"

"He is due back the day after tomorrow. Fatinah and I were going to Alexandria to meet them when they dock."

With his nose bandaged, the wounds to his back tended, Rafiq entered a private room on a gurney. Sabir was waiting anxiously for him to arrive.

"Jameel, this is the second time you have operated on one of my sons."

"Sabir, he is going to be fine. He is in shock and I do not expect him to be conscious for several hours. I gave him something to help him sleep. He needs rest. There is nothing more to be done tonight. Go home, get some sleep."

Alex had arrived just as they were wheeling Rafiq out of surgery.

"He is going to make it?"

"Yes, he will be very weak for a few days, he should be fine. How badly wounded is your prisoner?" Sabir asked.

"I do not want his wound tended until Asad has had a chance to question him. I am going to his room. Henry Ewing and Asad are with him now. Between those two, I am sure he will tell us everything he knows. Call the police and post a guard outside Rafiq's room. We lost the two Russians that left just before our attack. The van never came back and we lost the tail on the second man in heavy traffic. We believe it was Boris, the ringleader. They must have gotten a call before we killed or captured everybody at the church and managed to escape. We will find them. They are Russian."

"I will alert hospital security to watch for any strangers entering the hospital. It is late at night and no visitors should be in the building."

Chapter 39

Dov arrived at hospital and wheeled into a room on a gurney where Henry Ewing and Asad were waiting for him. He was in a great deal of pain.

"I know you," he shouted when he saw Asad, "You are not dead. You are a traitor, Yuri. I would know you anywhere. Someone called Yuri in the basement as I was leaving."

Asad looked at him, "I am afraid you are mistaken, sir, I am British and my name is Asad." He spoke in perfect English without a hint of a Russian accent.

"I would recognize you anywhere. If I ever get out of here, I will tell Boris, and he will kill you slowly. You are a dead man, Yuri."

Henry Ewing interrupted, "It is of little concern who you think this man is. We are both British MI6 and you will tell us everything you know. All of your companions are dead or in our custody. We know you are Mossad and acting illegally in Egypt to traffic women for the sex trade. You will not escape and you will not report to anyone. We already know about Boris and his brother Mikhail Schochat from another Mossad member we are holding."

"You lie, my friends would say nothing. I need my wound taken care of immediately."

Asad walked over, grabbed Dov's arm, and squeezed tightly causing Dov to scream, "Stop, that is illegal. I insist you follow the conventions of war."

"I am sorry to tell you that we British, like the Americans consider you an enemy combatant and can hold you for as long as we like. The Geneva Conventions do not apply. You do not exist outside of this room. No one knows if you are dead or alive." Asad answered him.

"I insist the Israeli Embassy be notified."

"Notified of what, that we are holding a member of their Mossad who is a rogue agent working covertly with the Russian Mafia. Be careful what you wish. Once your operation is exposed, the scandal will reach all the way to the Knesset in Tel Aviv. You are safer with us than with them. Do not worry, we won't tell them. You are our prisoner, you will talk to us or die in isolation, and no one will mourn your passing. Terrorists have no rights. They will believe you were killed in the attack at the church. Besides, your passport identifies you as Russian. Good forgery, Mossad is very thorough." Henry added.

Dov shut his eyes and fell silent.

Dr. Gaafar entered the room, "Is this one of the bastards that tortured my son?"

Henry looked up at him, "Yes, Sabir. This is one of them. Would you care to remove the bullet from his shoulder?"

"Yes, I think I could do that. Probing for the bullet will help me pay him back for the torture my son endured."

Dov opened his eyes, "Do you think I am stupid. Your son is dead, such a wimp, could not stand the punishment. He screamed like a woman. He is dead. I cut him down and carried him to a room myself."

Dr. Gaafar walked over to Dov, grabbed his arm, and pulled the edges of the wound apart. Dov screamed in agony.

"Who is the wimp now? You scream like a little girl. I will enjoy this surgery like no other. If you pass out, we will bring you around and start again. You have just begun to suffer."

"Move this man to operating theatre seven. I want Jameel and Helen to assist me." He leaned over Dov. "The only thing I will guarantee is that the surgery will take place under clean conditions and no infection should occur. Of course, there is a patient suffering from a staph infection on the fourth floor in isolation. We could have his sheets put on your bed."

"That is not legal."

"Neither is the beating, torture, and whipping of my son."

Dov continued to shout and Alex put a gag in his mouth.

"I do not want you disturbing other patients. This is a hospital. Cover his head with a sheet and move him to the operating room."

The operating room was cool and Jameel was fully prepared as was Helen when Dov entered the operating theatre.

"Strip him and bind him tightly to the table. I do not want him moving around."

Dr. Gaafar entered wearing his scrubs and a mask. "We will begin by cleaning the wound. Use the strongest antiseptic we have. I would not want our patient to get an infection." He sneered.

Helen began to clean the wound and Dov tried to hold back his anger, but he was in immense pain from the strong antiseptic Helen swabbed on the wound pressing deep into his shoulder.

"Stop, stop, you are killing me."

"Now you can appreciate what my son went through. It will hurt a lot more before I finish."

Sabir began to use a probe to find the bullet lodged in Dov's shoulder. Dov let out a piercing scream and fell unconscious.

"Bring him around. I want this man to suffer. This goes against everything medicine stands for, but this is personal. My son suffered more than this man is suffering." Dov came around and the surgery continued. He writhed in pain, after about twenty minutes the bullet was in Sabir's hand, and the wound sutured.

Dov pleaded, "Please, no more. Give me something for the pain. I will talk. My name is Dov Zahavi and I am working for an organization outside of Mossad. The regular Mossad does not know our group exists. We are a secret organization. Please, no more pain. I am sorry about your son. I thought he was dead."

"The human mind shuts down after too much pain. You almost killed him, but my son is strong. I will give you something to ease the pain slightly if you continue to talk with us. If you stop talking, I can always open your wound again and do a little more probing."

"That man I saw in the room is Yuri Berezovsky. He is part of the trafficking ring and should be arrested."

"We know him as Asad. He has been with us for years. He must resemble this Berezovsky. I checked, we had a man by that name brought here with two wounds received in a military action in the Sinai. He died on the operating table." Sabir continued.

Asad walked over to Sabir, "Before you leave, you need to remove a capsule concealed in his arm. If captured, this group has orders to commit suicide by biting into their arms and swallowing that capsule. It should be just above his wrist. I am sure you will find an old scar."

"Hold his arm; I think I may have missed something earlier."

"Stop, how do you know about that?"

"Do you think you are the only member of Mossad that the Egyptian authorities have had to deal with? You will not commit suicide while I am your doctor."

Sabir quickly located the scar and cut Dov's arm with the scalpel. The capsule was small and in a dry pack so it would not break free by accident.

He carefully removed it so as not to release the contents and sutured Dov's arm.

"That is the end of my surgery on you for tonight. We will let you rest for a few hours before interrogating you. Asad and his two companions will conduct the interrogation. I am sure you will tell us what we need to know. I could always remove your appendix or spleen without anesthesia. I would be glad to assist them in helping you to tell all."

Dov swore in Hebrew, "Asad translated for them."

"Asad is a linguist we hired years ago. He speaks six languages fluently. If you tire of speaking in English he can interrogate you in Hebrew, Russian, Arabic, French, the list goes on. He is very good at what he does."

"I still say he looks like Yuri Berezovsky."

"You may think what you like, but his name is Asad and he is British."

Asad and Alex left Dov's room. Dr. Gaafar left Helen in the room with Dov.

"You do know that this man must never be freed. My life would be worthless and Helen would be in great danger. I have known this man for the four years I was with them. He is very clever and a deadly assassin. The man Boris, he mentioned is near the top. His full name is Boris Schochat. His operation is outside of Mossad, and operates secretly. These men are all members of Mossad and if Mossad knew of their secret organization, they would eliminate them. Boris lives outside of Moscow and has a villa on the island of Cyprus high in the mountains with his brother Mikhail. If the group is still together, the others are Dror Caspit, Amir Harari, and Ofer Inbar. If I study the bodies from the basement, I may be able to identify them and give you the name of the man you hold in Scotland." Asad cleared his throat as he continued to brief Alex and Henry. "My own uncle is part of this group, but never played an active role. He has influence with well-paid officials in the Duma who look the other way and have unofficially sanctioned this business. I need a guarantee; this man must never be free. If they know I am alive, my life and that of Helen is forfeit."

"Asad," Henry interrupted. "I will personally guarantee this man will never be freed. We will officially record his death from loss of blood. He will die in a private prison at an undisclosed location that we keep for men such as him. This is an interesting group. You were once one of them until Alex found you. He told me that you contributed greatly to the success of this operation. Let me assure you that you and Helen are safe. This man may be dead to the world, but will serve us for some time to come but may not survive his internment."

"Alex told me you are a man that can be trusted. He said he placed his own life in your hands once by telling you something that could have ended his career."

"That he did," Henry, confirmed what Alex had told him.

Alex said nothing.

"Someday he may tell you what happened and you will better understand him. Let him tell you when he is ready."

Alex nodded at Henry, "When we return to your apartment tonight, Asad, I will tell you. My life will then be in your hands."

"Thank you for trusting me Alex. I will continue to help your organization. I have come to regret the last four years of my life, but it cannot be undone."

"There is no more we can do here tonight. Helen will stay with Dov the night. He is shackled hand and foot to the bed. She speaks Hebrew and will get us the information we need. You know how skilled she is."

"Yes, I do. I am not worried that Dov will make a pass at Helen. She is not his type, a male nurse or a very young boy maybe, but not Helen."

"Are you saying he is homosexual?" Alex asked.

"Yes, he is *peedarahss (homosexual)* and has some perversions that I do not understand, mainly his preference for little boys and young men." A look of disgust crossed Asad's face.

"I will see you in the morning Alex." Sabir interrupted, "I am spending the night in Rafiq's room. My wife will join me in the morning."

Alex and Asad left together and drove to the apartment. While they were driving, Alex told Asad the story of how his wife Catherine died, and how he almost lost his mind after contributing to her accidental death.

"I could have handled her leaving me, but when she told me of the abortion, I totally lost it."

"I am glad I rescued Magdalena. Now I understand why you were so sensitive to the plight of a pregnant woman. We will see this through. Dov confirmed that Boris is still active along with the others. I thought they might have retired wealthy men by now. If possible, I want to keep my uncle out of this in return for his cooperation. He has already revealed the names of Boris's contacts in the Duma and others in his group. These men are politically connected and will do anything for money. Russia is a poor country. People jump at the chance to make money, legal or not. It is the law of survival in capitalist Russia. Do unto others before they do it to you, is a way of life here. My uncle is not active; but he knows who these vulnerable men are and how to tempt them with financial rewards. When I returned home from Singapore and my father abandoned me, my Uncle Petrov helped me. I have not seen him in over a year. He is the only family I have. The Russians believe that Mikhail, Boris's brother, is dead. He is wanted for crimes against the state."

"Do you believe he is dead?" Alex asked.

"They think that I am dead. Anything is possible. Both Boris and his brother are very resourceful men with money and contacts."

"No promises, but we will try to keep your uncle out of this. You and I are leaving for Switzerland in three days. I have made the arrangements. MI6 is quite anxious to see the proof you have."

"When you see the pictures of the documents I photographed, you will realize how high this goes both in Russia and Israel. Keep in mind though; this is the only group I know about personally. There are many groups involved. I have no knowledge of the others, but I have suspicions. We could make a sizeable dent in their operation."

Moments later, they arrived at Asad's place, parked the car in the garage and went upstairs to an empty apartment. It was eerily quiet after the firefight at the church and the commotion at the hospital. "It is not the same when Helen is not here."

"Would you like some whiskey before retiring?"

"That I would Alex. We make an odd team. I suspect when Hassan returns and finds out what they did to his brother, he will want revenge."

"That is why we are not flying to Switzerland until he returns. He may not want to continue the hotel business full time. With your connections in Tel Aviv and Moscow, we might really have a chance to reduce the trafficking of women into this area."

"I would like to do that. Count me in."

The two men retired for the night and Helen stayed in Dov's room.

Chapter 40

Angus and Tim entered the dungeon at dawn and kicked their captive in the leg to wake him up.

"Your fellow Mossad member, Dov Zahavi has been talking quite a bit. We captured him in Cairo."

"I do not believe you."

"How do you think we got his name? He said your real name is Amir Harari. He made a deal with us since you are the only other member of your group still alive. He traded your identity and other information on Boris Schochat and his brother Mikhail for a chance to live. He confirmed that Boris is the Russian he reports to in Moscow and that Boris and Mikhail were in Cairo when we captured Dov."

"That bastard, we swore an oath."

"Oh, that reminds me. I am to remove the capsule from your forearm so you will not be tempted to commit suicide. He told us about that."

"That fucking coward."

One of the men opened a pouch and removed a surgical scalpel. "We know approximately where the capsule is embedded, but we might do a little exploring to persuade you to talk first. I am not a surgeon, but I have exact directions on how to cut and how deep."

"Hold his arm Angus, I would not want to cut a vein and have him bleed to death all over Alex's floor."

Angus held Amir's arm and Tim looked for the telltale scar. He found it and cut into Amir's arm.

"That hurts," he grunted in pain. "It did not hurt that much being implanted."

"Hold still or I could cut too deeply."

Amir held still and they removed the capsule.

"I see you have been struggling against the cuffs. You have cut both of your wrists. It is useless to struggle. You cannot break free. Why were you planning to kidnap MacKay's woman?"

"We were going to use her as a hostage. In return for calling your dogs off for six months, she would be returned unharmed."

"You and I both know if you kidnapped her, you would sell her to a pimp and whip her into obedience like the rest of the women you kidnap or lure into your filthy business."

"I had orders to kidnap her and drive her to London. There I was to be contacted and given directions as to what to do with her."

"Who is your contact in London?"

"I do not know. I call Boris on an encrypted phone and he gives me a number to call or an email address to contact."

"Who was your contact in London that told you to come to Fettercairn, Scotland?"

"He is a janitor in the headquarters of MI6. He finds information when he is cleaning. No one pays attention to a cleaning man with mops and buckets. He does it for the money."

"I need his name."

"I do not know his name. He has a code name, which is the only name I know."

"The code name."

"Translation into English is 'the bee'."

"Give us a description. What hours does he work?"

"He is short for a man, maybe 153 centimeters tall, skinny, graying hair, wears glasses, slightly stooped, works the night shift when the building is quiet."

"I cannot believe it. You just described Paully, Paul Crawford. I wondered where that old man got that Rolex he wears. I never believed his story."

"Tim, go make a phone call. Paully will be scrubbing floors somewhere else for the rest of his life. He was always so friendly. I gave him a bottle of Scotch last Christmas."

"I gave him twenty pounds myself. Hope he enjoyed his spying life. The government does not treat its spies kindly."

"Tell us more about Boris and Mikhail."

"I want clothes and a descent meal before I tell you anything else. I am freezing in this bloody dungeon of yours."

"I guess we can arrange that."

"How about a shower and access to a bathroom? I am cooperating."

"I think it is time you were transported to London. We will make the arrangements. Our high security prison has everything you asked for. Sit tight. Do not go anywhere. We will return in an hour." The two men laughed.

Tim and Angus left the dungeon, bolted the door, and left Amir in the dark.

"It is cold as hell in that dungeon. I hate having to be there asking him questions. Bastard looks terrible. He cannot stop shivering. We will transport him as soon as proper transport can be arranged."

Angus placed the call. "Send us a chopper. We want to transport this man immediately. He has given us some information, but I think he knows a lot more. We need to get hold of Paully Crawford. It seems he likes to sell information and obviously knows his way around a computer. We have reliable information from a rogue Mossad agent that he has been selling information for some time. He seemed like such a nice old man. You cannot tell these days. When I asked him about his Rolex, he told me his friend died and left it to him, lying old scoundrel. Where he is going, he will not need a watch."

Angus hung up the phone.

"The chopper will be here in two and a half hours."

The two men packed their bags and were about to have lunch when they heard a helicopter approaching.

"They are early. They must have made good time the chopper is here. This weather is terrible. I hope they can fly him out of here."

The helicopter landed in the courtyard of the castle and a British trooper exited the chopper and met Tim and Angus.

"I will take it from here. Where is he?" The trooper wore a heavy coat, helmet with goggles that hid his face and leather gloves.

"In the dungeon."

"Dungeon, you have got to be kidding."

"No, it really is a dungeon, cold, damp, and unheated. Our Israeli is shivering so badly, he claims he will die if we do not give him clothes and a hot meal. He even wants a bathroom."

"He wants too much." The man answered in a gravelly voice.

They entered the dungeon and Amir was shivering so badly he was almost unconscious. His lips were blue.

"I think he is going into shock," The trooper said.

"Do not trust him. When we release him from his chains, immediately shackle him hand and foot. Wrap him in a blanket and take him as he is to London."

"Probably right, they will only strip him, and do a deep body cavity search when he arrives."

The trooper strapped on the new shackles, before releasing Amir from the wall of the dungeon, wrapped a heavy blanket around him, and led him out of the dungeon across the courtyard to the chopper. Amir shuffled along beside the trooper.

"Want to have breakfast before you leave."

"No sir, thank you. I have orders to take him to London immediately. This weather is closing in fast. The pilot wants to get airborne as soon as possible." He loaded him into the chopper.

"Wish we had a dungeon like that still in use in London. Those bleeding hearts would have a fit if they knew about this place. We will keep it in mind the next time we want to chill somebody down." They all laughed.

The chopper took off for London.

Albert had a huge breakfast ready when they came into the kitchen.

"They did not want anything to eat?"

"No, he was in a hurry; said he had orders to fly to London immediately."

"I am so glad that man is gone. I was tired of living in that safe room. I like windows and natural light. It was more like a prison than a refuge."

Magdalena came into the kitchen. "I am glad to see daylight and smell fresh air again. Have you heard when Alex is returning?"

"What the, it sounds like the chopper is returning." They looked out and another British helicopter was landing.

"There should not be a second chopper landing here so soon after the first one. Albert, you take Magdalena back to the refuge room. Tim and I will investigate. Something is wrong."

Tim and Angus drew their weapons and went out to meet the troopers walking toward them. The rain was coming in torrents and the wind had picked up since the first helicopter took off. This time there were three troopers; two of them were carrying a gurney.

"Why the guns?" They asked.

"Who are you?"

"We came here to transport that Mossad agent to London. He is to be rendered unconscious and strapped to this gurney and not told where he is being taken."

"Show me your identification soldier."

The soldiers showed Tim and Angus their identifications.

"We have a problem. Another chopper landed about half an hour ago and took your man with them. Call out an alert. We just handed him back to Mossad."

They made an immediate call to headquarters.

"You what, did you get identification before handing him over?"

"No sir."

"We will need to post a contingent at Alex's castle. They will obviously try again. I cannot believe they walked in and you politely handed him over to them."

"It looked like a military chopper."

"How many guards were there?"

"There was only one trooper and the pilot."

"Did you ask his name?"

"No. We talked about the dungeon. He was in a hurry. The weather was falling apart. There is a gale blowing and the pilot thinks he will have to wait out the storm before flying out of here. We did not even dress our prisoner, wrapped him in a blanket and he was out of here in less than fifteen minutes."

"The Mossad is good. We underestimated them. We did apprehend Paully Crawford and he told us everything. Said they threatened to harm his family if he did not get the information for them."

"Why did he give us Paully so easily?"

"They probably were finished with him. By now, they have someone new. Paully really did not know much. Seems a different man met with him each time on four separate occasions. He does not know their names and that all he wanted was the money."

"We have a bigger problem. How did they know we were transporting that man today?"

"They have compromised our communications. Contact Henry Ewing. Tell him how they rescued their man here in Scotland. They may try the same thing in Cairo. We must be on alert. The man they took knows Dov is in Cairo."

Angus placed the call to Henry in Cairo.

"We had a problem here. Mossad masqueraded as British military and we handed our captive over to them. They know we have Dov in Cairo. Be prepared for anything that might be suspicious."

"I am on my way to the hospital immediately. We will move our captive tonight. They are good. I will tell Alex."

Chapter 41

Helen entered Dov's room. He was wide-awake and staring out the window. She greeted him in Hebrew. "*Shalom*."

"I did not know they had Jewish nurses in an Egyptian hospital."

"My father was Jewish and Russian. I am Egyptian and speak Russian, Hebrew, Arabic, and a little English."

"Can you loosen my cuffs? They are cutting painfully into my wrists."

"I will have to have one of the guards do that. I am merely a caregiver. You are a wounded prisoner and you are to be restrained and not allowed to leave the bed, even to go to the bathroom."

"Bring me something to drink."

"Do not order me around," Helen snapped at him. "I am a nurse, not your slave. They told me why you were here. I do not like slavery or the people involved in it. You want me to help you, try being polite."

"I apologize. I am not myself. Please may I have something to drink?"

"That is better. I will see what is allowed."

Helen left the room and went to the nursing station. As she was about to ask, the phone rang. It was Alex.

"Helen, Asad and I are en route to the hospital. Let no one in Dov's room. Trust no one except the two guards at his door. If new guards arrive, call security. Get back to his room immediately. Tell the guards to be alert. The Mossad freed the man held at my castle. Be careful. Asad and I will be there in fifteen minutes."

Helen hung up the phone and raced back to Dov's room. The same two guards were at the door and she gave them the information.

"If you have a relief show up, chances are they are imposters. Trust no one. Alex MacKay and my husband, Asad will be here in a few minutes. No one, absolutely no one is to enter this room. If you see what appears to be a relief guard contingent, bolt the door; call security. They are ready to help. I will wait in his room until Alex arrives."

"Yes, we will be alert. I do not like Mossad. I have heard how clever they are but will not be fooled."

Helen returned to Dov's room with a glass of orange juice.

"They said you could have some juice. I will hold it for you so you may drink. You are to remain shackled hand and foot."

"Would you call the Israeli Embassy for me? They are holding me illegally. I have rights. I will see you are rewarded for helping me. The income of a nurse in Cairo has to be insignificant. I can make you a wealthy woman, one phone call."

"Sorry sir, I would have to be paid first. You did not have anything with you when you arrived. I like money, but I must have it in hand before I do anything."

Helen had no intention of helping, money or not.

"I will give you a number. They will give you the money."

"I do nothing without money."

"You miserable *pizda*. When I get free, I will return and make you my personal slave. I enjoy punishing uncooperative bitches like you."

At that, Helen took the juice and threw it in his face.

"Do not refer to me as a cunt. *Peedardiss*. They should have sent a male nurse. Enjoy your juice, you bastard. I can see why they wanted you bound to the bed and unable to move."

"I have to pee."

"So pee. I have things to do." Helen turned and walked toward the door.

"You bitch. Come back here," he screamed.

The guards smiled as she left the room. "He does not sound like he enjoyed his juice, Helen."

"It must have been too cold when I threw it in his face. He is a very hateful man. I will be glad to see him leave. They are moving him as soon as Alex and Asad get here. Any sign of a relief contingent?"

"No, wait, there are three men I do not recognize coming down the hall."

"Call for back up. I will go back into his room. Give me your back up hand gun."

The one guard handed Helen a 9mm Glock; she returned to Dov's room, and pulled back the slide and loaded the chamber. She walked over to his bed and he began to shout at her.

"Why the gun, are you going to shoot me again?"

Helen grabbed a small towel and stuffed it into his mouth.

"You are disturbing the other patients."

Helen picked up the phone and called security from the room.

"There are three men approaching Dov's room. The guards are ready. I believe it is a rescue attempt. Get here immediately. They are dark, black hair, wearing jeans and pull over dark blue jerseys. They are most likely hired mercenaries. I am in his room and have a gun in case they get past the guards. Have the nurse's lock down the criminal detention area on the floor."

The men arrived at Dov's room.

"We are your relief. This man is very dangerous and may try to escape." He spoke Arabic.

"We are not due to be relieved. Show us your identity papers and orders," barked one of the guards. At that, one of the three men shot one of the guards at point blank range. Brain matter sprayed against the wall. The other guard managed to get off two shots and took out two of the three men. The third man shot and killed the second guard. The sound in the hospital corridor was deafening and the smell of gunpowder and blood lingered in the air. The remaining imposter searched one of the dead guards and found the key to the room. Helen crouched behind the bed and took aim at the door.

The remaining imposter unlocked the door as shouts rang out in the corridor.

"Stop where you are," a security guard from the hospital shouted.

The imposter turned and fired, but missed and instead was shot in the leg by one of the advancing security guards. He managed to open the door to Dov's room, stumbled in and locked the door behind him. He did not notice Helen aiming a gun at him.

"Drop your weapon!" Helen shouted in Arabic.

The imposter turned and aimed his gun at Helen, but she shot first hitting him in the shoulder causing him to drop his weapon. Helen dashed around the bed and kicked his gun to the side. Hospital security broke the door down, grabbed the imposter, and dragged him from the room bleeding from his wounds.

"Helen stay here. We are cleaning up the mess in the hall and posting new guards. I cannot believe they thought they could get this man out of our custody. The Mossad is relentless."

Alex and Asad arrived and after showing proper identification entered Dov's room. Helen was standing with gun in hand aiming at the door.

Asad walked toward her, took the gun gently from her hand, and held her in his arms. "I guess we arrived a little late for the party." He smiled and handed the gun to Alex.

"We are moving him immediately from this room. There is a holding cell in the basement of the hospital. We took out an ambulance in the parking lot on our way to the room; that is why we were a little late. We called in the license plate and the ambulance was reported stolen. They had a man ready to drive them out of here."

"Did you capture the driver?"

"No, he put up a fight and Asad shot him."

"This man will never see the sunshine again. His would-be rescuer is on his way to surgery. They do not think he will make it because of loss of blood, must have nicked an artery. You are a damn fine shot Helen."

"Thank you. I never shot anyone before. Asad, please take me home." Helen was trembling and tears cascaded down her cheeks as he held her close.

"Go ahead," Alex urged him. "I will wait until we get this man out of here. I want to check on the assailant that Helen shot. I will see you back at the apartment when I am finished here."

Helen and Asad called a taxi and left the car for Alex.

"Are you all right? You look a little pale."

"I will be okay. I need to go home, Asad. I hope I never have to shoot anyone again. I know it was my life or his, but it did not make it easy. I received training from the police, but it does not prepare you for the real thing."

"I do not want you in harm's way again. You are off duty and staying at home until after the baby arrives. If I have my way, you will retire. I do not want my wife and mother of my children working."

"Asad, I do not want to work ever again."

When they arrived at the apartment house, Asad picked her up in his arms and carried her into the elevator, and pushed the button for the seventh floor.

"I never should have agreed to allow you to go into that man's room. I am so sorry."

"It is not your fault. I knew the Mossad were dangerous, but I had no idea they would invade a hospital and try something like that considering the security we had in place. The other patients on that floor must have been terrified. I know it is a secure wing, but shooting rattles even criminals."

"Can I get you anything? I am going to wait here for Alex to return. Hassan is due back tomorrow. I do not know how he is going to react to the news that his brother was almost beaten to death."

"How is Rafiq?"

"His father is with him and said they gave him something to knock him out and will not be conscious until tomorrow morning. They wanted him to rest completely. Given the severity of the beating, he will be in pain for some time. The lacerations on his back are deep. His father knows an oral surgeon that does implants. It will take a couple of months for him to completely recover."

"I am so tired, stay with me until Alex arrives. I do not want to be alone."

Asad lay next to her and held her in his arms. Her body was still trembling as he whispered words of love in her ear. She fell asleep just as Alex arrived.

"Be quiet."

"Is she okay?" Alex asked in a concerned tone of voice.

Asad replied, "Helen is a strong woman, but shooting that man was unsettling. I wish we could have saved her from that. When we go to Switzerland, she will need a bodyguard and a companion. I do not trust the Mossad."

Alex assured him, "I have spoken with Henry. He is working with the Egyptian authorities and they are moving Helen to a safe location until we return. They are taking no chances. The Egyptians do not like the Mossad invading their country and discussions are going on between Egypt and Israel. The Israeli's are saying this was unauthorized, and making all kinds of apologies."

"What happened to the imposter that Helen shot?" Asad asked.

"He died on the way to surgery. She shot him in the shoulder and the security team shot him in the leg. He bled out."

Asad asked in a troubled tone, "Where did they take Dov?"

"He is in a holding cell, but will shortly be on his way to London. The world will never hear about him again. Officially, he died in Cairo. We notified the Israelis. They stated they knew none of the men. Boris and Mikhail Schochat and Amir Harari are still at large. We will find them. There is no word as to where Mikhail is hiding. He may be headed to Cyprus."

"If Helen had been injured, I would have killed Dov with my bare hands." Asad stated emphatically.

"I would have helped you."

"I told you once before, we have a lot in common."

"I have to agree with you."

"Alex, I am going to bed. See you in the morning." Helen will have a restless night.

"Henry posted two lookouts across the street, and there are men at the front and back doors of your apartment house. I think we can sleep safely tonight." Alex assured him.

Chapter 42

Amir was barely conscious and looked at the trooper for the first time.

"Boris, how in the hell did you find me?"

"When you did not call in, we did some checking. One of my men hacked into a database and found a transmission concerning a helicopter flight to Fettercairn. We figured our helicopter could get there before the military chopper they were sending. It was close. They probably have landed by now. By flying low over the water toward the city of Wick, their radar should not find us. It is a thirty-five minute flight. We should be able to land, get on board our charter to Iceland, and be gone before they figure it out. This weather is getting worse by the minute."

"They have Dov in Cairo. He talked, the lousy traitor. He gave them my name, your name and everybody else's name. He even told them about the suicide capsule. If Dov is ever freed, I will personally kill him myself."

"We attempted to free him from the hospital, but we got word just before we landed that everything went wrong. They were expecting us. All our men are dead."

"What about Dov?"

"Do not know. The hospital is in lock down and I have a feeling they are going to move him immediately. They took out our ambulance driver as well. The other lookout panicked and ran. I gave orders to shoot him on site. I cannot stand men who disobey direct orders. You look like shit."

"You would too if you had been sitting on a stone floor in a dungeon chained to a wall with no clothes for all those hours."

Boris pulled out a bottle of vodka and poured Amir and himself double shots.

"This should help warm you up. When we get to Russia, we will have to go into hiding for a while. We both need new identities. I will try to rebuild the organization, but we will have to operate outside of Russia.

Tel Aviv and the Mossad will not tolerate our existence. The Mossad is probably looking for us as we speak."

"How long until we are in Russia?"

"We will have to fly an evasive route. I am sure the Brits have their radar working over time trying to find us. We only have a fifteen-minute head start. Our first stop is Wick, Scotland. There we will board a ferry flight to Iceland and fly to Russia from there. This weather is terrible; we are in for a rough ride."

Boris left Dov, entered the cockpit, and talked with the pilot.

"Any sign we have been noticed?"

"Lots of activity but at this altitude and given the weather they will have a hard time seeing us. We are no more than two meters above the water. It will be close. The weather is closing in, but that will not stop their radar. I may have to climb higher," the pilot responded in a frightened tone of voice. "I do not want to go too low and be swamped by a high wave. The sea has a mean chop. I can barely see where I am going. The ocean this time of year is rough and unpredictable. We are flying too low. I am going to have to climb to a safer altitude."

"You will keep at this altitude. You try to climb, and I will take the controls and you will go for a swim. Understand." Boris shouted.

"The waves, I have to climb. This mission is not worth my life." The pilot shouted in an angry voice.

"If I knew you were this unreliable, I would have flown myself and not used a pilot. Get out of the chopper."

"What the hell."

Boris pulled his gun and shot the pilot. He put the helicopter on autopilot long enough to open the door and kick the pilot out of the chopper.

Boris took the controls and flew a little lower while constantly watching the control panel. He checked his GPS. It showed an arrival in fifteen minutes. He called back to Dov through the speaker system.

"That damn pilot was going to give our location away. I have the controls. Hold tight. It is going to be rough"

"Can you crank up the heat? I cannot stop shivering."

"No, we will be there shortly."

Just then, a wave crashed across the front of the chopper and Boris almost lost control. He pulled the helicopter a little higher, but the weather was getting worse and he was having difficulty seeing where he was going.

British Spotter Plane

"Any sign of that helicopter? We know they headed out to sea. What's the range of that chopper?"

"It has a range of a little over a thousand kilometers, but I think they will set down sooner than that. They will be looking for an airport and a flight to Russia."

"Contact Aberdeen air control, tell them to report any helicopter approaching from the east. Inform them of the danger and that they are dressed as British troopers. They cannot fly undetected in this weather. They had a fifteen-minute head start. Choppers do not fly that fast. They cannot be more than seventy kilometers ahead of us. This weather is closing in and we will have to ground all flights."

"No sign of them. If they are flying at wave height above the sea, we will never find them."

"A major storm front is coming in from the East. Visibility is less than a kilometer. They have their radar searching, but no hits."

"Keep me informed. I do not want to lose that bastard."

A man rushed into the room shouting.

"A fishing boat called, a helicopter was spotted flying just above the waves headed toward Wick. The fisherman said he thought the chopper was going to collide with him, but changed course at the last minute."

"What's the location"?

"Chopper will land in about ten minutes if that's its destination and it doesn't crash into the sea."

"Notify Wick control that these men are highly skilled killers. They stole the helicopter they are flying, and they killed the crew outside of Aberdeen, Scotland. Take them alive if possible but our first priority is to stop them-dead or alive."

On Board The Chopper

"We are taking a pounding. Almost hit a fishing boat. I hope he does not notify anyone of our location. If he does, they will know we are headed to Wick." Boris spoke into the speaker connected to Amir's headphones. "I have no visibility, flying instruments only. Radar should pick up the airport in about five minutes. I have contact with the charter plane."

"Just do not ditch us. I would not survive the cold water. I cannot get warm. I do not want to die."

"Shut up. I need to concentrate."

The chopper shuttered, Boris panicked and jerked the controls. The chopper bounced up about thirty meters and then leveled off then started to shake buffeted by the strong winds. The rain lashed across the windshield making visibility almost impossible.

"I am losing it. Hang on. Have to ditch. Prepare to abandon the cabin. There is a life raft in the back. Crawl back there and get it ready."

"You son-of-a-bitch, you are going to kill us both. What made you think you could fly in this weather? The pilot was right."

"Get that raft ready."

A crosswind hit the chopper, and Boris lost control, but managed to set down in the water without causing any structural damage, and turned off all power. Immediately the chopper began to fill with water. Boris raced into the cabin. Amir, wearing a life jacket, got to the raft, but was too weak to move it. Boris pushed Amir out of the way, grabbed the raft, and hauled it to the door. The cabin was now awash and the chopper was sinking fast as Boris forced open the door. Amir, shocked by the icy cold water, screamed.

"You bastard, do not leave me to drown."

"Sorry."

Boris leapt into the raft and was no sooner away than the chopper sank beneath the surface of the wildly tossing sea taking Amir with it. Boris tried to orient himself. He knew his last location before ditching, but was still about ten nautical miles from Wick.

"Damn this weather," Boris shouted into the wind.

The raft bounced on the troubled sea and Boris held on for dear life. Suddenly the bow of the fishing boat perched atop a huge wave crashed down flipping the raft and dumping Boris into the sea. Boris secured to the raft with a safety line, managed to get it righted and pulled himself back aboard.

"Hey, on board the fishing boat. I need help," Boris bellowed as loud as he could. The men on the fishing boat were inside the wheelhouse and his cries went unheard. "You bastards, I am here."

Boris watched, as the fishing boat moved away until it was lost in the fog and rain. He huddled in the bottom of the raft and managed to put up the canopy, only to have the wind tear it from his hands. The rain stung his face and the wind howled like the sound of a screaming banshee as the raft tossed on the churning sea.

Almost as suddenly as the storm came, it began to quiet down. The wind was beating down the sea and the fog started to lift. The rain was still coming in torrents, but Boris was able to see a distant inlet. The high waves were crashing against the rocks. The current carried the life raft toward the beach, but it plowed into the rocks and dumped Boris into the still raging sea. He cut his tether line and managed to swim to shore.

Boris saw the raft coming ashore and raced to where it beached. He checked for supplies and found a flare gun, emergency water, and some prepared food packs.

Boris had made it alive but blood was running down his face from a cut to his head from the jagged rocks and he was exhausted from his ordeal and barely able to walk. He shambled along a narrow road until he arrived at a small house with a car parked on the side. Boris knocked on the door.

An older man opened the door, looked at Boris, and exclaimed, "My God man, what happened to you?"

"My boat was caught in that storm. Could you give me a ride to Wick?"

"I plan to go to Wick in the morning. You are welcome to stay the night. That cut looks serious. I'll get some first aid supplies."

Boris pulled his gun and hit the old man over the head, tied him, shoved his unconscious body into a closet, searched the small house for keys to the car, and found them. He raided the fridge, put some food and beer in a bag, and got into the car. He checked a map and drove in the direction of Wick. As he approached city, following the signs to the airport, he noticed military trucks and police cars ahead of him.

Boris put the car into reverse and turned around. He slammed his fist onto the dashboard, and looked at a map of the area. "Damn them. I am going to have to drive south, go on less traveled roads, and make my way back to Glasgow or Edinburgh. It is less than 300 kilometers to Edinburgh. If I can get there without being stopped, I can make arrangements to get out of this miserable country."

Boris began to drive toward Edinburgh; he figured the trip to London should take him about four hours from there. Rather than drive directly to London, he decided to drive to South-End-on-the-Sea and go into London via the Thames on a boat.

Four and a half hours later Boris arrived in South-End-on-the-Sea and ditched the car in a dark alley. He walked along the banks of the river until he spotted the right boat for his trip into London. There was a motor yacht anchored in the harbor, a twenty-meter cruiser. Boris put his possessions into a waterproof bag he salvaged from the life raft and swam to the boat. No one was on board the craft. He went below decks after jimmying the lock on the hatch. The boat was equipped with the latest in marine technology and seemed to have deluxe accommodations including a walk-in engine room with a new C-18 diesel engine. One thing that troubled him was there was food on the table and dishes in the sink. The boat had obviously just returned from a cruise, but no one had taken the time to clean up the mess. Boris checked out the electronics and was about to up anchor and motor away when a dinghy nudged the side of the boat. A teen boy and a girl, possibly his sister were climbing on board the yacht carrying several bags of supplies. The young girl was about 160 centimeters with shoulder length red hair and a face covered with freckles. She was wearing boat shoes, jeans and a long sleeved top with a storm gear slicker in bright yellow. The boy had brown hair and was about twenty centimeters taller, wearing glasses and a slicker the same as the girl. Both teens looked about sixteen or seventeen. Boris concealed himself in the master cabin.

"Why doesn't Dad pay someone to clean the boat, why does it always have to be us? I think he bought too much food. What does he plan to do go home now or travel along the coast first?" Jane complained to her brother.

"Jane, he told Mom that we would be home tomorrow."

"I will be glad when this vacation is over. Boating with Dad is too much like work. Mom is lucky; she gets sea sick and always begs off on these excursions."

The two teenagers began to clean up the mess in the galley while Boris listened as they went about their work arguing.

"When is Dad coming on board?"

"He said he would leave first thing in the morning. We can spend the night on the boat or go back to the hotel with him."

"I would rather stay on the boat John; I want to be away from Dad for awhile. He thinks he is an admiral or something. He is always giving orders. He should help clean the boat once in a while."

"Stop complaining. He takes us cruising every fall. Says it is cooler and no tourists. You have to admit we have seen most of Europe from the water."

"I wish we had a newer boat. This is an antique. I would rather have one of those sleek newer boats with more power so we could water ski."

"Dad loves tradition. I am going to the hotel tonight. I do not think you should stay on board by yourself."

"Oh John, I hate that hotel. The room has a strange smell. Besides I am fifteen and I can do whatever I want."

"It is only for one more night. We will be back in Dover tomorrow."

"I am staying on the boat. Go back to the hotel if you want. I need some peace and quiet."

The teenagers finished cleaning and John rowed the dinghy ashore. Jane fixed herself some dinner, put a CD in the player and turned up the volume.

Boris waited until Jane seemed absorbed in the music before making his move. Quietly he made his way from the master cabin to the galley and grabbed Jane from behind with one hand around her neck and his other hand across her mouth.

In English, he whispered in a low gruff voice, "You should listen to brother. Now you are mine. You will pleasure me on our trip to London; I need company."

Jane tried to struggle and pull away from Boris, but he held her tightly. He removed his hand from across her mouth and pulled her arms behind her back.

Jane screamed, "Let me go you creep."

Boris slapped her hard across the back of her head, and jerked her around to face him. She began to sob.

Boris shook her and slapped her several more times across the face.

"You will do what I tell you. Make one more sound, and I will really hurt you."

Her lip split and blood trickled down her chin, her eyes began to show bruising, as Jane managed to say something, "Please, don't hurt me. Who are you?"

Boris slapped her again and bound her wrists behind her back with some small line he found in a drawer in the galley. He grabbed a small cloth, made it into a gag, and stuffed it into her mouth. He fastened it with duck tape, dragged her into the master cabin, and tossed her roughly onto the bed.

"As soon as I get this boat headed to London, I will see that you pleasure me. I might keep you for myself for a while. Have you ever been to Cyprus?"

Jane sobbed and her body shook. Boris walked over to her and ripped off her clothes. He took another piece of line and bound her ankles to each side of the bed. He then took another line, wrapped it around her neck, and tied it off on a post at the end of the bed.

"I will be back. I bet you are a virgin. Not for long my little captive." He laughed as he slammed the door to the cabin and went topside to up anchor and head the boat toward London.

Chapter 43

The phone rang and Asad picked up.

It is Sabir, "Rafiq is awake and in a lot of pain, but he will recover. Jameel is driving to Alexandria to meet Hassan and Emunishere. I want you to ride along with him. Do not tell him anything until you are back in Cairo. I want to be the one to tell him about his brother."

"What about Alex?"

"Tell Alex to come to the hospital as soon as possible. We want to interrogate Dov before we move him to London. His flight leaves in about two hours aboard a private plane we chartered."

"I want you to guard my son and Jameel. Fatinah and Helen are coming to the hospital with my wife. I have arranged security and a driver."

"I will tell Alex."

Alex walked to the bedroom door. "What is the plan for today?"

"A driver is bringing Sabir's wife and Fatinah to the hospital. They are picking you and Helen up on their way. Henry wants you to interrogate Dov before they fly him to London. Jameel is due any minute and your ride will be along in about ten minutes. They did not say where they are holding him."

Alex handed Asad an Uzi and two spare banana clips. "In case you need something heavier than a hand gun. These men are ruthless and capable of anything."

"I do not expect trouble, but I will be alert. What happened to the helicopter and the agent in Scotland?"

"Henry called. The helicopter crashed and they found the bodies of two men washed up on the rocks. One was the Mossad captive named Amir, and the other we think is the body of their pilot. That means that Boris Schochat is still missing as well as his brother Mikhail."

"Boris is a very dangerous and clever adversary. He will try to get to Russia by any means possible. If he gets a car, he will drive to Edinburgh and onto London. I know he has a Russian contact there and another two agents in Glasgow. If he makes it to London, we will never find him. He may also head to Cyprus to join his brother Mikhail at his villa in the mountains. A lot of the Russian Mafia own property in the mountains of Cyprus."

"Give me the names of the agents in Glasgow and Edinburgh."

"Sorry, I do not know their names or locations. I have a number to call in case I found myself stranded there. You can have it; it is all that I have."

Asad handed Alex the phone number when their came a knock at the door.

Alex took out his gun and went to the door. Who is there?"

"It is Jameel. I am to pick up Asad."

Alex opened the door and Asad took his weapons and left with Jameel.

"Look out for Helen while I am gone. We should be back in Cairo this evening. It is a 225-kilometer drive to Alexandria each way, and we have to secure the yacht before we leave. See you this evening."

Alexandria, Egypt

Asad and Jameel arrived at the Port of Alexandria just as the *El Jumanah* was docking at its permanent slip. Asad and Jameel went aboard the yacht while their driver parked the SUV.

Hassan was standing on the deck waving to them.

"Come on board. We have to talk before we leave for Cairo."

"You look stressed. I expected to see you happy and relaxed after being on your honeymoon. What is wrong?"

"Come into the main salon and I will explain. Until last night, I was happy, relaxed, and so in love. I never thought I could love a woman this intensely ever again and be this happy."

The three men went to the main salon where Emunishere was standing chatting with a young woman who appeared to be in her early twenties. She was shorter than Emunishere by several centimeters, brown shoulder length hair, light complexion, and wearing a skirt much too long for her.

"This is Anne Cranston, an American from Colorado. She came on board the yacht last night just as we were leaving for Alexandria. She is a victim of the slave trade. Her story is a little different. Men kidnapped her while on a cruise ship along with her friend, Jennifer Green, and they were beaten and held captive. Anne managed to escape, but her friend is still being held by these bastards."

"Let's talk as we drive to Cairo. Things have been happening in the two weeks you have been gone. We must get back as soon as possible."

A crewmember carried their luggage to the SUV and the two women sat in the back. The three men sat in the first row of seats behind the driver.

"How did this woman get on board your yacht?"

"We were getting ready to leave our berth and this soaking wet woman, wearing only her underwear came running down the dock toward the yacht. She shouted, 'Help me, help me' as she was running, I was standing on deck, reached out to her, pulled her on board, and hurried her into the cabin. I told the crew to leave the dock and head for Alexandria. As we were leaving the port, I looked back and saw several men hurrying along the docks. Fortunately, we left Rhodes about the same time as two large cruise ships. We saw the men looking at the cruise ships. Fortunately, we were alongside one of the cruise ships hidden from their view. I do not think they saw me pull her aboard *El Jumanah*."

"How does a woman get kidnapped on a cruise ship?"

"It seems that this cruise ship has a very limited clientele. All of the passengers are wealthy businessmen from all over the world. The cruise is very expensive and for a ten day cruise of the Greek Islands, Istanbul, and Kusadasi, the price is $20,000 American money."

"If all the passengers are men and the cruise is so expensive, how did this woman and her friend get to be passengers?"

"They had reservations on another ship. When they were about to leave the hotel in Athens for Piraeus, the concierge gave them a message that their cruise had been overbooked and they would receive deluxe accommodations on this cruise ship called the *Apollo*. They were taken to the ship in a car provided by the hotel."

"What size is this ship?"

"It was small for a cruise ship only 225 meters long, but everything was deluxe."

"When were they kidnapped?"

"They were given a welcome aboard drink and shown to their cabin where a basket of fresh fruit was waiting for them. As promised in the note, the suite was a luxurious."

"Didn't they realize they were the only women on board?"

"There were other women on board the ship, all of whom were held captive and forced to sexually pleasure the male passengers. The clients were free to do with the women anything they pleased. Unbelievably, they even had a torture chamber below decks that the clientele used to punish or torture the women. Some of the women danced, and provided entertainment in the lounge. The men in the audience would pick the woman they wanted and took them to their cabin for sex. Some women chosen on the first day stayed with that client."

"What happened to the women after the cruise?"

"Some of the women would continue with the next charter. If they were not cooperative or sick and unable to perform because of severe treatment, they were removed from the ship in Kusadasi, Turkey, and transported to a gypsy camp and sold."

"How did they subdue them?"

"Either the fruit or the drinks were drugged. When they woke up, they were in an area resembling a dungeon. They had been stripped naked and bound to whipping posts."

"Their identity papers, passports, visas were destroyed while they watched. Their captors explained in very bad English that they were there to service the men on the ship. They were to do whatever was requested and not complain. If they refused, they threatened to beat them into submission and told their families in the United States would be in danger. Then to convince them, they whipped Anne and Jennifer with multiple tailed leather floggers that left red marks on their bodies. They screamed at each stroke of the whip. This punishment continued for at least twenty minutes before their captors stopped. They were released, told to shower, and prepare themselves for pleasuring the men on the ship. Anne talked back, and each of the two men that had whipped them took turns sodomizing her. She was then beaten a second time. Her friend was taken sobbing from the chamber and that was the last time Anne saw her."

"How did Anne escape?"

"A wealthy man took a fancy to her; brought her to his cabin on the third day and treated her well, but had sex with her three or four times a day. When the ship arrived at Rhodes, the women were locked in their small cabins while the passengers went on shore to visit Lindos and the other sites of the medieval city. The man Anne was with did not want to go sightseeing, but insisted on shopping for clothes and jewelry with Anne and took her with him into the city. Anne asked to go to the bathroom and noticed a narrow door next to the ladies' room. It was open and faced an alley behind the shop. She slipped through the door and hurried on foot toward the harbor. She slipped out of her clothes, got into the water, and hid behind a fishing boat until they left. Back on shore, she got dressed without drying off in an effort to avoid attention."

"He did not notice she was missing?"

"Realizing she had been gone too long, he summoned another man that had accompanied them from the cruise ship to help find her. Anne said she heard angry voices shouting at the shopkeeper about the open door. The two men then proceeded to check all the shops and patrolled the waterfront searching for her. Her captors had promised to find her if she attempted escape and that she would be tortured and sold to the gypsies in Kusadasi, or worse yet, killed."

"The cruise ships had started to leave and she heard the voices of the two men getting closer desperately searching. Anne was a good swimmer, a member of the college swim team. Spotting a dock with private yachts a short swim from where she was, she stripped to her underwear and slipped unseen into the water. Upon reaching the dock, she climbed out of the water and ran toward our yacht. Hearing her pleas for help I stretched my hand and pulled her on board."

"We will try to find out everything about this cruise ship when we get to Cairo. Do you know where the cruise ship was registered?"

"Anne didn't know, but said she thought it was Greek. Most of the crew spoke Greek and the signs on the ship were in Greek, French, Arabic, and English."

"You said we had to return to Cairo immediately, what is happening?"

"We shot and killed several members of Mossad who were searching for Yuri. We captured one of them alive and moved him to London for security reasons. We released word that an Israeli man at the scene was shot and later died from his wounds at the hospital. The head of the group, Boris Schochat, managed to escape. We had captured another man, but to make the story short, he died in a helicopter crash while trying to escape near Wick, Scotland. We suspect Boris is trying to return to Moscow or flee to Cyprus to join his brother, Mikhail. We have not found either of them."

"What else happened?"

"I will let your father tell you the rest. I promised I would let him tell you," Jameel answered.

"That hints of a major situation. Does this affect me personally?"

"We will be in Cairo in just under an hour. We will go directly to the hospital. Trust me. It is best your father tells you. Helen and Fatinah are in a safe location. Emunishere will join them," Asad assured him.

"What about Anne? She has no money, no identity papers. What is to become of her?" Hassan asked.

"We will make arrangements for her to stay at the America Embassy in Cairo until they can repatriate her and send her home. They will notify her family that she is safe in their custody." Asad replied.

"We were going to try and notify the Americans from the yacht, but thought the men looking for her might overhear our transmission using sophisticated equipment and come after her at sea."

"That was wise. We will contact the American Embassy when we reach Cairo." Jameel answered. "Marine radios are open to anyone listening on that channel and not encrypted."

"Not to change the topic, but your honeymoon was good." Asad asked.

"Emunishere is an amazing woman. She is a fabulous artist. She has been filling sketchbooks as we traveled. We went to all the Greek Islands, spent a few days in Athens, and visited Istanbul. Rhodes was our last stop before leaving for Alexandria."

"I am so happy for you."

They packed the car and started the drive to Cairo.

For most of the trip, Emunishere and Anne sat quietly listening to Asad and Jameel explain what had happened in Cairo.

"If anyone can help you Anne, it is the three men in this car. They are on a mission to stop the slave traders." Emunishere entered the conversation. "They have been working with a group from Cairo with my father-in-law to stop the sex trade from Eastern Europe through Egypt and across the desert to Israel. We will see that you are safe at the American Embassy as soon as we arrive."

Hassan turned to Jameel. "This is a different group of traffickers kidnapping unsuspecting female tourists and using them for their sea going brothel. We must notify the Greek authorities that there is a ring operating out of Athens preying on tourists using a private cruise ship and possibly hotel staff."

Asad spoke to the women, "Anne, we will see you get back safely, but I do not know what we can do about your friend. From what you have told us, the ship will sail to Istanbul first, and stay a couple of days before heading to Kusadasi. We may be able to rescue her when they leave the ship. I make no promises."

"Thank you. I feel bad about Jennifer. She is my age, but she very, very naïve, and at twenty-three, still a virgin. We are both from a small town in the Rocky Mountains. The men on the ship were planning to sell her for a lot of money. They discovered her virginal condition when they stripped her. She was whipped the same as me, but she was not raped. I do not know where they are taking her. They told her she would be untouched until the ship reached Kusadasi where they planned to sell her for a lot of money to an Arab. I do hope you can rescue her."

"We can promise you nothing, but we will try. Working through the Turkish authorities, we may not be able to act that quickly. The cruise ship, even with a stopover in Istanbul, will be in Kusadasi in three days."

"Please try. She must be terrified."

The car arrived at the hospital, Asad, Hassan, and Emunishere hurried to Sabir's office. Jameel took Anne to an examination room in the hospital.

"Anne, I am a doctor. I would like to examine you and check if you have any injuries. I know you have had a difficult time."

"Everything hurts. These men were not gentle. One of the passengers sodomized me with a carved phallus and then whipped my bottom for long periods. I know there is bruising. Another man was rough and caused me to bleed. I am still in pain."

"A nurse will get you ready so that I can examine you. I will be gentle and give you something for pain. Trust me. No more harm will come to you."

Jameel examined Anne thoroughly.

"You have been bruised from the rough sex and there is a slight tear. Nothing is severe. I will give you medicine to prevent infection and a painkiller. You will feel much better in a couple of days. I will also check for HIV, but doubt that will be a problem. Most wealthy men, such as you described, are very careful. I am sure they checked your blood before exposing you to the men on the ship. These men would not succeed in business if they had women with HIV in their service. I also know you are in shock and a few days in the hospital under observation will help. I suggest you talk with one of our counselors who can help. She is very good and speaks English; she has helped rape victims in the past. We have contacted the American Embassy and they are notifying your parents. A representative from the Embassy will be here shortly."

"I do not know how to thank you."

"Seeing you safe is thank you enough. We will try to help your friend, but there is very little time to mount a rescue and we will have to cut through a lot of bureaucratic red tape. If she were here in Cairo, we would stand a better chance. Turkish officials are seldom fast to react and if sold to a Saudi, there is no return from the Kingdom of Saudi Arabia."

Jameel left her and went to Sabir's office. When he entered, Sabir had just finished telling Hassan about his brother.

"I will take you to his room. He is still in a lot of pain, but he will be back to work in about two weeks. He will be glad to see you." Sabir placed his hand on Hassan's shoulder reassuringly.

"I cannot believe they kidnapped Rafiq from the hotel. These people are ruthless. It is lucky you found him. With all that has happened I am convinced that my future lies in helping the victims of this heinous trafficking of women." Hassan's voice was angry. "I know some investors that will help Rafiq with the hotel, but I want to actively hunt down these criminals. This has become personal; I cannot rest until we find the man responsible for beating Rafiq."

"It is difficult to comprehend the enormity of human trafficking. Even cruise ships are not safe. We no sooner close down one operation and another one crops up." Asad added.

Hassan left accompanied by Sabir to check on Rafiq. His brother lay sleeping in the bed with tubes connected to his arm and chest. Bandages covered his face. Bruises covered his body from the horrific beating he had endured. Hassan walked to his bedside and squeezed his hand awakening Rafiq who opened his eyes and smiled.

"You are back," he exclaimed. "Father told you what had happened?"

"Yes, I am so sorry it had to be you, it should have been me at the hotel that day."

"You should not blame yourself. For so long you have denied yourself the chance to be happy. Emunishere has given you that. I am so happy for the both of you."

Hassan fought to hold back the tears.

"Your suffering will not be in vain, I promise you. The man responsible for this will be found and dealt with. You have shown great courage"

"Be safe my brother, Allah has given me a second life."

"Rafiq, I will let you rest. Alex and Asad are flying to Switzerland tomorrow to retrieve the pictures and other documents implicating officials in Israel and Russia." Sabir added.

"I would travel with you, but I must get back to work. I will see that Emunishere joins Helen and Fatinah." Hassan then asked, "What about Anne?"

"She should stay at the hospital for a few days. The Embassy will move her as soon as she recovers. The shock of what has happened to her will trouble her for years."

Jameel interrupted. "Her parents are flying to Cairo and should arrive late this evening according to the Embassy. Her friend's parents were notified, but are staying in Colorado."

They left Rafiq's room. Alex, who had joined them and Asad along with Emunishere and Hassan drove to where Fatinah and Helen were staying at the safe house.

Helen put her arms around Asad and hugged him, "This slavery of women has to stop. You are doing everything possible and I am so proud of you."

"I am trying to make up for the last four years of my life. Alex and I fly to Zurich this evening to pick up the evidence I told you about. We will not be in any danger."

Alex entered the conversation, "Your man will be home safe in a couple of days. We are all proud of what he has done. With his help, we have made great strides toward stopping these criminals who victimize women for profit."

"Thank you Alex, Asad and I owe you our life together. Be careful."

Helen kissed Asad and Alex before they left for the airport.

"Don't worry about us," Emunishere answered. "We girls will anxiously await your safe return."

Hassan added, "I'll watch out for all of them until you return."

Alex and Asad left for the airport.

Chapter 44

Later that evening Alex and Asad arrived in Zurich, Switzerland to retrieve the documents Asad had hidden in a safety deposit box. Asad would leave for the bank in the morning to retrieve them.

"How do you plan to access this box, you were officially declared dead and now you have a new identity?"

"It is not under my name. I have identity papers with an assumed name to verify that I am that person. It was too dangerous to hide this information under my own name. Over the years I have met people who can arrange for new identities."

"Does anyone else know this identity?"

"The only person who knows is the man I got the papers from in Athens, Greece four years ago. He had no knowledge of what I was using it for at the time. My uncle suggested I make these arrangements before I joined the Russian Mob. He told me someday I might need a new identity. You are the only other person I have told."

"Is it possible either the man in Greece or your uncle has been contacted by the Mossad to track you through this identity?"

"I did it before I joined them. I told no one what name I used, not even my uncle. He does not know where or if I obtained the identity papers. He told me how to find people that did this type of work. I did not want to use anyone in Russia."

"You are well suited for espionage work. It is a shame you chose the slavery business."

"After my experience in Singapore I had a hate on for women. I had never been successful with relationships. Loving a woman is preferable to brutalizing them, but I never really loved any woman until I met Helen. Cassandra was lovable, but much too naïve and still tied to her father. I knew that Jameel would never abuse her."

"I will go to the bank tomorrow alone. No one but the owner of the box may enter and remove the contents. Once the bank opens, it will only take a few minutes. We will be on our way to the airport before three o'clock. Remember, they have your name and description. They found your home in Scotland. Boris will not forget or forgive the loss of his men. He will come looking for you once he is safe."

"I have protection arranged in Scotland. We must capture this man as soon as possible."

"Dov is the only permanent member of his group that worked from within the Mossad. He has others on his payroll outside of the Mossad. It will take him time to rebuild his organization. The Mossad do not like complications and will be looking for Boris, Mikhail, and Dov."

"Where will he go to regroup?"

"If he can make it to London, he will first go to Russia where he has a hide-away. I do not know where it is located. From there he will make his way to Cyprus to join up with his brother who is in hiding in the mountains since killing a government official. I was there only once but could find it again, but it is very dangerous to go there. The Russian mobs have a great deal of influence with the Cypriot officials. They are paid well to keep these men and their families safe from all intruders."

"Does he have another identity?"

"I believe he does, but I never found out what it was. Boris speaks Hebrew, Russian, Arabic, Greek, and some English. He might seek refuge in Israel after lying low in Cyprus for a while. My guess, he will not resurface for three or four months. He is a very wealthy man, but he is not about to retire. He loves the excitement and he has a psychopathic personality and enjoys torture and killing just like his brother. I'm sure he watched or even participated in the beating of Rafiq." Asad drew a deep breath. "I saw him beat a man to death that had overcharged him for a hotel bill in Athens six months after his visit. He is like an elephant; he never forgets. He is a psychopath, a very dangerous man. Be assured he will come looking for you and Magdalena, if not this year, perhaps a year from now. Trust me; you and your family are in danger, as long as Boris is alive."

"When you retrieve those papers tomorrow, we must take them to London before returning to Cairo."

The next day Asad entered the bank in Zurich carrying a large suitcase and presented his identity papers. Ivan Sovanovitch was the name on the passport.

"I have a safety deposit box here, and wish to retrieve the contents."

The bank associate, a young man in his late twenties wearing a conservative gray suit, light blue shirt and contrasting tie in a darker shade of blue, looked at the papers and led Asad to the vault.

"Your key, Mr. Sovanovitch. Will you be closing the box?"

"Yes I will. Here is my key."

Asad handed the man his key and went to a private viewing room. Asad opened the box and looked at the pictures remembering each moment that he snapped the photos. The first was a picture of Boris with his uncle that he tore up and destroyed. The second was of Boris kissing a naked blonde. He put the photo in an envelope. The third photo was of an assistant to the president of Russia posing with a naked woman he had bound and gagged; he was whipping her severely with a bullwhip. Asad added it to the envelope. The third photo was a prominent member of the Duma and another blonde beauty whipping him, as he stood naked chained to a rack. Again, Asad slipped the photo into the envelope. The fourth photo was of a ledger page showing the profits for 2005 and 2006 from the sex trade. They had kept copious records. The next four photos were of high-ranking members of the Israeli government, all prominently pictured with lovely blonde Eastern European women. One woman was crying as a man held a knife to her throat. Another showed her on her knees giving one of the men a blowjob. Two other women were shown naked, the official was whipping one, while the other woman could be seen whipping the bottom of a naked member of the Israeli government bent over a chair. Asad slid the photos into the envelope with the others. Asad studied a photo of high-ranking Israeli officials shown leaving a brothel in Tel Aviv before adding it to the envelope. Next was a photo of another ledger page showing a $2 billion dollar profit from the trade of, 'disposable goods'. Yuri thought carefully before adding it to his collection. When he finished, he had a series of twenty-five photos incriminating high-ranking Russian and Israeli officials pictured with attractive women and another twelve photos of ledger pages showing enormous profits from the sex trade. The evidence in Russia went deep into the Duma and in Israel included high-ranking police, army officers, and went all the way to the Prime Minister before he had a stroke and fell into a coma and died.

Asad emptied the remaining contents of the box icluding a stack of cash placing everything in the metal suitcase he had brought. Now he had enough evidence to incriminate these men and guarantee his freedom. This would fulfill his end of the bargain. He canceled the box, took the suitcase and left the bank. The case was heavy due to the large amount of cash. He returned to the hotel after doing some shopping.

When he entered the room, Alex was impatiently waiting for him.

"Where have you been? You are late."

"Sorry. I stopped at a jewelry store and bought a wedding and engagement ring for Helen along with a diamond encrusted Swiss watch. I have not given her anything but assurances."

"You have the photos?"

"As promised; I think we should return to Cairo immediately. The only loose end is Boris and his brother. I worry for your family. These men are deadly assassins. I know. According to my uncle, Boris was responsible for my father's death. I want him as much as you do. Even though I had a falling out with my father, he was my father and deserved better. We will make plans en route to Cairo."

Alex looked at the photos and was amazed at the records.

"I cannot believe they kept such accurate accounting."

"The Russians and the Israeli's were greedy. Everything had to be documented."

"How did you get photos of these men such compromising positions without being caught?"

"The women were paid very well by me and used miniaturized photo equipment I purchased in Germany."

"If they knew you had these; they would have tortured you into giving them the location."

"I destroyed photos that included my uncle. He is a clever man and never got directly involved with anything the mob did. He merely provided them with the names of officials that could easily be bought or bribed. My entire life he protected me. I owe him everything. It is a shame he will never know I survived."

"He must never know you are alive."

"I know it. Our next problem is to do away with Boris before he comes after you and your family. I owe you my life. You can count on me to help you. Until Boris is dead or put away, you have my word, we will kill that son-of-a-bitch and kill or capture his brother. Mikhail will avenge his brother; they are fraternal twins. Boris will contact him the first opportunity he gets, unless he has already spoken with Mikhail and given him some details."

"We have three hours before our flight. I promised Magdalena some chocolates and a music box. I imagine Helen would like a music box and what woman does not like chocolates."

"I saw a music box once that was a bird in a cage and it sounded just like a real songbird. I think Helen would like that. There is a shop that sells music boxes and chocolates across the street from our hotel."

The two men packed their suitcases and Alex took the large envelope with the pictures from the bank that Asad gave him and tucked it into a small attaché case he was carrying.

They entered the shop and both men bought large boxes of truffles and gourmet Swiss chocolates.

Asad bought an antique Swiss birdcage music box with singing birds for Helen along with a smaller music box that played three pieces of music by Tchaikovsky and Alex bought a more traditional music box that played three songs from *Phantom of the Opera*.

"I think the girls will love their gifts, but I insist Helen share the chocolates." Asad laughed.

"I can hardly wait to see Magdalena. I call every night and she tells me she is sorry and is in love with me. She said something the other night, but didn't tell me what it meant."

"What did she say?"

"*Miluju Te.*"

"Of course she said that to you. It means I love you in Czech. I know how to say I love you in at least fifteen or twenty languages. I will teach you sometime."

"Something you picked up the last four years."

"No, I have always been in love with women. I learned as a teenager to say I love you in every European language along with Arabic and Chinese. Helen is the only woman I told I love you that I really meant it. She is my only love."

"You are a romantic. I will take Magdalena to Edinburgh and buy her a ring before we are married."

Alex and Asad boarded the flight for London to deliver the photos to MI6. Asad would continue to Cairo and Alex would return to Scotland, check on Magdalena, and move her to safety until the baby was born. Then he and Asad would go in search of Boris and his brother.

Chapter 45

Boris checked his navigation instruments and set a course for London. He knew that come morning the yacht he was on would be reported missing and the girl as possibly kidnapped. He planned to be in London by three or four in the morning and by then he could set the boat adrift, take the girl, and be on his way to Russia or Cyprus.

Once the boat was on course, Boris set the autopilot and returned to the cabin to check on his captive. Jane was still sobbing when he entered the room. He walked over to the bed, ripped off the duck tape, and removed her gag.

"Now my little lady, you will learn to make love to a man. Are you a virgin or are you experienced as are most British girls today?"

Jane screamed at him, "Don't you touch me. My father will find you and kill you when he catches you."

Boris slapped her, released the rope on her ankles, and turned her on her stomach. He secured a rope around her neck again, and tied it to a hook in the wall at the head of the bed. Because of the rope around her neck, she could not move very much, but tried to kick him. He grabbed first one leg, tied a rope around her ankle, pulled her leg to one side of the bed, and fastened it securely. He then grabbed her other leg and did the same. Jane laid there her body trembling. Boris found some petroleum jelly, took a large glob, massaged it into her backside, and roughly thrust his finger inside of her and then he pushed a second finger into her. Jane tried to squeeze her butt closed, but he smacked her bottom hard with his free hand and shouted at her, "Relax or I will whip you senseless, you little cunt."

Jane continued to squirm; Boris removed his belt, stood over her and in rapid succession whipped her bottom at least twenty times. Her bottom erupted in shades of red streaked with red stripes from where the belt had struck.

"You are difficult to convince. You are mine now. I will do whatever I wish with you."

Jane stopped screaming and whimpered as he resumed his rough treatment. He pushed his fingers into her vagina and discovered she was a virgin.

"You will not lose your virginity to me, but you will enjoy anal sex with me. Your tight little ass will give me immense pleasure and when I am done with you, you will sell for thousands of dollars. I know wealthy men who will pay 10,000 pounds or more sterling for a virgin of your obvious charms. I will personally train you in the ways of love. You will do whatever I tell you to do. When I sell you, you will be submissive and an expert in oral and anal sex. The thrill of losing your virginity, sadly, will not be mine. I need the money to get home."

Boris went back to buggering her bottom with the smooth handle of a screwdriver. He pushed it in and out and wiggled it side to side despite her screaming. He tossed the screwdriver across the room and little by little, his hard erect manhood entered her to the quick. His movements became more rapid and it seemed to bring him to a rage. He smacked her as he plunged in and out of her body and finally came with a spasm and lay wet with sweat across her body. Jane was exhausted and past crying or screaming and made only quiet moans as he lay across her body. Boris got up and struck her another twenty times with his belt bloodying her bottom in several places, left the cabin, and shut the door behind him. She lay there whimpering like a whipped animal and cried herself to sleep.

By now, Boris could see the lights of London and seeing a place to dock pulled into the bank of the river. He looked around and saw several cars parked along the street. Because of the early hour, the houses were still dark. He went below and retied Jane's ankles and wrists together, released the rope from around her neck, placed the gag into her mouth, and secured it with more duck tape. After wrapping her naked body in a sheet, he tossed her over his shoulder, placed her on the bank of the river, and with some effort set the boat adrift. He picked up Jane and found an unlocked car. He tossed her on the floor in the back, managed to hot wire the engine, and drove slowly toward London. It was four in the morning. No one would miss the yacht yet, and the car would not be reported stolen for at least two hours. By then Boris knew he could make contact with his friends in London and manage to secure transport to Russia or Cyprus with the girl. He did not care if it was by slow steamer. He would have that much more time to enjoy Jane. By the time they arrived in Cyprus Jane would be fully trained in the art of making love and fetch him a lot of money. He smiled at the thought of buggering her for another week and whipping her into the perfect concubine. When he finished with her, she would not try to escape and would definitely comply with her owners every wish. He thought to himself. "If I didn't need the money, I would take her virginity myself."

Boris drove into a section of London not far from Hyde Park and made a call to his contact. The first number was not working. He dialed the second number and got an answering machine but did not leave a message. He dialed the third and next to last number before a sleepy voice filled with irritation growled into the phone.

"This better be life or death. Do you know what time it is?"

"Shut up," Boris snarled back. "This is a matter of life and death, my life or your death; you make the choice. This is Butcher. I need to get to Cyprus. I think Russia may be too dangerous. I have to lay low for awhile."

"I was expecting your call. Your adventures and failures have not gone unnoticed. Russia is too hot for you. The Russians and the Brits are looking for you and the Mossad is pissed off. Cyprus is a good idea. Your brother may be the only person in the world glad to see you. You have made many enemies. Mikhail is in Cyprus."

"Mikhail made it to Cyprus?"

"He has gone silent and is also being hunted. There is a steamer leaving for Istanbul tonight. I think transport for the right price is possible but it will be expensive."

"I have five hundred pounds."

"I do not think that would get you on board as a crew member. What else might you have? The captain loves women and as I recall you are in the business."

"How about a lovely young virgin in exchange for transport? She is fifteen, and I am training her to be a concubine. She should be worth the price of passage."

"I will see what I can arrange. The captain has his perversions and a young virgin may be your ticket to Istanbul. From there you can make your way to Cyrus on a fishing boat. Call me in an hour. I will have an answer for you."

Boris drove slowly through the city keeping to back alleys and side streets. In an hour, he called again.

"Go to the wharf and park at the warehouse marked D53. The steamer is at the loading dock in front of the building. The captain will see the woman and give you an answer. He is one mean son-of-a-bitch. Be careful around him. He has been known to shoot people he doesn't like and sounded irritated that you had no money and only a young bitch."

Boris arrived, picked Jane up, tossed her over his shoulder, and walked into a small office near the back of the building. A sea captain wearing a fisherman's cap and a pea jacket was waiting for him. The captain was in his fifties with steel grey hair and a full beard. His eyebrows were bushy and formed an unbroken line above his deep-set brown eyes. His hands, scarred and heavily calloused from a life at sea, clenched a coffee cup. He was slightly less than two meters tall and weighed over one hundred kilos.

"Put the package on the floor and unwrap it," snarled the captain in a voice made hoarse from too much smoking.

Boris removed the sheet and Jane lay on the floor with tears streaming down her face looking up at the captain.

"What a little beauty we have here. You sure she is a virgin?"

"Guaranteed she is a virgin. She is fifteen and I have begun to train her. A few more whacks of a belt or whip and I am sure she will do anything you want her to do. She has a real tight ass. That port I christened myself." Boris laughed.

The captain leaned over Jane, grabbed her face in his rough hand, and looked into her terrified eyes.

"She'll do. Get yourself a berth with the rest of the crew. I expect you to work on the ship. You will follow my orders on the way to Istanbul and train as a deck hand. I have a whip too, and a lot of crew men who do not like Russians."

"I have done hard work before. Just get me to Istanbul. Enjoy the girl. She is too skinny for me; I like a more rounded bitch."

Boris left and was escorted on board the steamer and shown to his cabin in the crew quarters by a burly giant of a man who tossed some work clothes on a bunk.

The ship was a 200-meter rusting hulk that had seen better days. "Put on. Come with me. We have to shove off."

He grabbed Boris's hands and looked at them. "You have hands like a woman, soft. You will toughen up between here and Istanbul. The captain does not like you. That is why he gave you to me. I do not like Russians either. My name is Alekos. I will direct you; if you do not do as I ask I will whip your ass into submission and give a taste of what it feels like to be severely whipped like the young girl you brought aboard. I have no use for men that abuse women. That young woman was severely beaten, her eyes are filled with terror. The captain will have lots of sex with her and may whip her, but not as hard as you did. Some of those lines on her bottom were bloody. Even a whore trains without scarring their body. I, on the other hand, will not tolerate disobedience and will beat you bloody if you do not do what I say. My men and I will see to it that you work hard. Give us a hard time and I will make a bitch out of you." He laughed and shoved Boris in the back as he walked toward the deck.

Boris knew better than to fight back; he was outnumbered, but he was already planning his revenge against the captain and this man Alekos.

Chapter 46

As soon as Alekos and Boris left the deck, the Captain ordered a crewmember to take Jane to his cabin.

"Lay her on the bed and I will be down shortly, I do not want to clear the harbor yet and tell the pilot boat not to get underway. Leave her bound, but remove the gag."

A muscle bound crewmember wearing a striped shirt and blue jeans picked her up and carried her below. He removed her gag and said something to her in Turkish, put a sheet over her body and left.

Jane stared at the ceiling of the small cabin. It was neat, and the sheets were clean. On a desk sat a bottle of whiskey, a large astray was filled with cigar ashes, and a large cigar laid there only smoked half way.

"Oh what is to become of me?" She thought. "Anything will be better than that repulsive Russian. He is a filthy beast."

She did not have long to wait when the door opened and the captain entered the cabin and took off his hat and sat on the edge of the bed. He reached over to the desk, poured himself a shot of whiskey, and relit the cigar. A blue cloud of smoke rose to the ceiling of the cabin and the aroma of a good cigar filled the area.

He looked at Jane. She looked like a ghost shivering under the sheet and her eyes were wild as she stared at the captain. She was afraid to say anything. The silence was broken when the captain moved closer to her and asked in a concerned tone of voice, "I am Captain Vasilli. I have a daughter that is your age. Who are you? "How did that animal get hold of you?"

"My name is Jane Taylor. He kidnapped me and stole my father's yacht. My brother went ashore, but I insisted on staying on the boat overnight. I should have listened to my older brother. That horrible man attacked, sodomized, raped, and beat me. He drove me to London in a car he stole and then to your ship. I do not think my father knows I am missing. He is wealthy. He will pay you a lot of money to return me to him. Please, please don't hurt me." She sobbed.

"Where is your father?"

"We were staying at a small hotel in South-End-On-the-Sea. We were to set sail to Dover this morning. He and my brother should be heading to the boat about eight o'clock."

"I will see to the man that abused you. He will suffer for what he did to you. I am going to see that you are on your way back to London on the pilot boat. I will try to contact the hotel and talk with your father. Do not be afraid, you are safe. I've asked a crew member to find you some pants and a shirt that might come close to fitting you."

"Thank you. I thought you were going to rape me."

"The thought crossed my mind, but when I saw the terror in your eyes and lashes to your young body, I could not. You remind me of my own daughter."

He untied her and massaged her wrists and ankles where Boris had tied her tightly. He gave her a bottle of mineral water, patted her on the head, and turned to leave. "Use the head. There is a sink in there and I will contact the pilot boat. The clothes will be brought to you."

Vasilli went to the wheelhouse, radioed the pilot boat, and told him there was a woman on board to be returned to London. He got on the satellite phone he always carried and called the police in South-End-By the-Sea. They quickly located her father and brother and her father called back.

"My daughter is safe thanks to you. I will see you rewarded. Do you have the man that kidnapped her?"

"I do, but do not be concerned. This man will not kidnap anyone else's daughter."

The father replied in an angry voice.

"He should be turned over to the British authorities and punished for what he did."

"On board my vessel I am judge and jury. I am a sea captain and he is under my control while he is on my ship. Do not worry about his punishment; I have handled ruthless men like him before. It will be my pleasure to bring him to justice. Men of the sea have their own system of justice. Enjoy your reunion with your daughter."

"Can I do anything for you in return?"

"Let me punish the man who abused your daughter. That will be satisfaction enough. I have a daughter her age and know what you must be feeling, but let me dole out the proper punishment. Glad I could help you sir. Your daughter will be waiting for you in London. The authorities will tell you where to meet her. Good bye."

Vasilli hung up the phone and summoned Alekos to the wheelhouse.

"Alekos, find some clothes for the girl and take her on deck and help her onto the pilot boat. When she is safe and the pilot boat away, take that Russian scum to the brig. Pick a real husky crewman to help you. Strip him and give him a hundred lashes. Throw him in the brig and we will leave him piss and moan for a while. When we get out of sight of land, about mid way to Istanbul, weigh him down and introduce him to the bottom of the Mediterranean. He is garbage."

"That is an order I welcome captain. That girl's bottom will bear permanent scars from where he beat her."

"See that our friend is conscious for all one hundred. If he passes out, bring him around. He deserves no better."

Alekos chose Petros, a heavyset man in his early forties and the two of them grabbed Boris and dragged him to the brig. Anastas held Boris and Petros softened him up with several hard blows to the stomach and two or three to the jaw and another slam broke Boris's nose.

"You mother fuckers. When I get free, you will suffer."

"What makes you think you will ever get free? You are a dead man; you just do not know it yet."

Boris tried to pull away, but he could not fight the two men that restrained him. They tied his wrists together and attached them to a pulley that pulled his body taught, and left him standing on his toes. Alekos ripped off his clothes and threw a bucket of salt water over him. He and Petros took turns lashing Boris's body with the whip. Boris groaned and screamed in anguish as the lash tore at his body exposing it to the salt left by the water. After forty lashes, Boris passed out. They left him for an hour, returned with another bucket of salt water, and tossed it over his head. Boris snapped to and the beating began again. They lashed his back so badly that his skin was shredded and blood streamed down his legs. Boris was beginning to convulse. His eyes rolled back, his head slumped onto his chest, and he hung limp from his wrists.

"How many lashes was that?"

"I don't know. I was not counting."

"Bring him around again and give him ten more. I will get the captain. I think it is time our friend goes for a long swim to the bottom of the sea."

Captain Vasilli and Petros arrived as Alekos laid the last punishing lash across Boris's back.

Boris, his face dripping blood, his eyes swollen, and his body cut and bleeding was barely conscious. "You bastards, why? I gave you the girl."

"She reminded me of my daughter. I sent her back on the pilot boat to her family. The Mossad also paid me a lot of money to take care of you. You have made some very bad enemies back in Israel. When they found out about your little group inside Mossad, the word went out worldwide to find you. I wanted you to suffer first. I cannot imagine that anyone will miss you. I will notify the authorities; you slipped, and fell overboard. Sadly, we will tell them, you disappeared beneath the sea."

"You bastards, may you rot in hell. My brother will avenge me."

"Your brother is also being hunted. Care to tell us where he is; maybe we wouldn't kill you?"

"Kill me; my brother will avenge my death."

"The Mossad will find him no matter where he goes. Wrap this scum in some of that spare chain and sew him into a heavy canvas bag." Vasilli pulled out a digital camera and took pictures of Boris front and back. "We should be able to slip him overboard as soon as it is dark. What a piece of crap."

Alekos and Petros brought the chain, wrapped it tightly around Boris's ravished body, lifted him off the floor by his wrists, slipped a heavy canvas bag over him and sewed the bag shut at the top. Petros and Alekos picked up the whip again and laid another twenty lashes onto Boris through the canvas bag. When the bag went limp, they stopped and left him hanging from the ceiling of the brig and went topside.

"Captain, it is done. As soon as it is dark, we'll slip him overboard."

"Did you kill him?"

"We sewed him into the canvas bag and whipped him until he went limp. We left him hanging. Does it matter?"

"No, I would like to think he is alive and feels himself drowning. He deserves no better. I never did like Russian Jews. The Mossad contact in London arranged the contract to do away with him. They are paying us very well for what we have done tonight. It would be a bonus to find his brother."

"The photos of Boris have already been sent to the contact in London," the first mate reported.

"It seems he got on the bad side of the Russian mob and the Israelis at the same time. Poor bastard, he pissed off the wrong people."

At ten o'clock that night, they released Boris from the hook and dragged the canvas bag topside. Boris was so weak he could hardly move, but managed to plead in a weak voice, "Please. I have money in Cyprus."

The captain shouted, "You do not have enough money to buy your way out of this. Good-bye Boris. Your friends in Tel Aviv send their best."

Alekos and Petros each took an end of the heavy bag and tossed Boris overboard. The bag immediately sank in the wake of the freighter as it steamed toward Istanbul.

Captain Vasilli called the London port authorities, "Is the girl okay?'

"Yes, she is fine. Her father still wants to know your name. He wants to reward you."

"That is not necessary. Tell him that this man Boris was not used to the wet decks of a freighter and regrettably slipped and fell overboard. We could not find him in the dark. Maybe he will be rescued at sea, but I doubt it. There are no ships near us and he was very tired from working all day."

"I will let the Russian authorities know that one of their citizens was drowned at sea."

"Ships are dangerous. Give my best to the girl and her family. We are continuing onto Istanbul. I will send a full written report when we dock."

The connection was broken and the man turned to Mr. Taylor. The captain sends his best. The man that allegedly abused your daughter fell overboard and was presumed drowned. They could not find him in the dark. Ships are dangerous."

Mr. Taylor gave a knowing nod, hugged his son and daughter, and left for Dover on his recovered yacht.

Chapter 47

When Alex and Asad landed at Heathrow airport, Henry was there to greet them.

"I have some interesting news that just came over the wire. Boris stole a yacht and kidnapped a fifteen-year old girl. He tried to escape on a freighter bound for Istanbul. The captain rescued the young woman that Boris had severely beaten and she is safe with her parents, but Boris had an accident at sea. The captain said he put him to work with his crew and seems he slipped on a wet deck and fell overboard."

"Sounds like he may have had help."

"That is not our concern. Boris will not bother your family or anyone else's, ever again. He was a dangerous man. Mikhail is still out there, but with us, Mossad, and the Russians looking for him, he is a dead man."

Alex handed Henry the photos that he and Asad had gotten from the bank vault in Zurich. Henry looked at the pictures as he sat behind his desk. He spread them out in front of him and shook his head.

"These photos will expose these people for what they are, criminals and enablers of those who would profit at the expense of innocent women whose only crime is trying to make an honest living by leaving their homes to perform menial labor. I wonder how many groups these officials conspired with over the years. There must be well over three billion dollars in transactions documented in these journals. I cannot believe they kept such good records."

"You know that the Israeli and the Russian mobs are only concerned with money. They want to count every dollar and have the proof of where it came from. I think a few heads will roll when these are released."

"Knowing the Russians, a few men will not be serving in the Duma anymore, and will find Eastern Siberia as uncomfortable as ever."

"What about the Israelis?"

"They may come down on some of the men responsible, but those at the top will be exonerated. They always manage to find a fall guy. It is not our problem. These documents will go to the proper authorities and their governments will handle it. We have done our job. You gentlemen look like you are in need of a rest."

"With your permission, I am going to Scotland and to be with Magdalena for at least a week. What about you Asad?'

"I am on my way to Cairo; Helen is waiting for me."

"I want both of you to be ready to go back to work as soon as possible. We still have a lot to do. I want to find that cruise ship and see what we can do about finding other groups still operating in the area. Asad, you have been of great service to us. I want you on our team permanently. Will you help us?"

"Retirement is not what it made out to be; I have found a purpose for my life and a woman I love. People like Boris must be stopped. I will call you from Cairo. I am afraid that other kidnapped woman from the cruise ship is most likely gone by now. I do not think we will ever find her, but we may be able to free the others on that ship and shut down their operation."

Anne gave us the name of the hotel that changed their reservations and we are trying to find out more about the *Apollo* cruise ship. We have sent some agents to Kusadasi to try to locate the gypsy camp, but so far no luck. Gypsies move a lot and never stay in the same location for long periods. We have an agent that is twenty-four years old; she has volunteered to go undercover, and see if she can find her way onto the *Apollo*. She is unmarried."

"Isn't that too dangerous for a woman?"

"This woman is very good at what she does and has driven to succeed. Her older sister was kidnapped five years ago in Turkey while on vacation. When her body was found, it was determined she had been a victim of the sex trade. Bridgett joined MI6 after she graduated from college. Her father works for Harrods in London and knows many influential men. When the older sister was killed, her mother who was a hair stylist had a total nervous breakdown. We have hidden a small transmitter subcutaneously in her leg. She will communicate with us by satellite phone. She is aware of the danger, but wants to find the people responsible for these heinous crimes."

"When is this to take place?"

"The *Apollo* is due in Piraeus in a week. If they kidnap Bridgett, I want you and Asad in Piraeus. Jameel has volunteered the use of his boat and crew. Hassan is prepared to help once his brother is fully recovered and able to run the hotels on his own. Hassan has already fought side by side with Alex on one other occasion. The three of you along with three of Sabir's trained fighters masquerading as crew should be able to get aboard the *Apollo* and keep an eye on the ship and Bridgett. The ship makes several stops throughout the Greek Islands and spends three nights in Istanbul. We have been working with the Turkish authorities and will make our move in Istanbul."

"How many men are booked to sail on the *Apollo*? Sixty-three men have booked passage and come from America, Europe, South America and Saudi Arabia. They are there because they enjoy the sex and depravity. They will be no help in rescuing these women. Anne thought there were about a forty or fifty crewmembers and eight or ten officers in charge of the operation."

"When the ship docks in Istanbul, the passengers always disembark and spend an overnight in the Istanbul Hilton. We have an eighteen-hour window. Anne said the man she was with had taken the cruise several times before, and even though he was taking her ashore in Rhodes for shopping, no women were allowed off the ship in Istanbul. Other women on board told her that the women were regularly disciplined based on negative reports from the wealthy men that enjoyed them during the trip. A select few crewmen were given the privilege of beating and torturing the uncooperative women; the remainder of the crew and officers were allowed their way with the women that were not disciplined. It was their reward for keeping silent. Those that were to be sold, were bound, gagged and nailed into crates to be off loaded and delivered to the gypsies in Kusadasi. They bragged to Anne that some of the crew beat these women so badly, they never made it to Kusadasi and were weighted down and dropped to the bottom of the sea at night. If a man wanted to purchase a woman he particularly liked, she was put into a cell, and untouched by the crew. These purchases were made before the ship arrived in Istanbul. The passengers then re-boarded the ship and continued on to Kusadasi. After ten hours in port, the ship sailed for Piraeus and the passengers went their way. Very few women were ever purchased by these men, and the ones that remained on board were given two or three days to rest in their cells on board the ship or until the next cruise."

"The crew is vulnerable and we should be able to take them without too much trouble. The Turkish authorities had only one requirement; the crew be handed over to them, along with the ship. The men who had booked passage, because of their status as wealthy businessmen, would be fined a huge sum of money, and held until their fines were paid. Those not paying the fines would be sentenced to ten years in a Turkish jail."

"I think these men will gladly pay, rather than face the embarrassment of their actions going public and the thought of a Turkish prison for ten years would be a great incentive."

"Call me in a week and I will make the arrangement for arrival in Piraeus. Asad will come by boat with Hassan and Sabir's men. Alex you will fly to Athens from Aberdeen. Jameel's yacht will shadow the *Apollo*."

"What about the woman operative, Bridgett?"

"She will gather as much information as possible and try to escape before the ship makes port in Istanbul. If Bridgett is unable to get away, hopefully the crew will not beat and torture her before we can rescue her in Istanbul. The risk is great, but she is a very determined woman and quite capable of taking care of herself."

"Your assignment will be to dock near the *Apollo* in the islands and watch for the women if they are taken off the ship for shopping and sightseeing. You will have no difficulty in recognizing Bridgett. She is almost 180 centimeters in height and has natural light blonde hair that falls below her waist, light blue eyes, and a gorgeous figure. She is quite buxom and carries herself like a model."

"How will we know if she is kidnapped?"

"If the concierge at the hotel notifies her of a change in her cruise ship reservation, we know they will take her. As soon as this happens, she will contact us. The satellite phone will be disposed of and no further communication between us will be possible. Bridgett is well trained in the martial arts and if given a chance to break free before Istanbul, she will escape. You have a week before the *Apollo* is due to sail. For now, relax with your ladies and plan to be in Piraeus a week from today."

Alex and Asad left Henry's office. They drove to the airport. Asad flew to Cairo and Alex flew to Aberdeen.

Alex rented a car and drove to Fettercairn to spend a week with Magdalena.

Magdalena met him at the door, threw her arms around him, and held him close.

"I was so stupid. I love you. Forgive me. *Miluju Te*, that means I love you in Czech."

"I know, you said it before and I asked Asad, he told me what it meant. *Miluju Te*."

Alex held her tightly and whispered the phrase Asad had taught him and his tears mingled with hers.

"I will be here for a week before I leave for Athens. We will get married when I return. I want to hold you, make love to you, and spend the week planning our future together. I thought of you every day I was gone. Forgive me for rushing you."

"Oh Alex, I looked forward to hearing your voice every night when you called. Albert has so understood my emotions. He is the caring father I never had. His wife Samantha is adorable, and knitting a baby blanket. We have gone shopping several times and are preparing a room as a nursery. I find out if it is a boy or girl next week."

"As promised, I brought you something from Switzerland."

He handed her a package neatly wrapped in paper. She opened it and smiled at him. The aroma of expensive chocolates drifted from the box.

"I love chocolates. They are almost too pretty to eat."

They opened the delectable box of truffles and each had one of the delicious gourmet chocolates.

"I bought you something else."

He handed her a large box.

"It is heavy."

She carefully opened the box, set the exquisite Burl wood music box on the table, and opened it. The music of Phantom of the Opera drifted through the room.

"Oh, Alex, I have never seen such a music box. The music is mellifluous. I know that song; it is one of my favorites."

She put her arms around him and they kissed passionately.

"I am taking you to Edinburgh tomorrow. If we are getting married when I return, you need an engagement ring."

"Oh Alex, I do love you."

They retired to the bedroom for the rest of the day. The week sped by and Alex was on his way to Athens.

Asad rushed to the apartment as soon as he got off the elevator. Helen had the door open before he could knock. She put her arms around him, hugged, and kissed him before he had a chance to say anything.

"I have missed you so."

"I never thought I could love a woman, as I love you. It was only a few days, but it seemed so long ago. I have brought you some gifts. I have never given you anything before."

"You did not have to give me anything. You gave me your love. That was enough."

"I think you will like this."

Asad handed her a small package neatly wrapped in white paper. She opened the box and tears ran down her face as he took the two rings and placed them on her finger.

"I knew you liked yellow gold and the emeralds are green like your bewitching eyes." He kissed away the tears as she cried and he held her close.

"Asad, they are stunning."

"I brought you something else."

He handed her another box. Inside was the ornate gold watch with each hour marked by a glimmering diamond.

"I will wear this always. You are too good to me."

Asad handed her the large box with the two music boxes. She opened the birdcage first, set it on the table, and listened to the birds sing as they moved on their perches like real birds.

"Oh Asad, they seem so real. I love the sound of birds singing. It is something we never hear in Cairo."

"There is one more package at the bottom of the box."

Helen opened the package, set the Swiss elm box on the table, and opened the lid. The music of Tchaikovsky filled the room.

"It is lovely; she sat there with tears streaming down her face. Asad hugged her and held her close.

"I loved buying you these gifts. I missed you so. They do not need me for another week. My next assignment is to shadow a cruise ship used for entertaining wealthy men with kidnapped women who are forced to have sex with the passengers. Before I go we will shop for an apartment in Alexandria with a view of the sea. Will you miss Cairo?"

"I will miss nothing as long as you are with me. Cairo is no place to raise a child."

Asad and Helen spent the week apartment shopping in Alexandria and looking for a fishing boat. At the end of the week, they had purchased a three-bedroom apartment in Alexandria with a view of the sea from their balcony.

"Helen, we will move when my assignment is completed, then I will purchase a yacht. You and I are going to relax for two weeks when I return. I love to fish; we'll have wonderful fresh caught fish every night for dinner."

"Asad, I wish you did not have to go to Greece and shadow that cruise ship. Call me whenever possible."

"I promise that I will call you every night and during the day whenever I have time. This assignment is not dangerous."

He kissed Helen goodbye and saw her safely into the hands of a security team.

To be continued winter 2012

Retribution

CPSIA information can be obtained at www.ICGtesting.com
Printed in the USA
LVOW081916071011

249616LV00001B/9/P